Leaping Wolf
JP Harker

Published By JPH
Copyright © James Thomas 2017

ISBN 978-0-9955219-1-9

Cover Art by Creative Covers

Prologue

Ierryn tramped down the *Leviathan*'s gangplank and wondered how he would adapt to a life without raiding. The boards beneath his feet were dry and solid and made barely a creak as the big man strode along them, trying his hardest not to limp. A Gaian sword had scored a long cut across his thigh at Nantwyn, and mere scratch though it was it still pained him to put weight through the limb. Ierryn grimaced and scolded himself for his whining. He had lived to see his island again hadn't he? The chieftain took a deep breath and then sighed it out again, taking in the familiar smell of his home port as he did it; salty air, damp cloth, and the heavy aroma of raw fish. Trethoer was one of the largest towns on Niswyn, with a broad front of trade-houses and drinking halls before the scores of round houses began, dotting the green landscape beyond like so many stars at midnight.

Ierryn stepped from the boards onto solid ground, whispered a quick thanks to Morannan for his safe return, then continued to mull as he walked. He'd been raiding the mainland since he was barely fourteen, and in thirty years he had made a fearsome name for himself. Ierryn the Black, High Chieftain of the Dariniae, was a name known and feared from the Breiryn in the south to the Gorvicae in the north, though the Caderyn in the centre were his most favoured target. He had no particular grudge against that tribe, but their coastline was close and thus the easiest to attack, and he had taken grain and tribute from them more times than he could count. Not that they were an option to him anymore.

3

He took another deep breath as he walked along and unclasped the brooch that held his heavy cloak, tossing the garment to Fearghal who walked behind him. After Kyran, the First Man of the tribe, Fearghal was probably the best fighter Ierryn had, but he was a naturally humble man and didn't mind carrying his chief's cloak as well as his own. Like Ierryn he wore a Gadarim's tattooed battle-marks along his arms and body, snaking up his neck onto his jaw. Any tribesman could paint his skin with such designs in simple woad of course, but only the elite Gadarim were permitted to make their marks permanent. Like Ierryn, Fearghal also bore the tiny scar below his eye, testament to their tribe's unique rituals for their warriors. Unlike his chieftain however he was lean of build, and his long hair and beard were chestnut brown rather than black. Both men carried themselves with the easy grace of the skilled fighter, though neither one expected to find trouble today. *But then, real trouble may soon be a thing of the past.* Ierryn only half-believed that but it was a serious possibility nonetheless.

The Dariniae, the Gorvicae and the Caderyn had formed an alliance of Lurian tribes against the aggression of the Gaians, something akin to a single tribe that had been called the Caledon. Ierryn was returning from a decisive battle with the legions which had forced their would-be-conquerors to agree to terms of peace. Most of his warriors he had left behind with Kyran to lick their wounds but Ierryn knew that Niswyn needed its chieftain back; to explain to them how their way of life was about to change forever. He did not look forward to it. Part of the agreement, bound in with Ierryn's own word in sight of his brother Gadarim, had been for the Dariniae to cease their

4

raids against the other tribes of the Caledon. The various headmen of the island would hardly greet such news with enthusiasm.

Niswyn was fertile enough in places but there was not sufficient farmland to feed the whole population, or not easily anyway. It was by raiding the mainland tribes that the Dariniae kept their own tribe going, and the good news of the Gaians' defeat would be tempered by resistance to the new alliance. Ierryn frowned to himself. He'd had his doubts about all this as well, but Reaghan the druid had convinced him of its wisdom, and the Wildcat had convinced him it could work. He scratched at his beard as he thought of her. Rhianwyn daughter of Carradan was the unofficial chieftain of both the Caderyn and the Caledon, and he had to give it to her, she would probably be good at it. She'd proved herself as a Lurian warrior but had spent time with the Gaians as well, and would understand them far better than most. *A bit skinny for my taste but a fine woman nonetheless – best of fortune to her sorting all of this out.*

Ierryn strode on, ignoring his injured leg with an effort of will, and his frown deepened as he recognised the three figures walking towards him from the town. His nephew Caserach was striding at their head. Ierryn almost sighed. *And best of fortune to me in sorting my own people out!* He slowed his pace a little and the men around him did the same. He was clearly not going to be able to avoid talking to Heuryn's son, and he made doubly sure that he wasn't limping. It was always important to appear strong when speaking as High Chieftain, especially in front of potential malcontents like his nephew.

Caserach was tall and strong with black hair and a trimmed beard, the very image of his father, and seeing his nephew sometimes made Ierryn regret that he'd had to kill him. Heuryn had tried fighting his brother for his position as High Chieftain, and Ierryn had reluctantly buried him for it. Caserach had accepted his father's fate in public but had done so with poor grace, and his would doubtless be the first voice to object to their agreement with the Caledon.

As he approached Ierryn once again resisted the urge to sigh aloud. This would not be easy. He would have to emphasise that there was no rule against raiding the Breiryn further south, or they might even take their ships around the Gorvicae coast and raid the Sarrac tribes of the Black Mountains. They were practically as foreign as the Gaians were and fought enough among themselves that they would be a challenging target. Plenty of Dariniae headmen would be glad to try their hands against them, simply to prove to one another that they could. *Now we are at peace, we could even re-supply in Gorvicae ports along the way.* Yes, that would have to be the first thing that he brought up when council was called; it would soften the blow of telling them that Caledon lands were now forbidden.

He almost smiled to himself. Change was never easy and he'd felt old for most of the journey as he'd pondered all of this, but tonight he would call Tegian to his room and she would make him feel young again. Since the death of his wife Ierryn had taken three lovers so far, but Tegian had been the best of them and she alone had shared his bed for a year. *I should probably do the decent thing and wed her soon before I get a bastard on her. She's a good girl and she deserves a more decent reputation.*

Caserach and his companions stopped just in front of their chieftain and nodded their heads respectfully, Caserach more shallowly than the others. The one to his left was a lanky, hard-faced warrior named Idwal, while to his right stood Fearghal's sister by law, Aerona. She was hardly a great beauty but had a nice, homely sort of face, with broad hips that had already brought forth at least four children for Fearghal's brother. She stepped closer to the Gadarim and started talking to him, probably to complain about his brother again, and Ierryn didn't listen too closely. Caserach was looking at his chieftain impatiently and Ierryn knew he would have to speak to him first, and that neither one of them would enjoy the conversation. But it had to be done and so he took a deep breath, ready to get in early with his argument.

'Nephew,'

But that was as far as he got. His instincts screamed out a heartbeat too late and he twisted on the spot just as the knife was thrust under his ribs. At first it felt like nothing more than a solid punch to his torso, but soon the burning pain began and he let out a coughing gasp. A group of men had slipped behind them with short daggers beneath their cloaks, and even as Ierryn turned he saw two of his guards struck down. They were Gadarim, the finest warriors that a Lurian tribe could make, but they were also unarmed and taken unawares, and iron plunged into flesh before any man could draw his sword. Fearghal was staggering with Aerona's knife stuck in his side and Ierryn too found himself struggling to stay upright.

Rage flooded through him and he grabbed his attacker by the throat, smashing his other fist through his face before the coward could stab again. Teeth cracked under the impact and blood dribbled to his chin, but Ierryn didn't stay in place to pummel him. Instead he shuffled around him, his side burning horribly, and shoved him into his nearest comrade before turning to face a third. To their credit his Gadarim were not dying easily and were battering at their attackers with fists and heads, though the fight was lost, and Ierryn knew it. It was more than half a dozen knifemen against four wounded warriors, and brave though they were the Gadarim were as good as dead already.

Ierryn grabbed another of the craven bastards and clamped his hands onto his head, bellowing in righteous fury as he drove a thumb into his eye. The man screamed and stabbed weakly at him but Ierryn knew that he was dying and he paid no heed to it. He would cross Annwn's Bridge with his head held high, and no feeble wounds from cowards would slow him down. His thumb was wet up to the base before he let the wretch go and he was searching for another foe when more knives plunged into his back. Without even looking he knew that Caserach was behind him and he whirled around, his arms flailing out.

His nephew dodged back quickly and he clipped Idwal's jaw instead, and the tall man was knocked sideways. Ierryn tried to charge at Caserach but Idwal recovered too quickly for him, and he grabbed the chieftain by the hair, pulling him into another stab. Ierryn snarled and lunged for him, catching him by the flesh of his cheek and dragging him in close. Another stab almost took the fight from him but he clung on like a madman and the two men collapsed to the ground. Ierryn almost cried out in pain as his wounded body struck the hard earth but he was too angry to care about that and simply snarled as he sank his teeth into Idwal's ear. The lanky man let out a yelp but he could do nothing to shake him off, and Ierryn ripped the ear free with a vicious jerk of his head, the metallic taste of blood almost sweet on his tongue.

The something very hard struck the back of his skull. Then again. And again. Bright spots appeared in front of him and he lost his grip on Idwal. His enemy wriggled free, howling in pain, but Ierryn didn't follow him. He couldn't. His head and torso were a screaming mess of blood and pain, and try though he might he couldn't focus his eyes. The best he managed was to roll over so that he was facing upwards, and for a moment he saw Belenos shining down from the clear blue sky. Then Caserach's boot struck his head again, and Ierryn knew no more.

Chapter 1. The New World

It didn't feel like autumn. The leaves were on the turn and the blackberries were ripe, but still Gawan couldn't quite believe that summer was done. Belenos was blazing hot in the sky above, and the air around him felt thick and heavy. The Gorvic hadn't needed his green cloak for days and even at the column's easy pace he could feel himself sweating in the heat. He ran a hand through his hair and it came away wet, and he felt a little pang of sympathy for his mount.   Gawan was not a man known for his sympathetic side but while he would happily belittle a *man* for griping about the heat, his attitude to the ponies was quite different. The beasts were not just walking out in the hot sun but were carrying big men on their backs as well, or heavy bundles of supplies or stolen weapons.   The Second Battle of Nantwyn had yielded a great deal of Gaian equipment to the Caledon, and what gear hadn't stayed at the hillfort was coming back with them to Bryngarth.

Gawan reached for his waterskin and took a quick gulp. They shouldn't be too far from the Caderyn's capital by now and then both he and the horses could enjoy a rest from the road. Along the column in front of him he saw dozens of riders in a similarly overheated state, and a quick glance behind him showed several hundred more sweating bodies. Most were Caderyn fighters heading home after the battle, and despite their tribes' alliance Gawan felt uncomfortably outnumbered.   With their common enemy defeated, for now, keeping the Caledon together would be a challenge to say the least, and he was only half-convinced of the wisdom of it. The Caderyn had been his enemy long before the Gaians came, and were it not for the terrible battles he had seen recently he might have thought the fledgling Caledon had already outlived its usefulness. But he *had* seen those things, and so long as there was any chance of the Gaians coming back it made sense for old enemies to become partners, even if they could never be truly called friends.

He was lost in his thoughts when Emeryn spoke beside him, and she had to repeat herself before she got a response.

'Gawan?'

He turned in his saddle.

'Hmm?'

Emeryn shook her head.

'I'd swear sometimes that you can sleep standing up for all the attention you pay.'

Gawan shrugged, not quite apologetic but acknowledging his rudeness at least. He had found himself growing fond of Emeryn, and she was one of the few people with whom he'd make an effort to be polite. She was the childless widow of a fellow Gorvic and though she was still young enough to bear sons, she had not re-married as yet. Why Emeryn had chosen Gawan as a lover was still something of a mystery to him, given that he was a grim-faced man almost a decade her senior, but for some reason she had. She was still waiting for him to answer but Gawan was enjoying looking at her. Like him she was dressed in plain tunic and breeches but somehow she managed to make herself appealing in them, being as well-shaped in her body as she was pretty in her face. To many men her looks alone would be enough to draw them to her, but Gawan knew from long experience that the world was full

11

of pretty girls, and most of the ones he'd met had tried his patience. No, far more important than Emeryn's looks, at least as far as Gawan was concerned, was the woman's temperament. She had a mischievous nature that ought to have been at odds with Gawan's stoic one, but somehow it managed to complement it instead. He kept looking at her. Her straight hair was shining blonde, a stark contrast to his own black tangles, and he wondered quietly if anything about them was actually the same. *Well, we share maybe one or two interests...*

The First Man of the Gorvicae answered casually.

'I was just thinking.'

Emeryn looked cynical.

'Well think on something useful; you've been this way before, how far do you think we have left to go?'

Gawan thought of the other times that he'd been to Bryngarth, first as a prisoner, then as a victorious enemy, and finally as a reluctant ally. *And what am I now? I am Gorvicae and Gadarim before all else but am I also Caledon now?* He put the thought aside and scratched at his beard, considering.

'Not far now, I'd say we should see the hill before dusk.'

Bryngarth wasn't actually that far away, but the country was all little hills and valleys and they were currently riding through one of the dips. For all the limited view ahead Gawan had to admit that the landscape was pleasant, though as usual he compared it unfavourably to the Gorvicae lands of the north. Up there the grass was more vibrant and the trees stood that much prouder, the air was clear and the mountains tall. *Or perhaps that's just your pride talking? Perhaps the Caderyn lands are just as fine as yours?* Gawan's lip twitched. He doubted it.

12

Emeryn nodded her head.

'So long as we're there soon, my arse is killing me.'

He'd never admit it but Gawan's legs and rear were aching too, though probably not quite as badly. He was accustomed to this sort of thing. He'd spent much of his life riding far and wide in the company of Baercban, the last Gorvicae chieftain. *Until you killed him that is.* The thought was not a welcome one and he pushed it away and tried to think of something more pleasant.

'Does that mean you'll do nothing but lie there tonight?'

Emeryn smiled a little.

'And act like some clueless new-wed? Come now, some things are worth a little discomfort, provided *you* are up to the task of course?'

Gawan almost smiled back. He was not a man prone to smiling but if anyone could bring it out in him, it was Emeryn. He was aching plenty himself, less from the ride and more from the various blows he'd suffered in the battle, but his lover was right; some things were worth the discomfort.

'Behave yourself and I'll maybe show you later.'

Emeryn winked at him.

'How bored would you become if I behaved myself?'

She took out her waterskin and drank, he suspected to draw attention to her mouth. He felt himself start to harden thinking of her and tried to put his mind somewhere else. It was never comfortable to ride in such a condition.

He was still uncertain about the whole idea of the Caledon, but tried to comfort himself by thinking that the Caderyn at least had always been a decent enemy. Both the Gaians and the Dariniae had shown themselves to be

13

untrustworthy but the Caderyn had always fought with pride and honour. He remembered the fight he'd had with them at Broken Stream, what was it... five, six years ago now? The two sides had battled fiercely and it had ended with a duel between the Gadarim, with Gawan son of Dearg fighting Madoc son of Derfel; the Leaping Wolf clashing swords with the Smiling Fox. It had been a fine fight, and Madoc had beaten him fairly and called an end to the battle.

Gawan frowned a little. Madoc was dead now, as were most of those who'd fought that day, both Caderyn and Gorvicae. Many had died during the massacre at First Nantwyn, where Gorvic and Gaian had fought side by side thanks to the deal Baercban made with Lepidus. It wasn't a memory Gawan treasured. Most of the rest had died at Second Nantwyn, when the Caledon had united against the Gaian shieldwalls. Gawan sighed. Victory or not it was a gloomy thought. He realised he'd not spoken for a while and looked back to Emeryn.

'We shall have to make the most of a decent bed while we're there. It should only be a few days before we head for home again.'

The only reason Gawan was coming to Bryngarth at all was to take part in the Wildcat's testing. He had named Rhianwyn to the Gadarim but the rules of the warrior elite meant she still had to be tested. Since a First Man had already named her certain allowances had been made, but the rituals of the Gadarim were sacred and the Caderyn's future chieftain could be no exception. Emeryn nodded in agreement.

'That we shall. My back is too old for rutting in pine-groves these days.'

Gawan smirked. Emeryn had seen barely thirty winters but she loved to complain about feeling old. She probably just did it to tease her lover, who had seen his fortieth.

'*I* am still young enough to try it.'

Emeryn gave him a mock-stern look through her brows.

'Then you can bloody well go into the woods on your own on the trip back. We'll see if you can make the badgers blush.'

He gave her arm a playful shove and she held up the waterskin as if to throw it at him, but he knew it was an empty threat. It was too hot to waste the water. Instead she took another gulp then stoppered the leather flask.

'Do you think we will catch up with Duran when we go north? The legion aren't all mounted after all.'

Gawan shook his head.

'He said he'd leave Nantwyn only a day or two later than us. Unless he lingers on the journey he'll be home long before we get there.'

The Wildcat's Gaian husband, Marius, had taught the Lurians to fight in formations the way the Gaians did, and though Gawan had never liked him, the man had known what he was doing. The Gorvicae cohorts of the Dragon Legion would now be making for White Ridge and then on to Graigarw, probably leaving some of their number at the edge of Gorvicae land. Treaty or not the Gaians were still far too close for comfort, and whoever became the Gorvicae's new chieftain would want his borders well protected. Emeryn either read his thoughts or was thinking along the same lines anyway.

'Who do you think will stand for Baercban's Chair?'

Gawan shrugged his shoulders.

'I would say either Karadoc or Taliesyn, or maybe Boryn if he puts his name forward.'

Emeryn nodded slowly.

'Do you know who you will choose?'

The Gadarim shrugged again. As First Man he would have a voice in the moot but it would be the headmen and the druids who truly made the decision.

'Boryn's a decent man but he is contented where he is and may not stand. I know little enough about the other two.'

Emeryn spoke again.

'Whoever becomes High Chieftain will want you on his side. They will probably all seek to be your friend in the days beforehand.'

Gawan pressed his lips together irritably. Lurian politics were fairly simple affairs but they existed nonetheless and he did not want to get involved in them. Emeryn had tactfully left out the fact that whoever became High Chieftain would remember that Gawan had killed his predecessor over a matter of principle, and he would want to be sure that his First Man respected him. Gawan still felt sad for having had to kill Baercban but he harboured no real regret. He'd had no choice and the chieftain had known that, and Gawan liked to think he reached the Otherworld without a grudge. Baercban had been weak in many ways but he'd not been an evil man, and Gawan hoped that Annwn's Bridge had been broad for him.

He turned his attention back to the conversation.

'They may seek all they like.'

Emeryn smiled.

'But you are not an easy man to befriend?'

She said it in jest but it was fairly accurate. Gawan was on good terms with his brother Gadarim and had few living enemies, unless you counted his real brother, but he could count his true friends on one hand. It was how he liked it. It meant fewer names and stories to have to remember. He snorted at her little.

'*You* seemed to find it easy enough?'

Emeryn raised a golden eyebrow.

'It may cause a stir if they befriend you the same way I have. Besides,' she tossed her hair casually, 'I may tire of you soon.'

The gesture revealed a long length of her neck and Gawan was tempted to stop right there and drag her from her horse into the trees. No doubt she would complain about rutting on hard earth and not a soft bed but she wouldn't really object, and he considered it seriously for a moment. She was obviously teasing him on purpose and it might be just what she wanted him to do. But he fought back the urge. The rest of the column would hardly thank them for holding them up so close to home, and if they sated themselves now Emeryn might be less keen to couple later on. *And admit it man, you too prefer a straw mattress to hard earth and wet grass. You may not be ancient but you're no romping youth either.* He settled for leaning close and running his hand along one of her legs.

'You'll be tired all right by the time I am done with you.'

Emeryn gave him one of her wry looks.

'You men and your promises.'

Gawan was thinking of what to say back to her when Gwydion, one of his fellow Gadarim, came trotting up. Like Gawan his limbs were covered in tattooed battle-marks but where Gawan was stocky Gwydion was lean,

17

and while Gawan's thick hair and beard were black, Gwydion's were blonde and fine. He was a few summers younger than the First Man but very nearly as experienced in warfare, and he was someone Gawan respected. Even if he did have a habit of grinning like a fool at the slightest excuse. The fair man wasn't grinning now however and he nodded to them briskly. Gawan returned the gesture.

'Problems?'

Gwydion had been scouting the countryside since Nantwyn looking for any stragglers from the scattered Panther Legion. The Blackbird Legion were looking for them too, claiming they were rebels that they would bring to justice, but Gawan for one had little faith in Gaians of any sort and had made sure to have his own people keeping an eye out for them. Gwydion shrugged his shoulders.

'Likely nothing but I felt you should know; Tarwyn heard from a local that Gaians had been seen north of here. The man said they wore no armour so they may just have been enforcers fleeing Caderyn lands.'

Gawan frowned a little. During the occupation the governor had employed various mercenary peacekeepers, most of whom had left quietly when the Caledon had been formed. There were bound to be stragglers about the place. *All the same...*

'Has he gone after them?'

Gwydion nodded.

'He took a few of the boys with him to see. Like I say, probably nothing.'

He was probably right, though Gawan still felt pensive. The Panther Legion had been men twisted by Lepidus' sorcerer, and armoured or not they were still inhumanly dangerous.

'If you've heard nothing by dusk send someone out to bring him back. We cannot be too careful with those bastards.'

Gwydion dipped his head.

'As you say.'

The blonde man eased his mount's head around and made his way back along the column, leaving Gawan looking thoughtful behind him. He hated to admit it but the men of the Panther Legion had frightened him. It was perfectly sensible to feel fear for such men of course, given their strength and bestial nature, but all the same Gawan didn't like acknowledging it. He might have started brooding but Emeryn knew him well and decided to take his mind from it before he could. She sighed and jerked her head towards the west.

'I wonder how it will feel to make love in the fortress of an old enemy?'

Gawan showed his appreciation with a small smile, glad of the change of subject. On reflection it would probably be a strange feeling indeed. *But then being there at all is a strange feeling.* Just a few years ago the tribes of the Caledon had been killing each other, yet tonight the First Man of the Gorvicae would sit among the most honoured of the Caderyn's guests. Not there as a prisoner or a mistrusted ally but as a war hero and a friend. He shook his head a little, still struggling to believe it. The Wildcat had done something exceptional in making this happen, there was no doubt about it. *But how long will this new world of hers last?* Gawan couldn't guess, and he didn't really want to.

19

*

Emeryn was back to complaining about the ride when Gwydion returned, though she fell silent as she saw him canter up. Once again the blonde man's face was unusually serious, and Gawan didn't waste time with pleasantries as his brother slowed his mount.

'Well?'

Gwydion answered through heavy breaths.

'Tarwyn found something.'

Gawan resisted letting his hand stray to Heartreaver's grip.

'Trouble?'

In the corner of his eye he saw Emeryn's face grow concerned, but he kept looking at his fellow Gadarim. Gwydion shook his head.

'Not anymore, but you may want to take a look all the same.'

Gawan saw Emeryn's shoulders drop in relief as he turned to face his lover.

'I'll be back soon.'

They both knew that Emeryn would be in no mood for a gallop back down the column and she simply nodded to him with a smile.

'I will try to manage without you for a while.'

Gawan's lip twitched slightly and he swung his pony around. Gwydion had already turned his and Gawan followed his lead as he spurred his mount into a canter, first back east along the track and then veering northwards to the beginnings of a beech wood. They made it there in swift order and slowed their horses as they broke the treeline. Both men dismounted after a few more paces, with Gwydion still leading the way. The trees were not quite so thick as to make riding impossible but it was easier just to walk and guide the ponies by their bridles. In any case, Gawan found it was nice to be out of the saddle.

Gwydion spoke as they walked.

'Tarwyn's boys found him trekking roughly southwest. I doubt if he knew where he was going.'

Gawan nodded slowly.

'Panther?'

Gwydion simply grunted and nodded back.

'Any of ours hurt badly?'

Though not so deadly as the Aborans the Panther men were still dangerous, and Gawan had lost enough of his people already. Gwydion shook his head.

'They took him unawares and made sure to work together. Tarwyn says he took some bringing down but he'd discarded his mail and helmet and they managed to bleed him out. Hewin took a heavy clout but nothing more.'

Gawan was quietly relieved that they had come off so lightly, though he felt a stab of annoyance that they would not be gaining another mailshirt. A few Lurian smiths were trying to learn the craft of making them but most had been occupied in forging swords and shield-rims for the Dragons and besides, the process was time-consuming. Every mailshirt worn by the Caledon's legion had been looted from a Gaian corpse, and even after the carnage at Nantwyn they were still in shorter supply than he'd have liked.

He kept his disappointment to himself and they walked on a little way, and soon the pair came to a small clearing, and the first thing Gawan saw was Tarwyn cleaning his bloody sword on a cloth. His fellow Gadarim was dark-haired and dark-eyed, plainly dressed in grey tunic and breeches, and though he was already a tall man he appeared taller still because he was so slender. Nearby him young Pryder was trying to help the much larger Hewin onto his pony, the latter's injured ribs making it a painful process for the both of them. Between them, lying at the base of one of the thicker trees, lay the soldier.

He looked young, but then with the beardless Gaians it was always harder to tell. His cheek was dark with stubble and his short hair ragged, the skin tanned a little browner than one tended to see among Lurians. There was blood all over his body and limbs and Gawan noted the ragged cut that ran across the dead man's throat. He felt no pity for him. The Gaian would have done far worse to them given the chance.

As Gwydion had said the man had abandoned his mail but he'd apparently kept his short sword which lay a few feet from his hand. Perhaps he'd thought to be less conspicuous without the armoured shirt but had been reluctant to discard his weapon. He was still wearing the thigh-length green-and-black tunic of the Panther Legion, though it was now torn and stained with blood in several places. Gawan felt his gorge rise. Green was the colour of the Gorvicae, and seeing an enemy wear it always felt like a stab to his pride.

The others were standing about looking rather uncertain and Gawan took command of the situation.

'Right, first of all get that tunic off him. We can keep the belt and sword but I'll want the shirt burned when we get to Bryngarth.'

There was a heartbeat's hesitation before the Gadarim complied and Gwydion gave him an uncomfortable look before speaking to Tarwyn.

'Did he have a dagger on him?'

The tall Gadarim bobbed his head, his voice laconic.

'He never drew it though, it's still in his belt.'

Gwydion nodded.

'Very well. We'll dig a pit for the body and throw the knife in with him. I know we need swords but he ought to have *something* to give to Annwn.'

Gawan couldn't help but sneer at that.

'Why waste time and iron? Do any of you think this bastard would ever cross the bridge in safety?'

The others shuffled uncertainly for a moment. They must have known that the chances of Annwn allowing such a man into the Otherworld were slim, but nevertheless they were clearly feeling awkward. Tarwyn, his eyes serious, spoke for them.

'Likely he would not, but that is not for us to say.'

Gwydion and the others nodded their agreement. Gawan scowled. Truth be told they had a fair point, but few men hated the Gaians more than Gawan son of Dearg. He shrugged his shoulders.

'Very well. Let's get him off those roots and onto some clear earth.'

Pryder wrestled the tunic from him before Tarwyn and Gwydion took an armpit each and hauled the legionary up, his head lolling forward. He wasn't that large a man and the two Gadarim were strong, and they moved him to the open ground with relative ease. Gawan didn't pause even for a heartbeat. In a single smooth motion he drew

Heartreaver from its sheath and brought it down onto the Gaian's neck, severing the head in one stroke.

It hit the ground with a dull thud and rolled in the dirt. Gwydion and Tarwyn dropped the body in shock, the headless corpse crashing onto the grass. Both men stumbled a pace and then glared at Gawan. They knew his skill well enough to know they had been in no danger from his blade but they looked at him with quiet anger all the same. The First Man ignored their disapproval and then ignored his aching legs as he leaned down. He grabbed a fistful of dark hair and picked up the dripping head before gesturing contemptibly at the body.

'Bury that much of him if you wish.' He tossed the head to Pryder who almost fumbled it, clearly discomfited. 'Find an old spear and stick that on it, and put it on the road facing back east.'

Gawan doubted many Gaians would be travelling this way by road but if even one of them saw it the message it was enough. The younger Gorvic seemed ill at ease but didn't want to contradict him, and the injured Hewin came to his rescue.

'Hand it here lad. We'll go back to the road together then you can come back here with some spades.'

Pryder nodded thankfully to the big man and took his pony's reins. The two men left the clearing, leaving the other three in an uncomfortable silence. Tarwyn made as if to speak but Gawan cut him off.

'Someone will bury the head too sooner or later, and then this damned Gaian can go to wherever it is his gods like to send murderers.'

Neither Tarwyn nor Gwydion seemed particularly appeased but neither one argued back either. Gawan sighed. He didn't like having to throw his weight around when it came to his fellow Gadarim, but soft warriors were no good to anyone and these cursed Gaians had earned no kinder fate. This one could wander blind for a while as he searched for his afterlife, and have his head back when some passer-by took pity on his spirit. Gawan felt no sympathy for the soul of such a man as for a moment he remembered Nantwyn, and the dreadful slaughter he had witnessed there at their hands. *Let him travel to the next world in a dozen bloody pieces. It's no more than the bastard deserves.*

Chapter 2. Bryngarth

The hill of Bryngarth was broad and flat, its green slopes dotted with patchy grass and clumps of heather. They had made good time, and the sun was only now sinking behind the mound of the Caderyn capital. Rhia felt barely a drop of relief at the sight of her old home but she tried to remain positive as she urged her pony onward. Bryngarth was where she *belonged* at least, even if it might never truly feel like home again. Back when it had been home Rhia had shared it with two brothers, two sisters, a mother, a father, and a husband. Now only her mother and Olwyn were left alive. She bit back tears as she thought of all the family she had lost these past few years.

First had been Dane, killed at First Nantwyn along with Rhia's first husband, Bevan. Gwen had fallen to her death in Tamora, taking her terrible Gaian husband with her and saving Rhia's life in the process. Ewan had been killed by Gaian enforcers during the occupation and Carradan, their wonderful father, had been murdered by Sedryn, the son of Baercban. *You had vengeance on him at least, but for all the others, and for Marius...*

Rhia held the tears at bay, they would come back later anyhow, and held on to little Lucan that much tighter. Even in the worst fits of her despair, she could always hold her son and see a tiny speck of light in the blackness. If Lucan found the extra squeeze uncomfortable he didn't show it, but rather continued with his lecture to Owain. Meghan, riding beside them, had been keeping him occupied on the long ride by teaching him the names of various flowers, and Lucan was at a stage where he loved nothing more than to repeat everything he knew to anyone

26

who would listen.   Right now he was speaking to the Caderyn's new First Man and educating him on every plant he could remember.

'That one's a faerie's glove,' he pointed his little hand towards a clump of purple flowers, 'and you mustn't eat them, you know.'

He spoke with an adorable earnestness in his voice and Owain played along perfectly, though Rhia suspected his heart was melting as much as hers was.

'Must I not?'

Lucan shook his head.

'No. It'll make your insides all bad.'

Meghan smiled knowingly.

'You could say the same of too much strong ale and milkwine but that has not stopped him yet!'

Owain simply smiled and shrugged but Lucan gave them both a confused look. Rhia wondered if she ought to try to explain but then the boy decided it didn't really matter.

'That one there is a bower-leaf...'

He carried on like that, revelling in showing them all how much he'd learned, and requiring only a smile or the occasional 'yes' to keep him going. Rhia smiled at his efforts, glad that his grasp of his native tongue was so good. He'd been born in Tamora and had spoken Vulgare for most of his short life, and though Rhia had made sure to teach him the Lurian tongue when she could, she had worried that he would struggle to speak it all the time. But the boy was clever, and he liked to talk, and on the rare occasions when he struggled for words most Caderyn knew enough Vulgare that he was still understood. The Gaian language had been a wise thing to learn during the occupation.

Rhia's mood was in danger of dipping again but Owain's question took her mind from it.

'So, are you feeling nervous?'

He was referring of course to her Gadarim tests. In truth Rhia was indeed feeling anxious about them, but she was not about to show him her fears. Instead she smiled.

'Maybe a little, but then if *you* can do it surely anyone can?'

Owain grinned at her. As the new First Man of her tribe's Gadarim he would preside over the rituals that would confirm her within the warrior elite. She had already been named to them, and already she had blue battle-marks tattooed around her forearm, but nonetheless traditions had to be honoured. She looked at Owain and couldn't help but compare the tiny dragon and lion chasing each other around her wrist to the dozens of swirling battle-marks that covered the veteran's body. Owain's marks covered both his arms and his hands and she knew that beneath his tunic they spread across his chest as well. *And every mark hard-won in battle.*

The needle allowed them to be more intricate than the painted woad worn by other warriors, though mostly his tattoos were of the same simple patterns, the occasional lightning-bolt being the most detailed design he wore. Though she'd seen the occasional dragon tattoo before, Rhia had been unusual in requesting specific animals to be marked on her. She wondered briefly if it would start a trend, but then she remembered that things like whims of fashion were things of the Gaian world. Even now it sometimes felt odd to be away from that society, where every day some new dress or exotic dish became something of vital importance, only to be forgotten again before the moon had turned. Meghan chuckled a little beside her, bringing her mind back to the present.

'My man is strong at least, we must give him that. Though whatever else these tests are, you can be sure there will not be too much thinking involved!'

Having once spied on the Gadarim rituals in her youth Rhia had a pretty good idea of what to expect from them, but the memory of it still made her feel ashamed and she'd never spoken to anyone about it, not even to Meg. The stocky Gadarim shrugged.

'I leave the thinking to the druids. Fighting and rutting are what I do best.'

Meg frowned at him a little and looked significantly at Lucan, but the boy was still merrily pointing out flowers to anyone who would listen and clearly hadn't taken in what was said. All the same Owain took the hint and changed the subject back to something more suitable.

'You have fought in three battles now, yes? At Broken Stream and then twice at Nantwyn?'

Rhia nodded and Owain furrowed his brow a little, glancing at her forearm.

'Given how well you fought and the size of the last two, I would say you have earned enough to mark the rest of that arm, perhaps even on to the upper chest as well?'

Rhia nodded again, wondering what exactly the Gadarim rules were for permanent battle-marks. Owain's body was liberally covered in them, and Gawan's even extended to coil around one half of his face. Rhia pressed her lips together for a moment. She always felt confused when she thought of the Gorvicae First Man. On the one hand it was he who had named her to the Gadarim, and she was grateful, but on the other he would always be the man who had killed Dane all those years ago. The memory of that black day threatened to invade Rhia's thoughts, despite her best efforts. He had wounded Bevan as well of course, though his death had been no fault of Gawan's. *Nor of mine*, Rhia told herself firmly, *and nor was what happened afterwards!*

Once again it was Meghan who called her back to reality, giving her man a mock-chiding look as she spoke.

'You keep your eyes off her chest Owain!'

Rhia was of slim build and far from voluptuous, especially next to Meghan, but the Gadarim gave her a quick stare out of pure cheek before transferring his gaze to the redhead's impressive bust.

'As you say.'

Rhia laughed and even Meghan struggled to keep up her disapproving expression. The two were clearly in love and Meg had confided in Rhia that Owain had asked her to kiss palms with him on their return to Bryngarth. They would need to ask Reaghan if the omens were good of course, though with the senior druid having ridden off west a few days ago they might have to consult with Bael instead. Rhia was wondering if the younger druid might end up performing the ceremony when a shifting of weight on her pony made her start, and before she knew what was happening Lucan had slipped from the horse's back and was scurrying from the path, heading towards a little clump of field-lilies.

For an irrational second Rhia panicked and almost grabbed for him, but she restrained herself with an effort. *He is among friends on a slow walk across a field, no-one is going to hurt him.* Rhia took a couple of deep breaths as Lucan paused to pick a handful of golden flowers. Owain was beside him in moments and casually scooped the boy up and onto his own mount. Lucan was completely unconcerned and started chattering away to him about the field-lilies he was holding.

'I'll give these to mama later, and she'll like them because they're *rare*.'

He spoke the word with a very serious face and seemed to be waiting for Owain to ask him what this word meant; Lucan had clearly not known it for long. Owain shared a smile with Rhia before playing along with him.

'What does that mean?'

The boy embarked on a very patient explanation to the Gadarim and Meghan spoke quietly to Rhia, not wanting to interrupt.

'He is *adorable*, Rhia.'

Rhia smiled and whispered back.

'I know. But I do worry for him so.'

The redhead placed a gentle hand on hers.

'I can understand your worry, after all that you've lost. But he is safe with us.'

Rhia nodded a little, agreeing without being entirely comforted. Meg was right; having lost so much Rhia often felt that Lucan was all she had left. He had his mother's blue eyes but beyond that he was the very image of his father, and the thought of Marius threatened to bring tears to her eyes again. She shook off the thought of him. There would be time for grieving later.

She sighed and half-listened as Lucan's high voice went on. *Yes, my son and my duty are all I have left. And that duty will be his one day.* Though she was calling a moot to confirm it out of courtesy, Rhia was the accepted heir of Carradan and one day Lucan would be hers. He would be the half-Gaian chieftain of the Caderyn and perhaps even of all the Caledon. *My little boy may be the best chance that we have of living together in peace.* Rhia half-smiled. The child earnestly teaching Owain about yellow wildflowers would one day be the great hope of his people. Her smile became a frown as she was struck by conflicting emotions. She wanted her boy to grow up brave and strong and be the chieftain he was born to be, yet at the same time she wanted nothing more than for him to stay as he was right now; a chatty little boy with no more cares in his heart than to remember which flower was which.

Rhia blinked a few times and tried to clear her head of all that. She tried to push away her worries about her responsibilities and her son's; tried not to think about the looming Gadarim tests and the dreadful duties that awaited her when she reached Bryngarth. It was a fine day in Caderyn land and she was surrounded by her friends and by her precious boy as they made their aching way back to her home. *Enjoy the simple pleasures of a quiet ride, my girl. You'll be missing them soon enough.*

*

They had arrived earlier than she'd expected but much had been prepared already. The line of torches had been lit, the mourners gathered, and the barrow made ready to receive the last High Chieftain of the Caderyn. Rhia was tired and tearful, as were most of her people, but she had sworn to herself that she would do this before anything else, and so she set her jaw and stood up straight as the tears ran silently down her cheeks.

They were standing at the bottom of the town's north-western slope, the sky blood red as Belenos sank on the horizon. The green of the grass was slowly turning to grey and the unmistakable smell of early evening mixed in with the smoke from the torches. Bael was standing in front of the chieftain's barrow, a solemn expression on his young face. Rhia wished that Reaghan could have been here for this. The elder druid had been a father to them all and had known Carradan since the chieftain was young. But none were certain where exactly Reaghan had gone. Aside from a vague comment about communing with the gods he'd given no explanation for where he was going, and if Bael knew anything he had not shared it. Rhia suspected that he knew where his senior had gone but for all their benevolent nature the druids were still secretive, and what little she knew of their ways she struggled to understand.

Bael was dressed in his flowing white robe, his feet bare and his oak staff held in his hand. Rhia couldn't help but think that, were it not for the darkness of his beard, the young man might have passed for Reaghan in this half-light. Both had beak-like noses and piercing blue eyes, and both projected the same aura of calm authority. Bael was shaking his staff and making the iron rings on it jangle, chanting slowly in the ancient tongue as the body was brought forward. Only the druids truly understood the old language, and though Rhia knew the odd word she couldn't hope to follow what he said. She knew it was a blessing though, and that was all that mattered.

Rhia cast her eyes across the green-grey humps that were the barrows of her people's chiefs. She looked out past them a little further to the humbler graves of Bryngarth's people, mainly as a way to put off having to turn around.

She didn't want to look at the wooden frame that was being carried towards them. She clenched her fists as subtly as she could. *You are no coward and you owe him better than this. Turn and look at him.* Rhia tore her eyes from the distant landscape and looked back towards the huddle of her people. A red cloak had been placed over her father's body but just knowing that he was under there was enough to make her want to sob. Carradan had been so strong, so assured. A big man with a big heart, the High Chieftain had taken good care of his tribe, and had loved his family as dearly as any man could love anything. He'd been wise in peace and fearsome in war, and had been named to the Gadarim when still a very young man. The name Charging Bull had been renowned throughout the tribes, and even among his enemies he had been treated with respect. Until Sedryn, the honourless son of Baercban, had stabbed him in the back in his own hall.

Rhia fought back her anger and tried to maintain her composure. No Lurian would judge another for weeping at their father's death but Rhia knew that if she dwelt on it she might end up screaming in rage. Sedryn, she hated even his name, had gone against everything his people had stood for and even his own father had been ashamed at what he'd done. *Not enough to stand aside though. But then would I step aside and let him be killed if Lucan did something so shameful?* If anything that thought was more unwelcome than her grief and she shoved it away, focusing on the covered corpse that had once been Carradan.

The Gadarim of the Caderyn bore him up to the entrance to the barrow and paused before the holy man. Bael continued his muttered chants, waving his hands over the body while he jangled the rings on his staff. After a few moments he stopped and raised his arms above his head, speaking in common Lurian in a loud but unstrained voice.

'Carradan son of Cadog, the Charging Bull, will tonight cross over to the green pastures of the Otherworld. May Father Camelas and Mother Marna look upon him with favour, and may Annwn and Damara both greet him as a friend. May he cross the bridge unharmed.'

Rhia joined the others in placing a hand to her chest and echoing the blessing.

'May he cross unharmed.'

Bael nodded.

'Bring forth your gifts.'

Men and women stepped forwards carrying great wicker baskets full of offerings. Every soul in Bryngarth had given something to their chieftain for his journey to the next world, each man according to his means. There were loaves of bread and wheels of cheese, strings of sausages and bowls of oats, chickens, eggs, sheaves of wheat, jugs of milk, and a huge barrel of finest mead with a gold-banded drinking horn on top of it. The opening to the barrow was not large but it was big enough that Bael and the Gadarim were able to carry them inside where they would sustain Carradan on his final journey. Bryngarth's Gaian administrators, who'd remained at Rhia's order after the enforcers left, had on their own initiative collected a small number of silver coins and these too were placed in the barrow. Rhia doubted her father would be needing them in the Otherworld but it was a kind offer and she had thanked them accordingly. Even their occupiers had wanted to show respect to the great man.

After that, and a few more blessings from Bael, came the moment she had been dreading. Stepping forward she took hold of the wooden frame along with Olwyn and Myrna, their mother, with Owain and the Gadarim assisting them. Even with help it was heavy, holding a big man dressed in furs and thick bracelets, and the golden torque he had never worn in life, but Rhia didn't let the strain show as she carried her father to his grave. The opening to it was dark and, though she was loathe to admit it, terrifying, but Bael went before them with a torch in his free hand, chanting all the while in words she didn't understand. Ugly, cold thoughts threatened to invade her mind and Rhia tried to shut them away. She tried hard not to think of her own death, or to dwell on the fact that she would never hear her father's voice again in this world. It was difficult, *very* difficult, and she felt her hands begin to shake despite herself. Rhia snarled quietly and clenched her free hand into a fist. She was here to honour her father; that was what she should focus on.

They placed Carradan with his feet facing west, that he might look up to see through the barrow wall to the red-and-gold sunset beyond. They said the Soul Bridge could be found to the west if a man sailed far enough, but as yet none had found it and come back to tell the tale. *But then, who would?* Last of all, Owain placed Ironhorn beside its former master.

'You lived and died with honour, Charging Bull. Mabonac is made proud.'

When Carradan met Annwn he would hand him his sword, and the God of Death would hold it and know what deeds it had performed. Carradan had always been noble and had never used the weapon unjustly, and Rhia knew beyond a doubt that Annwn would smile when he held the blade. *And then my father will leave it with him and walk*

36

*on into the Otherworld, where none will ever need to hold
a sword.*

Rhia felt more tears coming as the Gadarim blessings
were made, and she made no effort to hold them back. She
held hands with Olla and her mother for a few moments
and all three cried together as they looked down at the
body. Their family had known so much grief already that
Rhia sometimes thought they should be immune to it by
now. But her mother, wise woman that she was, had said
that only through grief could they truly know how much
they had loved. Horrible though it was Rhia could not
deny the truth of it. She wept on.

After a few moments Bael gently ushered them out and
the three women emerged onto the grass. Rhia looked to
where Lucan and Siriol stood, neither child really knowing
what was going on but knowing well enough that it was
something sad and serious. She looked at her son's face
and once again saw Marius there, and when Bael gave her
the nod it was a moment before she was able to speak.
Lurian funerals did not require the oratory of Gaian ones
but nonetheless it was only right that she make a blessing.

'Fellow Caderyn, tonight we mourn for Carradan son of
Cadog. He was my father, and a father to us all. He was
noble and strong, and we can best honour him by living as
he did. Let us weep for his death but take solace in his
life, for he was a good and joyous man, let us remember
him as such.'

She wasn't sure what more she could add to that but it
didn't seem like there was much more to be said. Nothing
that wouldn't reduce her to more tears anyhow. *And
you've more to shed yet tonight.* Once again she placed
her hand on her heart and around her others did the same.

'May he cross the bridge unharmed.'

The blessing echoed back at her and she stepped aside to let Bael continue his chants. He did not go on much longer and soon enough he was calling the family and Gadarim back to him and indicated the pile of stones that lay beside the entry. One by one, beginning with Myrna, they took up a stone and kissed it before placing it in the entryway. Olwyn went next with Rhia following, and as she placed the stone down she tried to remember Carradan's smiling face, his booming laugh and his kindly eyes. She managed it for only a moment before the present came back to her again, and she stepped aside to let Owain pass. Slowly the stones piled up and the yawning opening to the barrow grew smaller and smaller. Rhia watched as her people walled her father in to his last resting place on this earth, and tried to brace herself for what would come next. Already she felt like she was standing neck-deep in a river and the current was buffeting her off balance. And there was more to come.

The barrow was sealed and there was a period of silence for all to give a last few thoughts to Carradan. Rhia had no idea if he could hear her before he crossed but she decided to try him anyway. *Father...* she wasn't sure what she ought to say next and it took her a moment before she could continue. *Father, I hope only to do as you did and lead the Caderyn and the others with fairness and wisdom. I could never hope to be the leader you were but I promise,* she balled her fists again, *I promise to try with everything I have. I know that is what you would have done.* She paused another second, once again lost for words, and settled for the simplest thoughts that came to mind. *I love you. I miss you. May I have even half of your strength or your kindness.*

Rhia wiped away some of the tears that stained her face and shared embraces with both Olwyn and their mother. She bowed politely to Bael and began walking south around the slope of Bryngarth's hill, her heart in her throat. Within easy sight of the chieftains' barrows a great pile of dry wood had been set up, and Rhia's second funeral of the day was waiting for her.

Gaian nobles burned the bodies of their loved ones after death, and Rhia had sent instructions ahead of the column to make sure that all was ready. She knew only a few of the rituals involved but she had lived for five years in the city of Tamora and had seen more than one nobleman lain to rest. She had spoken to Bael and he had agreed to do what he could in the absence of Gaian priests, saying he would appeal to both their own gods and to Marius' for his safe passage. The young druid followed her as she made her way to her husband's pyre.

Rhia was short but the pile of wood was not high, and she was able to look down at the face of Lucan's father. His death had been bloody but the herbwives had cleaned his body and dressed him in a fresh blue tunic. Gaians generally liked to wear white for things like this but in the west, white was the colour of the druids. Marius wouldn't mind. Rhia reached out and brushed a strand of dark hair away from his face. He looked peaceful, she decided, though perhaps that was just because she *wished* that he was.

Bael stepped close to the pyre and spoke quietly, his words a strange-sounding mix of Lurian and Vulgare.

'Marius Dessidus Antonius, we wish you safe passage to the golden fields of Elysium. May Camelas and Gron, Marna and Cassio, Taran and Vulco, Mehine and Sulis all be with you and guide you on your way.'

Rhia heard the words but kept looking at Marius, hoping they were doing right by him. She remembered how the Gaians priests had said that gods were the same the world over and that only their names became different. They'd said that Camelas was just a Lurian name for Gron, and Sulis merely the Gaian name of Mehine. Rhia had even owned statues that represented them both, back in their great house in Tamora. Rhia genuinely didn't know what to believe any more on that score, but however many gods it took to get Marius safely to the next world, she would pray to them.

She looked down at his face and let more tears fall from her eyes. For so long she had convinced herself that she did not love him. Their marriage had been arranged and they had made the best of it, and in time they had grown friendly and even fond of one another, but never had she told him that she loved him, nor had he declared it to her. Only after she had seen his bleeding body hit the ground that day had she realised how wrong they had both been. There had been no thunderclap, no moment of blind passion, no searing heat of lust as there had been with Bevan, but nonetheless love had somehow grown between them. Through their years together that love had become something she could never deny, but she had only understood it once it was gone.

Rhia put her hands on the pyre and grasped the branches tight. She would not succumb to anger. She was here to grieve and pay respects to her loved ones, not to rail at the world for its unfairness. In the corner of her eye she saw that Owain among others had come with her to the pyre. Marius had after all fought alongside the Caderyn and been named a Gadarim after his death; it was only right that his brothers attend his final rituals. She paid them no mind for now though as she fumbled in the pouch at her belt. When she and Marius had fled Tamora they'd taken as much gold with them as they could and she still had plenty of it stored up in the longhouse. The coin she took from the pouch was thick and heavy, with the Emperor's head on one side and a wreath of oak leaves on the other. The oak was as sacred to the Lurians as it was to the Gaians and was preferable to Tiberian's face, so Rhia put that side of the coin to her lips and kissed it softly.

She had learned that the Gaian beliefs were not so very different to those of her own people, but while the Lurians saw the way to the next world as a bridge across a chasm, the Gaians saw it as a river with a ferryman. No Gaian, no matter how poor, was lain to rest without *something* to pay their boatman, and a rich man was expected to pay in gold. Perhaps it was foolish, but it explained why the Gaian scribes had given coins for Carradan's barrow. Rhia only hoped that wherever Marius was, she too could go there after her death. Either the druids didn't know or they wouldn't tell whether the Gaian Underworld and the Lurian Otherworld were one and the same place, but Rhia hoped and prayed that they were. For a moment she felt conflicted, since Bevan was surely waiting for her in the Otherworld as well, but she put her confusion aside for the time being. She and Bevan had loved each other dearly but she had mourned for him years ago; tonight was for her Marius.

41

Carefully, she opened his mouth and placed the coin inside, whispering what was probably a mangled blessing but one that she felt ought to be said.

'Cross your river unharmed, Marius son of Glaucus. And cross with my love.'

She gently laid her hand on his forehead and might have stayed that way forever had her fellow mourners not approached. Owain, Elfed and Bedwyr appeared to her left and laid their hands respectfully on the pyre, with Gawan, Gwydion and Tarwyn appearing on her right. It wasn't strictly a part of the Gaian ritual but Owain produced Marius' recovered sword and placed it beside him on the wood, with Gawan supplying the Gadarim's blessing.

'You lived and died with honour, Roaring Lion. Mabonac is made proud. The Dragon God will guide you home.'

The other Gadarim echoed him, Rhia included.

'He will guide you.'

Rhia struggled to keep her composure as she watched the Gorvicae warriors bow their heads in respect. Not all the Caledon had liked Marius, he *had* once fought against them after all, but Gawan especially had hated him. Yet the Gorvic had named both Marius and Rhia to the warrior elite, and now he offered blessings on this man he had so reviled. She nodded both to him and to Owain in silent thanks. Behind them she glimpsed Lucan and Siriol, both hiding behind Meghan's skirts looking scared and confused as they watched. She knew she probably ought to say something to her son, something to comfort or explain things to him, but she couldn't bring herself to do it. It was hard enough keeping from breaking down already and if she spoke to Lucan about his father she knew it would open the floodgates.

Bael passed her a burning brand and she took it without a word. This was it. Like placing the last stone in Carradan's barrow, this would be the final moment before her husband's soul could rest. She held it close to the wood but hesitated before lowering it. She was still wearing Marius' Vulco amulet around her neck and she wondered if she ought to place it on the body. The silver sword-and-spear was the only symbol she had of the gods of Marius' ancestors, and it seemed right that he should wear it in death. But then Gaians didn't really hold with such practices and in any case, Rhia was loathe to part with it. The little trinket was like a link back to her husband and, selfish though it felt, she knew his spirit wouldn't mind her keeping it.

Once again Rhia found herself wondering if where he went and where she went were the same place, or even places close by to each other. She liked to think that no god that cared for them would allow them to be kept apart and she prayed to Lurian and Gaian deity alike in the hopes that they might one day be reunited. She almost smiled. Marius would never stand for being kept from his wife and son. She could almost hear him arguing with his gods, calm and eloquent, and explaining to them firmly why it had to be as he said. And her clever husband would get his way.

The smile actually appeared as she banished her fears for his soul. Both his holy men and hers agreed that the gods loved those with courage and kindness, and no man could doubt that Marius was rich in both. Either Annwn would make a wide bridge for him or else his boatman would ferry him to safety. She gently placed the brand onto the pyre and stepped back to watch the flames dance up from the kindling. Fresh tears still rolled down her cheeks but despair could not keep a hold of her. She still had her boy; a living statue of her husband, and Marius would be safe in whatever afterlife awaited him. And one day she would see him again, if she lived a tenth as nobly as he had. Rhia watched as orange flames engulfed her husband's mortal form and felt the heat on her skin as the pyre burned. *You will cross unharmed to the next world my love, and one day I shall see you there. Be patient my Marius. I love you.*

Chapter 3. The Longhall

Gawan was as close to contented as he ever got, lying in a comfy cot bed with Emeryn in his arms. The straw mattress beneath them was old and shabby but it was soft enough, and a welcome change from sleeping beside the road. His back felt comfortable for the first time in days and he stretched his legs out until his feet poked through the blanket, grunting quietly in satisfaction. Emeryn stirred a little beside him but did not wake. A lock of hair had fallen across her face as she slept and for some reason Gawan was reminded of his mother; in her face Emeryn was nothing like her but her hair was the exact same shade of golden yellow. Before he could stop himself he was thinking of his brother too, who sported the same colour in his hair and beard, but Gawan shoved his image aside before it could form. He had no wish to think about Rylion.

His mind wandered instead to the funeral rites of the night before. Carradan had been a good man and a good chief. He might have been a Caderyn but he had always seemed strong and just, and Gawan found that he was sad that he was gone. The Gaian on the other hand... he'd had his strengths; he'd been brave and bold, and he'd done a fine job turning their warriors into a legion, and Gawan had no regrets at all about having called him Gadarim. But nonetheless he could not say that he missed the man. He'd been arrogant and self-satisfied in that manner that the Gaians did so well, and though he'd just about come to respect him, he had never for a moment liked him. *He deserves to be at peace with his ancestors though. He earned that much at least.*

Gawan found himself wondering what would happen to the soul of that Panther legionary whose head he'd taken. He knew little enough of Gaian gods but if they had any sense of justice they would punish men like that for their crimes. *But are they gods of conscience though? If they are, their people don't seem to listen to them much.* He put it from his mind, such philosophising was for druids anyway, and instead enjoyed his memories of the night before.

On another occasion he might have been invited to sleep in the longhall but it was filling up with Caderyn chiefs coming to Bryngarth for the moot. Instead he and Emeryn had been put up in one of the long houses on the other side of the town, along with a couple of score of others. Like most hillforts the Caderyn capital contained several simple longhouses for use in time of war, when all the nearby clans would abandon their villages and gather at the hill. Such need had always been rare but for times like this the houses were ideal. *And treaty or not the Gaians still look westwards. Who knows when these houses may be needed again?*

There was little enough by way of privacy here but nobody seemed to care that much. Gawan and Emeryn hadn't been the only ones to enjoy themselves on proper beds last night, and though it was somewhat improper for them to be doing so unwed, that was a rule mainly observed in the case of youngsters. Both Gawan and Emeryn had been married before and there was no loss of innocence in their intimacy.

Gawan found himself in danger of thinking about his former wife, something he was in no rush to do, and so instead he distracted himself with other thoughts of his home. He wondered what would be happening at Graigarw this morning, and whether chiefs and headmen had been called yet to decide on a new High Chieftain for the Gorvicae. He did not look forward to sitting in on the moot, any more than he looked forward to being present for the Caderyn one, but he was a First Man and it would look amiss if he was not there. *Well you'd have far less of this to do if you hadn't killed our last High Chieftain!* Gawan grumbled at the criticising voice. He'd been right to kill Baercban, it was just a pity it had made everything so complicated.

He sighed to himself. First things first, he needed something to eat. The stone longhouse was built with two great hearths, one at each end, and fires had been lit at both. Emeryn was notoriously difficult to wake in the mornings but still Gawan took care not to disturb her as he eased himself out of the simple bed. His lover let out a snuffling snore but gave no other reaction as he swung his legs from under the blanket and hauled himself to his feet. He was aching, as he generally did, but not nearly so much as he had done after sleeping on the road, and he felt worlds better after a few stretches. It wasn't cold and he threw on his brown breeches and tunic without needing anything heavier to go over it. He clasped on his belt by its pawprint-shaped buckle, but left Heartreaver with his cloak and boots as he looked about the long room. Tarwyn and the others were squatting beside the nearest hearth and he started off towards them, picking his way through the forest of beds and blankets.

Gwydion and Hewin were cooking sausages on sticks and Gwydion held one out to him as he approached, with Tarwyn passing him some bread. The First Man made the mistake of taking the sausage first and winced as the hot meat burned his fingers. He almost dropped it to the floor but managed to snatch the bread from Tarwyn and place the scalding sausage on that instead. The others smirked but said nothing as he blew on his fingers, and he suspected he was not the first of them to do something so stupid that morning. After the long ride that had followed the worst battle any of them had seen, this chance for rest would be making many people complacent.

Gawan shook his hand a few times and eased himself down to join them. Gwydion offered him a mug of brown ale and he nodded his thanks before he sipped. It was decent stuff he supposed, though nothing like what Anryn could brew up of course. He looked over to see young Pryder helping a Caderyn local to manhandle a massive cooking pot, while two others struggled behind them bearing bags of oats. In all fairness to their hosts they were doing their best by them, though it must have been a strain to have the Gorvicae to feed on top of so many of their own people. Tarwyn spoke through a mouthful of bread.

'Good send off last night.'

There were mumbles of agreement but no real conversation started, not that it really mattered. They had known each other long enough to enjoy a comfortable silence and Gawan chewed quietly on his sausage. It was still hot but not too hot to eat, and the flavour was rich and pleasant. *Erivon back home makes better ones of course, but these aren't bad. Not bad at all.* He noticed that there were several more on a wooden plate waiting to be cooked, and he picked up a long stick and skewered one of them before shuffling closer to the hearth. Almost at once he felt the familiar illusion of his back being cold simply because his front was closer to the fire, but he ignored the sensation and held the meat out to the flames.

He was watching it go from pink to brown when Pryder sat down next to them.

'I was just talking to some of the Bryngarth boys. You know Rhianwyn is calling her chiefs for a moot today?'

It was in fact fairly common knowledge but Gwydion spoke before Gawan could comment on Pryder's slowness.

'I don't see the point, myself. She's Carradan's heir after all.'

Tarwyn shrugged without looking up.

'Her brothers may be dead but she *does* have a living sister. Her elder too, judging by the funeral.'

Gwydion snorted.

'Well I've never heard of her. If she wanted to be chief she should have come to Nantwyn with us, it's too late to start challenging Rhianwyn now.'

Gawan only half-turned from the fire to speak.

'It is nothing to do with her sister. Rhianwyn knows she was only accepted as their leader because we were at war. She will want to make sure her headmen are happy with her remaining as chieftain now that we are at peace.'

Saying the words felt odd and Gawan found himself wondering what a real peace might mean. What would the world be like if there was no more fighting between the tribes; no more scrapping with the Caderyn or raids from the Dariniae and, Taran-willing, no more attacks from the Gaians? He knew he ought to be happy about it but he found himself frowning at the flames. *Without war, what use is there for Gadarim?*

The others either nodded or shrugged noncommittally and Hewin was the next one to speak up.

'What of the Caledon then? Is she to be chieftain of that as well?'

The question was asked of the group but they all looked to Gawan for the answer. The First Man rolled his shoulders.

'When Carradan was made leader of the Caledon even Reaghan agreed that he was only to lead it while we were at war. If the Gaians mean to keep their word we should need no single chief.'

Gwydion snorted again.

'I'll lick my own balls before I trust a Gaian to keep his word.'

Tarwyn raised an eyebrow, the serious man's equivalent of a smirk.

'But then you've been trying to lick your own balls for years?'

Gwydion looked ready to reply but Hewin leaped in first.

'I assumed he was just trying to suck his own shaft again, Tar.'

Gwydion threw a handful of crumbs at both of them.

'With a member like mine I'd barely have to bend my back to reach it! But with so many girls keen for a taste, why make the effort?'

Young Pryder held up a sausage that was barely the length of his finger.

'Perhaps because they want a bit more than *this*?'

The blonde Gadarim grabbed Pryder and slapped the meat from his hand, only for Tarwyn to catch it expertly and wave it towards him.

'It feels a bit soft to me as well Gwyd; you know my grandfather chewed goatweed to help him with his, maybe you should try it?'

Gwydion was still happily grappling with Pryder, trying to topple him.

'I've not felt as many sausages in my life as you have Tar!'

Gawan watched them bicker and smiled with just his eyes. He rarely engaged in banter like this but he always enjoyed listening to it. Hewin and Pryder had been fighting beside them for most of seven winters, and Gwydion and Tarwyn had known each other for twice as long. After all the blood and death they'd seen, it was nice to hear them laugh.

Hewin, his stubby fingers wrapped around another sausage, grinned at the group, his voice low.

'Between us, I'd not say no to this new chieftain getting a feel of mine.'

Gwydion smirked.

'Well I hope you and Karadoc are very happy together!'

Hewin looked ready to throw the meat then remembered his stomach and settled for shaking a hollow fist at his friend.

'*Their* chieftain you plough-end.'

Tarwyn raised an eyebrow.

'The Wildcat?'

Hewin took a bite and spoke as he chewed.

'Are you saying you *wouldn't*?'

Tarwyn just shrugged but Gwydion grinned.

'Maybe; assuming I survived to tell of it! Would you want her claws turned on you?'

The others chuckled and Gawan smirked to himself as he drew the stick from the fire and dropped the sausage into some bread. Rhianwyn was appealing in a forest-sprite sort of way but she was nothing to a woman like Emeryn. And of course, he'd never wanted to *kill* Emeryn. He looked over to their bed. The blankets weren't thin but he could still see the outline of her body through them, and as he watched he saw a length of pale leg come into view. Emeryn seemed to be coming awake and Gawan felt himself stir at the sight of her flesh.

He poured out a second cup of ale and rose to his feet.

'I'll see the Wildcat at this moot no doubt, I'll make sure to pass on your affections.'

Hewin looked slightly shamefaced but couldn't hide his smile, and the others grinned or shoved at him good-naturedly. Gawan nodded towards Emeryn.

'Meanwhile I have concerns of my own.'

His fellow Gadarim chuckled as he walked off and he heard Hewin mutter to his companions.

'I swear, some men have all the good fortune.'

For a heartbeat Gawan felt his good mood punctured as he thought of how very wrong that sentiment was. But then Emeryn's dark eyes met his and she beckoned to him lazily, and his mind was taken up by other things.

*

Gawan hated to admit it, but this young Caderyn druid looked every inch the equal of Hywel. The Gorvic holy man must have seen threescore winters at least, and his grey hair and beard were testament to his years of experience and wisdom. He wore his white robes as though born in them and the hands that clutched his oaken staff were almost as gnarled as the wood. His eyes were deep and dark, his features long and serious, and the impression Gawan had always had was one of quiet dignity and knowledge. And he spoke to Bael as though addressing a peer, not an acolyte. The Caderyn seemed barely older than his soon-to-be chieftain, yet something in how he carried himself belied his lack of years. Gawan knew that there were druids among the Caderyn who were older than he but they seemed not to have objected to Bael's representing them here, and it was not difficult to see their reasoning. Though there was no hint of silver in his hair or beard his blue eyes were full of wisdom, and Gawan couldn't help but think he was a worthy stand-in for Reaghan.

They were standing about in Bryngarth's longhall and besides the two druids the only people there were a handful of Gadarim and Rhianwyn herself. Many of the headmen had been sleeping there of course but they had stepped outside with another of the druids for a blessing before the moot began. Gawan took the mug of ale that Owain handed him and the pair strode towards the high table. Though he'd only been there a few times in the past, it was strange not to see Carradan's blocky frame in the chieftain's chair. He'd not been a tall man but he'd had a certain presence about him, and the lean figure of Rhianwyn looked almost comical in his place.

The two druids stopped their talking as the Gadarim approached but not in such a way as to seem suspicious or secretive. They had probably been talking of things that Gawan and Owain wouldn't understand anyway and the warriors both nodded politely to their tribes' holy men.

53

The druids nodded back but said nothing and the Gadarim continued to the table. Gawan briefly pondered what the druids thought about the idea of the Caledon, and decided fairly quickly that most were in favour of it. It had been Reaghan's idea in the first place after all, and druids were fond of saying how Lurians killing one another should be avoided. *Their say in things will go far in persuading the tribes to stick together. But druids for all their influence always stop shy of commanding men, and plenty of chiefs will have doubts about remaining as allies.*

Gawan leaned on the table near the place he'd once sat years ago, when he'd come to Bryngarth as a prisoner after losing at Broken Stream. He'd had a choice few words with Rhianwyn and her first husband that night, and once again he was struck by the strangeness of seeing her sitting in the chieftain's chair. Owain moved to sit beside her while Kyran took a seat near to Gawan. The Gorvic looked at his fellow First Men and wondered if they could have seemed more different. Owain was pale-haired with a broad and honest face, his body stocky and short-limbed, almost like a Carrock. Kyran on the other hand was tall and lean, with a hard, gaunt face that made Gawan think of predator birds. His hair and beard were dark and below one eye was the tiny scar that marked the faces of all Dariniae Gadarim. Like his fellows he was covered in permanent battle-marks but Gawan found himself wondering, as he often had, how the islanders' rituals differed from his own.

The Caderyn's First Man addressed his chieftain.

'Have you given any thought to what we spoke of earlier?'

Rhianwyn looked a little awkward for a moment and scratched the ears of the brown dog who sat beside her chair.

'I am still considering it.'

Gawan was only mildly curious but apparently Kyran was more interested. Though the Darin's voice was naturally harsh, like cold iron scraping on rock, his tone was courteous enough.

'May I ask what this is?'

Rhianwyn didn't answer and so Owain turned to his comrade.

'With Madoc and Marius both dead, it will be down to me to teach the boy Lucan about our ways. I had been wondering if we should talk about where to start, and when.'

Kyran nodded his approval.

'Quite right.' He faced Rhianwyn. 'You will want him to join the Dragon Legion one day, I assume?'

The chieftain looked hesitant.

'I want him taught our ways of course, but to join the legion? I am not sure. He still has family in Tamora and I had thought to send him back there to be given a Gaian education. He will need it if he is to treat with the Gaians, which he will inevitably have to do someday.'

Gawan's brow furrowed slightly and he decided to weigh in.

'You will do the boy no service by making him into one of them. Nor will your people stand for it if he is to become High Chieftain after you.'

He put a very subtle emphasis on 'your' as opposed to 'our'. He was still far from convinced about how long the Caledon would last, let alone this so-called treaty with the

Gaians.   Rhianwyn had her answer prepared.   *She probably knew this argument was coming.*

'We are fools not to keep on good terms with the Gaians. Lucan's being educated in Tamora is our best hope for keeping that.'

Owain took over the argument against her, his voice a fraction more respectful than Gawan's had been.

'If he is to be our chief he must be raised Lurian and be *seen* as Lurian by all.'

Kyran nodded gravely.

'Already too many people see him as the soft-handed son of a Gaian.'

Rhianwyn held in her temper but Gawan could see it bubbling beneath the surface.

'He *will* be Lurian because he *is* Lurian. I promise you that he will learn our ways and be a part of us but a Gaian education will take him far, as will his being known in Tamora's society.   In his time there he may build friendships to help secure our treaty for another generation.'

Gawan suspected that few enough of them trusted the notion of this Gaian 'treaty'. Rhianwyn, to her credit, had done her best to ensure that they honoured it, even going so far as to write it down as was their tradition, but there was little enough cause for mutual trust between Gaian and Lurian. Owain seemed about to say something of the kind but Rhianwyn cut him off.

'Lepidus was but one man. Not only should we not judge them all by his standards, but we must also remember that *he* was a man acting alone. We fought him off true enough, but the Emperor is another matter.   Should Tiberian decide he wishes all of Daeria to be conquered then our one legion would be no match for the armies he might bring. But he will not commit troops and resources to a campaign that is not necessary.'

She turned from Owain to address the group.

'Whether we will it or no, the Gaians rule the world. They are the future, and if we do not seize this chance to be their allies then a year or ten years or twenty years from now we *will* be destroyed as their enemies.'

Gawan could see that even as she argued she was denting her own pride, and he half-sympathised with her for it. But his own pride was stung just as hard, and he found himself speaking at the same time as Kyran.

'We have won before.'

'We stopped them once.'

It was a stupid thing to say and Gawan knew it but he couldn't stop himself. The truth that she was speaking was making all of them feel helpless, and he had lived his life as the predator, not the prey. Rhianwyn was clearly frustrated and was rescued from speaking by Hywel. The grey-haired man spoke quietly but everybody listened. No-one ignored a druid.

'We stopped two legions, one of them under-strength and frenzied beyond discipline, and another that withdrew largely by its own will.'

Gawan grudgingly agreed with him. He was still uncertain as to why the Lions who'd been flanking them had fallen back near the end of the battle, but then they'd been less tampered-with than had the Panther Legion. Perhaps their leader had thought to keep their formation intact and had fallen back to guard their fleeing general. Gawan almost snorted. *For all the good it did him.* Lepidus had been stabbed by his own slave as he tried to escape the battle; a Basian that the Gorvicae had subsequently taken in. Apparently he was an odd little fellow but he had done them a great service, and had been welcomed into the tribe with open arms.

Hywel continued in his patient voice.

'But the Blackbirds alone could decimate our damaged legion, and the Gaian Emperor has many more legions with him across the water.'

Rhianwyn nodded to him respectfully.

'Indeed, father. When last I heard tell of it Tiberian had seven more serving legions in Caspea and as you say, even those Gaians here now could cause us serious trouble. Not that they will.'

Gawan scowled. The Blackbird Legion were still far too close to them for comfort, for all that Rhianwyn was friendly with their general. They had allegedly marched into Caderyn lands to stop Lepidus and to deal with the rebel Gaian legions; the Lions by escorting them home to be judged, the Panthers by hunting them down and killing them. *Though these clever Gaians seem to have missed a few!*

Owain and Kyran wore expressions similar to Gawan's. They too hated to feel helpless but the fact of it was that a Gaian legion was almost unstoppable if it managed to maintain its discipline. More than a match for the battered Caledon. Gawan might have known the truth of it but still resentment swelled up in him at what Rhianwyn was saying. *She has seen them for what they are. Has she no pride?* He was unpleasantly reminded of Baercban and his voice didn't rise but still it came out hard.

'How far can you trust these men who have used sorcery to butcher our people? Would you first beg them for their mercy and then deliver them a hostage?'

There was a silent beat as blue eyes bored into Gawan's grey ones. For a woman who'd not seen thirty winters Rhianwyn had a glare to match most men. *There is strength there, no doubt about it. Whatever the Wildcat argues for, she does not do it out of cowardice.* All the same the Gorvic didn't look away when she spoke, her voice very cold and hard.

'They are not all alike, Gawan.'

The silence that followed this was awkward and Gawan eased his tone a little.

'Not all of one tribe share one mind, true. But the only Gaian I even *half*-trusted was burned to ash on this very hillside.' Rhianwyn looked like she might say something to that and Gawan held up a pacifying hand. 'And no doubt he crossed his river unharmed. But even *if* there are more decent Gaians out there, I do not trust those who they allow to lead them. And I have good cause to feel so.'

He suspected that the other Gadarim agreed with him but only Kyran nodded along while Owain remained motionless. Bael, who had been watching all this in polite silence, spoke up.

'There is truth in what both of you say. Lucan must indeed know our ways and be seen as one of us, yet we would be fools to think the Gaians will hold to their peace while they see us as strangers. All men fear what they do not understand and that fear can all too easily turn to hatred.'

He cast his piercing eyes around them and Gawan had the distinct feeling of being judged. He spoke as respectfully as he could but couldn't quite bring himself to call the young man *father*. It was a term for elders after all, not just for druids.

'I hate them not through ignorance but through experience.'

The others looked disapproving that he had answered back to a druid like that, but Bael was completely unfazed.

'You have experienced *some* of them comrade, and even you have said that not all think alike.'

The young man had referred to him as if part of his own tribe, countering Gawan's rudeness with courtesy. Gawan wanted to argue with him but he stayed silent. The druid continued.

'We would be wise to let them see that our chieftain is one who understands them and can deal with them. Rhianwyn has shown this of herself but,' he gave her a soft look, 'she will not live forever. An experience of Gaian life would serve the boy well, and through him it would serve us all.'

Hywel nodded his head in accord. Gawan still didn't like it and found something else to be stubborn about.

'What of when he marries? Our own people will be right to expect that he marries one of his own yet the Gaians may expect him to wed a Gaian.'

Rhianwyn looked both irritated and conflicted and Gawan got the feeling that this thought had crossed her mind already, and that she didn't have an answer to it yet. Owain spoke gently from beside her.

'For that matter Rhianwyn; will you be marrying again? Camelas knows you have lived through hard times and of course there is no hurry but all the same, you are still young.'

Perhaps Owain had meant to give her something else to talk about but deliberate or not his question raised another, unspoken concern. It was not rare for children to succumb to sicknesses and Lucan was an only child. Gaians or not, a chieftain needed an heir. Rhianwyn was indeed still young and fair, and there would be no shortage of volunteer husbands, either for the woman herself or the prestige of fathering a potential High Chieftain. *But then she was married to the Lion for five years and had only one child from it. It could be that one of them at least was none too fertile.*

The Caderyn chief kept her voice confident, though Gawan suspected it was a bluff.

'I am in no rush to hear another man's snoring as I try to sleep. I may choose to wed again, I may choose not to.'

It was said with finality and Owain fell silent on the matter. Bael spoke up quietly.

'And Lucan?'

A line appeared between Rhianwyn's brows and once again she scratched at the sitting hound's ears.

'He has not yet seen his fifth summer. Such things can wait.'

Gawan wondered whether or not he ought to speak again. This was Caderyn business after all, even if it might affect them all. The decision was made for him when the doors at the far end of the hall swung open and the first half-dozen Caderyn headmen came in. The huddle at the high table knew their conversation was over, at least for now, and that the moot to decide the new leader of the tribe was about to begin.

Gawan knew only a few of the men who would decide their tribe's fate. Some had come with them from

Nantwyn while others had come to Bryngarth from across Caderyn territory. The two senior men he recognised as Merwyn and Alraig. The former was the eldest of all the Caderyn chiefs and frankly, he looked it. While not much bent with age his hair was whiter than Hywel's, and he walked with a subtly stiff-legged gait. He wore several thick bracelets but beyond that he was plainly dressed, wearing a buff tunic and a sleeveless sheepskin coat that seemed to meld with his hair and beard.

Alraig was not that much younger but the years seemed to have been kinder to him, and he strode through the hall with strength and poise. His hair was still mostly brown, though he had streaks of silver at his temples and another running down the middle of his beard. He wore a deep red cloak, a dark tunic, and what looked like the studded belt of a Gaian legionary. He had not brought a sword with him of course but a second glance showed Gawan that a legion-issue dagger was sheathed at his hip. *I wonder, did he take that from a Panther or a Lion?* He had not been a part of the Dragon Legion but Gawan knew he had been present at Nantwyn, fighting with a group of his warriors up in the town itself.

Behind these two came others and Gawan vaguely recalled a few names. The lanky one he thought was called Gwynfor, the wild-haired one was Rhys, and the man with the scar across his nose could only be Uthyr. Beyond that the Caderyn headmen all blended together into a mass of faces that he had seen but couldn't name. One man he *did* know well was Boryn, one of the few Gorvicae chiefs who had come with them from Nantwyn. Rhianwyn had invited him to the moot out of courtesy, and as a way of showing unity between the tribes.

Boryn was of a height with Gawan but a little narrower in the shoulders and much greyer in his hair. His beard was trimmed close to his chin but his moustache drooped heavily over his lip as if to compensate. Naturally he was wearing a green cloak over one shoulder which he had fastened with a swirling brooch of yellow gold. Gawan gave him a polite nod of his head. While Boryn had his humorous moments he was generally a very serious man, and he returned the nod with his face grave. He was probably feeling both honoured and awkward at having been invited to this moot and would want to represent their tribe with dignity.

A rumble of conversation began which Owain would soon silence when he called for the moot to begin. Gawan got the feeling that things would go well for the Wildcat today but that a lot of old men would do a lot of talking before they were finished. He took a sip of ale and sank onto a bench. It all had to be done he supposed, and it was right that he should be there as it happened, but that didn't mean he was in for an interesting time of it. He sat up as straight as he could and put his cup down on the table, and told himself firmly not to let his boredom show.

*

Fearghal was fairly sure that he was dying. His wound had been bleeding intermittently for days and even if that did not kill him, in his weakened state something else almost certainly would. He found himself wondering about what would happen when he crossed over. Ordinarily he would have been confident that Mabonac would guide him safely; that his bridge would be broad, and that Annwn would welcome him as he handed him Hardbiter. He'd served his tribe well after all and had done little enough to displease the god. Now he was not so sure. Besides his many other faults he had abandoned his chieftain to die and had run away from a fight instead of rushing towards it. *But you had little choice in that and you did right by coming here, you know that.* He grimaced inwardly. The words were a hollow comfort.

The boat hit the stony beach and Fearghal winced as his wound bit at him again. He cursed Aerona's name for her cowardly attack but reminded himself that cursing wouldn't bind his flesh together. He tried to focus on the dragonfire in his body's centre but even that was fading fast. He sighed. It had been blind chance that he had fallen from the pier and been able to crawl to a boat, and even more so that Dyfan had been in it and able to tend to him. He should be grateful to the gods for that blessing and not waste what favour they gave on impotent cursing at his brother's wife.

Dyfan, a simple but decent Darin who'd been horrified by what he'd seen, had hidden Fearghal from sight and bound his side up as best he could. He'd then gone a step further and sailed him over the Glaswair Sea, landing them both on the Caderyn coast. If Fearghal was to redeem himself to Mabonac and Taran then he had to get word to Kyran, who was presumably at Bryngarth. It was a long damned way and he might well die before he reached him, but the First Man had to be warned that Caserach had murdered Ierryn, and would even now be seizing all of Niswyn in a stranglehold. The Dariniae were strong-willed but they had lost many warriors and headmen, and many would follow Caserach because they saw no other choice. Even

Fearghal, if he were honest, could see few other options open to them. But that wasn't the point. Ierryn had been murdered, and by his own kin no less. He had to be avenged and their people saved from this treacherous bastard.

Dyfan leaped from the boat and began making it fast to something. Fearghal wasn't paying much attention. What Dyfan lacked in conversation he made up for in the milkwine he made, and Fearghal was hardly able to focus his gaze on anything. He was reasonably sure that enough of that stuff would eventually make him blind, but it also managed to dull the pain in the wound that bitch had given him, and he had the feeling that 'eventually' was not a problem he would have to face up to. But that didn't matter, so long as he reached Kyran. If he could at least set things in motion for vengeance against Caserach then he could say to Mabonac that he had done all that he could. It might not make his bridge that wide but it should be enough that he might cross it in safety. *Perhaps*.

Fearghal shoved the doubts from his drink-sodden mind and tried hard to focus his thoughts. Mabonac's fire was dim but it was still there and he tried to kindle it in his centre. It was a long journey to Bryngarth and he would not get there without the Dragon God's help, and certainly by sitting here and fretting. With what felt like the effort of scaling a mountain he heaved himself to his feet and looked out to see the green grass and rolling hills of Caderyn land. *There'll be a lot of that to cross before I get to Kyran. Mabonac please, just keep me alive until then.*

Chapter 4. Preparing for the Dragon God

It had indeed taken a damned long time but Rhianwyn had eventually been confirmed as High Chieftain of the Caderyn. Gawan shook his head at the futility of it. The only ones who might have come close to challenging her were Merwyn and Alraig, and Merwyn had stated from the beginning that he was happy follow her, with Alraig agreeing to the same before the moot had even sat down. All these clan chiefs had trudged all the way to Bryngarth only to trudge all the way back home again, having done nothing but confirm what everyone else already accepted. Madness.

Gawan leaned back against the stone wall of the longhouse and looked out across the green hills to the west. Belenos was sinking but there was still plenty of light left, and the Gorvic had to admit, it was quite a view. *Though nothing to the view from White Ridge of course.* Beside him Emeryn was sipping contentedly at some sweet mead, her golden hair looking reddish in the evening light.

'So what did they say about the Caledon?'

Gawan tilted his head a little.

'Nothing definite. The alliance is to stay together it seems and none objected when she suggested drawing up some common laws, with important issues to be taken before the whole of the Caledon. She will be seen as a figurehead but has sworn not to seek to rule the other tribes and to respect the rights of her fellow High Chieftains. Even Boryn and his fellows were content with it.'

Emeryn wrinkled her nose. It was quite a pretty thing for her to do, not that Gawan would ever *tell* her that of course. He'd never hear the end of it.

'I still don't know about all this. I mean, we've been fighting the Caderyn for years, what happens when they remember that? And what happens when the Dariniae start raiding the coast again?'

Gawan shared some of her doubts but thought he might as well tell her the arguments that had been made to him.

'Hopefully we will all remember how much stronger we are when we fight together, and besides, some good may yet come of this. It would make it harder for criminals to flee from punishment, for one. If Rhianwyn has her way we shall have one set of laws and a man caught anywhere in Caledon territory will face the same justice as if he were at home.'

Though she was also in favour of putting these things, among others, in writing the way the Gaians did, which Gawan did not like. If they needed to wave about a piece of paper to show that something had been agreed, Gaians either had bloody short memories or else their spoken words could not be trusted. *It might be their way, and peace and trade with them might be nice ideas, but the Wildcat mustn't forget that* our *way is most important.*

Emeryn nodded half-heartedly.

'I suppose it makes sense. But if the Caderyn think they can tell us what to do in our own land then they have another thing coming.'

Gawan almost smirked. Emeryn might look fair but she had a fierceness to her that a man was foolish to underestimate. She'd fought Caderyn, Dariniae and Gaian alike in her time and had been a credit to her clan in every battle.

'That I don't deny, but Rhianwyn's not fool enough to risk warring with us again, not with the Gaians still bitter about defeat.'

Rhianwyn could call the Blackbirds friends all she wanted, Gawan knew fighting men and he knew they would be feeling resentful that an army of barbarians had defeated Gaian legions, rebel-led or otherwise. Emeryn shifted slightly to look at him more directly. It gave Gawan a generous view down her tunic and he suspected that was part of her reason for doing it.

'Did she say that she would make the Blackbirds leave?'

Gawan nodded, bringing his eyes back up to meet hers. There was a hint of satisfaction mixed in with the curiosity on her face.

'In a way. They are permitted to remain here another moon's turn while they hunt down more missing Panthers. After that no Gaian legion may cross Caledon lands again.'

Emeryn looked approving and Gawan didn't blame her. It had been a popular decision, and even Gawan hadn't minded its being written down. Rhianwyn had already had the Blackbird general put his mark on it and she insisted it would bind him to the words of it. Just *how* bound he'd be might remain to be seen but it was a good idea at least. Emeryn took another sip of her mead.

'I'll be glad to see the backs of those bastards. If nothing else we'd bleed hard if we wound up having to fight them.'

Gawan was reminded of yet another reason why he was so fond of his lover. She was no fool, yet still she had absolute faith that if it came to another battle her people would be victorious. So many Lurian spirits had been crushed by defeats, and while Second Nantwyn had done much to restore their courage, they still had a long way to go. In all honesty even Gawan wasn't quite so confident as Emeryn was, given how battered the Dragon Legion now was. Not that the prospect of losing would stop him from trying if it came to it. His tribe had been servants of the Gaians in all but name, and the shame of that still made him want to punch every Gaian he saw. He took a slow breath. *But we are at peace with them now. We are at peace with everyone.* Once again Gawan wondered what a Gadarim would do in such a time but was spared from having to dwell on it by Emeryn's next question.

'Did she say if she'd be marrying again?'

Gawan shook his head.

'I doubt it.'

Emeryn frowned.

'You would think she'd want a father for her boy.'

Gawan tilted his head a fraction but said nothing. He didn't like thinking about fatherhood. Emeryn continued, half to him and half to herself.

'She's still young, and she'd be wise to bear more children.' She nudged him with her elbow. 'A strong Gorvic in her bed would do her all sorts of good.'

Gawan wasn't well-known for his humour but Emeryn was good at bringing it out in him.

'Well I'm afraid I am spoken for, but I can ask some of the boys?'

Emeryn gave his arm a playful slap. If she'd noticed the hint about his intentions, or *possible* intentions anyway, she didn't mention it.

'I was thinking of Karadoc or Taliesyn. It would show that she takes us seriously.' She slapped his arm again.

'And don't go thinking that I'd have you anyway! Gwydion's closer to my age and I can tell he likes what he sees.'

Gawan knew she was teasing and merely shrugged again.

'He's not quite the fool he seems, I suppose.'

Emeryn sat up straighter and shoved him a little.

'For a man so besotted with me you show an annoying lack of jealousy!'

She pouted prettily. For a grown woman she could pout remarkably well and but for her eyes she might have passed for a flirting maiden. But Gawan could see all too clearly that she was mocking him, and herself, by her act. He knew the best thing to do now would simply be to take her in his arms and kiss her but the sound of movement nearby made him hesitate. He turned on the spot to see Gwydion and Tarwyn making their way towards him, both of their faces serious. Gawan resisted the urge to frown. He might be annoyed at their timing but the duty they had tonight was important. Emeryn was clearly annoyed as well but simply gave his hand a quick squeeze.

'Taran go with you.'

Gawan nodded his thanks as he heaved himself up. His two comrades stopped a few feet away and Tarwyn didn't waste time with pleasantries.

'Are you ready?'

Gawan nodded again.

'Always. Where is it to be done?'

This time it was Gwydion who spoke.

'They have gathered at the bottom of the slope, near to the treeline. Kyran is already on his way there.'

Gawan had taken off his belt to sit down and left Heartreaver leaning against the wall. Emeryn passed it up to him and Gawan took it without a word. The leather around the scabbard was soft and worn, and the weight of the iron weapon was comfortingly familiar. He let out a slow breath as he fastened his belt and shifted the sword into place on his hip. *You and I have work tonight my old friend. Taran and Mabonac guide us both.*

*

The sun was all but gone as the Gadarim gathered at the base of the hill. From the east the sky above was growing steadily blacker and Gawan even saw a star or two appearing in the north. Mabonac's rituals were always performed at night, since one of the many legends about him told that he and Belenos had been rivals in the distant past. They had fought a great battle over who could truly be called the Master of Fire, and the world had suffered terribly as a by-product; having to live without fire's warmth as both gods used all their strength to fight each other. They had eventually made peace for the sake of mankind's survival but even after this, Mabonac had resented walking the earth beneath Belenos' light. *A quarrelsome fellow; Mabonac. But then what else would befit a god of war?*

Gawan looked about him. Standing in the shadow of the darkening woods was the largest gathering of Gadarim he had ever seen. It was not unheard of for Gadarim of different tribes to attend one another's rituals but it was a pretty rare occurrence, and tended to involve only one or two visitors at most. Tonight Gadarim from three whole tribes had come together, with the First Men of the

71

Dariniae, the Caderyn and the Gorvicae all present. *Such a thing must not have happened for generations.*

A fire had been lit in an iron brazier carried down from the town, and the orange light made the battle-marks on the warriors' skin seen almost black. They were talking quietly amongst themselves for the moment but they would all fall into silence when the testing of Rhianwyn began. Gawan found himself thinking back to his own first ritual, more than twenty long winters ago yet still as fresh in his mind as though it were only yesterday. Like Rhianwyn he had first been named to the Gadarim by his merit and courage alone, when at only sixteen he had saved his chief's life from a wolf that might have torn the old man apart. It had already killed one of the headman's dogs and even now Gawan could still see the hunger in the grey beast's eyes. Young fool that he was he had leaped upon the beast and crushed its skull with his axe, too brave or too stupid to know how dangerous wolves could be. Their First Man, Hedrin, had named him the Leaping Wolf right there and then.

He looked down at the blackish-blue spirals on his left arm, the first battle-marks that had been made permanent on him. Even now he sometimes wondered if perhaps he'd been named as one of Mabonac's sons too early. He'd fought in battles before he'd killed the wolf and he'd gained a fearsome reputation since but all the same, to be named a Gadarim so young was a rare thing indeed, and for all his testing he had never been quite sure. *But then perhaps old Hedrin always intended it that way? Perhaps he saw potential in me and knew that giving me my name would make me work that much harder to earn it?* He almost smiled. It was the sort of thing the sneaky old sod would have done.

Of course he'd still had to face the trials just as Rhianwyn would have to tonight. He could still remember the days leading up to them, listening to every word that Hedrin and Ioan had said as they tried to prepare him. They could not tell him the details of the tests themselves of course, but their teachings on calming his mind and the blessings of the War Gods had been vital. *Owain will have done the same for the Wildcat these last few days, teaching her our ways and our legends. He'd best have done it well.*

Gawan took a breath of the evening air and caught the distant smell of the trees over the woodsmoke. He thought back to when he'd first walked into a circle of Gadarim, waiting to be tested before both them and his people's gods. He'd been so afraid on the walk towards them, unarmed and naked but for his painted marks, more afraid of what was to come than he could ever recall fearing an enemy. All his life he'd been a fighter and the tremor of combat was a fear he could easily conquer, but this… this had been something else entirely. To be Gadarim meant more than simply battling your way through people. It was to be a part of a brotherhood that went beyond everything, even a man's tribe, and simply being a bold scrapper was not enough to be counted as one of them.

But old Hedrin taught me well, or else Mabonac had plans for me. Or both. Though his heart had hammered like a maddened smith as he'd approached the ring of men, the moment he'd found himself among them he'd felt the Dragon God's fire in his belly. Mabonac had entered his spirit, and though Gawan had felt the eyes of gods and warriors watching him, his fear had been calmed by his focus. Looking back now he could remember how the tests had gone but at the time there had been no conscious thought at all, only instinct. He half-smiled, half-grimaced. *And pain!* Even through his focus the Test of Strength had been brutal, and the next morning he'd been struggling to walk. Though even that was nothing to the dreadful pain of the Test of Will. He looked down at the old scars on his hand and remembered the horrid, searing feeling of hot iron on his flesh. But then the pain of the tests had been good in its own strange way; it had been earned, and Gawan would not have wished away a single bruise.

He let out a sigh and hoped again that Owain had prepared their new sister well. If she failed it would reflect poorly on him, and it would be a bad omen for her tribe and for the whole Caledon as well. A few of the other warriors seemed anxious as they waited, though all of them were trying hard to conceal it. Gwydion and Tarwyn were chatting quietly enough but the set of their shoulders betrayed the tension they clearly felt. Hewin and Pryder were both shuffling their feet and more than one of the Caderyn men was pacing. Nearby stood a pair of female Dariniae that Gawan didn't know, but he suspected that behind their blank expressions they were silently praying to the War Gods. Women were rare among the Gadarim simply because young warriors were so rarely accepted and then later on, once they had children, women's priorities would naturally change. But all too many people assumed that females were so rarely accepted because they were weak, and for all that they might be of a different tribe, Gawan was sure the two Dariniae would be wishing Rhianwyn all the best. They would be glad of another woman wearing Mabonac's marks, another living example of the strength of their sex.

Gawan took care not to show his own apprehension and calmed his mind as he'd been taught to long ago. He focused on his body centre and felt the dragonfire smoulder within him. A glance around showed him that the more experienced warriors were doing the same thing, the same expression of calm readiness on their faces. The conversations died down as the warriors sensed that the time was coming, and soon the only noises were the wind in the trees and the crackling of the fires. Before long Gawan saw dark shadows against the pale grey of the hillside and soon enough, a pair of figures entered the circle.

Owain, First Man of the Caderyn, walked slowly and steadily as he escorted his new High Chieftain. But for her painted marks Rhianwyn was naked, as was the custom, and as she stepped into the firelight Gawan had to stop himself from staring. Next to Emeryn she was only a skinny little thing, but the sight was still pleasant and he felt a tiny stab of guilt. He regained his focus within a couple of heartbeats but all the same, he knew he ought not to have looked at her so. He saw other men around him in a similar position, looking once and then bringing their minds back swiftly to the task at hand. A little spark of pride in them banished his moment of guilt. *We might all enjoy the sight of a pretty girl undressed but every one of us here knows that duty is before all. First and foremost we are the Gadarim, the sons of Mabonac and the favoured of Taran, and this woman is to become our sister tonight. She will be treated with the respect she is due.*

75

Rhianwyn walked in amongst them with no fear in her eyes and Gawan was proud that he had given her her warrior name. He prayed quietly to the gods that she would pass her tests, as it was proper he should, but he had no doubt that she would succeed. He had seen the strength in the Wildcat too many times to doubt her now, and he was certain that his decision had been right. Gawan moved towards the two Caderyn with his face a solemn mask, but his spirit quietly confident that his faith had been well-placed.

Chapter 5. The Tests

There was almost no breeze, in fact the evening was quite warm, but all the same Rhia struggled to suppress a shiver. Belenos had set and the last ribbon of red had vanished over the horizon, the sky above her now a blue that was almost black. The grass beneath her bare feet was cool, and the woad of her battle-marks was still wet and cold on her skin. She walked towards the firelight with Owain beside her and tried hard to keep her hands by her sides. Besides all her other cares she was feeling horribly exposed and had to force herself to appear calm and relaxed.

Rhia never used to be nervous about her nakedness. When she was young she had swum in the river along with half the town of Bryngarth and no-one had cared a damn about their bodies. There would be some ogling and tittering, among the youngsters especially, and a fair share of joking and laughter, but no-one had really cared, and Rhianwyn least of all. They were all as the gods made them after all, what cause was there for embarrassment?

But that had been before. Rhia held her arms more firmly at her sides. That had been before a man she'd once thought good and decent had forced himself on her while she lay helpless. Before hollowness and shame had filled her soul to the point of drowning her, a feeling that even years later still plagued her dreams some nights. A good husband, a beautiful child, and a re-kindling of her pride meant she had kept that shame at bay, but the scar had never fully healed, and she often felt it never would. With Reaghan's help on top of everything else she was more at peace than she'd have ever thought possible, but still that terrible day had left its mark, and tonight she was all too aware of it.

Rhia ground her teeth and stuck out her chin defiantly. The greatest counters to the shame had always been the love of her family and her pride in herself, and that was exactly what she reached for as she strode towards the fire. Marius might be gone but he was still with her in her heart, and the thought of Lucan's face could always bring her back to herself. She almost smiled at the thought of him. Yesterday she had been teaching him about the Lurian names of the gods; of Belenos and Taran, of Camelas and Marna, as well as spirits like Karanon Lord of Mountains and Mehine the Lady of the Woods. He loved to hear the stories and then speak them back to all who would listen, taking great joy in everything he knew. Only that morning he'd been talking to everyone about Mehine and her dryads and was even swearing that he had seen one in the woods. It was already a happy memory but Rhia forced herself to put it aside. Now was not the time.

She walked on towards the warriors and what flutter of nerves she still felt at her nakedness she banished with a burst of stubborn pride. She was Rhianwyn daughter of Carradan, High Chieftain of the Caderyn and accepted leader of all the Caledon. She had a duty that extended far beyond any emotions, and if her spirit were to break, so too would that of her people.

She walked forwards into the firelight with her head held high, or as high as a woman of her height could hold it, and remembered the pride of her family and people. *And besides*, she thought as she strode on, *you are not naked. You wear the battle-marks of Taran and of Mabonac on your skin. You are as clothed as if you were wearing mail and furs.* For a tiny moment she wondered what would happen if she were to fail these tests. Would the skin on her arm have to be scraped off because of the marks already tattooed there? She'd once seen a man flayed alive in a Gaian prison and the dreadful image flashed unbidden before her eyes. She shoved it away. She would not fail. Her people were depending on her and failure was not an option tonight.

For all her determination she still felt nervous as they came to a halt, and she practiced focusing her mind as Owain had instructed her. It was without doubt the most valuable thing that he had taught her, though she had learned much and more the previous day from the new First Man of her Gadarim. First she had been told a legend she had never heard before; that of Taran and Mabonac's great duel. She had known of the Dragon God's feud with Belenos but had never before heard of the struggle between the two Gods of War. *Mabonac clearly liked to pick fights, even if he didn't hold grudges.* It seemed, back in the Ancient Days, the two had quarrelled somewhere up in the Black Mountains, and the night sky had burned as bright as day as the battle raged on the crags. The Dragon God had raked with claws as long as spears, and gnashed with teeth as sharp as sword-blades. He had sent red fire in gouts as thick as a man's waist and had flown in circles around Great Taran's head.

But the son of Camelas had skin as tough as leather and wore a cloak of wyvern scales. He could leap as high as the dragon flew and strike harder than a quake of the earth, and his mighty hammer, Morthyg, had battered at Mabonac with the strength of a thousand men. By midnight, Taran had struck the dragon a hundred times but

79

still he would not yield, and his fires were undimmed no matter how hard and swift the blows of Morthyg fell on him. In the end Taran announced that for all his might he could not defeat Mabonac, even if he continued the fight for a hundred years and more. The two had bowed deep to each other and had agreed upon a truce; Taran would keep his title as the God of War, but the finest warriors would all do homage to the Dragon God, in honour of his great spirit.

Rhia had listened spellbound to the tale, and to the tales of the first Gadarim when they had fought the wicked Sidhe, or battled snake-headed demons and giant spiders the size of mares. Some would have questioned legends of such amazing foes and deeds but Rhia had seen and felt the magic of the world, and had no doubt that there was truth in what she heard. But of course, the most important thing she had learned was how a Gadarim controlled himself through focus, and thus kindling what Owain called dragonfire in the centre of his being.

Though it was a mystery to most, Reaghan had once told Rhia about the magic that flowed through the world, the ava, and how the Gadarim touched that magic in their rituals without even realising it. Even so, learning how to use it had been something entirely new to her, and she had listened and practiced carefully with Owain. As she put her thoughts into her stomach and felt the glowing ball inside her, she was sure it was this same force that the druid had told her about. It was warm and soft, and yet undeniably powerful, and confidence flowed through her as she felt it.

Owain held his arm up high and raised his voice to the assembly. Rhia knew more of what was in store for her than most potential Gadarim and had heard these words spoken before. All the same, it was strange to hear the words being said of *her*.

'Brothers, Rhianwyn daughter of Carradan comes to us in the sight of Taran and Mabonac, that she would be confirmed in the ranks of the Gadarim. Who will be witness for this woman?'

Gawan, who Rhia thought was probably best described as her dearest enemy, spoke up.

'I will be the witness for this woman. I am Gawan son of Dearg. I am the Leaping Wolf.' He turned from Owain to face the others. 'With my own eyes I have seen her fight with courage and skill, both against my own people and beside them.'

Rhia looked around and was surprised to see not a single face showed any sign of awkwardness or resentment. The orange light flickered on a score of calm expressions, with no indication anywhere that these people had once been deadly enemies. *But then the Gadarim have always placed themselves above tribal rivalries. It's just strange to see it from so many of them.* Gawan continued speaking.

'I have seen her devotion to her people and seen her triumph against fighting men as well as against unnatural sorcery.'

He licked a finger and drew a circle in the air with it, and the Gadarim all copied the gesture. Rhia did the same a heartbeat later, though once again she was surprised by what she saw around her. The ward was a common enough thing to do when speaking of witchcraft, but normally people did it with a sense of fear or foreboding. Yet the Gadarim here were stone-faced and steady as oak, as if daring some evil spirit to try to break the protective charm.

'After the Second Battle of Nantwyn I named her to the Gadarim, as is my right as First Man of the Gorvicae. I say she is the Fearless Wildcat.'

Rhia still found it odd to hear her warrior name, but she didn't have time to dwell on it as Owain spoke back, his voice solemn but not harsh.

'Yet the tests have not been passed, and none may join our ranks who have not faced them. Do you wish to name any of the five virtues as proven, Leaping Wolf?'

Rhia controlled her nerves with an effort. What tests would he name, if any? Gawan would be allowed to declare two tests of the Gadarim virtues as already passed in combat, but would he? The man himself spoke clearly.

'Rhianwyn daughter of Carradan has done much for all of our tribes in the war against the Gaians. I say her Test of Loyalty is done. I say her Test of Courage is done.'

Rhia breathed out a little. She'd seen Ossian's courage tested and had not been looking forward to it. All the same, she'd not yet seen a Test of Strength. Owain nodded gravely and addressed the group.

'Very well. Three tests shall be carried out.' He turned to face Rhia. 'Prepare yourself for the Test of Strength.'

Rhia wasn't quite sure how to do that beyond continuing to breathe steadily and focus on the fire in her stomach. It seemed Owain did not expect much more because he nodded and then spoke again.

'Stand as I stand.'

The Caderyn First Man placed his feet wide apart and sank down until his thighs were in line with the ground, his back straight and his arms held out in front of him.

Rhia dutifully copied him and suspected she was not going to like what was to come. She put her mind into her body centre and took comfort in the warmth that she found there. Owain stood up again and stepped back, and the test began without warning. Kyran appeared at her side as if from nowhere and delivered a savage kick to her bent leg, slamming his shin into her thigh with bone-juddering force. Rhia winced as the muscle screamed out at her but she kept her stance strong and tried to block out the pain. The Darin moved around her like a stalking predator before striking her other leg just as hard, and Rhia worried that the limb would buckle. But she set her teeth and fixed her eyes on the fire ahead of her, stalwartly ignoring the pain. It was only the beginning.

Kyran repeated his attack a dozen times more before Owain raised a hand. The Caderyn then approached her with a handful of iron bracelets and carefully placed a pair of them over each of Rhia's wrists. The hoops were large and Rhia was small, and she might easily have fitted both her forearms inside just one of them. Her shoulders began to burn almost at once, and a part of her almost smiled. *At least it's taking my mind away from my legs.* The smile did not come.

As soon as Owain had stepped away Kyran began again, with vigour. His shins battered into Rhia's aching thighs until the muscles felt like raw meat being tenderised for stew. She wanted desperately to cry out, or at least drop her arms and straighten her legs, but she forced it back. This was her chance to count herself among the greatest warriors alive, and no mere pain was going to keep her from realising that dream. Though it came damned close. Four times more Owain added rings to her arms and four times more Kyran pounded at her burning legs. Rhia wanted to cry, wanted to scream, but she kept her eyes locked forward and her mind in her body's centre, until at last she heard Owain's voice again.

'Bloodhound, are you satisfied?'

Rhia was shaking as the Dariniae's First Man spoke to the crowd, and had to fight hard not to bite her lip in pain.

'Does any man here doubt the strength of Rhianwyn daughter of Carradan?'

There was no answer to Kyran's harsh-voiced question and Owain nodded to Rhia a second later.

'You may stand, and prepare yourself for the Test of Focus.'

Rhia let her arms drop and heard the thud and clang of the rings hitting the ground as she tried to straighten up from her painful posture. Her legs and shoulders were on fire and for a moment she thought she would collapse. Owain subtly moved forward a pace and Rhia knew he was offering for her to lean on him if necessary, but she wasn't sure how that would look to the watching Gadarim. She clenched her fists tight and forced herself to stay on her feet. Her respite was only brief however as Owain gestured for her to step forwards, and Rhia resisted the urge to pre-empt his request. She knew from watching Ossian what the next test would be and she waited patiently to be told what to do.

'Kneel here, on both knees.'

Lowering herself down was agonising and her thighs screamed in protest as she sank into a kneeling position. Owain's voice was patient but still too formal to be called friendly as he squatted down on his haunches in front of her.

'Close your eyes and relax your mind. Keep focus on your fire and breathe slowly and evenly.'

Rhia did her best to obey, though the beating she'd just taken made it more difficult than it might have been. She couldn't decide if it was good or bad that she knew what to expect. Her nervousness threatened to return to her and it was all she could do not to twitch in anticipation, but she banished those thoughts with an effort of will and focused her mind as Owain had said. All that mattered was that she stayed calm, that she breathe slowly, that she...

Her senses flared and before she knew what she was doing she had thrown herself into a roll. She couldn't describe what had prompted her, she simply felt grass on her back and a moment later she was up on one knee, facing back the way she'd come with fists up and eyes wide. Gawan was standing before her, his arms stretched forward and his face grim, the tip of Heartreaver buried in the earth where Rhia had been kneeling a heartbeat earlier. She found herself breathing hard as for a moment she remembered the day *she* had held that sword. The day she'd killed Sedryn and avenged her murdered father.

The image was gone within a second and she was back to trying her damnedest not to shake. She remembered how she'd seen Ossian do this all those years ago and wondered, as she had at the time, whether the cutter could have stopped himself if the kneeler had not moved. She had never known a warrior who had gone for his testing and never returned but all the same, like Madoc before him, it seemed that Gawan had struck with such speed and purpose that even a man of his skill could not possibly have pulled back the blow. Her heart was pounding so hard she felt sure that it would burst as she locked eyes with the Gorvic and forced her face to remain calm. Gawan tilted his head the barest fraction before raising his voice to the assembly.

'Does any man here doubt the focus of Rhianwyn daughter of Carradan?'

Once again the only sound was the sighing of the breeze, and Rhia wondered if Mehine might be watching her from the woods. There was no time for musings though as once again Owain approached and she eased herself to her feet, her legs still throbbing.

'Prepare yourself for the Test of Will.'

Rhia tried not to but she couldn't help but swallow nervously. Once again she knew what to expect from this and despite her focus felt a cold prickling on her skin. This would be the worst test, the worst by far, and her aching legs felt like water as she was led to the fiery brazier. *You can do this. You are the chieftain of your tribe, not some cowering little girl. You are Gadarim. You are strong.*

She saw Kyran approach the fire and thrust a sword into the flames. There was no leather around the grip and the iron blade was plain and ugly, but Rhia knew that this was not a sword for fighting with. Owain indicated that she should kneel in front of the brazier and Rhia obeyed. Her legs protested loudly and the fire was hot on her face, but she kept her expression blank. Her first man spoke quietly.

'You must grasp the sword.'

Despite the fire's heat Rhia came close to shivering once again as she imagined the pain she was about to endure. She ground her teeth together and clenched her fists tight, and forced herself to take a deep breath through her nose.

86

She let it out slowly. *You can do this. But first things first.* Rhia felt guilty for the deception but she knew she had to keep her prior knowledge hidden, and so she reached forward with her right hand. She was expecting it but nonetheless she felt relieved when Gawan appeared at her side and took hold of her wrist.

'Use your left.'

It was odd to feel him touch her but she simply nodded without speaking. Now was the time. Rhia pictured Lucan's face and drew strength from her love of him, and poured all the focus she could muster into the centre of her body. The ava, or Mabonac's fire or whatever this magic was, felt warm in her belly, and after only a heartbeat's hesitation she reached out her left hand and wrapped her fingers around the sword's hilt.

The burning metal seared her flesh and Rhia almost screamed despite all her preparation. Every instinct in her body was begging her to let go of the hot iron and she desperately, desperately wanted to. It felt as if her skin was melting at the touch and she clenched and unclenched her right fist frantically. Owain had moved to stand in front of her and began to speak, his voice calm. Rhia fixed her eyes on his, focusing her mind harder than she ever had before. *You are Caderyn. You are Caledon. You are Gadarim!*

'Will you defend your land and your people with all of your might?'

Her answer came through clenched teeth but she made sure to make it loud.

'I shall.'

The pain was almost unbearable but she held on nonetheless. *I am the leader of my people. I will defend them with my life. I can take a burned hand damn it all!*

'Will you balance fury with mercy as it pleases Taran and Mabonac?'

Some foolish part of her felt like saying that all she could feel right now was the fury part but she forced it away along with the pain and answered once again.

'I shall.'

'And will you honour all Gadarim as your brothers beneath the gods, and live your life proudly by their code?'

Rhia wanted to scream and felt sure her body would betray her will at any second; that she'd give in and let go and weep in pain at her ruined hand. She shut her eyes tight and thought of Lucan, then of her father and Marius and dear sweet Gwen. This was not just about her, this was a debt she owed to all of them to prove herself a worthy chieftain, and though her answer came out loud her voice did not break.

'I shall!'

She opened her eyes as Owain's voice bellowed out to all of them.

'Then Rhianwyn daughter of Carradan, I say that you are Gadarim. May you live and die with honour!'

Rhia could think of nothing but the pain in her hand but she faintly heard the words being echoed by the warriors around them.

'May you live and die with honour!'

Owain spoke again, his arm outstretched towards her.

'Rise, sister.'

For a panicked second Rhia realised that her hand was stuck to the metal but with help from both Owain and

Gawan she managed to let go of it. The pain didn't recede but she did her best to keep her face from showing it. Beside the other First Men she saw Kyran holding a bandage that smelled strongly of honey, but the ritual was not over yet. From behind him Owain produced a sword that shone with reflected firelight, and he held the hilt of it out to her with a nod.

'This sword is yours.'

Rhia took hold of Silverbite with her good hand. Her sword felt almost unbearably heavy but she somehow managed to hold it up. Many Gadarim were presented with a new sword when they passed their tests, but Silverbite was as much a part of her as her screaming left hand and the notion of setting it aside for a new blade was inconceivable. Besides the pain she felt relief and a swell of pride inside her chest as she realised she had done it. It was over. She'd been proud when Gawan had named her after Second Nantwyn, but the rawness of her grief and the knowledge that these tests were still to come had taken some of the shine from that feeling. But tonight was different. Tonight in the sight of all these warriors she was truly counted among the Gadarim, the warrior elite, the Mighty. She was a daughter of Mabonac the Dragon.

Owain spoke out again, a note of joy in his voice, and Rhia felt her spirit soar as she heard him speak her warrior name.

'Rhianwyn daughter of Carradan, we the Gadarim lend our voices to that of Leaping Wolf: You are Gadarim. You are the Fearless Wildcat!'

Once more the crowd echoed the First Man's words, and the night sky was filled with the sound of their voices.

'The Fearless Wildcat!'

Chapter 6. News of Treachery

Bryngarth's longhall was full to bursting with men and women of all tribes as they celebrated the last day of their all being there together. The Gorvicae warriors would be leaving the next day and the Dariniae shortly after them. Gawan couldn't say he'd be sorry to leave. He'd been glad to have taken part in the rituals for Rhianwyn, but the north was where he belonged and he was eager to get back there. He took a pull at his applewine. He had to admit, it went well with the flavour of the pork in his trencher and he supposed he was as contented as he was likely to be in this hall of his former enemies.

With many of the Caderyn chiefs having returned to their homes there was space for Gawan and Emeryn at one end of the high table, where the best of the food would always be brought first. Already Gawan had eaten half a chicken and a handful of sausages that he grudgingly acknowledged were probably the equals of those that were made back home. They were thick and just slightly blackened with no breadcrumbs to pad them out, just tender meat and a few choice herbs, and the Gorvic had wolfed them down quite happily.

Beside him, Emeryn was hunched over a trencher of roasted chicken, and from the way she went at it he suspected she too approved of the cooking. Gawan was well aware that only a fool would interrupt her during a meal at any time but tonight she seemed particularly ravenous. Though for all her enjoyment of the hospitality he had no doubt she too would be keen to be on the road. Alliance or not she was surely as uneasy as he was in the Caderyn town. She had trained here with the legion but beyond that this was her first time staying at Bryngarth, and even Gawan still had the vague feeling of being on foreign soil. It must have been worse for her and for the others. *Or maybe not? Plenty of other Gorvicae seem relaxed enough in our enemy's capital. Maybe it's just me who still feels like a stranger here?*

He looked around the packed hall. The smoke from the fires meant a subtle grey haze was forever hanging in the air, and the whole place smelt strongly of burning wood. Mixed in with it were the smells of roasting meats and sweating bodies, and the air was filled with sounds of chatter and merry music. The local bards were writing a new song to celebrate their victory, and men cheered and dogs barked as they experimented with the tune. A couple of the drunker tribesmen were even dancing between the tables, a Caderyn harpist capering along with them.

He saw Tarwyn and Gwydion further up the tables matching horns with Elfed and Bran; Gorvicae and Caderyn drinking and laughing together. The other warriors of his cohort were doing much the same, and he even saw a Gorvic girl on the lap of a Caderyn man; both old enough to have fought against each other before the Gaians had come, and now kissing fit to make a pair of new-wed youngsters blush. *Perhaps this Caledon notion is less of a foolish dream than you had thought?* He knew some people saw it as some kind of new summer after the bleak winter that had been Gaian occupation, but he had always put that hope down to mere post-war relief. *But what if you are wrong? What if this is something that will last, and it is just you who still feels the tension?*

He drained his horn of applewine. Few brewers in the north had given much thought to this type of drink and if nothing else, Gawan felt this was something he could get used to. Unprompted, Owain reached across and refilled his cup from a pitcher. Gawan nodded his thanks and the stocky Caderyn smiled back. In all fairness, Gawan had grown to like some of the local Gadarim, at least as much as he generally liked anyone. Owain especially was open and friendly without being a grinning fool about it, and Gawan knew from experience that the man was a solid fighter. They'd spoken together a fair bit after Rhianwyn's ritual, when the Gadarim of all three tribes had drunk until Belenos returned. He took a sip at his fresh-poured wine. His brethren here he could at least get along with.

Without really thinking he looked across at their newest sister and the fresh battle-marks tattooed along her arm. He'd watched Elfed, the Caderyn's best tattooist, putting them on after the ritual was done, spreading the whirls and spirals almost all the way to her neck. It had taken a while but he knew full well that she wouldn't have cared. No Gadarim ever did. The scar on her hand, now gesturing casually to Merwyn, was still ugly but healing fast, courtesy of Bael's impressive healing skills. Druids might not use their powers all that much but they were always happy to assist an injured warrior. For a moment the image of the Wildcat's naked body came back to him, but he quickly pushed it away from his thoughts. She was nothing next to Emeryn. *Or Bronwen for that matter*. He shoved that thought away even harder, determined not to think about his wife. *She and Tegwen are part of the past, and if today is about anything, it is about the future.*

He returned to his meal but was soon distracted by Emeryn beside him. She was holding her chicken up in front of his face, trying to keep it out of reach of one of the snuffling dogs that prowled the hall for scraps. She held the meat up high and moved it around a lot before finally giving in and tearing a morsel free, throwing it into the middle of the hall with the beast bounding happily after it. She turned back to the table and grumbled at her lover.

'That's four times now he's come here and robbed me of my food. Bloody Caderyn dogs!'

Gawan remembered when he'd used those words to describe the people around him but he didn't mention it. Instead he took another bite of his pork.

'Well just think, soon enough you'll have Gorvicae dogs begging for food and you can complain about them instead.'

Emeryn threw a tiny bone at him.

'If *I* have to listen to your damned snoring at night then *you* can bloody well listen to me complain about thieving dogs.'

As if hearing her, the brown hound came trotting back up, tongue lolling and tail wagging, and she threw another piece of chicken for him. He scampered after it, loving the game.

'You do know that he'll keep coming back here now?'

Emeryn shrugged, and Gawan suspected that she didn't really mind. She loved dogs almost as much as she loved food and she probably managed to strike some kind of balance.

'It's alright. Next time I'll throw *your* food.'

He nudged shoulders with her but then looked up as Alraig spoke from across the table.

'Do you think you will make it back to Graigarw for your own chieftain's moot?'

Gawan nodded to the older man. He and Merwyn had been named as Rhianwyn's chief advisors, along with Bael, and as such enjoyed a high place at the chieftain's table. The young druid was not with them tonight, having left the town on some errand, and only Owain, some other druid, and Rhianwyn's mother were seated higher. Gawan jerked his head towards the lone Gorvicae chief.

'Likely they will delay it until Boryn and I get back.'

The white-haired Merwyn nodded sagely.

'As they should. Boryn is a good fellow and the voice of a First Man is always to be valued.'

Boryn, Owain and Kyran all bowed their heads to him, suitably humble, and Gawan gave a little nod as well. At a glance it looked like Alraig didn't exactly agree but he didn't contradict him either. Rhianwyn turned towards them and spoke.

'I assume your moot would be between Karadoc and Taliesyn? They're both senior men and most experienced in ruling large numbers of people.'

Gawan's instinct was to say that this was none of their concern but he decided he should be content to talk about it, at least a little. *We're not enemies anymore, remember?*

'Most likely,' he turned to Boryn, 'though you might put your name forward as well?'

The Gorvic smiled through his heavy moustache.

'If it were best for the tribe I might, but I'd say more of our headmen will want one of those other two.' He raised a cup towards Rhianwyn. 'I do not envy the High Chieftains their greater care.'

The Caderyn chieftain tilted her own horn back at him.

'I am still new to it as yet, who knows what I may later live to regret?'

There were some polite chuckles as the two drank but Alraig's voice remained serious.

'A strange thing that neither man is married. I understand that Karadoc once had a wife some years ago but that Taliesyn is a lifelong bachelor?'

Once again Gawan felt the urge to tell these people to keep their noses out of Gorvicae affairs but he managed to hold it back. He guessed that Alraig was bringing it up in the hopes of reviving discussion about Rhianwyn's marrying again but Emeryn's voice sounded out before anyone could comment.

'Bachelor he may be, but Taliesyn's bed is rarely a cold one!'

She'd not spoken loudly and Gawan suspected it had been meant only for him, but she had said it during a brief lull in the music and half the table had heard her as a result. A few awkward looks went around the chiefs but it seemed that Rhianwyn's mother was the least embarrassed of them all. She raised an eyebrow at Emeryn and half-smiled.

'Would you ever trust a man who *sought* a cold bed?'

The widow's comment eased the tension somewhat and most of those seated there smiled. Emeryn nodded politely.

'Probably not, mother.'

It was a remarkable courtesy for an outsider to the tribe and was greeted by several looks of approval. Gawan wasn't quite sure what he thought of it himself but the matronly woman had a wise feeling to her and he supposed he didn't object to her being treated with such respect. She and Emeryn shared a smile as the brown dog returned and began snuffling for more food. Sitting beside his own mother, the boy Lucan piped up in his high voice.

'Do dryads sleep in beds?'

The question came out of nowhere and, likely by blind chance, the boy was looking his way. Gawan wasn't sure if he ought to respond. He was spared from having to by Boryn, who leaned forward and spoke softly.

'In a manner my boy, yes they do. My da always told me that they slept on the softest leaves.'

Lucan seemed uncertain for a moment and looked up at his mother. Rhianwyn smiled down at him.

'It's true.'

The boy seemed satisfied with that and went back to picking at some food, curiosity sated. Rhianwyn was looking at him with adoration and Gawan wondered despite himself how it might feel to be a father again. He'd placed so little value on it last time and before he'd known it had been and gone but perhaps now... perhaps now it might be different. For half a heartbeat he found himself thinking again of how Rhianwyn had looked the night of her testing, naked, wide-eyed and fearless, but he brushed it aside with a grunt under his breath. Sitting next to him was a fine woman, a good Gorvicae woman who he could see himself kissing palms with someday. Men could father sons at any age and Emeryn was young and strong; it could happen. *I could be a father again with her help.*

He was staring into his drink as he contemplated that notion, but then the banging of doors from the far end of the hall caused him to look up. There were a few people in the way but they moved aside quickly and the chatter and music died down within moments. A little group of men, two of them supporting what looked like a half-mobile corpse, had entered the Caderyn longhall. They made their slow way up to the highest table, the supported man barely moving his feet and being carried more than assisted by his fellows. It was hard to tell but he seemed to be of middling size and was dressed in a simple tunic and breeches. His hair was dark and he had trimmed his beard so that most of the chin was shaved but for one small patch; the moustache above seeming to grow across his face like whiskers. There was stubble hiding it now but the styling made Gawan sure he was Dariniae, and the battle-marks on his lower arms showed that he was Gadarim.

The Gorvic looked to Kyran and sure enough the Darin was already standing up. A pair of Caderyn appeared from a bench with a straw mattress held between them, and they lowered the grey-faced man onto it as Hywel and the Caderyn druid rushed forwards. Gawan and every other Gadarim in the place stood up as well, eager to help, but Hywel waved an arm for them to stay.

'Do not crowd around him.'

The holy man leaned down and partly obscured him from view, but not before Gawan saw the rust-red stains that covered the Darin's tunic. He was hurt, and hurt badly, and he doubted if even a druid's skills might be of much help him now. He resumed his seat along with the others as an older newcomer with a long blonde braid addressed the high table.

'Forgive our barging in comrades, but this man bears ill tidings that cannot wait.'

Rhianwyn made her way around the table as Hywel examined the Dariniae Gadarim. She seemed both angry and slightly awkward as she spoke to the blonde man.

97

'Bradan? What has happened?'

He bowed his head.

'I was heading back to Mobryn after the moot when I ran into some of my men coming the other way.' He indicated his fellows. 'When I heard what they had to say I knew I had to come straight back here.'

Rhianwyn opened her mouth but Kyran had moved around the table by now and was speaking to the injured man.

'Fearghal? Fearghal can you hear me?'

He grunted out a few words that mostly sounded like pained curses, and a disapproving look from Hywel caused Kyran to back off a little. Gawan saw Rhianwyn tip a nod to her mother, who took young Lucan by the hand and led him outside without a word. The blonde man, Bradan, spoke again.

'He was badly wounded when Sawel and Gorin found him,' he nodded to the two Caderyn who'd carried him in, 'and I fear he has only grown weaker.'

Gawan looked at the two men. One was old and grizzled-looking with a pot belly and greying hair while the other was a lanky youth, little more than a boy, with watery eyes and a wispy moustache. Bradan gestured to a third man.

'This is Dyfan, who brought him to us from Niswyn.' He looked earnestly at Rhianwyn. 'They have come with terrible news.'

Most of the hall looked at the man he indicated but he shied away from their gaze nervously. Gawan got the impression that the Darin might well be simple-minded, and he cowered behind Bradan a little. Hywel and Kyran were gently raising Fearghal's head and it seemed they hoped to get some sense from him before he crossed the bridge. Now that he looked, Gawan could see that the man's breeches too were soaked through with blood and he was fairly sure he smelled corruption from his wound. He was not long for this world. The Gorvic druid shook his head at Rhianwyn, confirming Gawan's suspicions.

'We have taken much of his pain, but there is little more to be done. Had he come to us a few days ago maybe...?'

He tailed off with a gesture and what looked like genuine sadness on his face. No matter the tribe a druid cared for life above all things, and both Hywel and his Caderyn brother seemed distraught that they could not help the dying islander. Rhianwyn nodded back, her features grave but understanding.

'You have done all you can, father. We cannot ask more.' She turned her attention to the fallen man. 'Can you speak at all, um...?'

She seemed to flounder and Kyran, gripping the man's hand hard in his own, supplied the name.

'Fearghal!'

His voice was quiet as ever but there was anger in it, though whether at Rhianwyn's forgetfulness or at those responsible for his brother's wounds, Gawan couldn't tell. *Probably both.* The Caderyn chief looked suitably apologetic and spoke again.

'Forgive me Fearghal.'

The man still looked pale as death but he did not wince as he replied.

'I can speak.'

His voice was weaker than a child's and Gawan had to lean forward to hear him. Kyran held the man's hand even tighter.

'Brother, what has happened to you?'

For a few heartbeats he said nothing and simply stared blankly at his First Man. He seemed not to know where he was and blinked rapidly several times. Hywel placed a hand on his forehead and the Gadarim seemed to calm a little, his eyes turning towards where Rhianwyn stood. Then he took a few breaths and seemed to muster his nerve, and the dying man told her his tale.

*

By the time Fearghal was done all the Gadarim and half the hall were on their feet. Kyran's face was white with rage, and he was the first to speak as his brother sank back onto the straw, exhausted.

'Caserach will die for this, brother! I'll nail his head to a ship's prow and he can drink salt until his flesh melts!'

All around there were sounds of agreement and Gawan nodded his head along with the others. Former enemy or not the murder of a Gadarim, and a High Chieftain no less, could not be tolerated. He stepped up to Kyran and put a hand on the lean man's shoulder.

'I will come with you to avenge our brother.'

Similar promises came from a dozen other Gadarim, Gorvic and Caderyn alike. There were few enough Dariniae in the hall but they made their voices sound out louder than all the others as they swore vengeance for their slain chieftain. Behind him Gawan heard Rhianwyn calling out for calm, and even before Owain started banging on the table the hubbub began quietening down. She took a breath to speak but a nervous voice came out of the silence before she could.

'Could this not be a mistake? After losing so much blood...'

Like with Emeryn's comment earlier Gawan suspected he had not meant to be heard by everyone and Sawel, the young Mobryn man who'd spoken, looked shamefaced as his words carried through the hall. Tarwyn responded in a very controlled voice, and Gawan suspected there were few men there beside himself who would sense the anger beneath the words.

'Would a Gadarim lie to us about the murder of his chief?'

The boy shook his head and backed away a little. In all likelihood he had spoken purely out of fear, not wanting to believe what he had heard.

'Of course not, forgive me.'

Bradan spoke up, partly to cover his man's embarrassment.

'So, what are we to do? We are all of us sworn to the Caledon, should we not unite to help our neighbours?'

Kyran nodded curtly.

'Assistance would be appreciated. Caserach is not loved by my people but many will fear him and think they have no other choice for a leader, especially now he has shown that he is not above murdering his rivals.'

His normally hard voice now sounded like it might kill all on its own, and Gawan thought he would have spat in disgust had he not been in a chieftain's hall. Once again Rhianwyn began to speak but Alraig got there before her.

'I agree we must send help, but we need some greater plan than just rushing off to Niswyn this very instant.'

There were nods, mainly from the senior men there, and Rhianwyn nodded too.

'Fearghal, is there any more of help that you can tell us?'

All eyes went to the Darin but he was lying motionless and silent, and Hywel looked up and shook his head at them. He gently closed Fearghal's staring eyes with one wrinkled hand.

'It was a miracle that he lived as long as he did. He held on until he felt his duty done and now his spirit has moved onward.' He shook his head again with sadness in his eyes. 'A remarkable man. May he cross the bridge unharmed.'

The hall echoed the blessing and all around it open hands were placed over hearts.

'May he cross unharmed.'

Gawan spoke the next words only in his head, and he knew the other Gadarim would do the same. *Mabonac guide you, brother.*

Rhianwyn's voice was the first to break the silence.

'You may take his body home should you think it right, Kyran. But I offer him a barrow among the bravest of Caderyn fallen, should you wish it.'

The Dariniae's First Man had tears in his eyes but he bowed his head respectfully to the chieftain.

'Any Gadarim would be honoured to sleep beside men like Smiling Fox. I accept.' Rhia nodded back and Kyran turned to Alraig. 'A strategy would indeed be wise if you are to come to our aid, but I ride for the coast at first light.'

Gawan was the first to answer that.

'I shall ride with you.'

His offer prompted a dozen others, including Emeryn, to raise their voices in support, but just as many were voicing caution and the hall was soon chaotic with noise. Owain banged the high table hard enough to topple one of the jugs and eventually the arguing died down. Rhianwyn raised her hands to speak. She was too short to be seen by everyone but her words carried well through the crowd.

'I shall consult with my chief advisors regarding strategy, but Kyran is right in saying that we must not delay. The Caledon has a duty to protect all the tribes within it and more than that, Ierryn's spirit must be laid to rest. Without him and his people we might all have perished at Nantwyn. He served his tribe and the Caledon with courage and loyalty, and his bridge to the Otherworld will be a broad one indeed.'

The blessing for him had already been said but the Dariniae and a few others still placed hands over their hearts and muttered the words under their breath.

'But before he crosses it he will wish to know that justice has been done, and that the people of Niswyn are not ruled by this murderer.'

Gawan agreed, surprised that he did not feel more conflicted. For years Ierryn the Black had been the scourge of the coast, Caderyn and Gorvicae alike, and he had only been their ally for a moon's turn or so. Yet Gawan felt almost as angry as if one of his own people had died, not a lifelong enemy whose death he'd once thought he would celebrate. *But then the man was formidable, even among Gadarim, and without him we would have been lost. Foe or not he deserved a better end than a knife in his back from a kinsman.*

Boryn answered first. He lacked the obvious anger of Kyran but like Rhianwyn, he spoke with passion.

'I say we let Caserach and whatever traitors that stand with him feel the might of the Dragon Legion!'

Gawan nodded to his fellow Gorvic.

'Aye. My cohort and Kyran's together would scatter them like Samhain apples before a gale!'

Both cohorts were severely depleted after Nantwyn but nonetheless Marius had taught them to fight together in a solid shieldwall, and even weakened they were more than a match for a rabble of Dariniae. The hall rumbled with approval and once again, Kyran nodded his thanks.

'We shall be grateful for the help, but *I* shall be the one to take Caserach's head from his shoulders.'

His tone was not the type that invited argument and Gawan returned the nod smartly before clasping wrists with the man.

'Agreed.'

He turned to face Rhianwyn and looked into her eyes.

'Will the Caderyn come with us?'

For all that he was confident that his and Kyran's cohorts were enough, it would be good for Rhianwyn to show solidarity among the Caledon. *Besides, the greater the odds in our favour, the fewer loyal warriors will die.* Her face was grave but she nodded her head.

'I had hoped to avoid more bloodshed so soon after the horrors we have faced, but this crime cannot go unpunished, no matter how much we wish for peace. The Caledon must show this wretch what we think of those who murder their own kin. The Caderyn will send a cohort to march alongside the others, and Caserach will feel the Dragon's fire for this foul act of treachery!'

The cheer that went up was almost deafening and even the nervous-looking Sawel raised a fist and shouted with them. Cries to the War Gods, and of 'Caderyn!', 'Gorvicae!' and 'Dariniae!' went up, and Gawan was surprised at how many also shouted, 'Caledon!' or 'Wildcat!'

Belatedly, he thought about how the Gorvicae moot would now have to wait even longer. *And there'll be yet* another *one for the Dariniae after all this – what a bloody mess!* But that didn't matter for now; there was battle to be getting to. Emeryn was grinning fiercely between her cheers and Gawan struggled to keep a smile from his own face. Battered though it was the Dragon Legion would crush anything that Caserach could throw at them, and they would likely not fight alone in any case. There were plenty of fighters from each tribe who were not part of the legion but who would still want to come with them to Niswyn and deal out justice to this murderer. Gawan sneered quietly. This would-be chieftain would be a mound of sand trying to stop the oncoming tide.

He looked around and saw Tarwyn and Gwydion and the others, all bellowing out oaths and warcries as they clapped shoulders with warriors of the Dariniae and the Caderyn. *You wouldn't think they had only just come from the hardest fight of their lives.* Gawan felt a swell of pride in his chest to know these men were his brothers.

He looked to Rhianwyn, who was standing up straight with her face set firmly, but he was sure he saw a sadness in her eyes as she heard them roar. She was no coward but he could tell she wasn't keen to see more death. *You can hardly blame her for that I suppose, not after all she's seen. But this shouldn't mean too much bloodshed, at least not on our part.* Caserach would be cowed quickly and then she could go back to running the tribes in peace. Assuming they let her, which likely they would. For himself Gawan had no wish to see his comrades placed in

105

danger again, but like the others he was swept up in the eagerness for combat. After his fears of what a Gadarim would do with himself without warfare, here was perhaps his final chance to let Heartreaver taste blood again. The Caledon could be something for Rhianwyn to care about for a few days more, while he marched off to do the thing that he had always done best. He gave in and smiled down at Emeryn as she cheered away with the others, and let himself go in the euphoria of heading off to a righteous fight. The Dragon Legion would ride forth and destroy a foe who had damned well earned his fate. Gawan came perilously close to actually grinning. Caserach did not stand a chance.

Chapter 7. The Raid

The Caderyn headman kept a pair of hulking dogs at his longhall, probably thinking they would intimidate any would-be attackers. Many men who would gladly charge someone brandishing a sword or an axe would baulk at the thought of dogs being set upon him. But of course, Caserach was no common man. The first of the black hounds leaped at him with its massive teeth bared, but the Darin sidestepped neatly and swung a backslash into its ribs. Greyfang didn't bite deep but it was enough to make the animal yelp with pain and it tumbled to the ground behind him. The second beast was not so quick to attack and Caserach smashed the sword across its muzzle in a heavy two-handed stroke. The iron half-severed the black hound's jaw and Caserach's next blow hammered down onto its head, splitting the skull almost in two and spattering the Darin chief with canine blood and brains.

The warrior spun on the spot, careful not to slip in the pink-and-red mess, and turned to face the first beast that had charged him. It was on its feet and seemed ready to launch itself again but Idwal appeared from behind it with his axe already raised, and he buried the narrow blade deep into the hound's broad back. The dog whimpered pathetically but then another stroke crashed into the base of its neck and the black beast dropped, as silent as stone. The chief who'd set them loose came charging at them, screaming defiance, but he was a stout old man who had hidden behind his hounds and was no match for the Dariniae raiders.

The Caderyn tried to rush them but Caserach slipped left while Idwal went right, and the white-bearded man whipped his head from side to side, unsure of what to do. He jabbed out at Idwal before lunging at Caserach, but the Darin parried him with ease and scored a counter-cut on his shoulder. The man cried out and fell back, though he kept his blade up. He swung clumsily at Idwal but the rangy Darin shuffled back out of range, and before the chief could turn to face him again, Caserach had stepped inside his reach and hammered Greyfang's guard into his head. The old Caderyn crumpled, red blood staining his white hair, and his sword hit the mud a mere heartbeat before his wrinkled face. He was probably still alive and Caserach nodded to Idwal to watch him while the chieftain cast his eyes around the settlement.

The late afternoon sun was dipping in the west but there was still plenty of clear light to show the scene. Three Willows was a middle-sized village set on a low hill that was barely a bump in the rolling landscape. A little more than a hundred houses were dotted around the hillside and plain, and nearly every occupant who could hold a stick was fighting hard. Caserach had brought nearly two hundred warriors with him from Niswyn, and Three Willows had almost as many people of fighting age. On another day it might have been a fair fight, but as a rule that was something Caserach did not approve of.

In fairness to them the Caderyn had responded quickly to the raiders' attack, but the element of surprise had been a crucial advantage and the Dariniae clearly held the upper hand. Caserach liked to take credit for that but it probably helped that the islanders were the only ones wearing battle-marks, and so Taran was likely watching over them more keenly than he was the Caderyn. He smirked. Even so far from Morannan's waves the gods were still on his side. *But then the old words are true; the gods love the strong.*

Not that the Dariniae were having it all their own way. Caserach watched as a female Caderyn, with stringy copper hair and a face like a pig, hacked brutally into Gerat's stomach and spilled his entrails onto the mud. She thudded her axe into his belly a couple more times for good measure before whipping a knife across his throat, screaming in his face as he bled. Gerat toppled, and the ugly bitch yanked her axe free of his guts as he fell. She turned to face Caserach with a snarl on her lips.

She charged forward with a shout and tried a low swing at the Darin's midriff, but Caserach was a strong man and Greyfang stopped the blow cold. The Caderyn recovered quickly and tried to slash her knife at his head but the sword was back up in an eyeblink and the iron bit deep into her forearm. She cried out and Caserach took her by the wrist and pulled hard as he shoved his blade into her neck. The initial cut went in clean but then he wrenched it sideways to open up a gaping wound, and the woman staggered backwards, gurgling. She was already dying but Caserach's blood was up, and another swipe of his blade took her head clean off her shoulders. Her body thudded to the ground and continued twitching for a few moments, a dark pool slowly forming on the muddy grass.

The Darin looked around. It was as good as done by now and most would know it, but these Caderyn could be damnably proud and the fewer of them he left alive, the fewer people there would be to pay the tribute. So long as their best warriors were cut down in the fight, the rest of them should be cowed enough to do as they were told by the victors. Caserach half-smiled to himself. *Like any predator grazing a herd we take what we must without wiping them out. I for one don't feel like farming this land myself!*

But before that could be sorted out they had to call a halt to all this. The tall Darin stalked back to the fallen headman and dragged him up by a handful of white hair.

'Tell them it is enough.'

The old man gargled something unintelligible and Caserach dealt him three rapid punches to the face. His nose almost burst in two, streaming with blood which stained his straggly beard red before dripping from his chin into the mud. Darin shouted down at him.

'Say enough!'

If this kept up for too long not only would people who could be paying him end up dead but also, much more importantly, Caserach's own force might be further depleted. The old man croaked out what sounded like compliance but it was too quiet for anyone to hear. Caserach hauled him fully to his feet and raised his own voice above the din of combat.

'Enough! Enough!'

Faces turned to him and fighters backed away from each other, and Caserach let go of the headman's hair. He almost collapsed but Idwal held him upright and Caserach glared at him before shouting again.

'Enough?'

The white-haired man nodded feebly and dribbled more blood as he coughed out his answer.

'Enough.'

It wasn't loud and Caserach kept staring at him, and the old man repeated himself enough times that those Caderyn nearby were convinced. Word spread in a rumble around the rest of the tribesmen and they sullenly stepped back from opponents or else tossed weapons to the ground ungraciously. The Dariniae began to cheer amongst themselves and Caserach smiled along with them. Idwal passed the old headman into Grwnn's arms and joined the others in collecting bangles and trinkets from the beaten Caderyn, who handed them over with angry snarls but knew better than to object. So long as the Dariniae didn't try to take more than their due, they had no right to call the raiders' trophies theft. They had won the fight, albeit not *entirely* fairly, and tribute was the proper thing to offer.

Caserach wondered how much he could squeeze them for before they decided it was worth fighting again. The battered old man should be good for a boatload of grain at least, and he could probably be persuaded to send one every moon until winter came. Something like that would do wonders for his popularity at home, and that was something he was very keen to gain. *But home is something that can wait until morning. Today I have my new friend to impress.* He left Grwnn holding the sagging chief and headed off to the edge of the town.

Beside the last roundhouse stood the only men who'd not been fighting in the battle, their leader watching Caserach with an almost bored expression. He was a serious-looking fellow, his dark hair hanging raggedly over his long, horse-like face. His eyes were flat and dull and his beard was just a thin line of grey-specked black along his jaw. He was dressed in a drab, yellow-brown tunic belted in at the waist with a cheap bronze buckle, and the sword worn at his hip looked like it didn't see much use. For a prominent chief among his people he was a pretty shabby sight, but then what could you expect from a Breiryn?

Caserach approached him with a smile and tried his best to sound friendly.

'Well Asrec, are you convinced?'

From the looks of him he was trying to seem unimpressed but the Darin saw through the facade. Of the Dariniae who were loyal Caserach had brought only the best of them with him, and their little demonstration had gone well. Asrec nodded slowly.

'Your warriors are impressive, and the attack was indeed well-managed.'

He was putting it mildly but then he hardly seemed the type of man who was prone to enthusiasm. In truth, Caserach had timed things perfectly; attacking the town from one side before a second force pounced in from the other, catching the already surprised Caderyn between the hammer and the anvil. Combined with his forcing the headman to call it off, what might have been a bloody fight had turned into an easy victory. He kept the smile on his face.

'Then you will support us?'

The Breiryn still looked doubtful, though with a face like his it was hard to tell.

'Well, I think perhaps...'

All Caserach wanted to do was slap some spirit into this miserable piss-drinker but he wouldn't have got where he was now if he'd made a habit of giving in to instinct. Instead he kept the smile up and tried to sound reasonable.

'You wanted to see that we were as good as we claimed, have we not proven so?'

The horse-faced man nodded reluctantly.

'Aye, you have.'

Caserach ploughed on before he could say anything else.

'And you know what will happen if the northern tribes remain united as they are? Rhianwyn is practically a Gaian, and when her old friends are no longer a threat to her she will do as they do and look to conquer her neighbours.'

Asrec gave no sign of agreement, but he didn't contradict him either. Caserach continued.

'She will attack your territory over land and once your people have been enslaved she will attack mine over the sea.' He leaned forward, trying to look earnest without being threatening. 'But together we can stop her. If we can show that she is not so strong as she makes out, that her precious Caledon is a house built on sand, then the Gorvicae and those fools among my people who have been taken in by her lies will abandon her. Only then can we be safe from her ambitions.'

Asrec stroked his ridiculous beard thoughtfully.

'Hmmm. Many of my people might think the same but you, Caserach, are unknown to them. Even Ierryn, for all the troubles he caused, was a man of great renown. We know little enough of your reputation.'

The urge to knock the bleating bastard down flared up even hotter at the mention of his uncle, but Caserach had been prepared for this and kept himself calm, his shoulders down and relaxed, his palms together. He adopted an expression of manfully controlled grief mixed in with a tiny dash of offended pride.

'Do you not think that I too held my uncle in high regard? What was he to you but an enemy? To me he was as a second father.'

The lies seemed to take Asrec off-guard and Caserach followed up carefully.

'I tried to tell him of the folly of shackling ourselves to that Gaian bitch. I *begged* him to see reason but he would not listen. Having to fight him was the worst nightmare I could have imagined and I *wept* as he fell to the dirt.'

He locked eyes with the Breiryn chief and made sure to put in just the right touch of suppressed emotion.

'I was forced to kill my own High Chieftain, my own kin, to keep our people safe. Will you not lend us the strength of your warriors to do the same for both our tribes?'

Keep the look up now, let him see that you're eager to be his friend but that you'll tell the whole world of his cowardice if he refuses you. He's half convinced already, you just need to keep him on the line.

'Would you deny the strength of my warriors, their determination and courage? Would you not be proud to fight this tyrant with us?'

Once again, Asrec was trying to hide how impressed he'd been. Even Caserach had been pleasantly surprised at how well they'd done, given how few Gadarim he had with him. Most had gone to Nantwyn with Ierryn and had either died there or else were still with Kyran and the legion. *We shall have to deal with him of course, but one thing at a time.* Only a few of the warrior elite had remained to safeguard the Dariniae's home, and precious few of those had been willing to join Caserach. *But they will all come around, once they see I am all they have.*

Asrec nodded his head.

'They are indeed fearsome, and Rhianwyn should indeed be opposed.'

Caserach leaped in, smelling victory.

'All I ask is enough warriors to beat her broken legion; that Gaian obscenity she has inflicted upon honest Lurians.

Once that is done and the Gorvicae head north again we can demand all the tribute we want from the Caderyn, and sleep the sounder in our beds to know that she is undone.'

The cowardly fool stroked his beard some more. *Come on damn you!* You *may be as much use as a hog-spit made of grass but I need your men to get this done!* The Breiryn chief mumbled some nonsense to himself and Caserach was on the verge of arguing some more when the southerner looked up at him and extended his hand. Caserach smiled his best comradely smile and clasped wrists with him. He was completely unsurprised by how weak the grip was.

'Very well, Caserach son of Heuryn. We shall be allies against this woman. I shall muster the clans of my people to your aid.'

Caserach kept on smiling, the expression almost genuine this time; Edryd's promises were coming true. The Darin chief looked at the Breiryn and made sure to keep hidden the contempt he had for this man. *Asrec can secure your chair for you, you can put up with him for now. Later… later the raiding will be plentiful and the coastline will be ravaged, and this horse-faced fool will rue the day he tried the patience of the Dariniae!*

Chapter 8. The Proposition

Gawan wandered about the hill of Bryngarth, unsure of what to do. He had woken before the dawn, eager to be leading his cohort off to battle, but had soon realised there was nothing for him to actually *do* yet. The wagons were already loaded with supplies, armour and weapons, and his warriors would be waking soon enough. They would breakfast, which was already being prepared for them, and then be away in almost no time, heading south and east towards the enemy. There was nothing Gawan could do to hasten it, yet still he had left a soft bed and a loving woman to pace around aimlessly in the chilly morning dew.

He shook his head at his own folly. After all his years of fighting he ought to be used to this by now. A small war party might be quick enough to move but any large group of fighters would take time to get going, especially over a long distance, and one man rising earlier would make no difference to that. *More than twenty years as a Gadarim and still you leap for combat like an untested youth. You are not young anymore, Gawan. You really should have learned patience by now.*

He decided not to waste time scolding himself and instead went on with his walk, mainly to make the most of the chance to stretch out his legs. It was a long ride to the coast and they would all be sore by the end of it. He tried to look on the bright side; at least he wouldn't have to carry much on this march, a pleasant advantage of travelling in such large numbers. His mailshirt and shield were loaded up on the carts and his saddlebags would be light enough. *I hold the only things that truly matter anyway; a knife for my meat, the green cloak of my tribe and Heartreaver at my hip.* Gawan ran thick fingers across the leather grip, worn smooth by many years of use. He almost smiled. *What man could ask for more than this?*

The sensible part of him reminded him that a few hundred comrades, a shield and an armoured shirt might come in handy, but his mood was brightening and he refused to be dragged down. After an evening of good food and drink he'd shared a pleasant night with Emeryn and would soon be on his way to another battle, one that he stood a damned good chance of winning. *And after that we head back north, and home.*

He stared out to the east as Belenos began to rise. The smell of the morning was fresh in his nostrils and reddish light was spreading across the skies to light up the plains below. At the base of the hill the thick woodland spread out north like a mop of dark hair above the 'face' of the lighter grass. Once again he had to admit that for all his pining for the northlands, the Caderyn had picked themselves a nice piece of land down here. Though it was still a far cry from home of course. Gawan furrowed his brow a little. *But I wonder; will Graigarw feel the same as it once did?* For years he had lived in the Gorvicae capital, protecting Baercban in between the various fights with their neighbours. Would it still feel like home with Taliesyn or Karadoc in the chieftain's seat? His scowl deepened. It would probably still feel more like home than *home* could feel again.

The First Man felt his good mood evaporating and he turned away from the stunning view. He was spared from sinking into melancholy by the sight of Elfed approaching, though the urgency in his stride replaced Gawan's gloominess with concern. His fellow Gadarim was walking quickly with an anxious look on his age-lined face, and the Gorvic tilted his head as he drew near.

'Something wrong?'

The Caderyn nodded and kept his words brief.

'The chieftain has called us to the longhall, at once.'

The lean man beckoned and started walking back the way he'd come, and Gawan fell into step beside him.

'Do you know what this is about?'

Elfed shook his head.

'I know only that a rider got here sometime in the night, his horse half-dead so they say. I was sleeping but it seems Owain was summoned straight away and he sent for me not long after. He told me to fetch you while Bran went to find Kyran, the druids will likely be there as well.'

Gawan nodded and kept walking while his brain broke into a sprint. Whatever reason Rhianwyn had for calling her senior Gadarim at this hour, Gawan would wager his right hand that it was something very bad. All talk of logistics and planning for the legion had taken place the night before and there was nothing more to say on that score. Merwyn was organising for them to be supplied on the march and Kyran and Bradan had assured them all that they had boats enough between them for the crossing. Gawan had frowned as he thought of that. Many more Dariniae had come over than would be sailing back again.

They were as prepared as they could be, which meant either some problem had come up that none of them had foreseen, or this rider on his dying horse had come with some very serious tidings. Had Caserach crossed the sea and begun raiding Caderyn land? If so he was a damned fool. The sea was his only protection against the wrath of the Dragon Legion, and even if he managed to attack them on the crossing, Kyran and his warriors were well-accustomed to fighting on the water, as would be Bradan and his Mobryn men. So far as Gawan knew this Caserach was no fool, so what else must he have done?

The pair covered the ground across the hill quickly and the longhall was soon in sight. Gawan glanced off to his right and saw the Gaian-style building that the governor had built, back when they had occupied Caderyn lands. It was a good thing that Rhianwyn had not used it for herself; she'd merely left it to those Gaian clerks she had invited to remain to help the Caledon in their dealings with the Empire. What little face she'd lost by allowing them to stay she had saved by doing her ruling from the longhall of her forefathers. Gawan looked at the thick grey columns and the posturing statues. Portunus had clearly built it intending for it to look imposing, and to make the Caderyn feel envious when they saw it from their roundhouses. To Gawan's eyes it looked impressive but also hugely out of place; like a stag poking his antlers up in the middle of a dairy herd.

They reached the hall but rather than make for the main entrance, Elfed took them towards a side door that led into the back rooms. Presumably the main hall was still full of sleeping tribesmen, but nonetheless Gawan was not keen to go in this way. Elfed opened the door and the pair walked in, and Gawan tried hard not to look at a certain spot on the little room's floor. The stain had been washed away for the most part but still he could see traces of his chieftain's blood on the boards. It seemed like only the day before that Baercban had lain there with a red hole in

119

his chest. The hole Gawan had made. He reminded himself firmly that the killing had been just, and looked around to see who else had been summoned at this hour of the morning.

There were some half a dozen other people already in the room, all standing around with almost no noise of conversation between them. Rhianwyn was at their centre, standing next to Owain. The chieftain wore a dark red dress with a brown woven belt, and though her face was alert he could see that the belt had been clumsily tied, and her black hair was tousled from sleep. There too were Bradan, Alraig, Merwyn, and the stick-thin Caderyn druid Gawan had seen the night before. Bradan's braid was untidy and Merwyn especially was bleary-eyed, and Gawan assumed that they too had been dragged from their beds for this impromptu council. None of it bode well.

Along with the Caderyn were Boryn and Hywel, and Gawan exchanged nods with them and then the room in general. Before he had to think of anything to say the door behind him opened again to admit Bran and Kyran, along with two others that Gawan assumed were a druid and a headman of the Dariniae. The white-robed man looked ancient but broad, the chief beside him around Gawan's own age and lean-built like Kyran. Once all were inside and the door was closed, Rhianwyn spread her arms and addressed them. She wasted no time with pleasantries.

'Comrades, I am sorry to say that more bad news has come during the night.'

Gawan noted the lack of surprise in the people around him and guessed he hadn't been alone in his concerns. Rhianwyn continued calmly.

'Caserach has crossed the Glaswair. He and his followers travelled eastwards at great speed and have launched an attack upon Three Willows. They have killed many warriors and are extracting a tribute from Bleddin.'

There were several angry rumbles but it was Elfed who spoke first.

'Well I hope Bleddin gave him only his heaviest bracelets! The slower Caserach is when he tries to run home, the quicker we'll catch the bastard.'

There were sounds of approval and Kyran nodded his head.

'He was a fool to cross the sea in the first place. He might need the grain but as you say, tribute will slow him. He must be desperate to prove himself as a man to follow.'

The distaste was plain on the Darin's face and Gawan suspected once again that he was on the verge of spitting. But the Gorvic was also thinking quietly. Why indeed had Caserach done something so foolish? Had he assumed that Fearghal had died without telling his tale, and that the Caledon didn't know about his murdering his uncle? And even if he did think that, why attack the Caderyn now, when the Dragon Legion was still largely in one place and easily deployed against him? Battered though they were, the legion was still more than a match for whatever warriors he had gathered to him. Why provoke their wrath?

He voiced his questions to the room in general but it was Rhianwyn who answered, her eyes rueful.

'Caserach wants to goad us into battle. He would prove himself strong in the eyes of his people and hope that they forget how he made himself chieftain.'

Kyran and the Darin headman both looked grim at that but Bran just shrugged his shoulders.

'Let him try. We have more than enough warriors to crush whatever he has, and if we send riders to Mobryn now they might be able to hunt the coast for their ships before he can retreat?'

Bradan nodded and stepped forward.

'I can set off right now. With some fresh mounts I can be home in a matter of days.'

There were some encouraging murmurs but Rhianwyn held up a hand.

'Wait father, there is more.'

Gawan blinked. It seemed odd that she used such a title for a man like Bradan. He was younger than both Merwyn and Alraig after all, and looked only a few summers older than Gawan himself. But then the First Man took a closer look at the headman of Mobryn. His face, and his blonde braid especially, reminded him of a Caderyn he had fought some years before; a young man who'd tried to fight him in vengeance for killing Dane, Carradan's son. He'd been a bold enough fellow, and not unskilled with a blade, but had been no match for the Leaping Wolf. Gawan actually felt a little guilty about his fate, since he'd knocked the man to the ground only for Gaian soldiers to stab him there before he could rise. Their legions might be devastating, no doubt about that, but honour and glory were foreign words to the all-conquering Gaians, and not one of them had thought twice about killing a man who was already down.

That man, Gawan couldn't place his name, had been Rhianwyn's first husband, and now he looked at him more closely he saw that Bradan could be no-one but his father.

122

Even now Gawan sometimes felt that lying with Emeryn betrayed his wife's memory, and he thought about how Rhianwyn acted around Mobryn's headman. He could well understand why she felt so awkward. And why she spoke with such respect to her former father-by-law. But for all the discomfort she may have felt the Wildcat carried on, her voice clear and even.

'I fear we would not be facing Caserach alone. The rider who came to us spoke of at least one Breiryn at Three Willows. The man clasped wrists with Caserach when the fighting was done.'

There were a few intakes of breath and a good deal of frowning but Owain spoke calmly before anyone could comment.

'From the way he was described it sounded like Asrec, the headman of Reed Marsh. We must assume he is in league with Caserach.'

The name meant nothing to Gawan but then he'd had few enough dealings with the Breiryn. All of Caderyn land lay between his home and the southern tribes, and even Hywel showed no sign of recognition.

'Is he formidable?'

Rhianwyn shook her head.

'For himself; no. He has little enough personal reputation but his clan is large and he has ties by marriage to several others of equal size. Asrec may be a middling fighter at best but he can summon many warriors should he wish to. He could often be a stone in my father's boot, back before the Gaians came.'

The Caderyn druid spoke softly from beside her. He was younger than Hywel but older than Bael with a stringy grey beard and sunken eyes. His white robe hung about a frame that seemed almost skeletal but though his voice was quiet, it was not frail.

'It is only a guess, but I would say he could muster up to two thousand Breiryn if he had the support of his neighbouring chiefs.'

Gawan was no expert with numbers but he knew enough to know bad news when he heard it.

'How many will be Gadarim?'

The druid shrugged his bony shoulders apologetically.

'Alas I cannot be sure, but I have heard nothing of Asrec's clans containing any more than would be usual. All told we have barely thirty such warriors available to us, he could in all likelihood match that number, perhaps even better it.'

Gawan frowned. The druid's estimate was not far off, though not all of their Gadarim were fighting fit. The prospect of facing at least even numbers of Breiryn elite, along with two thousand normal warriors, was daunting. Legion or not, this was grim news.

'Do we know how many Dariniae Caserach has brought with him?'

This time Rhianwyn answered him.

'Our messenger was unsure, but he guessed at some two hundred at most with few Gadarim amongst them.'

Gawan quickly ran through his knowledge of the legion, his expression darkening further as he did so. Nantwyn had scarred them deeply, and of the four-hundred-strong cohorts that had been formed initially, few could now boast more than three hundred men, and some had suffered even worse than that. Many of those who had not fallen had later died of their wounds or of disease, and the army that had ridden home a few days ago had been a shadow of the one that had ridden to war.

Of those savaged units, one Caderyn company was still at Nantwyn with Bedwyr, while another would have to remain at Bryngarth. Rhianwyn could talk of peace and friendship all she wanted but she was not fool enough to leave such vital settlements unguarded while the Blackbird Gaians were still upon her land. The larger Gorvicae cohort had left for Graigarw with Duran and might well have already reached the northern capital. That left Gawan's cohort of some two and a half hundred Gorvicae, Kyran's Dariniae company which was in similar condition, and the Caderyn cohorts of Owain and Bran. Those two had suffered more than either of the others and even between them they would field fewer than four hundred warriors. *Perhaps seven hundred Dragon Legionaries against more than three times their number, and with equal numbers of Gadarim for us to face.*

Owain had either worked it out faster or else had already thought the numbers through.

'Even if more warriors are gathered we will be badly outnumbered, by at least three men to one. But in open field a legion is worth much more than irregular troops.'

Irregular troops? The man had spent too much time with Marius, not that he was wrong. *Not entirely.* Bran piped up from beside him.

'We would be wise to bring yours and my companies together into one; that would give us one unit at least that was almost up to strength.'

Owain nodded and began to talk of numbers and equipment with Bran, speaking with confidence. But Gawan suspected he was not alone in his continued concerns, and Hywel proved him right by speaking them aloud.

'None can deny that our people are brave, but can even the Dragon Legion succeed against such fearsome odds?'

It was strange that even Gawan, who agreed with him, wanted to tell him that of course it could. He'd taken pride in both training and fighting with his cohort and had seen with his own eyes the quality of the other companies. He wanted to say that the Dragon Legion was invincible, and the match for any other force, Gaian or Lurian. But he couldn't say that. The fact was that even before the butchery at Nantwyn, the Dragons had not been trained to the same standard as Gaian soldiers. In their current state he could not speak for their worth against such fearsome odds. He took a deep breath.

'We could give them a hard fight, but to win? Of those here and fit to fight we have barely half the legion.'

The words tasted bitter in his mouth and Owain spared him from speaking further.

'Even if we beat them back, which we may not do, our losses would be too great to then challenge Caserach in Niswyn, not to mention if the Gai...'

He pulled himself up short with a guilty look at his chieftain. Rhianwyn simply nodded slightly and an awkward silence followed. Kyran was the first to break it.

'I will not ask any to come with me who do not wish it, nor would I endanger the Caledon,' he dipped his head to Rhianwyn, 'but I am taking my cohort south, no matter what else.'

Several people took in breaths to speak, but once again Rhianwyn raised her hand. For someone so small she could command a room extremely well.

'We are *all* heading south with you, comrade. The Caledon must be together or we are nothing and that is an end to it. We will commit all those we can to your aid.'

None of the little assembly smiled but a few faces looked at her with approval. Gawan nodded his head and tried to sound positive.

'My own people are ready to leave at once. If we send word ahead of us perhaps some of your clans can send warriors to swell our numbers?'

It was a rather hopeful thing to say, given that the land had been drained of fighters already by the war against the Gaians, but he felt he had to ask. Both Bradan and Merwyn spoke at once and two conversations began across one another. Various ideas were voiced about how more men might be found but Gawan heard little that was practicable. He wondered briefly whether he could summon Duran and his company back from Graigarw but then dismissed the idea again. For one thing, by the time a messenger had reached them and Duran had marched his people back, Caserach could have laid waste to the whole length of the Caderyn border. For another, what guarantee was there that the Gorvicae headmen would allow him to come at all? This was after all a Caderyn problem first and foremost, and plenty of chiefs would object to their warriors being summoned by a Caderyn chieftain to help solve it.

He saw Rhianwyn looking pensive, listening to the conversations with lines across her brow, but listening only, not speaking. He wondered if she was thinking the same thing that he was. *Probably. She has a good head for these things.* He kept looking at her and saw her eyes darting quickly from side to side, as though weighing up

127

options or else arguing with herself; thinking up point and counterpoint. All around her the chiefs and Gadarim, and even the druids, tried in vain to think up ways to squeeze more able-bodied warriors from a land that had already bled away the flower of its youth. Gawan studied Rhianwyn as her eyes twitched and her brow furrowed, until at last her face froze in an expression of resolve, and if anything he got the feeling that whatever argument she'd been having with herself, she had somehow lost it. It took two or three heartbeats before his mind caught up with hers and he realised with a jolt what she intended to do. He stepped forward before she could speak.

'No!'

He'd not spoken loudly, but his voice had carried through the small room, and the other conversations abruptly ceased. All eyes turned to him and Rhianwyn locked eyes with him before she spoke.

'It is the only way.' She turned to address the room. 'There is another option.'

Gawan moved in front of her and glared as he repeated himself.

'It is *not* an option!'

She was a foot shorter than he and barely half his weight but the Wildcat did not back down.

'It is our only chance at avoiding a massacre.'

Gawan stared down at her but Elfed's voice came from beside him before he could speak again.

'What are you talking about?'

Gawan saw Rhianwyn try to answer but he cut her off, not even trying to conceal the anger in his voice.

'She would summon to her the only other fighters in the west. She would have us fight alongside the Gaians.'

*

In the storm of objection that followed this, another leader might have had to shout the others down by brute force. Rhianwyn just let them speak for a moment and then raised her hand again, palm open. They fell silent quickly, and even Gawan held back his protests while she spoke.

'General Galerian's legion still has at least one cohort nearby, hunting down the stragglers of the Fourteenth. They march swiftly and can be here in only a few days. The First Legion is one of the finest in the Empire and with their support we could crush Caserach and any number of Breiryn that Asrec could muster to him.'

There was sense in what she said but Gawan was in no mood to hear it. A glance around him showed that he was not alone in his attitude, and he kept up his glare at Rhianwyn.

'You would invite a Gaian legion to march through your land and then expect us to fight alongside them? Have you forgotten already what they did to our people?'

There were murmurs of support but Rhianwyn matched his glare and spoke back, her voice calm but firm.

'Galerian is not Lepidus. He has no ambitions of conquest and no sorcerous allies. He is an honest soldier. He can be trusted to assist us.'

Gawan wanted to say exactly what he thought of that but Alraig voiced his objection first.

'Would this not go against the laws that you yourself have set down?'

Merwyn nodded his white head in agreement and spoke softly to his chieftain.

'I helped you to make these laws, Rhianwyn. Alraig is right, the treaty you and Galerian swore to *expressly* forbids any Gaian from crossing Caledon land under arms.'

Rhia held up a finger as she answered, and Gawan suspected she had prepared for this when she'd been arguing with herself.

'Yet it was agreed that this was to take effect *after* the First Legion had withdrawn from our lands.' She opened her hands. 'They are still here, hunting down their traitorous comrades *as we agreed* they would be allowed to do. We would not be inviting soldiers into our land, merely asking assistance from those already here.

Owain looked distinctly uncomfortable but he spoke in her support.

'I suppose it could be said that they already fight our enemies by hunting the Panthers. It would perhaps not be so bad if...'

But Gawan cut him off. He didn't want to be disrespectful to him but he was too angry for manners.

'*Any* dealing with the Blackbirds would be bad! For one thing, they are missing far more Panthers than they are catching, and it would not surprise me if they are delaying on purpose as an excuse to stay here. For another, how do you think our own legion will feel, having Gaian legionaries with naked swords standing beside them when they fight?' He looked around. 'How many of you would trust a Gaian to protect your flank, or stand with you back to back against an enemy?'

He was pretty sure that none of them would raise a hand to that, but then Rhianwyn cut in with a comment Gawan had hoped would not be made.

'Of those of us here, how many have fought beside the Gaians before?'

The Gorvic's face darkened at the memory of First Nantwyn. At the time of planning he'd enjoyed the prospect of teaching the Caderyn a lesson, but from the moment that fight had started he had regretted ever agreeing to it.

'Baercban did not know what he was doing when he allied us with them, and my people paid dearly to learn our lesson.'

He remembered bitterly the way the Gorvicae had been treated by their former allies after Nantwyn, and the failed rebellion he had led against the Gaians. He remembered the warriors who had died at White Ridge when the legions had counter-attacked, and the maddened frenzy of the Panthers as they had torn into his comrades. Yes, the Gorvicae had been wrong to ever side with these people, but the gods had seen to it that they were punished for their folly.

'I am not proud of what my tribe did but it is done now, and we all of us know the Gaians well enough to see the truth; they cannot be trusted.'

Rhianwyn was about to reply, her face set, but Owain's voice cut in before a harsher argument could ensue.

'Against odds of three to one, better a Gaian at my flank than empty air.'

Gawan snorted.

'At least empty air could not stab you in the back.'

Bradan stepped in-between them, his palms raised.

'I like this no more than you do, Leaping Wolf. Camelas knows well I have good cause to hate the Gaians, but if it is this choice or else the deaths of more of our warriors, then we must take it.'

Owain and Rhianwyn both looked relieved to have heard some support, but then their faces fell as Hywel spoke against them.

'I am not so sure. Caserach aside, would we not be wiser in trying to make peace with the Breiryn? A peace with fellow Lurians sounds kinder to my ears than to trust the safety of our people to the Gaians.'

Alraig nodded along with him but said nothing, and Gawan was glad to hear a druid speaking for his side. Peace with the Breiryn might be difficult to manage, and Caserach would still have to be dealt with, but if it meant the Gaians stayed away then Gawan was all for trying it. Rhianwyn cast her eyes down for a moment before looking up at the druid, her words courteous but insistent.

'Caserach is keen for a war with us to secure his chair, father. He will not want to seem weak by making peace, either to the Breiryn or to his own tribe, and now that they have declared themselves, Asrec will feel the same way. They will lose all credibility among their people if they seek peace now.'

Kyran nodded, his face sour.

'It is true. He will need a victory to prove his worthiness to lead, and he is the kind of man who lives only to have power over others. If this Asrec is of the same mind then they will draw us into battle, no matter what.'

The Caderyn druid chipped in, speaking mainly to Hywel.

'I too desire no more bloodshed for our people, but Asrec is indeed a man who would not dare risk such a loss of face. To make peace with an enemy he would most likely have beaten will make him seem like the worst of cowards, and his reputation will suffer for it.'

Gawan felt his spirits drop as the Gorvic druid nodded sadly. Rhianwyn leaped on the opportunity.

'If anything this will work to our advantage, if we let it. Instead of chasing them through hills like bandits on the run, they will seek to fight us openly simply to show that they can. With even one cohort of the First to bolster the Dragon Legion, we would easily break their charge in open field.'

Kyran nodded very slowly, his harsh voice filled with resentment.

'I *must* defeat Caserach. If this plan can let me do that, then I will consent to it.'

Gawan reminded himself that Kyran likely held less hatred for the Gaians than the mainlanders did. They'd never come into *his* territory after all, never tried to impose their will upon his people. Gawan could hardly blame him, or Rhianwyn for that matter, who always let her love for Marius blind her to what the Gaians really were. He hated it, but there was even some wisdom in what they were saying. But still he couldn't stop himself objecting.

'If we allow them to cross Caledon lands like this then they will think that they still control us, and how long before they are back to their old ways?' Rhianwyn took in a breath but Gawan didn't let her answer. 'Besides, if we tell them that we need their help they will know how weakened Lepidus has made us. If we are to keep them out for good then they *must* be afraid to provoke us to war.'

Merwyn spoke again before anyone could argue against that.

'And again I say that to do this would break your own law. Regardless of the prowess of our cohorts, you are still new to us as chieftain, Rhianwyn. If you begin your rule by ignoring laws that you would have others follow then many will lose faith in you. They would think that perhaps we were wrong in granting you your father's chair.'

He spoke in a kindly way that made it clear that *he* did not regret his choice but all the same, the message was there. Alraig backed up his fellow headman in somewhat sterner tones.

'You yourself wanted to make punishments for lawbreakers that applied across Caledon lands. What would the Caledon then think if their chieftains broke those laws?'

His posture was very upright and he gestured easily with one hand, not aggressive but not deferential either. Gawan added his voice to theirs.

'It would be a sign to all those who doubt the Caledon that their leader is far friendlier with the Gaians than we would like. They might even think that you would have them come back now that Lepidus has been dealt with.'

Gawan didn't really think that was true, not after losing her husbands, brothers and sister to them, but the point had to be made. Rhianwyn raised her voice for the first time, her reply snapping out waspishly.

'Have you a better idea? Can you bring Duran back here tomorrow, or gather more fighters from the north in time?

Can you find me more Caderyn when my tribe has already been bled dry? Or would you sooner fight Caserach and Asrec alone, have what is left of our warriors die for no good reason, and then lie happy in your grave knowing that at least you went to it without asking for help?' Her glare intensified. 'Best you start practicing your excuses to give to Ierryn when you see him, and tell him that he could have been avenged but that you were too much of a stubborn goat to do it!'

Gawan felt his gorge rise, in no small part because he didn't really have an answer, but Rhianwyn carried on, now addressing the room.

'It is not without risk, I know that, and I would not turn to this if I thought we had another choice. But only with Galerian's help can we hope to prevail against Caserach and once we have, the people will forgive us for having called on him. Given time.'

Kyran and Owain seemed fairly convinced and even Merwyn was looking uncertain. The druids remained silent with their faces impassive, having given their views to the assembly already. The role of the druid, besides communing with the gods, was ever to advise, not to command. Having shared their wisdom with the headmen they now stepped back and listened, ready to give their counsel again only as needed. It had always struck Gawan as strange that the druids held such vast power, in every sense, and yet restrained themselves from ever truly using it. It seemed like such a waste. But he had no time for thinking deep thoughts. Alraig was speaking again, still firmly opposed to his chieftain.

'And does a victory justify a crime? If a man stole another's horse and then proved to be a better rider, does that mean that he was *right* to steal the horse?'

He was putting his objections far more eloquently than Gawan could, and he found himself feeling grateful that the headman was here. Rhia turned to him and spoke rationally.

'It is not the same thing, Alraig. We are *borrowing* a horse and then giving it back after riding it, and we borrow it to fetch grain for the very man we took it from. It is for the good of all and no true crime is committed.'

Alraig scowled and flicked his eyes to Gawan. It being a time of war he would know that the support of the Gadarim would be immensely important, and it seemed Kyran and Owain had already conceded. The First Man of the Gorvicae spoke up.

'I am no expert in law, let the chiefs worry about that. What I do know is that we cannot trust the Gaians. Galerian may not be Lepidus but their swords come from one forge. If we let the Blackbirds see we are so weak as to need their help, I believe the Gaians will attack us in our weakness.'

Alraig seemed pleased by that but the others remained uncertain, and Rhianwyn turned to look at Gawan, her blue eyes bright and blazing.

'Galerian gave his word when he made his mark on the treaty at Nantwyn.'

Gawan wanted to spit on the value of that but instead he decided to be clever.

'Is this the same treaty that *you* are now breaking because it suits your own purpose to do so? Why should he not do the same?'

Rhianwyn's voice hardened further.

'I act for our protection, not for conquest or for greed. Yes, it may go against the exact words of the treaty but it is for good reasons, Gawan.'

The Gorvic had to fight to hold back a sneer.

'Yet still you break it which means that he might do the same. And who can guess at what a Gaian thinks would count as a good reason?'

Rhianwyn answered confidently.

'*I* can.'

Gawan knew his next words would sting her but he didn't care.

'Are they all like Marius? Tell me now that every one of them is a man like Roaring Lion and I will ride off today and fetch them myself!'

There was an awkward silence for a few beats before Rhianwyn sighed.

'I cannot say that. But...'

But Gawan interrupted, smelling victory.

'There you have it! We all know the measure of the average Gaian and we have all of us bled to fight them off. If your Caledon is to survive it must be proof against them should they ever think to turn on us.' He pointed a finger at the chieftain. 'And if *you* are not seen to obey your rules of peace, then nor will they.'

Alraig nodded in agreement but Rhianwyn wasn't finished yet.

'The Gaians may be our only hope in this, and Galerian...'

Gawan snapped out his answer before she finished. She was clearly in the wrong, why couldn't she see that?

'Your bloody Gaian friends can all tumble into the Pit where they belong!'

Rhianwyn's eyes flashed and her hand twitched as if yearning for Silverbite. Despite himself a part of Gawan wanted to draw Heartreaver free as well, and show this Caderyn fool what happened when a wildcat faced a wolf. But before they could even say anything the door creaked open and a handsome woman entered from the side door. After a moment Gawan recognised her as Rhianwyn's mother. She paused in the doorway and cast her eyes around in surprise, clearly not expecting to see them all there. She recovered herself a moment later, ignored the obvious tension in the room, and nodded politely to the druids before addressing to her daughter.

'Forgive my interrupting, but I wanted to know if Lucan was with you?'

Rhianwyn's face was flushed but she answered calmly.

'He should be with Olwyn, she was going to take him in today.'

The older woman shook her head.

'No he isn't. She thought he was with you. She and Siriol came to the longhall to get him but he was gone. Then she came to find me, thinking I had him, but of course I don't. I sent her off to see if Meghan took him away somewhere while I came to ask you about it.'

Gawan saw Owain frown.

'I left Meghan asleep in her house before I came here, likely she still is.'

Any comments that might have been made about the two of them sleeping together unwed were kept for later. Gawan saw Rhianwyn trying hard to keep from fretting.

'No-one else would have taken him anywhere without telling one of us first.'

No friend would have anyway. Gawan's mind was moving fast. He was still angry with Rhianwyn but first things must come first, and an unpleasant thought had come into his head. He spoke to the group even as he crossed the room, heading towards the door to the main hall.

'That rider from last night, what became of him?'

Owain stepped to join Gawan as he opened the door. The room was filled with sleeping men but the Caderyn soon found the one he was after. He pointed to a bench on the near wall.

'That's him. We barely got a sip of wine in him before he collapsed into sleep.'

The figure did indeed look a haggard sight but Gawan was casting his eyes around the rest of the room, scanning across the scores of tribesmen as they slowly came awake. It didn't take him long to spot the pot-bellied Gorin, snoring quietly on a mattress not far from the door. Gawan quickly looked over the other Mobryn men before turning to face Bradan. He held the gaze of the blond-haired man and tried not to sound too accusatory.

'That youngster of yours with the thin moustache, just how well do you know him?'

Chapter 9. Missing

Rhia tried hard not to panic as Bradan answered the question.

'Sawel? Not so well as I know most of my folk. His family live in a little settlement further up the coast, near the beach where poor Fearghal was found. Apparently it was Sawel who first came to Mobryn with the news.'

Rhia's mind was racing but Merwyn, his voice calm, spoke her thoughts before she could.

'Has his family done much trading with the people of Niswyn?'

For all the raiding and squabbling that went on between them, the Lurian tribes were more often at peace than at war, and for generations the people of Mobryn had traded wool for whale with the islanders. It was a strange relationship to say the least, and it was said a Mobryn man never went to meet a merchant without a blade at his belt, but nonetheless trade was common enough, and if this Sawel was on friendly terms with some of the Dariniae…

Bradan was frowning, lines of worry appearing on his honest face. He reminded her so much of Bevan sometimes that it hurt to look at him, but she had no time to dwell on that right now.

'I know that they have done in the past, but then they are hardly alone in that.'

It wasn't much of a comfort and Rhia fought to keep her breathing even. What if Caserach had known about Fearghal's escape and had sent Sawel to infiltrate Bryngarth for him? What if he'd sent him to steal her son, to be used as a hostage against her? Or what if… what if… Rhia found herself gulping in a breath despite herself.

What if he means to simply kill him, to show his tribes that the Caledon's leader cannot even protect her own child? Few decent Lurians would be impressed by such a murder, but the Breiryn especially could be a backward and savage lot, and any sign of Caserach weakening her rule would be sure to make an impression on them.

Blood began rushing wildly through her limbs and her heart was hammering fit to burst her chest. She felt first cold and then flushed, and she didn't know if she was about to scream or faint or tear apart the next man she saw. She felt bile in her throat and had to hold back the urge to retch in sheer panic. Somehow her hand found the hilt of Silverbite and she gripped it hard, her knuckles turning white as she tried to draw comfort from the weapon.

Owain saved her from having to speak.

'If he has taken the boy then he must be found. When was Lucan last seen?'

He cast his eyes to Myrna but Rhia answered him, her voice tight.

'He was asleep when the rider came and I sent for you. Beyond that…'

Her fingers were aching on Silverbite's grip but she daren't let go. It was the only thing keeping her standing in place and not dashing for the door or collapsing into a quivering mess. *My boy… what has happened to my boy?* Merwyn's voice was still kindly but had a definite urgency to it.

'He cannot have travelled far in such a time, if we begin a search now we will track him down.'

Bradan nodded.

'If he is in league with Caserach he will either have gone south to Breiryn lands or back westward towards the coast.'

Rhia saw Alraig step forward and nod, his hands folded before him and his voice perfectly calm.

'South is where I would guess; Caserach is there at present and would doubtless want the boy with him and his followers rather than risk any loyal Dariniae sending him back to us. Besides, there is less open ground that way than on the road to the coast, and if Sawel makes it to the hills he will have good cover from pursuit.'

Rhia nodded back, trying to keep her face composed. Alraig was a difficult man sometimes but he was clever, and she did not regret naming him as one of her chief advisors. She held onto Silverbite but tried to keep her free arm relaxed as she spoke.

'Bran, set up a watch around the hill right now, see what you can see, and have a troop of men search any empty houses. It is unlikely but he may be lying low and waiting for us all to head out before making his escape.'

It took a lot of effort to say so much with an even voice and Rhia was fairly sure her anger and fear weren't particularly well-hidden. *But you must keep yourself in control. You are no use to Lucan running off without a plan, even if that's* exactly *what you want to do.* The blood was pounding in her ears and it was all she could do not to draw Silverbite free and charge straight through the door, ready to run this traitor down and hack the bastard apart. All she had left of Marius and Carradan was in that one precious boy. She had to find him.

Bran bowed his head once and left by the closer door. Rhia started making towards the one that led straight outside, turning to address Elfed as she did.

'We'll need a troop sent along the west road too.' She switched her gaze to Alraig. 'Unlikely though it is, I would send riders that way to be certain.'

The headman nodded approvingly.

'Agreed. Once the hill has been searched I will send riders along the east road as well, just in case he thinks to circle around to throw us from the scent. There are few enough empty houses what with all of our guests here; it should not take long before they can be sent.'

Rhia's face was still grim but she dipped her head in thanks. All the terrible things that might happen to Lucan were still crashing through her mind, and it was taking all her willpower to walk calmly to the door.

'Owain, get our horses and a dozen good trackers. We will head south and try to catch him before he makes it too far.'

The stocky man nodded and started away as well, but before they reached the door the voice of Gawan came from behind them.

'What can I do?'

He sounded genuine enough but Rhia had no time for him now. All he'd done since he arrived was to delay what must be done, and now the stubborn bastard was delaying her search for her only child. A part of her wanted to take out her anger by slapping him right there and then, and had he been two paces closer she might have done it. As it was she simply stormed out after her tribe's First Man and spat out a reply over her shoulder.

'My son is a Gaian, remember? He could tumble into the Pit for all you care!'

Chapter 10. The Woodland

Gawan stalked out into the early dawn, furiously ignoring the bustling Caderyn ahead of him. *Damn Rhianwyn and her spite!* All he'd done was to tell her what was best for their tribes and she had flung his words back at him with naked contempt. Well, she could tumble into the bloody Pit as well then! He had offered his aid to find her boy and the ungrateful bitch had ignored it. *Let her find him herself then if she doesn't want my help!* For a second he thought of Tegwen but he shoved the thought aside. Rhianwyn had made her choice, and her own people could do the work of finding their precious lost child.

He was so busy fuming quietly to himself that he was barely five paces from them when he noticed Tarwyn and Emeryn. His lover's hair was golden in the early morning light, and her face was fresh and smiling.

'We've been looking for you. Itching to be away?'

Gawan frowned.

'Something like that.'

Tarwyn looked around at the commotion among the Caderyn and the tall Gadarim raised an eyebrow at the First Man.

'Trouble?'

Gawan nodded. He pushed down his anger at Rhianwyn for a moment and explained the situation to the two of them. Likely neither of them knew any more about the Breiryn than he did but the mention of their numbers caused their expressions to darken, and Gawan found himself growing concerned again. The fact was that Rhianwyn had a point about needing help to fight them off, but he couldn't face the idea of fighting beside a Gaian legion again. The shame would be too much for him to bear. He'd given good reasons of his own about the Caledon appearing weak and the treacherous nature of the Gaians, but when it all came down to it, it was shame that motivated his arguments. He remembered the terrible carnage at Nantwyn, the first time, when he'd seen legionaries cut down Lurians like wheat before a scythe. There was no honour in how they fought; no glory. They fought with brutal efficiency and did it purely to subdue others, and Gawan hated himself bitterly for having once been called their ally. He skipped over most of that part of their conversation when he relayed it to his fellows. He just hoped quietly that men like Alraig would talk some sense into Rhianwyn on her return.

Emeryn looked concerned as she heard the news but it was Tarwyn who spoke, his voice casual. Gawan suspected that he knew that more had gone on than his First Man was telling, but the slender warrior didn't press it and instead asked some practical questions.

'I will inform the others. Do we know what road we will be taking? Or for how far?'

Gawan shook his head. He had no real idea of where Three Willows was but he took his best guess for the time being.

'Not yet. Likely we will be heading south but I know little else for now. I shall find out soon and pass the word on to you.'

Tarwyn nodded.

'Alright. I'd best go and kick Gwydion awake.'

He turned on his heel and started heading back to the longhouses but Emeryn stayed behind. She put her hand on Gawan's arm before looking up into his face.

'There is more to this. What's happening?'

For a heartbeat Gawan considered telling some half-truth or another but dismissed the idea almost immediately. There was no reason not to be honest with Emeryn and besides, her presence had done a little to calm his anger at Rhianwyn. *She can make you smile* and *calm you down. You really should kiss palms with this one before she gets away.* But this wasn't the time to indulge such thoughts. He took a breath and spoke quietly.

'Lucan is missing. Taken, from the looks of things; one of the Mobryn men is missing too.'

Lines of worry appeared on Emeryn's brow but her mind worked quickly.

'Mobryn is on the coast. They think he is in league with Caserach?'

Gawan nodded.

'Bradan does not know him well and there is plenty of trade between them and the islanders. The other Mobryn men are still in the hall, only this fellow Sawel is missing.'

Emeryn twitched her lip in thought.

'Could be he just went out for a walk or something?'

She didn't sound especially convinced and Gawan shrugged his shoulders.

'If he did then good for him, but the boy will still be gone and this is the best guess we have. None of his family have seen him and combine that with a missing stranger who knows the Dariniae...'

He left that hanging in the air for a moment and Emeryn nodded, her face now determined.

'Very well. What are we to do then; are we spreading out in a search or do we know which way he has gone?'

Gawan felt his resentment begin simmering again.

147

'They have already organised a search, we are not needed.'

Emeryn blinked, taken aback.

'In a search like this you cannot have too many people. We ought to offer Rhianwyn our help, she must be worried.'

Gawan wanted to snap something about bloody Rhianwyn but he kept his voice under control.

'The Caderyn don't *want* our help. Best we spend our time making certain that all is ready for the ride south.'

Emeryn frowned at him.

'The legion is all but ready to go anyway, all that is changed is what road we will take. Since there is nothing we can do to hasten it, we may as well be helping them to track down Lucan and this Sawel.'

Gawan repeated himself, keeping his anger at bay with an effort.

'They don't want our help.'

Once again Emeryn looked at him with disapproval.

'Are we not supposed to be on the same side in this? Would you refuse a Caderyn's help if he was trying to rescue your child?'

Gawan felt a pang in his chest. He confided in Emeryn more than he did in most people but he'd never told her the story of Tegwen. He reminded himself that he was never much of a father anyway, but then a part of him knew how much he regretted that. He scowled but Emeryn met his look with determination. The First Man almost spat out his answer.

'Alright. But they've no need for us in the main party. I will ask Bran if there is anything of use we can do here.'

Truthfully there probably wasn't much, but if they had to do this then he was *not* going to tail behind the Wildcat, not after what she'd said that morning. Emeryn nodded, her expression softening a little.

'Thank you. What is the plan at the moment?'

Gawan filled her in on the details and lines appeared on her brow again, only this time in thought rather than in disapproval.

'Hmmm, with the houses so full of people, searching them seems a bit pointless.'

Her lover shrugged.

'True, but Sawel might have known the boy would soon be missed and be laying low somewhere until the search parties have left.'

Emeryn nodded slowly.

'Yes, but why do that in a town filled with his enemies? Where could he go where he and the child would be unnoticed?'

She had a point, and Gawan started thinking on it. Lucan had been seen with Rhianwyn often enough that most of the people of Bryngarth would recognise him. If Sawel tried to hide him in the town then he would surely be seen and questioned before long. The Gadarim started wondering where he might go if *he* had to hide from these people, and found himself thinking back on his walk earlier that day. He beckoned to Emeryn and started heading roughly east, away from the main town and towards the edge of the hill. His lover followed curiously but didn't speak as they walked, weaving between the houses until they stood out in the open.

From there Gawan looked out on the sprawling green lands of the Caderyn but his gaze didn't linger on the sunlit vista. His eyes focused on the woodland away to the north and he struggled to suppress a little shiver. He'd never been there himself but he knew of the sacred ground that lay somewhere within those trees. There were sacred sites all over the land of both the Caderyn and the Gorvicae of course, but few held the same mystery as the legendary Ring of Stones, and Gawan had heard some tales about this place that made even him feel nervous. But for all that, or even because of it, the woods would make a damned good hiding place in a pinch. But would Sawel dare to go in there?

Emeryn followed his gaze and spoke from behind him, her voice quiet.

'You don't think...'

Gawan didn't turn but he nodded his head slowly. The spirits and Sidhe of sacred forests didn't like intruders at the best of times, and a pair of Gorvicae in a Caderyn wood would be a long damned way from welcome. *But the life of an innocent child is at stake; is anger at Rhianwyn or fear of ghosts enough that you will not at least go and look?* Gawan clenched his fists. He was right to berate himself and would go down there of course, but the thought of hostile spirits made his hands want to shake. *At least men, even the Panthers and Aborans, can be hacked down and killed with guts and effort. Ghosts on the other hand...* He ground his teeth and kept his eyes on the trees as he spoke, and wondered how deep they might have to go into the wood.

'It's a better place for him to hide than up here on the hill. There's only one way to find out.'

*

150

The Caderyn riders set off south at a gallop as the two Gorvicae tramped slowly down Bryngarth's hill. Gawan had considered seeking out Hywel the druid but it seemed he had volunteered to ride out with one of the searches, and the First Man wasn't sure what other druid he might ask. It was probably better this way anyway. Chances were they'd either forbid him or else delay him from going to look, and with every passing moment Sawel might be scurrying further away, perhaps intending to pass through the woods and come out the other side. Gawan wasn't sure if he ought to hope for some spirit to catch him first since, for all that Sawel no doubt deserved it, whatever ghost it was might end up harming Lucan along with him.

Gawan did what he generally did when faced with something he feared; he embraced his anger and used it to burn away some of the dread. It wasn't difficult. He was angry at Sawel not just for kidnapping a child but also, if they were right, for desecrating sacred ground by fleeing there after his crime. He was angry at Rhianwyn for snapping at him, and for countenancing letting Gaians fight alongside the Dragon Legion. Most of all he was angry at himself, partly for his hypocrisy after having already fought with them before, and partly for letting that get in the way of what might be their best hope of beating Caserach.

But before he could think on it further Emeryn held up a hand for them to stop. The ground was just starting to flatten out ahead of them but Emeryn was gesturing to their left.

'Look there.'

Gawan looked where she was pointing. On the pathway down the hill the earth was too well-trod to see anything, but Emeryn had been keeping her eyes peeled for any signs of footprints leaving the trail. She was generally better at this than he was and it took him a moment to see what she had seen. The tracks were faint but he just about made out two sets of footprints heading towards the trees, one large, the other very small. It was impressive that Emeryn had spotted them at all, but then she had tracked down Nomad scouts before now and Gawan could hardly have picked a better companion for this. She looked up at him.

'They're fresh. An adult and a child, walking this morning. The man is not large, his tracks are broad but not deep, and the child with him could not be more than five or six years old.'

They exchanged a grim look as their suspicions were confirmed, but Emeryn's eyes were soon back on the ground.

'The man's stride is fairly long, and the boy was walking fast to keep up with him.'

They began following the tracks and Gawan asked her questions rather than make guesses for himself.

'Dragged by the hand?'

Sawel hadn't looked strong enough to carry a child that size over any distance so it made sense that he'd have made the boy walk instead. Emeryn shook her head as they went on, her gaze still focused on the damp grass.

'I don't think so but I can't be sure. They are close together but I see no scuffing. I would say that they were holding hands, likely Sawel got him to come along by persuasion rather than force.'

Gawan remembered how the boy liked to babble and figured that Sawel had indulged him enough to gain his trust. *Sly bastard.* He held on to his anger but didn't let it overtake him, and as they approached the treeline he peered into the sacred woods. They were beautiful in their own way, mostly oak and birch by the looks of it, yet he couldn't help but feel a vague sense of foreboding. Emeryn had taken her eyes off the ground for a moment and Gawan could tell she was as nervous as he was. She spoke without much confidence in her voice.

'Whatever spirits dwell here, they will not love a man who steals a child.'

Gawan grunted. They had both heard myths of gnomes and goblins who would do the same and worse, but these woods were not known as a home to evil beings and he doubted the druids would use it if it were filled with foul spirits and ghosts. All the same he was still hesitant, remembering the tales his mother had told him about Jarinn and Echan, Sarwch and Brenyl, and any number of other wicked sprites and imps. He remembered Anryn's stories of sylphs who would tempt a man into their bower with fair words and soft flesh, only to drain his soul away as he slept. He snapped himself out of it. He was Gadarim, a son of Mabonac, and daylight or not the marks on his skin were proof that the Dragon God watched over him. *I am beloved of the War Gods. Any ghosts or goblins here should be afraid of* me*!* He knew Emeryn was watching him and he kept his face relaxed, striding into the trees as if he had no care in the world.

She followed him a moment later and he felt a surge of affection for her. He thought he ought to hold her and say something loving or encouraging but the moment they

153

crossed the treeline her eyes were back to the ground, studying the dirt and fallen leaves for tracks. If anything that only raised his opinion of her but he kept silent about it for now and let her step a little ahead of him. While Emeryn concentrated on the ground ahead Gawan cast his eyes about, ready to free Heartreaver at a moment's notice should anything come out of the trees.

The forest was dense, with oak, birch, ash and even holly growing close together. Gawan wondered about the holly trees, and whether Mehine might be lurking in them. She was no goblin; depending who you asked she was either a Sidhe or a goddess, but she was known to haunt the darkest woods and he was sure he'd heard something about her favouring holly. Mehine was also known as being not exactly *malignant*, but very impatient and unpleasant around uninvited men in her woods. To make matters worse, she was also more revered among the Caderyn than the Gorvicae, who generally looked more towards her husband, and rival, Karanon. Gawan wondered if he ought to be appealing to him now. Though she was the Lady of the Woods and he the Lord of the Mountains, it was said that they walked in one another's realms, and either one might be watching them right now. He shook it off angrily and focused on his body's centre, taking strength from the dragonfire he kept burning there.

Emeryn was still tracking, but rarely needed to scan the ground any more. The undergrowth was thick with bracken which might otherwise have frustrated them, but for tracking purposes it was ideal. Whenever they found a thick patch there was ample evidence of Sawel's passing, and only in those places where the ground was clearer did Emeryn find the need to look down. In one such place she squatted down for a moment, putting her hand to a fist-sized stone. Gawan saw that the moss growing on it was torn and ragged but she must have read something more there because she changed direction slightly, heading more towards what Gawan thought was roughly northwest. It was difficult to keep a good sense of direction in the middle of unfamiliar woodland.

They carried on for a little way, Gawan wasn't sure how far, and the more they walked unharmed through the trees the less concerned Gawan became about the ghosts. Emeryn was surely right that the spirits here were on their side, and would want to see a child-stealer punished rather than hinder well-meaning outsiders. All the same he only cleared branches or ferns from his path with his left hand. His right was always ready to reach for Heartreaver.

Soon enough he saw Emeryn squat down again but her eyes weren't on the ground or on the undergrowth. For a moment he thought she might have lost the trail but she raised a hand swiftly when she saw he was about to speak.

'Shhh. Listen.'

She was speaking quietly and almost lisping to keep her voice low. Gawan crouched down and strained his ears and for a moment he heard nothing. Then, very faintly, he made out what could only have been voices. They were too distant for him to understand the words, or even the language, but one seemed to be deeper pitched than the other, and that was all he needed to know. He and Emeryn exchanged silent nods and kept low as they moved forward, creeping carefully through the ferns. He was grateful that only bracken and not briar stood in their path, and remembered briefly the hard lesson he had learned about the difference. He'd paid little attention to his

155

mother and her wisdom when he was young, and had scratched himself something terrible after not understanding her warning. The memory of it almost brought a smile to his face but then he remembered what was happening and drew his mind back into focus.

The voices were still speaking as they slowly closed the distance. Gawan wasn't a clumsy man but Emeryn was making him feel like one, slipping through the thick ferns like an otter moving through water. He comforted himself that she didn't have a sword to restrict her movement but there was no denying it; she was better at this than he was. The voices seemed to stop and Gawan worried that their quarry might be moving away, but his fears were dispelled as they reached a little rise and he saw two figures in the clearing below.

It was Sawel and the boy, no doubt of that, and Gawan felt a mixture of relief and satisfaction. Soon he'd have the chance to pay this bastard his due for stealing away a child. *And we'll see how dismissive Rhianwyn is when two Gorvicae have rescued her boy!* Lucan said something to Sawel that was too quiet to make out but the answer of the Mobryn man was clear.

'No!'

His voice was sharp and Gawan saw him grab the boy by his arm, dragging him across the clearing in the direction they'd been travelling. The Gorvic wasn't sure what was going on but he'd had enough of watching, and he leaped out of the undergrowth with Emeryn pelting after him. He covered the open ground quickly as Sawel slowly turned to face him. He saw the Caderyn's wispy moustache twitch in alarm and his hand tighten on the boy's upper arm. He had no real time to react but Emeryn was taking no chances, and she hurled the rock she had found earlier at the surprised kidnapper's head. It bounced from his temple and the young man staggered, losing his grip on Lucan and swaying awkwardly off-balance. Gawan left the boy to Emeryn as he launched himself at Sawel, bearing him to the ground and pinning him down with his knees.

The Mobryn man barely had the chance to gasp before Gawan was hammering punches into his face. He tried raising his arms to defend himself but the effort was pitifully feeble, and Gawan kept battering down at him while the young man sputtered and bled. He had no intention of actually *killing* him, that was for his own tribe to take care of, but he would enjoy teaching the bastard a hard lesson about stealing children away from their parents.

Sawel's nose and mouth were a mess of blood before a noise behind him caused Gawan to pause. He turned and furrowed his brow as Lucan cried out again, his voice shrill.

'Stop hurting him!'

The boy was only about five paces away, struggling against Emeryn who was trying to hold him still. His eyes, so like his mother's, were bright with tears and anger, and Gawan got the very real feeling that he would actually try to fight him if Emeryn let him go. He hesitated a moment as the boy screamed out again.

'Stop it! Let him be!'

Gawan was unused to speaking to children but Emeryn's attempts to sooth him didn't seem to be working.

'Boy, you've been fooled if you thought this man was just playing a game. He meant you harm.'

Lucan tilted his head at him in confusion, forgetting to struggle for a moment.

'What do you mean?'

Emeryn spoke quietly into his ear.

'When he told you he was bringing you here, whatever reason he gave, he was lying. He was trying to steal you away.'

Sawel gave a gurgling cough and might have tried to speak but Gawan slapped his face hard before he could. Lucan started struggling again.

'But *I* brought *him* here! We're looking for dryads.'

His face was earnest and Gawan began to feel the fire in his veins dying down. His limbs felt almost cold in its absence and he exchanged a look with Emeryn. Sawel was trying to speak again, his voice thick and breathless as he dribbled out blood.

'He was talking to me this morning... said he was going to find one because no-one believed him... listen...'

He tried to sit up but Gawan shoved him back down impatiently. He looked pathetic, his ridiculous moustache stained bright red and one of his eyes already swelling. What he did *not* look however, was dangerous. Gawan glowered at him.

'Why didn't you just tell him no?'

Sawel couldn't shrug properly because of how he was pinned but he tried moving his shoulders a little.

'I told him to stay but he's a stubborn lad. My brother is like that... the only way is to indulge them or they just... wander off alone.' He squirmed under the Gadarim's weight. 'But look, you need...'

But Gawan glared at him harder and he was cowed into silence. The Gorvic found himself thinking about his own brother, and how little *they* were indulged when they were young. *What kind of fool can't stop a child that small from wandering off alone?* It seemed ridiculous, but then Rhianwyn was small he supposed, and stopping her was always a challenge. All the same, this Sawel was lying, stupid, or monumentally naive to think it was acceptable to take a stranger's child out for an indulging stroll in the woods. Another look at him made Gawan think the first one was unlikely, and it was probably some combination of the others that had led to this. Lucan piped up again from beside them.

'It's true! I just wanted to...'

But learning the foolishness of all this had done nothing for Gawan's mood and he growled at the child angrily. The boy recoiled a little and held his tongue. Emeryn was the one to speak, her voice calm in the child's ear.

'So, why was he dragging you off just now?'

Gawan allowed himself the tiny hope that this might all be a ruse after all and that he'd just given a beating to a kidnapping liar, rather than a stupid but innocent young man. Sawel was shifting uncomfortably under him and tried to say something, but Lucan answered first.

'He got scared.'

The boy was clearly wary of Gawan and so Emeryn spoke again.

'What was he scared of, Lucan?'

He gave an indifferent shrug and pointed at a spot just beyond the two men.

'Of that.'

Gawan followed where the boy's finger pointed as Sawel continued to squirm underneath him. He didn't see it at first, seeing only more grass and bracken around them.

But then the movement caught his eye and he was on his feet in a heartbeat, his left hand dragging Sawel backwards as he rose. By the second beat his sword was free of its sheath and by the third Heartreaver was point down in the ground, pinning the serpent's head to the forest floor. It all happened so quickly that the other two had barely started back before it was all over. Gawan took a moment to steady himself as he looked down at the snake, now writhing wildly in its death throes.

It was a naedr, what some people called a hatch viper or just a hatcher. It was a big bastard, thick in the body and almost as long as Heartreaver's blade. Its head was broad and flat, and the distinctive cross-hatch marks were plain to see on its dark brown scales. Herbwives and druids used snakes like this for all sorts of things but Gawan remembered the only thing the average man needed to know; they were poisonous. The venom was sufficient to disable a strong man, though he was likely to at least survive the attack. A child Lucan's size on the other hand...

The creature's spasms died away and Gawan pulled the sword free of the earth. He took a step away from the dead snake before wiping the blade on the grass, looking up at Emeryn as he did so. Her eyes were wide and she was holding Lucan tightly, though the boy had ceased to struggle against her. Lucan himself seemed completely unconcerned, if anything he seemed fascinated by the shining blade of Heartreaver, and was looking at it with undisguised envy. Gawan let his heart slow down as he wiped the iron clean. The snake had been damned close to the boy. Had Sawel not dragged him back he might be on the ground right now, his leg already swelling as the venom did its work. The Gorvic shook his head. He wanted to scream at the pair of them for being fools enough to come here in the first place. Lucan he could almost forgive, but young though he was Sawel was old enough to be called a man of his tribe; how could he have been so stupid? *Perhaps the Caderyn think their sacred woods don't hold the dangers that another wood might? Well, it seems their Lady Mehine isn't keen on male trespassers at least!* He was quietly glad that Emeryn was with them, and that at least no real harm had been done.

He stood up slowly and dragged Sawel to his feet. The lad was a mess and Gawan felt a little guilty for the beating he'd dealt him, but at least he wouldn't forget today and it might even have knocked some sense into him. He gave the younger man a curt nod.

'I apologise for striking you so hard.'

He ignored Emeryn's look of mock surprise from behind the Caderyn and kept his face neutral as Sawel answered him.

'Accepted. Good work with the snake.'

His voice was still thick and nasal, and Gawan suspected that when he told his tale it would need some repeating before anyone understood it. He sighed quietly. When this got out there was every chance they would all be subject to some ridicule for it, but if they brought the boy back he could at least rub that in Rhianwyn's face. Emeryn had finally loosened her grip on Lucan, though she kept hold of his hand and was clearly planning on keeping it. The boy looked first at her and then at Gawan and managed to sound both grateful and irritated.

'Thank you for that. But we've still got dryads to find.' He pointed off north. 'I think we should try over there.'

The little fool actually tried to start walking that way and Gawan's patience snapped like a dry twig.

'I'll give you dryads!'

He crossed to him in two quick strides and fetched him a sharp clip across his ear. The blow wasn't hard, barely more than a tap, but the boy looked as shocked as if he'd just been punched in the face, and Gawan saw that he was fighting to hold back tears. He got the odd feeling that maybe Lucan hadn't been hit before. *I suppose not getting hit enough as children would explain an awful lot about the Gaians.* Gawan put the thought aside for now and locked eyes with the boy, staring hard.

'If you ever wander off with a stranger again you'll *wish* you had been kidnapped when I catch up with you!'

Watery though his eyes were, the boy looked as if he wanted to answer back with something bold. But at the last minute his nerve failed him, and he simply nodded his head in silence. Gawan noticed Emeryn frowning a little and suspected that she disapproved of his scaring the child. But it had to be done. A lesson was no good unless you remembered it and hopefully he'd now think twice before doing something so stupid again.

Gawan gestured for Sawel to follow them and started back the way they'd come, relying on Emeryn to keep hold of Lucan. He tried to think once again of how he could crow over Rhianwyn when he entered Bryngarth with her boy, but found he couldn't take any joy in it. He was glad Lucan was safe but beyond that his mood was sour. He was embarrassed at the mistake that he and all the others had made in their assumptions, and was still feeling a prickling of guilt for having thrashed Sawel so thoroughly.

He tramped his way irritably through the Caderyn's sacred wood, and tried not to think too hard about anything.

Chapter 11. Back to the Hall

The riders sent out after her had been gone for a while, and Gawan guessed that Rhianwyn would be on her way back by now.   The Gorvic paced impatiently outside the longhall, keen to get this over and done with. He'd be glad to be able to show her how two Gorvicae had found her son, but given how harmless Sawel's intentions had been, it was hardly an achievement to brag about. Emeryn was standing nearby still holding Lucan's hand, though mercifully the boy had neither cried nor shown any sign of wanting to wander off again. Near to her stood Bran, Alraig, and the slender Caderyn druid, along with a bloodied and sheepish-looking Sawel.

The holy man had been surprisingly indifferent about their trespassing in the Caderyn's woods, and had asked only if they had entered the Ring of Stones. After Gawan had confirmed that no, they hadn't, he'd been not the least concerned about it, merely glad that they had found Rhianwyn's boy.   Gawan continued his pacing and wondered idly what had become of Bael, the younger druid. Along with Alraig and Merwyn he was one of Rhianwyn's closest advisors yet he'd not been seen for several days and the most that anybody knew was that it was on some sacred business. Gawan couldn't help but wonder if it was the same business that had called away Reaghan, the wisest of all the druids, but he put that from his thoughts before much pondering could take place. He'd let his mind dwell on gods and spirits quite enough for one morning.

He turned in his pacing and looked over at young Lucan. He'd not chattered all that much on the walk back up, though Emeryn had coaxed a few responses from him. He was clearly still wary of Gawan, though not nearly so much as Sawel was. The Mobryn man didn't seem to be holding a grudge exactly, but a blind man could have seen he was uncomfortable around the Gadarim. The atmosphere was tense and Bran seemed about to say something to try to start a conversation, but then the thudding of hoofbeats came from behind the buildings and moments later the first riders came into view.

They were coming from the west, presumably because that was the easiest slope to ride up, with Rhianwyn at their head, followed closely by Owain and Hywel. She was driving her pony hard and the beast kicked up a wave of pebbles as it skidded to a halt. As she swung down from her mount Gawan spotted Bradan and Merwyn appearing behind the rest, but for the most part his attention was for the chieftain. Her face bore a strange expression that was difficult to gauge. There was relief in there, no doubt about that, but also fear, grief, embarrassment, and no small amount of anger to go with them.

She strode up to them in what was almost a run and ignored the standing men as she rushed towards her son. Emeryn let go of the boy's hand and Rhianwyn half-lifted him in an embrace. She squeezed him hard for a few heartbeats and then set him down again, face hard and voice sharp.

'Where have you *been*?'

Gawan had originally intended to tell her what had happened, but given that the boy had been asked he felt it might be better to let Lucan speak for himself. He did, and in fairness to him he was entirely truthful, though he had

165

to ask Emeryn and Sawel to confirm one or two things for him. He ended by saying he was sorry for what he'd done and Gawan felt he deserved at least part of the credit for that apology. Rhia, after a distrusting glance at Sawel, turned back to her son and spoke firmly.

'You are never, *never* to do something like that again Lucan, do you understand me?'

The boy nodded his head but seemed comfortable now he had apologised.

'I won't, but it's all right mama, I've learned.'

He looked towards Gawan and Rhia turned to face him, tilting her head a little as she did.

'Meaning?'

Gawan hadn't expected this but he answered indifferently.

'I gave him a quick clip, it seems to have done him good.'

Lucan chipped in, his voice earnest.

'And I won't do it again mama, I promise.'

Though obviously wary of Gawan he didn't sound as if he were afraid of being struck again, and if anything he merely seemed keen to assure his mother that he had understood and had taken the lesson seriously. Perhaps he had his father's nerve when facing what frightened him? Gawan had noted that while Rhianwyn got angry when she was scared, Marius had always just looked through it as though it wasn't there, covering his emotions with a blank mask. If this Lucan had indeed inherited his courage he might actually make a good chieftain someday, provided *somebody* brought him up to be one.

The people around them didn't seem to react much to this but he saw that Rhianwyn's face had grown pale. She spoke to her own First Man over her shoulder.

'Owain, take Lucan inside.'

The Gadarim nodded and took the boy's hand. Rhianwyn's tone had been unmistakable, and when she approached Gawan the others seemed to take the hint that she wanted to speak in private. Alraig, Bradan and the others followed Owain into the hall while the other riders dispersed, leading their ponies away with them. Sawel took a moment longer to catch on to things but was saved when Hywel and the Caderyn druid offered to take him indoors and see to his bloodied head. Emeryn's face was set and she was obviously ready to stay, but Gawan gave her a little nod to indicate that she shouldn't. If Rhianwyn wanted to berate him about something he didn't need another's help to weather the storm. And he didn't want the Wildcat to think he needed it.

His lover gave him a tiny nod back before heading into the longhall with the others, reluctant but obedient to his wishes. Rhianwyn's voice was quiet but the rage in it was palpable.

'You struck my child?'

Gawan was in no temper to be put on the back foot and spoke in his most condescending voice.

'Someone had to.'

The Caderyn was keeping a tight hold on her anger but he could see that it was bubbling near the surface.

'Marius and I did not make a habit of beating our son, Gawan.'

The Gorvic shrugged, though he was confused by what she said about her husband. It seemed odd that a man so disciplined, and so apt at instilling it in others, would not discipline his own son as well. Or perhaps Gaians let their children run free in their youth, then let the centurions of their legions do the beating of them later? It was a curious thing, Gawan thought, but now was not the time for ruminating.

'Nor do I; I barely touched the lad. There is a difference between a clip and a beating, you know. Or you *would* know if you were raising your boy a Lurian.'

Rhianwyn clenched her fists but Gawan was feeling just as angry. The ungrateful cow ought to be pleased that he'd brought her son home unharmed! Why was she taking such umbrage with a single smack of her son; she surely knew that every child got one now and then? *Compared to what my brother and I used to get, I might as well have run a leaf across his ear.* The chieftain kept her voice low, though her eyes were wide and staring.

'If my child is to be disciplined then *I* will be the one to do it, not you. What the Dis made you think that you had any right?'

He didn't really know what she meant by that but presumably it was a Gaian curse of some kind. *Sometimes you are far too much one of them for your own good. Damn it all woman, remember who you are!*

'He wanders off with a stranger in the woods then wants to stop and play with a bloody hatcher, and after I bring him back for you, you lecture me on whether I had the right to teach him not to do it again? I gave him a sharp shock so he'd remember his lesson,' he pointed a finger at his own chest, 'and I had the right because it seems his parents have failed to teach him!'

Gawan knew his words were cruel but he was too angry to care. Apparently he was not alone in that mood because Rhianwyn's hand came up like lightning and the slap had already struck him by the time Gawan caught her wrist. His cheek stung and his temper flared, and the urge to crack her bones flooded through him. Her forearm felt tiny and feeble in his hand, though the glare she was giving him would have cowed a bull.

'Perhaps that will help *you* to remember your damned place around my son!'

Gawan held her gaze. He still had her wrist and he was aching to slap her back and knock the self-righteous bitch to the ground. She might be fast but there was no chance at all of her beating him in a fight, and they both knew it. For all her ferocity she was still a head shorter and stones lighter than him, and Gawan had over a decade of fighting experience on her. He could crush her right now and it would damned well serve her right! His free hand twitched ready to strike and he saw Rhianwyn register it, but though her posture shifted slightly she didn't break eye-contact. She knew as well as he did what would happen if they fought, but she showed no sign of backing down. Gawan sighed inwardly. He doubted if the idea had even crossed her mind. *Damn it all but she's a bold bitch!*

Gawan held his anger back, for the most part, and settled for flinging her arm back at her.

'If you want your boy to grow into a pampered Gaian then be my guest, but do not blame me when your people say he is not fit to be their chief. Soft lives breed soft men.'

It took her a moment to answer that, and Gawan hoped rather than believed that some of what he'd said had sunk in. Rhianwyn's words snapped out angrily.

'Do not pretend to understand, you are not his father!'

Once again he was tempted to strike her as the old pain bit into him but he held himself in check as he growled back.

'I may not know boys but I *do* know men, and if you ever want Lucan to be one you may be glad that somebody was willing to teach him a lesson or two.'

She must have known he was right but she kept arguing all the same, stepping in close and staring up into his face.

'He is *mine*. Touch him again and it will cost you more than a slapped cheek.'

Gawan wanted to tell her to try her hand against him and see what happened but he hauled himself back with an effort of will. They were about to go to war and if the tribes found their leaders fighting each other it would make a hard job that much harder. He remembered how he and Marius had almost come to blows before Second Nantwyn and it had taken a lot of quiet thought for him to realise how foolish that had been. All the same he spat back his answer.

'Do as you will then, but you can find him yourself next time he disappears!'

Rhianwyn glared at him murderously for a moment but then backed away a few paces. She closed her eyes and took a breath before speaking again, her voice tight but composed.

'I have riders to be sending and a legion to muster. I will expect you to be ready to leave when we are. We have battle to be getting to and you will be needed.'

A part of him wanted to snarl something at her but then he realised this was the closest thing to gratitude that she was capable of. *She knows I am right, but stubborn pride and hatred of me keeps her from saying it.* He told himself it didn't matter. The boy was not his concern, and had he known it would have led to this he would probably have just left him to Emeryn. The thought of her made him realise that he really didn't want to be standing here arguing anyway, and that he'd rather be wherever she was instead.

He gave Rhianwyn a curt nod and didn't wait for a response before stalking off in the direction of the longhouses. Even as he walked away from her, the image of her face flashed before his eyes, still filled with hatred and scorn. He frowned as he went. All this nonsense with the boy was unimportant and he had his warriors to attend to. He thought of Tarwyn and the others and all of a sudden got an odd, almost cold feeling in his stomach. He was all for justice for Ierryn and he knew Caserach must be stopped, but his conflict with Rhianwyn had reminded him of a very unwelcome truth; soon his brothers and tribesmen would have yet another battle to fight. And his Gorvicae would die protecting her Caderyn from their enemies.

Chapter 12. The Road South

He'd not spoken more than two words to Rhianwyn while on the road but Owain had been back and forth between the cohorts regularly, and according to him they had travelled thirty 'miles' today. Gawan had heard Gaians using the word before but he still barely understood it, and he resented Rhianwyn for using it now. They had ridden at good pace for a day and the Caderyn knew where they were now; that was all he needed to know, there was no need for all these foreign notions to prove that. He scowled to himself and let his pony graze a little more before walking him for a while, to stretch his own legs as much as for the horse's benefit.

Gawan sighed and tried to be grateful for small blessings; few people had seen the exchange between him and the Caderyn chieftain, and the three tribes on the march had remained on good terms with one another. Had their confrontation been witnessed it might have caused some serious discontent between them. In the absence of a High Chieftain, the Gorvicae looked to Gawan for their leadership more than anyone, and if discord was seen at the top it would inevitably trickle down. Fortunately the only rumour going around was that Rhianwyn was embarrassed that a Gorvic had found her boy first, and angry though he was at her, Gawan was happy enough to play along. It was better that way.

Better still was that her notion of summoning Gaians to their aid had been abandoned, though he suspected it was more due to Alraig's calm persuasion than to his own more spirited argument, and even so her new plan was far from ideal. It seemed they had reached a compromise whereby a request had been sent to General Galerian to move his people to defend Bryngarth should the Dragon Legion be defeated and the Breiryn begin moving north. How well they could be trusted to stand by that arrangement Gawan couldn't say, but it was a good thing that young Lucan had been left at the Caderyn capital. By his understanding, what loyalty Galerian and the Gaians had would be to Rhianwyn and her son personally. He doubted if they would give a crow's squawk for the tribes she was trying to rule.

He continued walking his pony and tried not to brood. The movement ought to have helped him to relax, but the First Man had a good deal on his mind. The legion was fairly confident, despite being outnumbered, and Gawan only wished that he could feel the same. They had suffered so much against Lepidus at Nantwyn, and to be tossed back into combat against such fierce odds so soon...

He was scowling to himself when young Pryder came up to him. Gadarim or not, as the youngest of their group he was given most of the boring work and was leading the other ponies in the direction of the stream. Gawan handed him his horse's reins without a word, settling for a simple nod of his head. Pryder didn't even try to engage him and nodded back in silence. It was a pity that Hewin hadn't been able to join them, the two were good friends, but he'd been in no state to fight after their clash with the Panther and had been left at Bryngarth in the care of the herbwives. He was likely kicking his heels pretty hard by now.

Gawan watched Pryder go for a moment before heading off through the various huddles of fighters. Before long he reached the fire where his fellow Gadarim sat, though a glance at the flames made him twitch his lip.

'Did Pryder do this?'

Tarwyn replied laconically, sitting with his long legs stretched out in front of him.

'That he did. And before you start yes, we told him. Gwydion is fetching some more wood now and Pryder's under orders to do the same once he's done with the horses.'

Gawan grunted and eased himself onto the grass, his legs aching a little as he sank down. Pryder might be bold but the lad was impatient. The key to getting a proper fire going was good preparation; you needed to do more than just light your kindling and stick some branches on top before you wandered off in search of more fuel. Unless in dire circumstances, the intelligent fire-builder would always have his kindling, twigs, branches and heavy logs all ready before he began. It was a fairly basic idea, but Gawan had found that young men these days were less fond of hard work than they used to be.

He might have begun ranting at the general state of today's youth but Tarwyn spoke first, quite possibly just to forestall him.

'So, from what I hear it'll be seven hundred of us against two thousand of them?'

He didn't sound worried, though with Tarwyn it was hard to tell, merely curious about the situation. Gawan smiled inwardly. Fear was as natural as autumn rain and the man who didn't feel it was either mad or just plain stupid, but no Gadarim worth a crumb would ever *show* it.

'Something like that. But then we've seen legions facing odds like that before.'

Tarwyn nodded quietly and Gawan suspected he was not convinced. He couldn't blame him. The fact was that they'd only seen *Gaian* legions fight like that, and for all his pride in the Dragons they had only been formed a few short moons ago. The legions he and Tarwyn had faced at White Ridge, and fought beside at First Nantwyn, had been made up of soldiers with years of experience of fighting in the shieldwall.

Gwydion came striding up before either of them had to comment further, a bundle of medium-sized branches held in his arms. He nodded in greeting before dropping them at the Gadarim's feet, and he and Tarwyn proceeded to build up the fire properly. The taller man pushed branches in from the outside while Gwydion placed more across the flames to burn through slowly. Gawan hoped that one of them would change the current subject but it seemed Gwydion too was thinking of the coming battle. *Are not we all?*

'Sounds like we'll have a hard job of it against Caserach and this Breiryn rabble. Do you think Broad Kellas will be there?'

Gawan blinked for a moment. He'd been so preoccupied with the numbers he'd forgotten about the one Breiryn name that he knew. Broad Kellas, he didn't know his birth name, was First Man of the Breiryn Gadarim, and had a reputation fierce enough to carry even as far as the Gorvicae. Named for the deadly kellas cats of the mountains, he was said to live up to his warrior name, being swift, strong and truly deadly in combat. Gawan had never met him but he knew him to be a rare big man by all accounts, and young for a tribe's First Man. Inevitably he found himself wondering if he could take him in a fight. In the last twelve winters only Madoc had beaten him man to man, and Madoc had been practically a legend. *Whoever this Broad Kellas is, he'll be no Smiling Fox, that's for sure.*

Tarwyn interrupted his thoughts, his voice as casual as ever.

'Maybe his chieftain won't let him come? Until Caserach can show his worth the Breiryn's leader might not want to be seen helping him?'

Gwydion nodded.

'You may be right.' He paused a moment and then said aloud what all of them had been thinking. 'Should we be hoping for his presence or not?'

It was an interesting question and Gawan mused on it a little. A Gadarim should not shrink from a fight of course but all the same, perhaps it would be better if he was not there. Even discounting the damage he might do personally, the presence of the tribe's First Man would be a sign that their High Chieftain was invested in this fight, and so might send more warriors to fight the Caledon later on. Better all-around if he stayed at home, doing whatever these damned Breiryn did with themselves all that way down south. Nonetheless, a part of Gawan wanted to test himself against this kellas cat, and prove to himself as much as to anyone that the wolf was still top of the predator's chain.

'Let us hope only for honour and victory. The gods can work out the rest.'

There were nods from the other men, Tarwyn's sombre and Gwydion's smiling.

'I'm sure they will.'

Gawan wondered if he ought to tell them about the plan to bring the Blackbirds to Bryngarth should the battle go ill for them. He'd had visions of the Dragons being driven back from Three Willows, wherever that was, and forced to retreat through Caderyn land towards the capital. He couldn't believe he was alone in worrying about this, and the knowledge that, should that happen, a legion would be there to support them might give comfort to his warriors. Then again, if they thought that everything hung on victory down here, it would strengthen their resolve to fight that much harder. Besides, he wasn't the only one to feel misgivings about Gaian support.

Tarwyn's face was serious and Gawan wondered what he was thinking. The lean man was arguably the sharpest of the Gorvicae Gadarim and had probably thought through this whole thing pretty thoroughly.

'We will need Mabonac's good will.'

Gwydion was still smiling broadly. The blonde man was no fool but around Tarwyn he could sometimes seem like one.

'I don't doubt we shall, but why the worry? Have you pissed on a snapdragon or something?'

Tarwyn raised an eyebrow. The bright flowers were, understandably, sacred to the Dragon God and the idea was plainly ridiculous.

'Bold words from a man who'd spill his seed on *mistletoe* if it meant a chance to touch his member.'

Gwydion looked ready to return the banter but Tarwyn continued, his voice serious again.

'No, I was thinking about how he would look on this battle.'

Gawan frowned a little. He didn't want to admit aloud how much the odds were concerning him.

'The legion is well-trained and experienced. They may have the numbers but our warriors are ready for them.'

He spoke with a confidence he only half-felt and the lean man nodded slowly.

'Oh I don't doubt that we have the better men, and hard though it will be, with a little help from the gods we should prevail.'

Gawan suspected that Tarwyn too was speaking with more faith than he truly had. The First Man tilted his head a little as the thoughtful man went on.

'No, what concerns me is *how* the battle is fought. Mabonac's love is honour, and what honour is there in fighting as the Gaians do? Hiding behind shields and stabbing out as real warriors charge is hardly worthy of Mabonac's chosen.'

Gawan felt familiar discomfort at the thought, but at least Tarwyn wasn't bringing up their chances of defeat. He replied casually.

'You had no such worries before Nantwyn?'

Tarwyn gave a tiny shrug.

'That was a legion fighting against other legions and besides, Lepidus would have destroyed us all given the chance. Mabonac understood that we did only what we had to. *This* fight is against fellow Lurians; men raiding another tribe as we all have done for years. How will he and Taran see it when we fight them the same way we fought the invaders?'

The conversation was becoming deeper than Gawan generally liked and he was glad when Gwydion answered first.

'I think they will remember that Caserach is a murderer. He would threaten the Caledon, which is all that stops the Gaians from coming again, and the man has no honour of his own. What more does he deserve than to be put down as we see fit?'

Gawan nodded in agreement.

'Besides; bringing so many warriors with him shows that he wishes to overwhelm the Caledon. *He* does not intend to give *us* a fair fight, why should we concern ourselves with using different methods to fight back?'

He felt odd, arguing for something he wasn't quite sure he agreed with. Tarwyn was quite the thinker and made an excellent point, to say nothing of the fact that the Breiryn were the Caderyn's enemies, not theirs. Once again he wondered at the thought of Gorvicae dying to help Caderyn, and his resentment of Rhianwyn re-surfaced. The Wildcat might be a strong leader but she thought too much of herself, and she could well create real trouble for his tribe once all this was done. *But better her than the Gaians, that's for damned sure. Her Caledon is important, at least for now, and if we've learned nothing else in these last few years it's that we survive only by unity.*

Tarwyn tilted his head in acknowledgement.

'True enough, in a way. Yet does his fighting foul justify our doing the same? If a man murdered my father am I right to murder his?'

Gawan wouldn't have called legion fighting *foul* exactly, though his brother was right about there being little honour in it. He wanted to curse Tarwyn for being too clever for his own good, but mercifully Emeryn arrived at that moment and the trio broke off their argument and turned to face her. She was carrying a huge bowl of steaming liquid in her hands, and the smell coming from it was deliciously rich. She smirked at the sitting men.

'I see you've made no effort to start your suppers yet?'

Gwydion smiled almost sheepishly and even Tarwyn's lip moved a fraction. The fire was still too low to cook anything, and Gawan had been content to settle for a boring meal of bread and dried mutton. Until the smell from Emeryn's bowl had reached his nostrils. Gwydion spoke for them, a beam across his face.

'We were living in hope that someone like you would take pity on us.'

Tarwyn rolled his eyes at his friend but Gawan was glad of the interruption. Emeryn pursed her lips at the blonde man and walked towards Gawan.

'Lydwen gave me this for you, though you'll have to fetch your own bowls.'

Gwydion had already fetched his from his saddlebag and tossed another one to Tarwyn, who caught it one-handed. Gawan made for his own bags to find his and Emeryn's bowls and spoke over his shoulder as his lover put the big vessel down.

'I hope you thanked her for us?'

Emeryn nodded and began ladling stew out for Tarwyn.

'Naturally, and she said it was a pleasure and to pass on her blessings.'

Gawan almost smiled as he nodded back. People often gave food to Gadarim when a tribe went off to war but if old Hedrin had taught him nothing else, it was to never take their kindness for granted. He dug out wooden bowls and spoons and shuffled over to Emeryn, who was now serving a smiling Gwydion. The stew smelled wonderful and Gawan paused only briefly to thank Camelas for his bounty before shoving his spoon into the liquid. It was hot but very welcome, with soft vegetables and a subtle seasoning that he couldn't quite identify. The meat in it was rabbit, chewy but delicious, and Gawan wondered, as he always did, whether it reminded him more of pork or of chicken.

Emeryn filled her own bowl and sat down beside him. She snuggled in close, and the little group was silent for a while, all enjoying and appreciating Lydwen's welcome gift. The feel of Emeryn next to him helped take Gawan's mind off things, and he found himself relaxing as he ate. He found he liked to just sit with her like this, not even needing to talk but just enjoying being with one another. It felt... right. *Perhaps you should just tell her that you love her? It's as true of her as it is of anyone isn't it?*

Eventually some quiet conversation resumed, and Gawan was glad that the subject of Mabonac's approval did not come up again. It wasn't something he cared to dwell on right now. Instead the talk mostly revolved around Gwydion and Tarwyn exchanging insults, with Emeryn joining in every now and then. Gwydion might be the more jovial man but Tarwyn had a cutting wit, and Emeryn could banter as well as anyone. They bickered happily for a while, with Gawan rarely passing comment, until Pryder arrived with some newly-filled waterskins, and then they all began mocking him instead.

For the most part Gawan just sat back and enjoyed it, the sound of his brothers' happiness washing gently over him. Combined with Emeryn's presence it did a great deal to calm his spirit, and he watched the fire contentedly as the darkness around them deepened. Eventually the other Gadarim kicked off their shoes and began to lie back with their feet towards the flames, the talk slowly dying down as they prepared themselves for sleep.

181

With the lack of talk some of Gawan's cares returned to him, and he thought of the test that the Dragons would soon face. Combined with his annoyance at Rhianwyn, and the Caderyn in general, his mood might have turned sour again had it not been for Emeryn. As Pryder's snores began to drift across the fire, she shifted closer and locked her gaze onto his. In the light of the flames her eyes were almost black, and her hair seemed to shine reddish-gold. Maybe it was that she'd sensed his tension, or maybe she was just feeling in an amorous mood this evening, but whatever the reason he read her eyes as easily as she would read tracks.

Without a word the First Man eased himself up and extended a hand to help her to her feet. Emeryn reached up languidly and took his arm, lifting herself up smoothly to stand close to him. He kept hold of her hand and began to walk, away from the flickering light of the fires and out into the night. They hadn't gone far before they found a patch of ferns and they walked around the edge of it, both stopping at the same time. Gawan made to lift his tunic off but Emeryn placed a gentle hand on his chest to stop him. She kept her eyes on his as she stepped away and began gathering up her skirts. Given that dresses were generally removed by pulling them up over the head, there were few women who were able to make the movement look even remotely sultry. But Emeryn was one of them. With a single smooth motion the green garment was up and off and Gawan stared at her nakedness in the silvery moonlight.

Her skin was naturally pale and almost shone in the night, her whole body tight with muscle yet still curved and feminine. Gawan stepped forwards eagerly and drew her

182

into a kiss, his hands beginning at her hips before running slowly up to her breasts. Her milky skin was as smooth as it looked and the flesh beneath was soft but firm. Gawan felt himself harden as the kiss deepened but then Emeryn backed off again, placing a long finger on his lips. Her mouth quirked up mischievously as she took hold of his tunic and drew it upwards. Gawan raised his arms above him and Emeryn paused as the garment was halfway off, leaning forwards to kiss his chest before removing it fully.

The moment his arms were free again his hands returned to the glory of her skin, stroking gently down her sides until he reached her upper legs. Her thighs and buttocks were both strong and firm, and Gawan smiled as he took hold of her and drew her closer to him. Emeryn continued kissing his chest as she pulled at his breeches' ties, teasing his manhood with her other hand as she did. Gawan wanted to tell her to just get on with it but he restrained himself. Back in his youth he had always rushed these things and while he'd never walked away unsatisfied, Bronwen had taught him the value of taking his time. For a moment he thought about his wife and he even saw her face flicker before his eyes, but he closed them tight for a count of three and when he opened them, only Emeryn stood before him.

She had finally undone the cords of his breeches and he stepped out of the garment, Emeryn's hands still toying with his hardness. He kept a hand on her flank while the other reached up to her hair, his fingers running slowly through the fine golden strands. Everything about her was perfect, and all Gawan wanted to do was to throw her down and take her right now, to use her body for his own pleasure; to make her *his*. They'd coupled like that before, like beasts driven by urgency and need, but tonight it seemed Emeryn was in a teasing mood, and if she could do it, then so could he.

He lowered her to the grass and followed her down slowly, letting his hands run along her skin so lightly as to be barely touching her. He felt her tremble with excitement but he didn't rush, and he started planting kisses along her neck. Emeryn kept stroking him but reached her other hand to his back, and Gawan felt the scratching of her nails behind his shoulder. He lowered his mouth to the swell of her breast and let his hand drift down to her thigh. Emeryn's breath was coming out shallower, more desperate, and when he finally touched her womanhood she arched her back and sucked in her breath. He teased her until her eyes were all but begging him to take her, but she was giving as good as she got, taunting him with her own touch until Gawan was longing to be inside her. When neither one could stand it any longer the Gadarim eased his lover back and slowly, gently entered her, revelling in her urgent gasps and the delicious warmth of her body. After that, the two became considerably less restrained.

By the time their passions were spent and they were just lying in each other's arms, all of Gawan's great cares were gone. He lay panting with Emeryn's golden head on his chest and felt nothing but ease and contentment. He was tired, but not uncomfortably so, and he allowed himself to drift into a doze, enjoying the gentle presence of his lover at his side. Already she was beginning to drop off and he wondered if he ought to tell her that he loved her tonight. It seemed the right time, and he was sure it would make her happy, and he took a slow breath in to finally say the words. Then Emeryn let out a quiet snore and he figured it would be a waste to do it now.

Instead Gawan let out his breath in a satisfied sigh, looking up at the star-filled sky above without a care in the world. For a brief while he forgot all about Caserach and the Breiryn, about Galerian and the Gaians, about tribes and wars and bloody Rhianwyn. Tonight he had Emeryn, soft and lovely, lying in his arms and snoring her quiet snore. Everything else in this foolish world could damned well wait until morning.

Chapter 13. A Clear Night

The warriors of her legion were drifting into a quiet slumber, and Rhia wished that she could join them in it. She had tossed and turned beside her fire for what felt like half the night but still sleep had eluded her, and eventually she had given in and decided to take a wander about the hill to clear her mind. So many thoughts were racing through her head it was a wonder she could walk a straight line. The coming fight, and the inevitable mess that would follow it, were of course foremost among them, followed closely by the fate of poor Lucan, on whose shoulders so much would rest.

She took a deep breath and tried to admire the view. From where she stood she could see the many copses of trees away to the west, and further south the range of hills that led towards Breiryn lands. Closer to she saw the hundreds of tiny fires that warmed her little army, turning the plain below into a mirror of the night sky above. The moon was bright tonight and the skies almost empty of clouds, leaving much of the land below her bathed in a silver-grey light. *My land.* For a moment she felt a surge of pride and a burning need to defend it, but this was soon dispelled by a sudden wave of sadness. Yes she was proud, and yes she knew that this land was hers to defend, but so often when she viewed the lands of the Caderyn she couldn't help but think of her father. Carradan had been the wisest and strongest ruler her tribe had known for generations, and living up to his reputation would be a something she would spend a lifetime struggling with. *Who are you trying to fool? You're not a chieftain worrying about living up to his legend. You're missing your father still, just admit it to yourself.*

Rhia was well-accustomed to self-criticism but all the same the truth of it irritated her and she tried to push the thought away. She had avenged her father and buried him with dignity; that was the important thing. *Lie to others if you want girl, but don't think to lie to yourself.* Rhia ground her teeth together. *Whatever I feel, right now I'll serve his memory best by keeping his tribe in one piece, now shut up and let me get on with it!* Her inner voice didn't seem to have an answer for that and Rhia took a slow breath, trying to marshal her thoughts into something constructive. If the gods, or more likely her own mind, wouldn't let her sleep, the least she could do was to make the most of the time.

She looked down at her sleeping legion. They would head south a while longer and then westward along the river towards Three Willows, since odds were good that somewhere along that route they would run into Caserach and his Breiryn allies. In many ways the Dariniae usurper's eagerness for a battle was a good thing, since at least they wouldn't have to seek him out or worry about his evading them. But all the same the numbers still made her nervous. Even with the legion's advantage in open field they were dangerously under-strength, and she had far fewer Gadarim with her than she'd have liked. Eurin and a few others she had sent to Mobryn to rally locals against potential attack, Bedwyr was still at Nantwyn, Elfed she had left at Bryngarth with Merwyn, and so many more had died at Lepidus' hands.

Rhia found herself clenching her fists tight at the thought of the Gaian general; the mentor that Marius had once trusted. The fact that he'd been killed by one of his own might have been a fitting end, and it had saved the Gaians some face, but still Rhia regretted never having ended him herself. Though worse than that was the thought of Praecus having escaped. The little sorcerer who had caused all of this had apparently come with Lepidus to Caderyn lands but he had not been seen among the dead, having presumably slunk away when things turned sour. The thought of that vile man still living when so many better men lay dead and buried made Rhia want to punch something. She took another breath to calm herself down.

She tried instead to think of those good Gaians she had known; those like Marius and Glaucus, or her friends back in Tamora like Vorena and Drusus, Narbo and Gregor. She'd been sorely tempted to send another rider off to the general, just to check that he'd received her message. She was confident he would not refuse her, but all the same terrible thoughts of what might go wrong rushed through her head, and once again her hands twitched and clenched as her fears threatened to overwhelm her.

She shoved it from her mind and focused on her centre, and took comfort in the dragonfire she found there. Rhia had been alive for less than thirty winters yet she'd seen more trials than most women faced in a lifetime, and she wondered now how she had ever endured them without this fire to help her. *Because for all your foolishness you've always had your stubborn pride beneath everything else, and you've had good husbands and a sweet child; people to love and be loved by in return.*

Rhia took a breath of the clear evening air and thought about her boy. He would be safe enough back at Bryngarth, though he'd desperately wanted to come with them of course. Her little soldier. Her eyes moistened as she remembered him playing with his tiny sword back at the legion barracks in Tamora. Half of Marius' cohort had dandled him on their knee, and he'd become a sort of unofficial mascot for the Tenth Legion. Not that Lepidus would have condoned such a thing of course. Rhia sighed. In some ways her critics were right; Lucan *was* a Gaian in so many ways, but what else could he have been, growing up as he had? Rhia had done what she could to set things right but it was a narrow path to walk. He had to be a true Lurian if he was to rule their people, but if this peace was to hold he would have to know the Gaians' ways as well. She remembered the old man at Glyscoed a lifetime ago, and how she'd ignored his warnings. And almost lost everything as a result.

She banished her regret by reaching for anger, her old friend, as she thought about what Gawan had done to her boy. It was partly the thought of his striking her child that angered her of course, but it was the mind-set behind it that had irked her more than anything. She and Marius had raised a fine young boy, and had seen no need to beat him to teach him lessons about life. He was clever and brave, and for the most part he was obedient, what bloody right did Gawan have for saying that he needed discipline? But then there was truth in what he'd said, both about learning lessons and about how Lucan must be seen, though Rhia hated to admit it. It was vital that Lucan appear as a strong Lurian to his people, even if he also had to remain part-Gaian to treat with their former enemies. She tried not to grind her teeth in frustration. It would be hard, for both of them, no doubt about it. She shook her head a little to clear it. The notion of Gawan being even partly right had only angered her further but she put him from her mind with an effort. Instead she concentrated on Lucan.

Rhia whispered a quick prayer to Cassio Marna to bless and keep him, and then others to Gron Camelas and Sulis Mehine. Lucan's gods would always be those of his father as well as his mother, and it made sense to pray to all of them for him. *Well, almost all*. Right now Rhia needed Mabonac, Taran and Vulco here with her. Beneath the stillness of the night there was a rumble of tension, subtle but certain, as seven hundred Caledon fighters readied themselves to defend the Caderyn's homeland. She would need every God of War on her side. Rhia straightened her spine, all thought of lost sleep forgotten, and looked out over her army, praying hard that the Caledon would survive this ordeal. She had already taken a terrible risk with her people's future. *Everything* depended on the next few days.

Chapter 14. Battle Looms

Gawan awoke with a jolt as Emeryn sat up suddenly from her sleep. Instinct meant he was already reaching for his knife but he stopped his hand mid-way to his boot. The camp was still dark, the dawn just barely creeping up on them, and besides his fellow Gadarim they were alone beside the embers of their fire. A thin line of light was showing from the hills to the east, but the sky was still dim and the world around them was grey. They'd been riding with those hills at their backs for two days now, following the river that marked the boundary of Caderyn land. The usual morning smells were wafting through the camp as the early risers began cooking breakfast or poking life back into their fires.

He relaxed a little as he realised there was no danger nearby, but then tensed again at the sight of Emeryn. She was sitting spear-straight and breathing hard, her dark eyes wide and haunted. Gawan reached across to touch her and she almost flinched away. Then he felt her fingers close around his hand and clutch it hard, as if making sure he was still there. Gawan met her gaze and squeezed back, lines of concern appearing on his face.

'Are you alright?'

It took her a moment but she nodded her head. She tried to smile and failed.

'Just a dream. A very bad dream.'

Gawan frowned but didn't press her, and she continued after a few slow breaths.

'We were standing together in a shieldwall, fighting in the battle, when something struck me in the side. It was...'

she furrowed her brow, concentrating, '... it was a beast of some kind. I don't know... I... I can't really remember.'

She was silent for a while and Gawan let her think in her own time. Soon enough she continued, making a distracted brushing motion with one hand.

'Anyhow, it came at me and I... I struck at it but I must have missed because the next thing I remember is feeling sharp teeth on my arm. I tried calling for you but no sound came out and then... then I felt its teeth in my leg.'

She gripped Gawan's hand even tighter and he shuffled closer to her, putting his chest to her back.

'I still couldn't cry out, and then whatever it was it clambered up as I fell and leaped straight for my throat.' Her free hand seemed to stray unconsciously up to her neck, then she shuddered and tried to give a nonchalant shrug. 'And then I woke up. Foolish of me to start at it really.'

Gawan nodded and kept hold of her. She was clearly trying to look indifferent but he could tell she was still feeling shaky. He'd once heard Merdryn tell Baercban that sometimes a dream was just a dream, but nonetheless plenty of druids put great stock in what they might mean, and a portent of the dreamer's death was generally taken seriously.

The First Man wasn't sure what he should do. He had little enough experience in comforting frightened women, and it disturbed him that a woman as bold as Emeryn had been so affected. He stroked her hair awkwardly, noting how even in such dim light it almost shone. He spoke to her as softly as he could.

'We all of us start when we are shocked from a dream.'

The words came out calm but Gawan's mind was racing. He couldn't help but wonder if the beast she'd seen had been a kellas cat. If it had been, then what if the dream was indeed a portent, and that Broad Kellas would be facing them and was destined to kill her in the battle? He kept stroking her hair and muttering what he hoped were comforting things, all the while resolving himself to let no Gadarim within arm's reach of her. He would keep close to her in the shieldwall; keep her safe. She leaned her head onto his chest and seemed to calm down a little, and Gawan wondered what he would say if anyone came and saw him like this. He had a reputation to maintain as a hard-faced bastard, one that had taken years of hard-faced bastardry to earn. What would his warriors say if they saw him stroking hair and cooing nothings to the woman in his arms?

He'd just decided that he didn't give a damn what anyone thought when Emeryn spared him from the dilemma by sitting up a little and smiling. She gave him a playful punch in the chest and did her best to lighten the mood.

'Don't think I don't know what you're doing there. A little more hair-stroking and I'll find my head being "accidentally" guided downwards!'

Gawan twitched his lip in what was dangerously close to a smirk. She was forcing the smile, that was clear, but it meant she was putting a brave face on something that scared her, and he was happy to play along if it made her feel better.

'At this time of the morning? That would be a rare treat, but what would the others say?'

Emeryn raised an eyebrow.

'They are still asleep.'

193

But even as she said the words he saw Gwydion start to stir and a moment later Pryder's eyes began to open. Emeryn shrugged her shoulders and did a fairly good job of looking casual.

'Ah well, too late.'

She let go of Gawan's hand but he gave her arm a quick touch before leaning back to reach for his boots.

'I shall just have to settle for a decent breakfast.'

At the mention of food Pryder sat upright. Tarwyn rose more slowly, clear-eyed but unhurried, while Gwydion started tugging on his boots, his face eager.

'Do you think there will be any pork left from last night?'

Mostly this was met with shrugs but Pryder chipped in eagerly.

'Gods I hope so. My belly's growing tired of porridge every morning.'

Gawan didn't comment. He'd lived on far worse rations than they'd eaten on this ride, though he had to admit the thought of pork was pleasant. The day before they'd passed a village who'd been convinced they would soon be overrun by marauding Breiryn, and the farmers had not only greeted them but made them a gift of more than three-dozen pigs. The noise of the slaughter had been loud and long but it had given the legion some precious fresh meat and, to her credit, Rhianwyn had shared it out equally.

Gawan was just wondering at what his past self might think of his being fed by grateful Caderyn when he heard the sound of commotion across the camp. A hundred muttered conversations were already underway as the warriors awoke and started chatting, but this was something else, something urgent. The others had noticed it as well and Tarwyn nodded to Pryder as he stood.

'Go and see what all that is about, will you?'

The younger man bobbed his head and hurried off into the camp. Emeryn and the Gadarim laced up boots or pinned on cloaks as they waited for him, but before Pryder could come back with any news of what was happening, a rider came trotting up to them and Gawan recognised him as Boryn.

The Gorvic headman swung himself from the pony's back and spoke through his thick grey moustache. He didn't waste words.

'Caserach has been sighted. His force is on the north bank of the river and is heading east, right in our direction.'

Gawan was already buckling Heartreaver into place.

'How far off?'

Boryn opened his hands noncommittally.

'All I know is that the scouts say he could be here before noon.'

With the dawn sky still grey most might think that was plenty of warning, but Gawan knew from experience how quickly time passed on days like this. Part of him wanted to ask if Broad Kellas had been seen among them but chances were that Boryn wouldn't know and besides, he had no wish to worry Emeryn. She was no fool and would likely have made the same connection he had.

'Is it known whether he spotted our scouts?'

It was Tarwyn who'd spoken, his voice relaxed as he rolled up his blanket. Boryn rolled his shoulders.

'I know little more than you do, comrade. He was no doubt expecting to run into us sooner or later but whether he knows how close we are, I cannot say.'

195

The sky above them seemed to be getting lighter every moment and Gawan saw that it was going to be a pretty overcast day. *Good thing too. Mail is all very well but the damned stuff makes me sweat like a hog.*

'If he moves around us he could pin us with the river to our backs. Have you spoken to Rhianwyn yet?'

Boryn nodded and pointed off to his left.

'I have. We are to head north a little ways before turning back west again. She says there is a ridge over that way that will serve us well as a place to defend.'

Emeryn piped up, her voice steady.

'Will Caserach attack us straight up a hill if we just stand there and wait for him?'

Tarwyn answered her first.

'He cannot afford to look weak or wary in front of his Breiryn allies, not with such a huge advantage in numbers.'

Boryn nodded, his face serious.

'Exactly. He must show himself to be bold or they may desert him.'

Gawan had been wondering about that, and whether the legion could survive a charge even assuming that they had good ground, but he was spared from brooding on it by the arrival of more riders. He saw Kyran and Owain, along with the Caderyn druid and a handful of headmen, all following Rhianwyn who was cantering at their head. She was dressed for war in mailshirt, tunic and breeches and even before she stepped from her mount he could see the fire in her eyes. She strode towards the little group, her left hand held relaxed on Silverbite's shining pommel.

He couldn't help but notice how well she looked, and how fearsome. Rhianwyn was merely pretty at best, but

196

with battle near at hand something about her seemed to change, her courage and ferocity shining through. For an unkind moment he compared her to Emeryn, who only moments ago had been trembling in his arms like a child. He slapped away the thought with a curse at his own head. It was unworthy of him; shallow and base, and he felt shame rising up in him almost immediately. He loved Emeryn and she was as brave as any warrior he knew, how dare he judge her now for a mere moment of vulnerability! All his life Gawan had detested weakness, in others and in himself, but to look down on one he cared about for something so petty was despicable. All the same, with that fire in her eyes, it was hard not to remember the sight of Rhianwyn's naked body.

He cursed himself again and looked away from her, ashamed, only to meet Emeryn's eyes as he did. His thoughts had taken what? A heartbeat? Two? And he was sure that he'd shown nothing on his face. Yet one look at his lover told him she'd seen *exactly* what he'd been thinking, and a horrid cold feeling crept into his gut. He took a step towards her, ready to ask her forgiveness, but in that moment Rhianwyn spoke, addressing him specifically.

'Gawan, I take it Boryn has told you the news?'

Her voice was hard and flat and Gawan remembered that for all her sudden appeal the woman was still an over-proud bitch underneath it. *She is nothing next to Emeryn, what were you thinking?* He answered her bluntly, hoping to show his lover how little he cared to speak to her.

'The enemy is on his way and we have some good ground to take?'

197

If Rhianwyn noticed his attitude she didn't mention it, and Gawan snuck a quick glance at Emeryn before she replied. His lover's face was as blank as a mask and Gawan wished that he could speak with her alone, just for a moment.

'Moon Ridge is not steep but it curves in such a way as to be difficult to flank. If we position archers well we can hamper such a movement and further encourage Caserach to attack us head on.'

There were a few nods but no-one spoke, and Rhianwyn continued after a beat.

'We can hope that the sight of us will make the Breiryn think twice, given that they have not seen a formation like this in action before. With good fortune they will be hesitant but will still move forward up the hill, coming at us in an uncertain charge. Should they choose not to attack we may be forced to charge at them, but we will still have the advantage of moving down the hill.'

Gawan frowned and was briefly distracted from his current dilemma by a shared glance with Tarwyn. No doubt he too was feeling torn between wishing for a battle on the hilltop that they might actually *win*, compared with the nobler notion of an honourable charge that would probably fail. He wondered if Owain or Kyran had considered the same thing, and whether his fellow First Men were thinking on what Mabonac might think. He only dwelt on that for a moment though before going back to thinking of Emeryn, but then this too was cut short as Rhianwyn began to outline her plan.

The Caderyn chieftain had drawn a blackened stick from the fire and was now drawing in the dust with it, first marking out the shape of a long crescent moon.

'We will form a line facing roughly southwest along the ridge, the Gorvicae cohort on the left, the Dariniae on the right, and the Caderyn in the centre.'

First Gawan, then Kyran and Owain nodded their heads.

'Behind them will be those warriors we have who are not part of the legion.'

Gawan saw Alraig dip his head. The Dragon Legion had been formed while warriors were still coming in from across Caderyn territory to face the Gaians. From what Gawan recalled, Alraig himself had been at Bryngarth for council, but most of his people had not joined them until the march to Nantwyn and so had not been trained to fight in the shieldwall. But judging by the legion belt and sword the headman wore, he and his had still given good account of themselves in the battle. Rhianwyn carried on.

'They will act as a reserve in case the cohorts are pushed back, and will counter-charge if necessary to give the legion time to reform.'

She was talking very much the way Marius used to, and Gawan remembered how frustrated he'd got at the Gaian's damned chatter of 'Tactica One' and 'Flank Reformation'. *In all fairness though, he knew his trade, annoying though he was about it.* There was a brief pause as people nodded or grunted in acknowledgement, and Gawan looked to Emeryn again. She was still standing where she had been, perfectly still, and he was pretty sure she'd been looking at him until he'd looked at her. Then her eyes dropped down to the sketch on the floor, her face blank and hard and cold. Gawan started to feel angry. Couldn't she tell it had just been a look, a tiny moment that was gone before it started? She ought to know by now how much he cared for her, did that count for nothing?

His anger simmered beneath the surface as Rhianwyn looked around at each of them.

'Are there any questions?'

There was silence from the little group. The plan was simple enough; Gawan just hoped it would succeed with so few warriors to execute it. Rhianwyn gave a curt nod, and judging from her tight expression Gawan suspected that she too was well aware of how hard this would be.

'Very well. The ridge is only a short way north and west of us, have your people ready to leave as soon as possible.'

The huddle bowed their heads again and set about their duties, the Gadarim all clasping wrists and patting shoulders before heading off. Each one gave the same simple blessing to his brother, regardless of what tribe they might belong to.

'The Dragon go with you.'

'And with you.'

After sharing blessings with Owain and Kyran Gawan turned to look for Emeryn, but she had already left the group and was gathering up their saddlebags. Gawan fumed quietly, torn between wanting to apologise and wanting to shout at her for taking offence at something so mild. *Damn it all!* His frustration must have shown on his face because Boryn appeared beside him and spoke in a friendly voice.

'Are you alright?'

Gawan shrugged at the grey-whiskered headman.

'I'm fine.'

Boryn noted where he'd been looking and smiled a little under his moustache.

'Romantic troubles?' He gave the First Man's arm a slap. 'Take some free advice my friend; whatever it is, assume you are in the wrong!'

He'd clearly meant it as something light-hearted but it did nothing to raise Gawan's spirits or quell his temper. He was sorely tempted to snap something unpleasant at him but he reigned himself in and simply nodded.

'I shall keep it in mind.'

He clasped wrists with his fellow Gorvic and the other man bobbed his head before heading away to organise their people. Gawan took a last look at Emeryn, who was ignoring him as she gathered waterskins, and decided he had to put her from his mind. They could talk later when the two of them had calmed down a little and besides, more important things were afoot. There was fighting to be done and if nothing else, he had to be on the lookout for Broad Kellas and the other southern Gadarim. He might not know what to do about upsetting her, but if there was any chance her dream was a portent he could at least make sure she was safe. *If nothing else, that's something you* can *do well!*

Chapter 15. The Dragons Form

Moon Ridge was much as Rhianwyn had described it; barely high enough to be called a proper hill but very wide, curving around so that it faced both the south and the west. At the western end the ridge dropped down steeply while the slope in front of the Gorvicae was comparatively gentle. *If Caserach has half the wits the gods gave a goat, this is where the hardest fighting will be.* The Gorvicae cohort were already dressed and formed into ranks, though the lines weren't particularly tight and most of the northerners had left their long shields on the ground. They still had time.

Gawan was the only one of the cohort still mounted, the rest having left their ponies with Alraig's men at the rear. He would take his place among them once the battle was imminent but for now he waited on his pony and looked around the hillside. To his left the long ridge continued a little way before easing off behind them into a bright, grassy plain. To his right, three cohorts of the Dragon Legion were set out in a long line, Mabonac's banners flying high over each one. The sky above was grey with clouds, but even in the meagre light the dragons on their shields and banners still stood out clear and fierce. Though the symbol was the same throughout the legion, a dark green dragon with broad wings and sharp claws, each tribe had painted the background of their shields in different colours. The Dariniae on the right showed their dragons on pitch black, the Caderyn in the centre on red and blue, while the warriors with Gawan had painted their shields the bright green of summer grass. The green of the Gorvicae.

The First Man adjusted the cloak that he still wore over his ringmail. No-one knew for how long this colour had been sacred to his tribe or even the reasons why, but Gawan had his suspicions. His home was in the north, where winters were hard and good crops often scarce, and for such a people green would always be the colour of hope. He cast his eyes across his cohort again. Thanks to the carnage at Nantwyn nearly all of them had mailshirts, short swords and re-painted Gaian shields. He sighed a little as he remembered the days when a sword had been a symbol of status. His father had often wrought such weapons on his old anvil back at Green Hollow, but he could never have made a living by it because such work was so scarce. Good price though he might get, swords were carried almost exclusively by chiefs and Gadarim, and it was a rare year when he was called on to make three. That general rule was still true for long blades, Gawan supposed, but lately the Gaians had taught them the deadly efficiency of the short sword at close quarters, and then obligingly provided them with plenty to go around. *Of course, the reason our legion has so much equipment isn't just because we scrounged a lot from dead Gaians. It's because there aren't as many of us as there used to be.*

It was a fairly grim thought and Gawan put it from his mind. The matter of numbers had been discussed and pondered enough already, and a battlefield was no place for defeatism. *And anyway, our people here are better trained and better spirited than the Breiryn, and that counts for a damned sight more than mere numbers!* He looked again at the lines of Caledon warriors, well-armed and fearsome with blue woad bright on their limbs and faces. The warpaint still felt wet on Gawan's own skin, having been painted over his tattoos to further draw Mabonac's eye. Like the other Gadarim of his tribe he had also bleached his hair with white lime, spiking most of it up and backwards like some great albino hedgehog, with the rest tied back behind his neck with a simple cord.

He looked across to see Gwydion and Pryder preparing themselves, the younger man's hands in his elder's hair. It was a tricky thing to do, and with a real danger of blindness of course, but the Gorvicae had long ago perfected the art of limewashing, using crownless, broad-brimmed hats to protect the face while the lime was applied. Further up the ridge the Dariniae were doing something similar, only they bleached their hair in streaks that always made Gawan think of badgers. Beside them, the Caderyn's Gadarim whitened their beards instead of their hair, putting leaves in their mouths as they did so to protect them from swallowing the lime. Pairs of warriors helped each other with this all along the curving hillside, or else applied more woad to one-another's faces, the better to gain the favour of the gods. The process was one of both bonding and of focus, giving the fighters a time of quiet to settle their minds ready for war. When he and Tarwyn had been painting one another's battle-marks Gawan had been kindling the dragonfire in his core, and he knew his brother Gadarim had done the same.

For the most part he'd managed that well enough, he'd done so a score of times before at least, but all the same Emeryn's face kept interrupting his focus. He'd tried to speak with her a few times but she'd avoided conversation and always busied herself with some other task. Right now she was painting woad on Senia's face, and Gawan suspected she was taking her time about it simply to avoid having to speak to him. Senia had already applied the warpaint to Emeryn and Gawan couldn't help but think how much more beautiful it made her; strong and fierce and ready.

Again he felt the mix of guilt and anger that had been plaguing him all morning but he shook it off with an effort as he looked down into the bowl below. Covering the grass were the seemingly endless Breiryn; a seething mass of yellow-brown tunics with a cluster of black-clad Dariniae on one flank. Beyond a handful of chariots they were all on foot, and Gawan vaguely remembered that while horses were generally larger down south, they were also fewer in number. He suspected the chariots were there as an attempt to intimidate them as much as for warfare, and that this Asrec character would be watching from one as things unfolded.

They were still a long way off but he could spot individuals among them, and the white hair of their Gadarim shone even in the grey light. From what he could see, the Breiryn elite favoured shaping their hair into horns, and there were far more of them down there than he had hoped for. *Enough of such thoughts! We are the better men here; we are Gorvicae!* He wondered if Broad Kellas was one of the men he now watched and decided then and there that the Breiryn's First Man was no match for him. It didn't matter that they'd never met and that his reputation was impressive by anyone's standards. Madoc was gone, and no other man of all the tribes had bested Leaping Wolf in over a decade. He thrust out his chin defiantly. *Let him try to reach Emeryn. I'll send him back holding his head.*

Gawan was straining his eyes staring down at them, and wondering which one was their tribe's First Man, when the sound of hooves behind him made him turn. Rhianwyn, along with Kyran, Owain and the headmen, was trotting towards them on a dappled pony. Having no beard to colour, she had limewashed a long streak down the middle of her hair, a broader band than the Dariniae favoured but not so thick as to make her look like a Gorvic either. The mail and woad looked well on her but Gawan took care not to stare. The Caderyn chieftain gave him a short nod and spoke quickly.

'It is time.'

Part of Gawan wanted to turn back to Emeryn to see if she'd noticed his lack of interest, but he realised how pitiful that would look and kept facing forwards. He still felt bad for having upset her, but this was no time for such trivialities.

'Let's be away.'

Rhianwyn didn't bother to reply and simply wheeled her mount around to face down the slope. The others fell in behind her and Gawan urged his pony forwards to join them. As they trotted towards the massing Breiryn the First Man of the Gorvicae put his lover from his mind and focused on Mabonac's fire in his belly. Soon it would be time for battle, but first it was time to get his first good look at Ierryn's murderer.

*

As the party rode closer to him, the first thing Gawan noticed was how much the man was like his uncle. Like Ierryn he was built both tall and strong with black hair that fell down to his shoulders. His features were a touch sharper perhaps, his nose a little longer and his beard trimmed a bit more neatly, but beyond that only his age showed that this was not the same man. He was older than Rhianwyn but Gawan guessed it wasn't by much, and he doubted if he'd seen his thirtieth summer. He rode a grey pony and was dressed in dark clothing, a heavy cloak of what looked like bearskin held at his shoulder with a silver pin.

Close by him rode a lanky man with a missing ear and a ragged mark on one cheek that looked ugly even through his woad. He didn't seem all that formidable but he had a mean and vicious look to him, and he struck Gawan as the sort of man who avoided fair fights if he could. Their Breiryn allies had come up with them in a heavy, two-horse chariot, and a man Gawan took to be Asrec stood and faced them from the wooden platform. He was a long-faced man with straggly dark hair, his beard thin and flecked liberally with grey. The blemished torque around his neck marked him as an old-fashioned sort of chief, but beyond that his dress was fairly plain. Like most of his people he wore a dull yellowish tunic, a sharp contrast to the bright blue of his woad.

But it wasn't Asrec that caught Gawan's eye, nor the tough-looking driver in front of him. His focus was purely for the giant of a man who stood grim-faced and steady behind them, his bulging arms straining against the bracelets wrapped around them. He was maybe ten years younger than Gawan himself and at least half a head taller than anyone in either group. His shoulders were broad and his massive chest bare, and he was covered in bright woad painted over his tattoos. Beneath the battle-marks Gawan saw that his forearms were criss-crossed with scars, speaking of a man who'd learned to fight the hard way but had come out more-or-less in one piece. Around his waist was a belt of what looked like green-and-black snakeskin, and the sword that hung from it was as broad as Gawan's palm. His face was flat, with wide cheeks and a stubby nose, and his dark eyes were hooded under a pair of heavy brows. Like his brothers he had limewashed his hair to a brilliant white and spiked it up into short, sharp-looking horns.

Gawan looked at what could only have been Broad Kellas with affected disinterest, sizing him up ready for potential combat. *He's big alright, and younger than you, and even without his reputation, a glance could tell you the man is experienced.* Gawan frowned slightly as he considered how best to fight him. Too many people, generally those who hadn't done much fighting, believed that big men had to be slow. Gawan wasn't fool enough to make such an assumption, but at the same time knew that he couldn't match him strength for strength either, and the younger man could probably outlast him if he dodged and weaved to try to exhaust him. At his size he'd have the reach advantage too, leaving Gawan with precious little left to work with. The only way would be to close in fast and take him to the ground. He was a big man but Gawan was no weakling either, and a grapple would at least remove the advantage of his height. *Yes, take his legs and then finish him fast before he can recover and use his strength.* The only edge the Gorvic had was his years of experience, and that hard-won knowledge was telling him this was his best chance.

But it isn't though, is it? Gawan's scowl deepened a little, annoyed that his inner voice was right. His best chance of beating him, assuming they met, was to stay in the shieldwall and hack him apart from relative safety, trusting in his cohort to take the giant down as one. The thought grated on him. No matter who he was, surely no Gadarim deserved to die like that? He remembered seeing the Gaians at First Nantwyn when they'd killed Caderyn warriors from behind their shieldwalls. Back then the Caderyn had been Gawan's enemies, and he'd killed plenty of them himself that day, but all the same his guts had churned a little to see fellow Gadarim slain without honour. He ground his teeth and tried to put it from his mind. The important thing was to keep Emeryn safe after all, and whatever it took he would make sure no Breiryn Gadarim got near her.

His thoughts only took up a few heartbeats and he broke off from sizing-up his rival when Rhianwyn began to speak. The Caderyn chief glanced up at the sky before looking at her enemies.

'It seems to be clouding over. You might be wise to get yourselves back home before it starts to rain.'

Owain smirked a little from beside her and even Kyran had a glint in his eye, though his narrow face was set and hard. Gawan might still be angry at her but he had to admit it; Rhianwyn was a cool one. Asrec looked on indifferently but Caserach spoke up. His voice was light, very different to the deep tones of his uncle, and for all his relaxed confidence Gawan detected irritation as well. Clearly he'd hoped that she would be intimidated.

'There are roofs nearby, I'm sure. We can have our pick of shelter before long.'

Kyran leaned forward before Rhianwyn could respond, his words quiet and deadly calm.

'Your only shelter tonight will be cold earth piled on your head.'

Rhianwyn frowned a little. She must have known that she had no hope of persuading him to leave in peace, but all the same she seemed determined to try. Caserach smirked at the Dariniae's First Man.

'And whose hands will be pouring it on me when your blood is swelling the streams?'

Kyran looked at him with cold eyes but Rhianwyn answered first.

'The warriors on that ridge will be taking turns to do that. Unless you turn your people around and leave our land in peace.'

Caserach scoffed at her.

'Your words are wind. I see the rabble gathered on that hillside, you cannot hope to match my numbers and well you know it.'

The Breiryn chief beside him spoke for the first time, his voice flat.

'Our people are many, yours are few. Concede and pay tribute and they need not die.'

He'd put a subtle emphasis on 'our' but beyond that his voice seemed almost bored. He struck Gawan as being a dull and quiet sort of man, but not quiet in Tarwyn's deep and thoughtful way; more like the grey and lifeless way that corpses and limp fish were quiet. Rhia answered very simply.

'The Dragons lately saw off an army of two full Gaian legions. Your warriors will die here if you challenge them. I say again, leave our land.'

Caserach affected to ignore her and turned to face Gawan and Boryn. His brow furrowed in feigned confusion.

'Why is it that *you* are here anyway? You are Gorvicae. Kyran here may have some cause to hate me and these Caderyn fools fear for their lands, but you? What need is there for Gorvicae to die on this ridge today?'

Gawan didn't want to admit that the same thought had occurred to him, but fortunately Boryn spoke for them first.

'*Some* Gorvicae may die here to defend our neighbours and avenge Ierryn.' He turned to Asrec. '*Many* Breiryn will die for the sake of one murderer's greed.'

The old headman put it well, his voice grave and dignified. Asrec opened his mouth to speak but Caserach cut him off, clearly annoyed that Boryn had turned away from him.

'You come to avenge Ierryn? What was he to you for years past but a Darin and an enemy? Before the Gaians turned you all to sheep you'd have clasped the hand that killed him, not bitten it!'

Gawan felt his temper rise.

'If you wish that hand to stay on your wrist you will keep a civil tongue when speaking to chiefs.'

Boryn might not have been *Gawan's* headman but he was a chief and a Gorvic, and this Darin piss-drinker had insulted the tribe. Caserach glared at him.

'Try telling me what to do, fool, and my man here will take *both* your hands right before he takes your head.'

He jerked his chin at Broad Kellas who simply nodded without speaking. Gawan sneered at him, his voice dripping with contempt.

211

'You're a bold man Caserach, threatening me with the actions of another. Perhaps once I've sent him to the Otherworld I will summon up the courage to face *you* afterwards.'

Broad Kellas seemed unmoved but Caserach flushed red with anger. Kyran spoke before the would-be chieftain could answer.

'You will have to wait your turn for that, brother. *I* am First Man of the Dariniae, and if any are to take this bastard's head, it will be me.'

Gawan was oddly glad to have his old enemy on his side, but this was clearly not going the way Rhianwyn had hoped it would.

'Enough of this! Asrec, turn your people around and lead them home, none need die today over this squabbling!'

Caserach breathed in to say something to her but Asrec raised a hand and the Darin checked himself. Gawan could practically *see* the resentment pouring from him as he did, but he was not fool enough to anger his only ally and so he held his tongue. Asrec's voice was just as dull and nasal as before.

'You speak out of fear, Rhianwyn daughter of Carradan. You know that you will lose here.' He nodded at the rail of his chariot and then patted Broad Kellas' huge shoulder. 'We are the mightier. If you give yourselves up we will take our tribute and let you live. If you fight us then you will all die.'

He said it without any hint of threat or emotion, but from a man like him Gawan hadn't expected much. Besides, Caserach added his own comment straight afterwards, and his words were angry enough for the both of them.

212

'I for one would sooner have it that you tried to stay and fight.' He slapped a hand on his sword-hilt. 'Greyfang is thirsty for blood.'

Rhianwyn looked ready to try talking to Asrec again but Gawan's patience was already short enough this morning, and Caserach was pushing it to breaking point. Numbers and peace and wisdom be damned; this man without honour had talked enough.

'I am surprised it knows the flavour. I hear it is your dagger that does your killing for you, and even *that* fears to stab at a man's front!'

He spat angrily at the ground before the Darin's grey mount.

'Either you or your giant there settle this with me here and now, or else run back to your warriors and hide behind them as they charge. I grow weary of your voice.'

He glared first at Caserach and then at Broad Kellas, both of whom looked surprised for a moment, but the Gadarim recovered his plain expression quickly enough. He was strong and skilled and had a horde at his back, why should he worry? Caserach on the other hand was reddening again and began to snap back an answer.

'You would dare to…'

But Rhianwyn interrupted, ignoring him and speaking directly to Asrec.

'This is your final chance, you can leave here now and…'

This time Caserach was the one to cut in.

'No-one is leaving here!'

Even his horse seemed to be growing angry, scraping its hooves on the ground and snorting. The rider jerked his head towards the ridge.

'Go back to your hill and cower behind your shields. Hide there while you can before I come for you!'

Gawan sneered. The man had completely ignored the challenge he had been offered. He clearly didn't want to look fearful by hiding behind Broad Kellas now that Gawan had challenged them personally, but neither was he man enough to fight the Gorvic himself. *Or maybe he's just clever enough to know he doesn't need to fight me to win?* Either way Gawan felt his contempt for the Darin grow, and would have said something cutting had Rhianwyn not spoken first. Her mouth was set in a firm line; controlled anger over bitter disappointment.

'So be it. Come if you dare.' She gestured behind her at the Dragon banners. 'Mabonac will smile as your warriors fall.'

Asrec still looked indifferent but Caserach was fuming. He took a breath to spout what would probably be more threats but Rhianwyn wheeled her mount around and showed her back to him, the rest of the Caledon party following her lead. The chieftain urged her pony into a gentle trot, fast enough to show that she was done with these people but slow enough to show that she didn't fear them either. Gawan exchanged a quick look with Broad Kellas before he turned to follow her, and thought back to Emeryn's dream. *You must keep him from her, no matter what else. You must keep her safe.*

He set his jaw and trotted back towards the ridge with the others, and tried to ignore the itch between his shoulders. He didn't know this plain-faced Asrec but Caserach had already shown himself to have no personal honour, and an arrow in the back for each of them would make this battle that much easier for him. But Gawan dismissed his fear.

Broad Kellas might be an enemy but he was Gadarim, and would not allow such behaviour in his presence. Caserach could ill-afford to offend the First Man of his allies. Instead of fear Gawan felt a contradiction coming over him as he followed the others up the ridge. He was eager to fight these people, he even yearned for a chance to test himself against the giant behind him, but at the same time he was so worried for Emeryn. He shut his eyes for a moment and shoved all guilt and fretting from his conscious thoughts. Now was the time for battle, concerns about lovers would have to wait.

Chapter 16. The Battle of Moon Ridge

They rode back up the ridge in silence, heading towards the Caderyn company in the centre. The sky above was an almost uniform grey by now, and Gawan suspected the rain would be coming at any moment. *Though that should be better for us than for them; they're the ones who'll be trying to climb a slope in the mud.* For all his temper he tried to keep that positive thought in his mind as they approached the long Caledon lines. Standing in front of them was Owain's woman, the curvy redhead, and she gave her lover a mirthless smirk as the party reined in before her.

'You spoke nicely then?'

Owain smiled back at her.

'I kept perfectly quiet, just as you said,' he nodded towards his fellow First Men, 'it was these two who insisted on causing trouble.'

Gawan half expected Rhianwyn to say something disapproving about that, but to his surprise she practically defended them.

'Trouble was going to happen no matter what was said, but we had to try.'

The Gorvic was tempted to add a comment of his own but the look Rhianwyn gave him stopped him short. She didn't look angry so much as tired. She didn't want another battle, and more death for a people who had barely survived the last war. She was a good chieftain to her tribe, for all her faults, and Gawan decided to hold his tongue. Rhianwyn seemed to appreciate that and spoke to all three of the First Men, her face now set and grim.

'To battle then. Tribunes form your cohorts.'

It sounded odd to hear them being referred to by their rank, only Marius had ever really used the term, but Gawan nodded all the same, as did Kyran and Owain. Rhianwyn nodded back to them and urged her horse up to each man in turn. She clasped wrists with them one by one, looking each of her brothers in the eye as she spoke her blessing.

'The Dragon guide you.'

Gawan repeated the blessing back to her, noting again both the hardness and the sadness in those deep blue orbs. Once done she wheeled her pony around without another word and cantered off behind the Caderyn formation, presumably to hand her mount over to one of Alraig's people. Gawan watched her go for a moment and then exchanged blessings with the other First Men. As he turned to go he noticed how lovingly Owain and the redhead looked at each other, and hoped quietly that they'd both make it through this alive. That made him think of Emeryn of course and so he closed his teeth and pressed his lips together, trying not to think on it.

He and Boryn made their way along the Caderyn line, heading back towards their own cohort. The wall of red-and-blue shields was coming together, with archers behind testing their bowstrings and druids walking here and there to give blessings to the warriors and pass hands over their weapons. Naturally the druids would not be using their powers in the battle, they'd been reluctant to do so even against the sorcery at Nantwyn, but they gave courage to the tribesmen and helped light dragonfire in their bellies, and that was enough for now. The Caderyn seemed ready and confident despite everything, and Gawan only hoped that he and his would be the match of them.

Soon enough he and the headman reached the green shields of the Gorvicae, and they dismounted in front of the line. Tarwyn, Gwydion and Pryder were waiting for them, along with a few of the other more senior warriors of the company. The pair dismounted and handed their ponies' reins to a young lad, who then led them away along the slope. Several nods were exchanged between the warriors but Boryn was the first of them to speak.

'What are your orders, Leaping Wolf?'

The grey-haired headman's voice was strong but respectful, as befit the situation. As a chief he would normally be above Gawan in the tribal hierarchy, but in war the First Man was second only to the High Chieftain and it was to him that the tribe would look for leadership. Gawan kept his answer simple.

'We hold here and wait for them to come to us, as we expect. Caserach is angry and will be keen to attack. Should they try to move around us the cohort will advance down the hill and leave Alraig's people to hold the ridge.' He paused for a moment before adding. 'Stay close and work together and we shall defeat them.'

There was another series of quiet nods and again, it was Boryn who spoke for them.

'That we shall. Let us prepare.'

He clasped wrists with Gawan and blessings or wishes of good fortune were shared before the little group dispersed. Tarwyn was turning back towards the formation but Gawan caught his eye and motioned for him to wait. The quiet man thumped Gwydion's arm before he could go too, and Pryder saw them stalling and took the hint as well. Gawan stepped closer to the three Gadarim. The cohort behind them was preparing itself noisily but all the same, he lowered his voice.

'Brothers, you are not to speak of this to anyone but,' he hesitated for a heartbeat before continuing, 'Emeryn believes that she saw a vision of her death last night. She says she saw herself die in the battle today, at the jaws of some dark beast.'

There was silence for a moment before Tarwyn, undeniably the quickest of them, answered softly.

'A kellas cat?'

Pryder was looking worried and Gawan suspected that Gwydion was more concerned than he was showing. The normally jovial man didn't look fretful but his face was blank and serious, which for Gwydion was practically a scowl. Gawan shrugged.

'She does not know.'

There was another silence and he noticed Pryder draw a little circle in the air with his finger, trying not to be obvious about it. The young man spoke to try to cover the gesture.

'Could it not have been just another dream?'

He didn't sound convinced, and Gawan didn't blame him. It was a strange truth that men who scoffed at omens from the comfort of their homes felt very differently when combat loomed before them. Perhaps this was nothing, perhaps it was something, but a dream of death before a battle was rarely a good sign, and better to be cautious and risk feeling a fool than to ignore what might be a warning from the gods. He didn't want to voice his next thought out loud but Tarwyn spared him the trouble.

'You keep close by her brother, and we will watch for any Gadarim who approach.'

Pryder nodded eagerly and Gwydion managed half a smirk.

'They're easy enough to spot with those bloody horns of theirs!'

Gawan allowed his lip to twitch a little and tried to think of something suitable to say. He was grateful for their help but wasn't quite sure how to put it, and so he settled for a simple bow of his head.

'My thanks, brothers.'

The trio returned the gesture and he knew he didn't need to say any more. These were men who knew him well and would understand his feelings. Then the sound of a horn from below them caused all four men to turn. Looking down into the bowl below, Gawan saw the yellow-brown mass was moving forwards, though the chariots were staying where they were. Likely Asrec wasn't planning on doing much of his own fighting today. The First Man wasn't surprised.

In the open air between the armies he saw the first droplets of rain begin to fall and a moment later felt the wetness on his head. Some of the Caledon warriors had taken helmets from Nantwyn along with mail and weapons, but most had drawn the line at wearing such headgear. Helms were for chieftains to show the tribe where they were and besides, the Gadarim's hair had to be on show. Gawan watched the horde as it reached the base of the slope and then turned back to his fellows.

'Alright, time to make ready.'

The three men nodded and made their way to the front line of the formation. Emeryn was standing there waiting and Gawan wanted to say something to her but he held himself back. She had the four best warriors in the cohort watching over her, which meant her life was as safe as it could be made. He could worry about reconciling with her later on; right now he had to focus on the task at hand. Gawan took his place beside her in silence, only bowing his head a fraction in acknowledgement. For a moment he thought she was about to say something but then she fixed her gaze ahead of them and kept her mouth shut tight.

Gawan put it from his mind and slowed his breathing, kindling the fire inside him. It only took a few breaths to focus Mabonac's power. The First Man pulled out a length of leather cord from beneath his mail, revealing the little wooden whistle he had strung on it. It being a Gaian notion Gawan didn't like to admit to it, but the simple whistle was a useful thing to have in this kind of fight. Shouted orders could be lost amidst the warcries and screams of combat, but the whistle with its piercing shriek would be discernible even in the chaos, better even than the blare of a horn. The Gaians had been clever indeed to see its use for telling their soldiers what to do. Before that though Gawan knew he ought to speak a few words. It was not his strongest skill but then the people here knew that, and they were keen enough to fight without needing a great speech to encourage them.

'Warriors of the Dragon Legion, you each know your role. They have great numbers but we have great skill, great courage, and the might of Taran and of Mabonac on our side. Stay together, trust your fellows, and fight like bastards!'

A cheer went up from around him and he looked through the drizzle to see the Breiryn start up the hill. They were moving at a walk but would break into a sprint when they got a closer, and it was time to make sure the cohort was

221

ready for them. Given the length of the ridge their formation was not as deep as he'd have liked, having had to spread out in a long line to cover the ground. Even then there was a gap between themselves and the Caderyn, and the cohort stood only five ranks deep. *But it will be enough*, Gawan told himself firmly, *it has to be*.

He gave three blasts on his wooden whistle, two short, one long, then shouted out the order for good measure.

'Stand to!'

The cohort closed up the gaps between warriors and raised their shields in readiness. All along the line Gawan saw images of the Dragon God, dark and menacing on their painted shields. Nearby the First Man stood Tarwyn, Gwydion, Pryder and Emeryn, with Boryn and his best warriors making up the second rank. Gawan found himself pondering as the Breiryn walked onwards through the rain. The only other time he had fought like this he'd been facing the Gaian invaders. He thought back to Tarwyn's comments the other night and quietly agreed that against his fellow tribesmen he'd have sooner fought the old way; man to man and sword to sword, rather than smash them with a wall of shields and butcher them with stabbing blades. It was unfair, and without honour, but damn it, it was effective. He wondered uncomfortably if this was how the Gaians felt when they conquered a new land and he felt almost stained at the thought.

He grimaced and drew Heartreaver from the scabbard at his hip and bellowed out to his people as the Breiryn ascended. The shout echoed back to him, and Gawan felt some pride return as he heard the name of his tribe.

'Gorvicae!'

*

When the clash came it was hard, and bloody. The Breiryn had climbed the hill as a disorganised mob, the weaker ones slowed by the slope while the stronger and more eager surged ahead. Once the southerners had closed to forty paces the archers behind the shieldwall had let loose a volley, and as warriors fell wounded or dying to the dirt, what little cohesion they'd had had fallen apart. The Breiryn had struck the Caledon shieldwall piecemeal and, as Gawan had expected, huge numbers of them had been slaughtered.

Heartreaver flicked out for the eighth or ninth time, stabbing out at a tribesman's exposed belly. The Breiryn dodged to one side only to be skewered by Pryder's blade, and Gawan hacked off his sword-arm just to make sure. The younger Gadarim could finish him off. Through the grey sheet of rain he saw a woman thrust a spear at him, at the exact same moment the man beside her swung a pick-like axe at his head. Gawan ducked behind his shield and the axe clanged on the iron rim, just as the spearpoint glanced along the curved wood. In the corner of his eye Gawan saw Boryn's hand reach out from the rank behind him, grab hold of the spear's long haft, and pull. He didn't quite jerk it free of the woman's grasp but it was enough to drag her off-balance and Gawan rammed his shield into her face. She fell to a knee, her face bright with blood, and Gawan whipped Heartreaver up in a swift arc that opened up the axe-man from groin to neck. He cried out and fell backwards as the woman tried to stand, but Emeryn's blade plunged down through her collarbone, and the

Breiryn's scream became a gurgle as the iron drove through her lung.

Emeryn looked beautiful when her blood was up, and even in the rain her hair was brighter than spun gold. For a ridiculous moment Gawan felt himself thinking of his mother, and wondering why he had inherited his father's black locks while Rylion was as blonde as she had been. He shook the distracting thoughts away with a snarl and readied himself for another attack. He was not waiting long.

A huge, dark-bearded man approached them but was foolish enough to lean back for a moment to swing his massive club. First Heartreaver pierced his stomach and then Emeryn's shield shoved him to the dirt. The next warrior to come at them lost his throat to a lightning-swift cut from Tarwyn's blade, and blood spattered them all as he stumbled back. Another southerner grabbed hold of Pryder's shield with both hands, trying to wrench it from his grip and weaken the wall. The young man stepped heavily as he was almost pulled over, but the moment his feet were set he heaved back, hauling the man straight into the Gorvicae wall. Gwydion's blade bit into his thigh and Pryder followed it with a solid thrust to his guts. His screams were almost pitiful.

Gawan knocked another southerner down and almost *felt* their resolve beginning to waver. A quick glance along the ridge showed the other cohorts were doing similarly well; the Caledon suffering losses here and there but nothing to the slaughter they were inflicting on their enemies, and the Breiryn were beginning to falter. He felt triumph surge through him and an actual *grin* spread across his face. Everyone who'd ever met him knew that Gawan's smiles were rare, but Emeryn and bloodlust were two things that brought them out in him.

Fewer and fewer southerners were launching themselves at the wall and Gawan knew that now was the time to press them. If allowed to retreat they might reform and try again, and carnage or not he didn't want the shieldwall to take another charge. The Gorvicae had taken few casualties compared with the Breiryn, but Rhianwyn needed her warriors more than Asrec needed his. In a moment of respite the First Man thrust Heartreaver into the dirt and grabbed for his wooden whistle, letting out three blasts on it, one long, one short, one long. *Advance!*

He took up his sword and as one the Gorvicae line moved forward, a warcry on every northerner's lips. It was enough for the Breiryn ahead to see good sense. They might not be moving quickly, tight-packed as they were, but the Caledon were coming for them nonetheless, and the southern tribesmen soon turned tail and started running down the hill. Gawan howled in triumph and all around him heard bellows for Taran, Mabonac, Gorvicae and Caledon. The First Man found himself increasing the pace, those beside him speeding up to match him, every one of them eager to show these people what happened to those who made enemies of the Gorvicae.

But then something surprising happened. Just as they were getting up their pace the Breiryn turned, and Gawan saw a giant appear from their midst. Even without his massive height there was no mistaking the flat face and snakeskin belt of Broad Kellas. Gawan snarled and would have called out had the southerners not charged again a heartbeat later. He had to admit it was an impressively bold thing to do, and the cohort had barely formed up

225

again before the Breiryn crashed into them. Only this time they had barely started cutting their enemies down before a deep voice bellowed a little way to Gawan's right and he saw Broad Kellas' head, high above the others, shouting along the Gorvicae line.

'Who will fight me? I am Gadarim, who will fight me?'

The battle around seemed to slow and Gawan felt himself tense up in readiness. If he could kill this man, not only would Emeryn be that much safer but all the Breiryn nearby would lose heart. They would flee again when they saw their First Man defeated, they might even call the battle to a halt and concede right there and then. One stroke and this could all be done. He forgot all about the logic of fighting safely behind the wall and took a deep breath in to shout back and accept the challenge. But another voice sounded out first.

'I will fight you!'

Gawan snapped his head around and saw Tarwyn, his face bloody but grimly set, stepping forward from the line of green shields. For a moment Gawan was struck dumb as the southern giant bellowed again.

'Then face me and tremble, for I am Broad Kellas!'

Tarwyn let his shield slip from his arm to thud wetly on the grass, and called out to the other man in a voice that was clipped and clear.

'Face me and tremble. I am the Eagle Owl!'

The fighting nearby ground to a complete halt and Gawan wanted to scream out in frustration. Why was Tarwyn doing this? *Does he think I can't take him? Does he think that* he *can?* Gawan gripped Heartreaver's hilt until his knuckles turned white. The challenge had been offered and accepted, and First Man or not he could not interrupt it

226

now. He watched, powerless, as the two men approached each other and exchanged a quiet nod before their long blades came up into guard. They began circling one another slowly, steps small and eyes keen.

Broad Kellas was bold, and Gawan had been right not to think that he'd be slow. The big man sprang at the Gorvic like the cat he was named after, his massive sword flicking left before centring on his opponent's chest. Tarwyn was light on his feet and recognised the feint just in time, dodging backwards and parrying as the Breiryn lunged forward. Broad Kellas recovered himself quickly and spun around to face his enemy again. Gawan could tell from his feet that he was solidly placed but the giant leaned back his torso as if he had become unbalanced. Against a foolish man the ruse might have worked, but Tarwyn was not so easily goaded and he stood his ground, ignoring the false opening. Gawan let out a sigh of relief. His brother was still in mortal danger but at least he'd forced the southerner to reveal one of his tricks.

But the big man had more to him than trickery and he soon moved in again, swinging high and then low. Tarwyn ducked the first cut but was too close to dodge the second, and iron clanged on iron as he blocked it head-on. The force of the blow pushed him back and Broad Kellas followed him, keeping the pressure on with his greater weight. For a moment it looked like the lighter man would be overcome and topple backwards, but Tarwyn shifted his feet after a few desperate paces and cracked his fist hard against the Breiryn's jaw. The big man stumbled and Tarwyn backed away, flexing his hand in obvious discomfort. The punch had been well-aimed and a weaker man would have been knocked cold, but Broad Kellas' skull must have been hard as an anvil because he recovered almost instantly, shaking his head and blinking but otherwise alert.

The drizzle was making the whole field look drab and oddly colourless, and all around him Gawan saw dark woad running messily down pale skin. The Gadarim's tattooed battle-marks were beginning to show through though, and even in the dull light their limewashed hair shone out like beacons. Gawan itched to go in and help his brother. He could tell what the tall Gorvic was doing; he was trying to tire and hopefully *wound* the bigger man rather than attempting to kill him outright. They were of similar age and Tarwyn had great stamina, and if anyone could fight with patience, it was him. But giving away the initiative was always a dangerous game. For all that his cautious moves might incapacitate the Breiryn with time, Broad Kellas was fighting to kill, and a single slip would cost Tarwyn his life.

Once again Gawan saw him let the other man move first. The Gorvic evaded a pair of cuts and then traded a few blows with the giant. Broad Kellas was clearly growing frustrated while Tarwyn's face maintained a mask of calm. The big man growled as he lunged once again and the Gorvic warrior scored a cut on him as he passed, catching him high on his shoulder. The Gorvicae around them cheered but Tarwyn's sword had barely drawn blood, and Broad Kellas wasn't slowed down for a moment.

Gawan glimpsed Emeryn shouting encouragement with the rest of them, but he had no time to think of her. He was absorbed in the dance, praying quietly to Taran and Mabonac that his brother would defeat this man. Tarwyn was good, his face granite-hard and his movements swift, but he'd done no real damage to the massive Breiryn warrior, and the big man wasn't even out of breath. The two slashed and parried at one another a few more times and the Gorvicae cheered again as Tarwyn's blade raked the Breiryn's side. Gawan did not join them, and his face grew pale as he watched.

Most people watched fights and let either fear or excitement take over them, looking on at the violence with fascination or with horror. Even experienced warriors often got caught up in the moment and saw nothing but a mindless blur. Gadarim were different. Many might give in to their lusts once they were in combat, but Mabonac demanded a focused mind as much as a bold heart, and a warrior of the Gadarim would watch a fight very differently. They would watch each move and counter-move, see the ground around the combat and the strengths and weaknesses of the men who fought. They would gauge the power and spirit of the warriors as they danced, watching for when a man was overconfident, or when he had lost hope. And they would watch for tricks.

Early in the fight Tarwyn's mind had been razor sharp, and had he been watching alongside Gawan he would have seen it too. But he'd been fighting hard and his blood was up, and even a man as shrewd as he was could miss things sometimes. To his credit, Broad Kellas had made the opening subtle this time, and had taken a dreadful risk in the process. It was a fine trick, and perfectly timed. On another day Gawan might have admired it.

As it was he simply watched in horror as the big man let Tarwyn's blade slide harmlessly along his ribs before stepping in close and cracking a headbutt into his enemy's nose. The lean man's face seemed to explode in a welter of blood, and Gawan could think of nothing but an overripe tomato being smashed with a hammer. Tarwyn staggered and whipped his blade up but Broad Kellas was too quick for him, and he slammed a meaty fist into the Gorvic's gut before backhanding him hard across the jaw. Tarwyn's feet left the ground and he seemed to hover in the air for a moment before crumpling to the dirt like a tossed-aside ragdoll. The Breiryn around them howled in triumph and their First Man held up his bulging arms in victory.

Gawan longed to wipe the smile from the bastard's face but Tarwyn was still moving, and he had to die or yield before another could step in. The lean Gorvic was groaning quietly and it was clear to a blind man that the fight was out of him. Broad Kellas stepped closer to his downed opponent, his blade up and ready, but he made no move to attack him. Tarwyn coughed painfully a few times and Gawan felt a stab of guilt in his gut. His brother had done this to protect Emeryn, and to keep his First Man from rushing in and risking his life. He tried to comfort himself by remembering how his fellow Gadarim had wanted to please Mabonac by fighting the old way, but it did little to ease his conscience. Tarwyn groaned again and tried to rise to one knee, but the effort seemed to be gargantuan. The crowd around them fell eerily quiet and Gawan chewed on his lip. *You're a beaten man Tarwyn; stay down.* But he didn't.

With a sudden cry the tall Gorvic sprang forwards, his pain forgotten and his long blade outstretched. Gawan's heart leaped to his mouth; Tarwyn wasn't as badly hurt as he'd made out! The cunning man had waited until Broad Kellas dropped his guard, and he now leaped forward with a lunge that would finish the Breiryn's champion. It was brilliant, it was lethal. And it almost worked. Gawan felt his surge of hope dashed brutally apart as the giant sidestepped at the last instant, Tarwyn's blade drawing only a thin line of red along his thigh. The Gorvic had no chance to twist away and the Breiryn's counter-cut landed with the full power of his arms, his shoulders, and his massive dropping weight. Tarwyn's head was split almost completely in two. The Gorvicae cohort looked on in horror as his blood and brains spattered on the grass below, and his body thudded lifelessly to the ground.

Gawan screamed in rage and surged forwards, but Gwydion and Pryder took an arm each and hauled him back. Broad Kellas had been blooded, and unless he challenged again he had every right to walk away to be tended to. But Gawan was far too angry to care about some Breiryn bastard's rights and he struggled against their grip, shoving Pryder hard to the side. He turned to strike Gwydion away but the blonde man took him by the shoulders and met his eyes without fear. For once he was not smiling and his face looked as grave as any funeral.

'*Wait* brother, wait!'

Gawan didn't want to wait, he wanted to charge over there and rip that piss-drinker's heart out, and he almost spat as much to Gwydion, but by then it didn't matter. From the corner of his eye he saw the big man begin to move, and when he turned to look he saw Broad Kellas limping off into his own people, the Breiryn cheering him as he went. Gawan felt his blood race even faster. The victor had not called for a hold, which meant the battle was still underway. The First Man looked down at the mess that had once been the wisest of the Gorvicae Gadarim,

231

and he forgot all about the Dragon Legion. He forgot about the Caledon, about sensible tactics and keeping his outnumbered force together. All he saw was the body of his friend, and his vision narrowed until he saw nothing through the rain but the retreating back of Broad Kellas. He sprang from his lines and brandished Heartreaver.

'Coward! Come back here, and fight *me*!'

Whether Broad Kellas heard him or not he couldn't tell, because the moment he moved forwards both tribes began bellowing out warcries again, and his voice blended in with a hundred others baying for blood. He felt Emeryn follow on his right while Gwydion advanced on his left, and before long the whole Gorvicae line was charging forwards into the Breiryn. Gawan saw three warriors straight ahead of him but he paid them little mind. They were just so much dry grass standing between him and Tarwyn's killer, and could no more stop the Leaping Wolf than a sheep could stop a gale.

He hurled his shield into the face of the first and cut down the other two in as many heartbeats, Heartreaver moving as if by some will of its own. The first man recovered himself but Gwydion's sword crashed through his head before he could even think to attack them. Another man approached from Gawan's right but Mabonac must have been watching because his foot slipped in the mud as he drew his axe back to swing, and the Gorvic rammed Heartreaver into his gut and then up under his ribs. He gave the blade a savage twist before ripping it free, blood spraying onto Emeryn's legs even as she cut down another of their foes.

He had lost sight of Broad Kellas in all the confusion and his eyes darted about, seeking the giant Breiryn's ugly head. He was nowhere to be seen and Gawan clenched his teeth and growled in frustration. But then the fire in his belly felt like it had been doused in cold water. In his eagerness to rush forwards the whole Gorvicae line had followed him, and he saw now that it had completely come apart. Where once a shieldwall had held against a tide of Breiryn fighters, now warriors fought alone or at best in small groups, and the northerners were becoming overwhelmed.

Gawan felt rage rekindle the fire in him, the anger directed at himself as much as it was at Broad Kellas. The only chance they'd had against such numbers had been to hold their formation together, and now his foolish anger had destroyed even that. Every fibre of his body wanted to damn the rest of this battle to the Pit and keep on moving forwards. Victory or loss he might still find the giant and cut him down for what he did to Tarwyn. *But you are not alone. More Gorvicae will die here if you do not pull them back. Is your anger worth the lives of so many of your people?* Gawan wanted to scream at himself but he knew he had no choice. He'd been fighting battles long enough to take them in at a glance, and a quick look around told him all he needed to know. Chariots and horsemen were coming up to support the Breiryn and along the ridge he saw the southerners were pushing the other cohorts hard. Their allies could not help the over-reaching Gorvicae.

An arrow from a charioteer whipped past Gawan's face to bury itself in Pryder's shoulder beside him. The young man grimaced and backed off, snapping most of the shaft with a grunt of pain. He would pay for that later when they tried to remove the head, but he could hardly keep on fighting with a length of wood jutting out of him. Another

Breiryn tried to charge them, but Gawan cut him down without even thinking. The other cohorts had kept their formations but were still in danger of breaking under the pressure, and his own was just a ragged mess of hard-pressed fighters. He snuck a fleeting look behind them to see that Alraig had already brought his men up, but even with their help they could not hope to stop this flood.

Gawan cursed himself as he lunged out and took another southerner in the leg, the man collapsing to the mud where Emeryn finished him off. A young woman charged at them with a rusty-looking axe but impaled herself on Heartreaver as Gawan brought it up. Her face came almost nose-to-nose with his and he saw her green eyes fly wide with shock before squeezing shut again as she screamed out in pain. The First Man punched her hard in the jaw and tore the weapon free as she fell. The woman didn't cry out as she slumped down, and Gawan assumed the blow had landed well enough to knock her senseless.

Emeryn, Pryder and Gwydion were still fighting hard beside him, but everywhere else he saw Gorvicae being struck down by the southerners. *We have no choice. We must pull back, try to reform.* It was a slim chance but it was all they had. Gawan backed off a pace and put his whistle to his lips, ready to blow the three blasts that would call his people out of there and back to some semblance of safety. He swallowed his pride and took a deep breath, trying not to think of the vengeance he was losing. That was when he heard the blaring of the horns.

Chapter 17. Carrion

Gawan whipped his head around, and he wasn't alone in forgetting the chaos for a heartbeat to stare back up the ridge. All around him warriors had backed away from one another to look for the source of the sudden noise; a single, two-note blast on a deep and brassy horn, loud enough to carry even over the sound of battle. The rain was still coming down but not so heavily as to block his vision, and as Gawan looked Belenos peeked out briefly from the clouds, shining a golden light upon the hill. The ridge above him was black with shields.

Despite the light the symbol on the wood was hard to make out, but Gawan didn't need to see it to know what it would be. Besides, above the line was a long pole surmounted by a golden eagle, beneath which hung a banner that bore the same device; a pitch-black raven, wreathed in subtle white flames on an equally black background, its single red eye the only real colour on the cloth. The First Gaian Legion, the Blackbirds, had followed them here, and even as he watched he heard the tinny echo of a whistle. Three blasts; one long, one short, one long. *Advance.*

There had to be at least a full cohort there, in lines maybe fifty men long, and they made their way down the hill at a brisk pace, their formation tight and disciplined. Behind the infantry he could just make out a little group of horsemen following the footsoldiers at a trot, and from their look the First Man assumed that they were officers rather than cavalrymen. For half a heartbeat Gawan was sure that the legion was coming for the Caledon, but their angle of advance soon made their intentions plain. The Gaians were attacking the Breiryn.

A rallying horn sounded from somewhere amongst the southerners and the Breiryn began surging towards this new threat, barely a handful staying back to fight the disorganised Gorvicae. Gawan wasted no time and bellowed out to his company.

'Pull back and form up!'

He darted forwards quickly to disembowel the nearest Breiryn and then backed up with the others, fumbling for his whistle. The cohort had almost certainly heard the order but Gorvic lives were precious, and it couldn't hurt to be sure that they all knew to disengage. He gave a long blast then two short ones to order the fall back, and as soon as they'd gained some distance he blew again with two short and one long; *stand to*. The Gorvicae were barely harried at all by the Breiryn, though a few of them tried their fortune and paid the price for it. Nearly every one of the southerners was more concerned with the black line charging down the hill, and Gawan didn't blame them for it. The Caledon company was too small and scattered to be an immediate threat. The Gaians on the other hand had brought some serious numbers with them, and the wall of shields was tight even as the soldiers jogged forward. Gawan tried to busy himself with making sure his own line was formed up, but like all the rest of his battered cohort, his eyes kept straying to the flank.

The southerners were charging forward in their hundreds, bellowing warcries to Taran and brandishing their many weapons. The Blackbirds advanced more slowly, maintaining their formation with iron discipline, and Gawan couldn't help but feel envious of their precision.

As the tribesmen closed in a hail of javelins flew from the first two ranks and struck down a good twoscore of the southerners, but their blood was up and their spirits high, and the Breiryn pressed through it and launched themselves at the Gaian shieldwall. The Blackbirds smashed into them like a rock dropped onto ants.

Gawan was proud of what the Dragon Legion could do. They'd spent endless days drilling under Marius or the Wildcat and were now well-used to fighting as a unit; to holding their line firm and focusing on overall victory over the old ideals of personal glory. The result had led to their defeating Lepidus at Nantwyn, and had allowed them to fend off a southern force that badly outnumbered them. Watching the Gaians now reminded him of just how little they had learned.

The Breiryn were hurling themselves at the solid black wall but the Gaians ground forwards like a plough over a field, short swords stabbing out as desperate southerners tried to hack their way in. Blades licked out for barely an eyeblink before whipping back behind the shields again, and Gawan watched with morbid interest as the tribesmen were cut down. These soldiers had none of the sorcerous frenzy that the Panther Legion had shown, and fought with a cool professionalism that was frightening to behold. It wasn't warfare so much as human butchery; the training and discipline of the Blackbirds a match for even the most skilled of Breiryn warriors.

Gawan saw white-haired Gadarim falling before the onslaught and caught a glimpse of a man so tall that he could only be Broad Kellas, striding forwards with his sword held high only to go down before the wall of black-painted shields. The Gorvic cursed under his breath that the Gaians had robbed him of his chance to avenge Tarwyn, but before he could dwell on it he saw the Breiryn starting to flee. First in ones and twos and then in larger groups the southerners began to back away down the hill, and soon enough the whole mass of them were pelting back the way they'd come, the Gaians advancing slowly in pursuit. The muddy grass they left behind was strewn with dead and dying, and short stabs from the legionaries soon made quiet any who cried out.

Many Gorvicae were cheering as they watched their enemies run but Gawan kept on staring at the Blackbirds as they came. They had moved forwards enough to leave the trail of corpses behind them, and he squinted through the rain trying to find a mail-clad body or a black shield left abandoned in the mud. He couldn't see any. Not one Gaian had fallen in that dreadful clash. *Not one.*

Gawan saw that his people were eager to charge again as the Breiryn fled back across the field. He felt the same keenness for battle and was reaching for his whistle when the sound of hoofbeats made him turn around. The little group of horsemen was trotting up to them, and even before his face became clear Gawan recognised their leader. General Galerian had been the one to negotiate with Rhianwyn after they had defeated Lepidus, and he looked just as fresh and relaxed on a battlefield in the rain as he had done in that longhall at Nantwyn.

Much like Marius he was sharp-featured and clean shaven, and though today his helmet covered it Gawan knew that his hair was short and dark. He was dressed in mail beneath an officer's leather breastplate, and both his tunic and his cloak were as black as the crest on his helm, the garments subtly edged in silver thread. He drew his mount up close to the group of Gadarim and spoke to them in clipped Vulgare.

'Good day gentlemen. I take it one of you is the tribune of this company?'

Gawan assumed he had recognised their status by their limewashed hair and he stepped forward a little. His grasp of the Gaian tongue could have been better but like most Caderyn and Gorvicae he understood it to a degree. He answered as best he could in the same language.

'I lead here.' The Gaian nodded but before he could respond Gawan spoke again. 'She sent for you.'

It was a statement more than a question but the general nodded anyway.

'Lady Dessida did indeed request our aid, and a good thing she did too. Your flank seemed under severe pressure. I hope you do not mind the assistance?'

He spoke slowly, presumably to make sure that Gawan understood him, but even so the Gorvic felt patronised by the man's tone. And angry at Rhianwyn. She had deceived them. They had argued against calling the Gaians to their aid and she'd gone ahead and done it anyway, and in secret. *But then if she hadn't, what might have happened here?* Gawan shoved away the reasonable voice in his head and balled his fists until the knuckles turned white.

'Let's just get on with it.'

Galerian frowned slightly.

'We might be wiser heading back up the slope. They will likely seek terms now that we are here, and there is no sense in losing men in a pursuit.'

There was logic in what he said but Gawan didn't want to hear it. Across the field he saw the Caderyn and Dariniae

239

cohorts pushing forwards, the Breiryn in front of them clearly losing the will to fight. *Damned if I'll march my cohort back while* they *charge forwards into battle!* He was about to say as much to Galerian when Emeryn spoke from beside him.

'Maybe Gaians would back off, but Tarwyn was just killed by these bastards. We will finish this.'

If anything her Vulgare was even more broken than Gawan's but Galerian seemed to understand it. He looked on disapprovingly as Pryder handed Gawan a fresh shield, and the First Man glared up at the general.

'You form beside us if you want. We are chasing them down. Join us if you want a fight!'

Gawan felt his strength flooding back to him as dragonfire spread from his belly to his limbs. He prayed quietly that Broad Kellas was only wounded and not dead; it might save some of their honour today if the Gorvicae brought him down. *And this time no voice will come before mine in the challenge!* The Gaian general was still frowning but he nodded his head slightly, little droplets of water falling from his crest.

'As you say.'

He turned to another rider and said something Gawan didn't catch but the man blew two short blasts on his whistle, and the Blackbird formation switched their front two ranks. It sickened him how smoothly and easily they did it, and how few of them bore even minor wounds from their earlier slaughter of the southerners. The Gorvic turned away from them and locked his shield with the rest of the line. His eyes met Emeryn's and she held his gaze for a moment before looking away. On top of everything else he dared to think there might be hope for them yet, and he held Heartreaver aloft as he bellowed the War God's name, his whistle forgotten as he commanded his warriors.

'Taran!'

*

Their line was ragged compared with the Blackbirds beside them but Gawan didn't care. The Gorvicae couldn't back away while Caderyn and Dariniae moved forwards and besides, the southerners were in disarray and Tarwyn had yet to be avenged. Gawan let anger fuel his muscles as he ran; anger at Broad Kellas, anger at Caserach, and his anger at Rhianwyn for her betrayal of her people's trust. They all combined to give him strength and before he knew it he had easily outpaced his neighbours, Heartreaver almost singing in his hand. To their credit the Breiryn tried to reform and come at them again, but they were a disunited rabble and stood no chance against the northerners.

A lean warrior with a hatchet in each hand came screaming towards him, a snarl on his face and Taran's name on his lips, but Gawan bulled forwards and rammed the shield into his chest as the charging Breiryn was in mid-step. The blow caught him just right and the man bounced from the wood, flying backwards awkwardly before hitting the ground hard. The Gorvicae were moving fast as they chased down their enemy, and the man was barely up to one knee before Heartreaver took off his head. Gawan screamed in triumph, forgetting his frustrations as he revelled in the violence. The Gaians were advancing too, but their pace was a steady lope to maintain their tight

241

formation and the Gorvicae were well ahead of them by now. *Timid fools! They are on the run, why hide behind our shieldwalls now?*

For all that the majority seemed keen to get away, the Breiryn were not without their heroes, and Gawan spotted a red-bearded Gadarim trying to rally some warriors to him. Like the others his hair was shaped into white horns, and though not a tall man he was heavy with muscle. Gawan grinned and made towards him but Gwydion beat him to it, charging at the southerner with a wordless cry. There was no attempt by either side to make a formal challenge; this was just two men trading blows until one of them was dead. The red-bearded man was strong but Gwydion was quick, and the blonde man took him down in the space of three or four heartbeats. Gawan felt proud of his brother but also a pang of disappointment. He'd not crossed blades with a single Gadarim today, and a good First Man needed good practice.

A stocky warrior tried to spear him but Gawan knocked him aside with ease, and a deft flick of Heartreaver opened up his throat. Gawan flinched as blood sprayed on him, and by the time he blinked his eyes clear another pair of Breiryn had appeared as if from nowhere. One man grabbed for his shield and pulled hard, dragging the Gorvic off-balance as his comrade lunged in. Gawan felt a knife glance from the mail over his ribs as he shouldered his attacker away, Heartreaver slashing out as he fell back. The knife-man threw himself backwards and Gawan saw Emeryn ram her shield into his flank, sending him sprawling into the rain-soaked mud.

Gawan turned his attention back to the man still gripping the rim of his shield. The Gorvic feigned pulling back for a moment then shoved forward when the other man pulled, knocking him off his feet into the dirt. Gawan rushed forward and gave his head a swift kick before facing off with another man who swung an axe at his side. He took the blow on the shield and thrust Heartreaver out, catching the Breiryn in the shoulder. He grunted and jerked back but Gawan followed up quickly, hacking the iron blade into his neck. Blood flowed and the First Man screamed out again as Mabonac's fire burned hot through his body.

'Taran!'

He spun around on the spot, eager for more enemies to kill. And then saw that Emeryn had dropped to her knees, her eyes wide and her face white. Her hands were clutching her stomach and were already drenched with blood, and a tall Breiryn was standing over her, his red-stained blade raised for a final strike. Gawan cried out in alarm and started sprinting towards them, but he already knew he would never get there in time. He saw the sword falling and roared in impotent anger, but then Gwydion appeared and crashed into the Breiryn, catching him by the legs and driving him to the mud. Part of Gawan wanted nothing more than to join him and rip the man's eyes from his skull, but instead he kept on running towards his fallen lover.

Emeryn had toppled onto her side, and Gawan's legs turned to water as he saw the grey ropes of intestines in her hands. She was already shaking violently and as Gawan reached her the initial shock of her wounding seemed to leave her, and she let out an agonised scream. Her arms flailed for a moment, sending drops of blood flying up into her face and hair, before clutching again at the ragged wound that gaped across her stomach. She looked down at it in absolute terror and Gawan fought to hold back his own panic. His heart was hammering twice as fast as it had been in the press and his brow was drenched in freezing cold sweat. With one hand he ripped away his green cloak and pressed it to the red gash, the other hand reaching up to touch her face. Emeryn screamed again, the sound almost unbearable in his ears, and Gawan tried to breathe steadily as he gently stroked her cheek.

'Emeryn! Emeryn can you hear me?'

Either she couldn't or else she simply didn't have it in her to communicate because all the response he got was another pitiful cry of pain. She was shaking uncontrollably, and though he tried his best to keep pressure on the wound her constant movement made it near impossible. Bright blood poured from her opened stomach like a flood, and Gawan bellowed out for help but no-one came.

'Emeryn hold on! We'll get you to Hywel and you'll be alright.'

But all she did was squirm in place and continue to scream, pawing weakly at the cloak that was pressed against her innards. Her beautiful face kept shifting from a grimace of agony to a mask of mindless panic, and Gawan saw more blood start to dribble from her lips. Tears of pain were smearing the woad on her cheeks and Gawan held her tighter as he fought to hold back his own. He tried to keep the tremble from his voice but it came out as a shaky whisper.

'Emeryn, don't do this! I love you Emeryn, don't leave me!'

Her eyes didn't meet his and kept staring around wildly as her limbs continued to thrash. Her breath was coming

244

in frantic gasps and whenever she wasn't screaming she was groaning softly, simply because she lacked the strength to cry out any louder. Gawan held onto her and looked desperately around for somebody, anybody, who could help him. But both his own company and the Gaians were still advancing down the hill and besides, nothing short of the greatest druid could possibly help her now. He felt tears in his eyes despite himself as he realised what had to be done.

Back before First Nantwyn, before even Broken Stream, a Darin had gutted one of Gawan's comrades during a coastal raid. Culhwch had been blind with pain and beyond any help, and Gawan had opened his leg up and held his hand while he bled out. It hadn't been easy, Gawan had known Culhwch well and had been hesitant to cut him, but this... this was something infinitely different. Emeryn was someone who could make him smile; someone who'd made him happy after years of surly melancholy. Emeryn was someone he'd wanted to settle down with and perhaps even raise a child with. She was someone he loved. He looked down at her as she writhed in agony and knew that if he truly loved her, he could not let her suffer like this.

At some point, he couldn't remember when, he had dropped Heartreaver on the muddy grass. But this wasn't a task for a sword anyway, and he slowly drew out a dagger from his belt. He considered opening her leg as he had for Culhwch but another cry of pain told him he couldn't do that. It might be the easy way but it would take time, and listening to Emeryn's screams was more than Gawan could bear. It would be better to cut her throat but he couldn't bring himself to do that either, and so

245

instead he pushed the cloak aside and braced himself to strike. There was no time for words, no final kiss or a last caress. Every moment he delayed the woman he loved suffered more, and Gawan fought back the selfish urge to hesitate. With a single thrust he plunged the knife under her ribs and into her heart, and he made himself look as her eyes flew wide again. Emeryn gasped in sudden shock and Gawan kept his gaze on her and held tight to her hand, staring into those dark eyes as the light slowly left them. It took barely three heartbeats for her to slump down to the ground, and though Gawan knew her soul had left her, for some reason he kept hold of her hand.

The First Man of the Gorvicae wanted to weep but he held it back. Instead he knelt there in quiet misery, oblivious to the battle raging below him. It didn't seem to matter all that much anymore. He knew he ought to find Heartreaver and go back to join his cohort. They were his tribe after all, and he their leader, and they might need him as they pressed the Breiryn back. But he didn't stand. He couldn't. Instead he held on to Emeryn's hand and cradled her head in his arms. It was a while before he could think and even then he couldn't speak the words aloud. So he gave Emeryn's final blessing as a quiet prayer in his head, uncertain if the gods were even listening.

I am sorry I never told you what you meant to me, Emeryn. I love you with all my heart. Cross the bridge unharmed.

Chapter 18. A Beech Tree in the Rain

The rain was getting heavier but Gawan didn't care. The water beat down hard and thunder rumbled in the distance, but the First Man had no time even for Taran today. Emeryn was gone, perhaps by his fault and certainly by his hand. What did the weather matter a damn? Gawan wandered across the muddy grass with no real idea of where he was going, ignoring the cold water that soaked his hair and beard. He just wanted to be away somewhere. When Hywel had come to take her body away the old man had tried to comfort him, but the Gadarim had ignored him. When Owain had come galloping from the ridge's centre to tell them how the Breiryn had yielded and the day was theirs, he'd not even looked up from the ground. Even when Gwydion had sat him down to scrub the lime and clay from his hair, he'd not shared a word with his brother. He didn't want their comradeship. He just wanted to be alone.

The Gorvic plodded onward in no particular direction and eventually found himself at the edge of some grey-looking woodland. Gawan didn't break his monotonous stride as he passed the shadowy treeline, and he walked in among the oaks and beeches without really looking at them. He paid just enough attention to make sure he didn't walk into anything but beyond that his mind was elsewhere. He wanted to feel angry. He could be angry at Rhianwyn for betraying their trust, or at Broad Kellas for the death of Tarwyn, or at Caserach for bringing this fight upon them. He even tried to embrace his anger at himself for leading his people into danger instead of keeping them safe. None of it worked. The hot comfort of anger eluded him as he stomped on through the trees, his hair and clothes dripping wet and his feet squelching loudly in the mud.

He'd never imagined he could feel this wretched again. Long ago, when he'd lost Bronwen, Gawan had resolved to never again feel such misery and had spent years making himself strong enough to overcome it. Mabonac's fire had given him that strength, and with it he had risen above his desolation to become a great war-leader of his tribe. He had forced his body and mind to become mighty and stalwart, and had he not proven time and again that he truly was the first among their men? His limbs were fast and his focus keen, and yet again he'd emerged from battle with barely a bruise to show for it. Of all the mighty Gorvicae, Gawan son of Dearg had made himself the mightiest. And what good had it done him? What use was the strength of his body if it could not protect Emeryn? What good was the strength of his mind if it could not control his heart?

He trudged on through damp leaves and sopping ferns and tried to picture her face. He tried to remember it bathed in firelight, laughing at some jest of Gwydion's or Tarwyn's. He tried to remember how her mouth had curved when trying to hold back smiles, and how her long hair used to shine like strands of gold. He tried to think back to the way her eyes could flash with sudden passion, or how she'd close them tight as she gasped when they made love beneath the stars. He tried to picture her in any way other than the way he saw her now. Right now he only saw her drenched in her own dark blood, screaming in blind agony as her innards spilled into her hands.

Gawan ground his teeth and tried to catch hold of the anger that might burn away his grief. It was anger at himself but he didn't care about that, what he needed was to feel the heat of fire in his blood, even if it meant hating himself. He already did anyway. He thought of Emeryn, a woman he had loved and who he was sure had loved him back, and remembered that her last clear memory of him would be one of jealousy; that when she crossed the bridge and met Annwn, her last thoughts of her former lover would be of a man staring at another woman as he had never stared at her. *Rhianwyn!* Gawan tried to focus some anger at her but it soon switched back to himself again. It wasn't the Wildcat's fault that he'd looked on her in such a way. *It is your fault Gawan. It is you who wounded Emeryn's heart long before the Breiryn tore open her flesh.*

He swiped past a young oak as images of her bleeding body washed over him. The thought threatened to drive him to tears but he clutched on to his self-hatred like a drowning man to a line, and slowly drew Heartreaver as he walked. Ahead of him was a great beech, its leaves brown but still clinging on to its branches, and with a wordless cry he hacked the blade down onto the nearest bough. The rain was cold but his whole body felt hot as he struck down at the wood again, the iron thudding through the tough bark and scattering chips of pale wood through the air. Gawan didn't see an enemy in his mind's eye as he hacked, only himself and his own weakness, and with every new strike he shouted out in blind fury.

The bough was almost cut through when the voice came from behind him, and Gawan spun on the spot like a startled cat, blade up and teeth bared.

'You will only damage it, you know.'

The speaker was an old-looking man, his face lined and his beard grey, but his green eyes seemed bright even in the rain. He was wearing a long cloak and held a gnarled staff in one hand, and despite the snarling Gadarim before him he was showing no sign of concern. His face was completely at ease and his posture as relaxed as if he stood before his own fire. Gawan sneered at him.

'Mind your business old man.'

He knew it was disrespectful but he didn't give a damn. His fury was well underway now and he didn't want to lose it and have to face his grief again. He began turning back to the brutalised tree but the old man spoke again before he could, looking first at the sword and then at the beech.

'You know, the sword is unique among weapons. Spears and bows were first made only for the hunting of beasts. Axes were made for felling trees and knives for skinning meat. Only swords were made for the sole purpose of killing men.'

He didn't say it as though he were a warrior speaking with pride, nor as a druid speaking in sorrow. He simply said it. Gawan curled his lip again and tightened his grip on the weapon.

'If you do not leave me in peace old man, you will find out *exactly* what this sword can do!'

It was a mostly empty threat but Gawan was keen for this meddler to leave. The old man barely shrugged his shoulders, still completely unperturbed by the warrior.

'It would at least be serving its purpose. It *is* a thing for reaving hearts, not for chopping wood.'

For a moment the only sound was the patter of the rain as Gawan stared at the old man. Those green eyes were still calm and his face was still relaxed, as though he'd said nothing out of the ordinary. But Gawan knew that he had meant to say exactly what he'd said, and he kept Heartreaver ready as he spoke to the cloaked stranger.

'How do you know me?'

Thunder rumbled in the distance and Gawan thought of woodland spirits, but the old man made no sign of being anything magical. He merely spoke again with the same calm, barely-interested voice.

'I know why you named your sword as you did, Gawan son of Dearg. I know that it speaks more of yourself than most men would think. And I know that for many years past the only love that you held was for your land and for your tribe. And for your pride.'

His words stabbed at Gawan like cold ice into his heart and he felt his grief coming back to him like a heavy black cloud. He pushed it away hard with Mabonac's fire and snarled at the old man, finally feeling the blessed heat of anger in his veins. Ghost or magicker or whatever he was, today Gawan's rage was enough to conquer any fear.

'Keep your thoughts to yourself! Either turn me into a frog right now or else leave me in peace!'

Once again the old man merely shrugged but Gawan thought he heard something slightly different in his tone; a subtle hint of urgency.

'You have a part yet to play, Leaping Wolf, and it will not be served by standing in the rain hacking at wood. You fate is tied to that of Rhianwyn and if you abandon her now, much harm will follow.'

Gawan scoffed a little to cover his unease.

'My fate is my own. Save your talk of destiny for druids.'

251

The stranger almost smiled though his mouth barely twitched.

'You need not worry my Gorvic friend, you are not a man of great destiny.' Gawan wasn't quite sure what to say to that but the old man continued before he could comment. 'But the Wildcat is, and the Lion Cub is. And both will need you before all is done.'

He laid his free hand on the beech for a moment, though he leaned no real weight on it. Gawan was still trying to keep his anger ahead of his confusion.

'Who are you?'

The man gave no answer, seemingly more interested in the tree, and Gawan tried a different approach.

'Why do you tell me this?'

This time the stranger looked back at him and his shining eyes were oddly unsettling through the rain.

'For the good of your people.'

Gawan furrowed his brow.

'*My* people? I am Gorvicae. Whoever you are, you are of Caderyn woods.'

The old man gave another of his almost-smiles.

'These woods were here long before that name was ever spoken. But we are not here to speak of the history of trees. If you value your people you will go to Rhianwyn.' He shrugged again. 'Or do not go to her, I care not.'

A fresh ripple of wind caught the hem of his cloak and for the first time he seemed to notice the foul weather around them. He sighed and spoke quietly in a voice that sounded part-annoyed, part-amused.

'I care a little.'

Gawan blinked at him for a moment, unsure of what to say. His words made little enough sense already without him now seeming to talk to *himself*. The Gadarim's precious anger was fast losing the battle with curiosity and he looked back along the way he'd come. He couldn't see far through the trees and the rain, but he knew that back there would be the village where the Wildcat and her people were licking their wounds. Should he go back there and speak to her? What would he say to her about this; that a stranger in the woods had told him to stick by her but he had no idea why? Even in his own head it sounded ridiculous.

The First Man started speaking as he turned back again. 'What do...'

But he got no further than that. The old man, whoever he was, was nowhere to be seen, not in any direction. The Gorvic spun around on the spot a few times, feeling both anxious and foolish as he did. There was no sign of him anywhere. Gawan felt anew the biting cold of the wind and rain, and it was only then that he looked at the forest floor. There were no footprints but his own in the muddy ground.

Chapter 19. Back to the Caledon

The rain was growing lighter but the sky was still grey and dark, making it hard to tell just how late in the day it was. Gawan wandered back to the village where many Caledon were taking shelter, a little cluster of homes beside a stream not far from Moon Ridge itself. It was a modest place but the people there had made them welcome, and locals were cramming warriors indoors as best they could. Cracks in doors showed the yellow lights of fires winking at him through the rain, and Gawan made his way towards them, his mind in a whirl of confusion.

If the old man was to be believed then he was fated to help the Wildcat in some way, but how? Who had the man been anyway, this disinterested woodsman who had known the name of his sword? Had he been a spirit of some sort, or a hermit-mage living alone in the woods to practice his unsettling spellcraft? If he was the latter then he almost certainly could not be trusted, but even if he was something other than a normal man, there was still no guarantee that his words had been the truth. Spirits and Sidhe might have access to great knowledge but many were also known to be mischievous, and fond of manipulating mortals for their own sport. He remembered the stories Anryn had told of Fynbar the Trickster, who had doomed the great warrior Caryx, and wondered if he'd just met a similar being.

He found himself remembering the legend as he walked. Caryx had been set to marry the fairest girl of all the tribes, Meiriannon, who was said to make the wood-nymphs pale with envy at her beauty. All was planned for the two lovers to kiss palms at midsummer, but Fynbar had lusted after her and so had tricked her betrothed into a bargain; if Caryx would fetch him a hundred mistletoe berries from the nearby woods, his farm would prosper for so long as he and his new wife shared a roof. Thinking the task easy, and keen for a prosperous marriage, the warrior had ventured into the woods and collected the mistletoe berries. But the Trickster had convinced the woodland Sidhe to slow time whilst he was in there, and while Caryx was gone Fynbar took on his shape and married Meiriannon in his place, having his way with her each night for twenty long years. He then abandoned her and let her age for a further twenty before allowing Caryx to emerge, the warrior still thinking that barely a day had passed. He returned to his wife and his appearance drove her mad, and three days later she threw herself from Machlyd Point into the sea. Caryx had railed against Fynbar for his deception, but it could not be denied that for those three days his farm had yielded finer crops than any other in the land. Fynbar had kept true to his word.

Gawan growled at himself for dwelling on ancient legends and splashed his way angrily into the tiny town. He had already planned what he would do; he would go straight to Rhianwyn and find out if some dire need was upon her. If the Wildcat needed something important done she would surely tell him so and if not, he would know to be doubtful about the old man's words to him. Gawan pictured her face for a moment, despite himself. She was a remarkable woman for all their enmity, and for all her many faults. Evan as he thought it he felt guilt stab into him like a cold knife to his guts, and he clenched his fists tight enough to make his fingers ache. *Emeryn is not even laid to rest and already your thoughts are straying like this again!* He wanted to blame his lack of control on the confusion still raging through his mind, but then he'd had no such excuse the last time this happened.

Gawan stalked on, staring furiously at the ground in front of him, and almost collided with a group of men coming the other way. He looked up just in time to see three figures in hooded cloaks, two green, one brownish-red. A step later he recognised Boryn, Owain and Gwydion walking through the rain, each one smiling in relief as they saw him. It was Gwydion who spoke first, concern undermining his attempt at humour.

'You know, some clever man invented hooded cloaks for a reason.'

Gawan knew his brother was well-intentioned. He would be grieving for Tarwyn more than anyone but still he was trying to be light-hearted for Gawan's sake. But the First Man was in no mood for such talk. He simply grunted what could only be vaguely called a greeting and nodded his head, water dripping down his face as he did. Boryn tried speaking next, his thick moustache looking sodden despite his hood.

'You ought to get yourself indoors to a good fire, my friend. We will all be heading back to Bryngarth soon and no march is made easier by damp clothing.'

Gawan ignored the friendly advice but tilted his head a little at the headman, curious despite himself.

'Will we not be leaving a cohort here? These southerners may rise again once the legions have gone.'

Gwydion turned to Owain.

'A fair point. I could stay here with our company if yours is taking Caserach back to Bryngarth? It might be more proper for the Caderyn to do it, it being your land that he invaded?'

Gawan frowned at him before Owain could answer.

'He still lives?'

His brother Gadarim nodded.

'Rhianwyn has taken him prisoner and wishes him judged by the headmen of the Caledon. Riders have already been sent to summon the chiefs of the Dariniae.'

Boryn's brow furrowed in concern but he spoke softly.

'Though with Ierryn gone and no other to contest him, Caserach will still call himself High Chieftain until his own tribe decide to depose him. To my knowledge no judgement of this kind has happened before. I suspect it will prove difficult.'

Owain nodded his head in agreement.

'True, but Rhianwyn will see justice done.' He turned to Gwydion. 'And my thanks for your offer to stay here, it is appreciated.'

Once again Boryn spoke quietly but the other men all listened.

'Perhaps it would be wiser for the Caderyn cohort to stay here and the Gorvicae company to escort the prisoner? Many Caderyn will be upset with Rhianwyn for calling the Gaians to our aid, they might take further offence to Gorvicae being left to protect them instead of their own people.'

Thanks to the old man Gawan's head was still a fog of confusion, but he was just about able to understand Boryn's point. Owain seemed to agree too and the stocky man nodded.

'As you say. I shall stay here to keep an eye on Asrec if your cohort is content to accompany the chieftain to Bryngarth on your way back north?'

Gwydion nodded back and spoke the words Gawan was thinking.

'What of the Gaians?'

There was a brief and awkward pause. They all knew they ought to be grateful both to Rhianwyn and to Galerian for saving their skins in the battle, but all the same none of them were comfortable with the idea of them. Boryn spoke simply and quietly.

'They have done what was asked of them and I am told they will be taking the road north with us.'

There were some uneasy rumblings at that but Gwydion changed the subject before anyone could say more.

'They should be holding the moot at Graigarw when we return. Will you be standing for it Boryn?'

The older man shrugged noncommittally.

'Perhaps. I am senior but have only a small settlement in my care. I am unused to ruling over large numbers of people.'

Owain made as if to question him further but Gawan spoke first. This could potentially turn into a long conversation and he wanted to get this over and done with.

'Where is the Wildcat? I must speak with her.'

Owain seemed a little uncertain as he replied.

'If you intend to pick a fight with her over the Gaians, you know as well as I do that...'

But Gawan cut him off irritably.

'I said speak, not shout. I wish only to talk to her.'

Owain didn't seem convinced but he turned on the spot anyway, pointing in-between the houses.

'She is at the longhouse now, just down that way and to the left when the ground starts to slope.'

Gawan looked through the rain at the identical-looking grey houses and nodded his thanks without speaking. Owain spoke again before he could start walking.

'Shall I come with you?'

The Gorvic shook his head.

'Get yourself somewhere dry and drink to your victory.' He paused a moment before adding, 'I will join you later.'

He was hardly in a fit temper for revelry but Owain was a fellow First Man, and Gawan had not been as respectful as he could have been. The shorter man bobbed his head again and Gawan started off along the muddy street. His head was still a mess of thoughts and he still wasn't quite sure what he should do, but speaking to Rhianwyn would be a good place to start and so he plodded on past the dull-looking homes. Soon he felt the ground beginning to rise beneath his feet, as Owain had said. He looked to his left and saw a hall that looked barely larger than a barn and he started squelching towards it, his jaw set.

The main doors looked ramshackle and they opened with a piercing creak, and Gawan blinked his eyes at the yellow light inside the hall. A fire had been built in the pit at its centre and a rush of heat washed over him as he walked further in towards it. The place was crowded with bodies, which only made the room feel warmer, and the heavy odour of sweat mingled with the sweet smell of damp clothing. Now that he was out of the rain his tunic and breeches felt clammy on his skin, and Gawan was tempted to stand by the fire for a while to dry off. But there were people there who might pester him with talk and besides, he was still angry at himself. He didn't deserve to feel

259

comfortable here, or to share the day's victory with his comrades. He would see the Wildcat and if he had a duty to do here he would do it. If not... he really didn't know.

He crossed the hall in little time and those few who tried to greet him were met with shallow nods and grunts. Rhianwyn wasn't at the high table but there was a door just past it that presumably led to some private rooms and Gawan made his way towards it. Just before he reached the door a young Caderyn sitting near it stood up and half-barred his way.

'I'm sorry comrade but the chieftain asked not to be disturbed.'

Gawan scowled at him. Owain was elsewhere in the town and no-one knew where Reaghan or Bael had got to. Anyone else that she cared to speak to could bloody well put up with the intrusion.

'She will want to see me.'

He pushed past him but the young man shifted to get in his way again. Gawan shot him a glare.

'We have just come from a battle that has further depleted the legion. I am the senior Gadarim of the three tribunes here and I am going in to see your chieftain. Either I walk in now, or you fall down clutching your face in pain and *then* I walk in. I don't care which.'

Part of him knew he should feel guilty for intimidating a comrade like this but he was in no mood to be patient. The young man rocked back on his heels and held his hands up, palms open.

'Very well, very well.'

He made as if to knock on the wood but Gawan had wasted enough time already. He shoved his way forward and through the door, shutting it behind him quickly before the fool could say anything else. The room beyond was small and crammed only with barrels, but there was another door just across from it and he barged through that one too. This chamber was occupied, and Gawan froze as soon as he entered it. Like the first it was only a small room, with a bench against one wall and a pile of flat-lidded chests against another. There was a small fire in a hearth opposite the door by which he had entered, sending flickering orange light onto the walls. Most of the space was dominated by a large and heavy tub, the kind one saw in any headman's house, which was filled with water that sent steam curling up into the rafters above. Gawan felt the heat of the place the moment he walked in, but it wasn't that which stopped him in his tracks.

Standing in the tub, naked and beautiful, was Rhianwyn. Firelight reflected from the water that ran down her body, just as firm and lithe as he remembered, with subtle but well-shaped curves that made Gawan stare despite himself. The battle-marks along her arm were black in the orange light and they stood out stark and bold against her skin. Another woman, Owain's red-haired lover, was standing just outside the tub, leaning over it to pour more hot water over her chieftain. Rhianwyn herself was washing one leg, running soap along her glistening thigh, oblivious to the intruder. She was not a tall woman, not by any means, but all the same the limb looked long and lean, the tight muscles highlighted by the shining water.

Gawan blinked and looked away, furious with himself, but before he could leave the redhead noticed him and gave a sharp intake of breath. Looking back Gawan saw Rhianwyn turn her eyes on him and the two stood still as statues for a heartbeat, neither one knowing what they ought to say. He had seen her as the gods made her before of course, but that had been different. At her testing he had been at best momentarily distracted, his focus on the task at hand pushing away all thoughts of desire. Now... here in this warm little room things were very different indeed. His mind, already mauled and baffled by what he'd been through that day, started racing for something to say to her. Fortunately Rhianwyn recovered herself faster than he did and she gestured towards her friend beside her.

'Pass me the towel, would you Meg?'

The other woman did as she was bid, though she kept her eyes on Gawan. The First Man stared deliberately at the wall, ignoring the naked woman as she began to dry herself. He spoke to her without looking, his voice croaking a little.

'I should not have intruded. I need to speak with you but... it can wait.'

He turned to leave but Rhianwyn spoke to his back.

'You can stay, just wait one moment.'

Gawan stayed facing the wall, hating himself quietly and picturing Emeryn's bloodstained face in his mind. He heard shuffling behind him for a few moments and then Rhianwyn's voice again.

'I believe I am fit for company now.'

She was clearly trying to sound unconcerned but he heard the note of tension in her voice. He turned to see that she had thrown on a plain dress of dark red, though her hair was still lank about her shoulders. Owain's lover still held the towel and she spoke quietly to her chief, never looking away from the Gadarim.

'Should I...'

Rhianwyn simply nodded to her and the redhead strode to the door. Gawan stepped aside for her to pass by him. He tried to keep his face impassive as she went but it was hard to contain the rage he was feeling. He had ruined his brief time with Emeryn by his staring at this woman, and now he had stood and gawped at her like a boy who'd never clapped eyes on breasts before. *Did you care for her so little you piss-drinking dog? Was the love you claimed to feel so weak that you lust after other women before her blood is even cold?* His anger must have shown because the redhead almost flinched away when his eyes briefly met hers, and for a moment he thought she might insist on remaining. But Rhianwyn nodded to her again and she left the room in silence, but not before a last look of disapproval.

Rhianwyn must have seen the anger that was simmering in him too because she spoke before he had the chance to say anything.

'I am told you lost some good friends today. I am sorry.' She paused and put a hand to her heart. 'May they cross the bridge unharmed.'

Gawan mumbled the response and Rhianwyn spoke again before he could draw breath to say anything more. She seemed refreshed and ready for his expected outrage, but she kept her voice calm and even.

'Doubtless you will want to criticise me for requesting Gregor's aid today. Well I had my reasons and they were good reasons, but by all means you may air your grievance about it.' She sighed a little. 'You won't be the last to.'

For all the weariness in her final words her blue eyes seemed to shine with spirit, and what might even have been a touch of wry humour. For a moment Gawan wondered if she was mocking him, then a thought managed to penetrate his guilt and confusion; was she goading him into a debate? She likely knew that he would ultimately see the tactical sense in what she had done, but she also knew that he'd be angry and saddened after the battle and would need to let that anger out somehow. And for all their differences, she knew him well enough to know that arguing with her would probably be the best way. Gawan almost sighed. After all the grief he'd caused her, she still had a moment of kindness for him. The gods knew well that if anyone understood the pain of loss, it was her. That she had stayed so strong through everything that had happened to her was nothing short of miraculous. *And perhaps she is grateful for your finding her boy after all, and this is how she is choosing to tell you so?*

Gawan looked at her, wondering how he should answer. He had plenty of opinions on warfare of course, and on the Gaians and her methods in getting them there, but none of that seemed to come to the forefront of his mind. Instead all he could think of was the strength and compassion of this woman, the woman to whom he was somehow bound by fate if there was truth in the old man's words. For some reason he felt more ready to believe it here in her presence than he had been out in the woods, and staring into her eyes he almost *wanted* to believe it.

He didn't know how it happened. He was tired, grieving, angry and confused, along with a dozen other emotions he could barely have described. His mind felt like it had been pulled in a hundred directions at once as it tried to make some sense of what had happened today. He was as weak, unfocused, and vulnerable as he could ever remember being. And before he even knew what he was doing he was kissing her. His hands took her by the shoulders and drew her close to him, his mouth finding hers and pressing hard onto her lips. For the briefest, tiniest moment, Gawan felt his rage and sorrows drain away as raw passion flooded through his veins. And then, almost before it had truly started, it was over.

Rhianwyn pulled away from him within a heartbeat, her palm pushing firmly onto his chest. She stepped back with a look of mixed anger and shock, and she struggled for a moment, searching for words.

'What... what did you...?'

Her eyes were still bright but Gawan couldn't look at them. He backed away from her awkwardly, horrified. *What are you thinking? Have you no concept of decency to your dead love? Is this what Mabonac looks for when he seeks his men of honour?* Rhianwyn was still staring at him, speechless, but Gawan was just as lost for what to say.

'I am sorry... I...'

He couldn't think of anything. He had no idea what had driven him to such a thing but he knew enough to be both angry and ashamed. Without pause the Gadarim spun on his heel and yanked open the door, storming through it without another word. He heard Rhianwyn call his name as he went but he ignored her and kept walking, crossing the next room in half-a-dozen long strides. She didn't follow him and he barged into the main hall alone, his mind brimming over with fury at himself. *You have to leave. Whatever that old fool said you had no business coming here, and now you have disgraced yourself beyond all hope of redemption!*

The First Man ground his teeth together and strode angrily through the hall, glaring murder at any man who came within an arm's reach of him. He reached the heavy doors in no time at all and hurried outside into the rain. It was pouring down by now and the sky was grey and grim, but Gawan couldn't give a damn for the weather. He hunched his shoulders and began stalking through the storm in no particular direction, hot shame burning painfully through his soul.

Chapter 20. Friends or Enemies

Rhia was almost glad that Gawan hadn't turned back at her call; she had no idea what she would have said to him if he had. He had kissed her. He had *kissed* her! This was a man who for most of their acquaintance would happily have seen her dead, and he had come in here and shared barely a word before taking hold of her as though they were lovers. She shook her head a little and walked around the room, just to give herself something to do as she tried to make sense of it. She knew that Gawan had a sort of grudging respect for her, but in all other ways he had at the very best *tolerated* her, and for the most part he had actively disliked or even hated her. What the Dis did it mean?

  She kept up her pacing as her mind raced, so much so that she didn't notice the water running down her neck. She had dried quickly and her hair was still wet enough to drip, and she absently dabbed a towel to her skin. No matter how she tried to figure it Rhia couldn't think of any reason that Gawan might have for doing what he'd done. He'd not been drinking nor had he suffered any headwound that she knew of. He'd lost comrades today that was true, but then he'd lost more at Nantwyn and hadn't resorted to anything like this. *Though it* was *after that that he gave you your name. Is it grief and loss that brings out the man behind all the sneers and taunts?*

  Rhia closed her eyes tight for a moment as she clenched and unclenched her fists. She did it out of nervous energy more than anything else and felt surprised that she wasn't feeling angrier. Ever since what happened with Delyn she'd been wary of the touch of man; before Marius the notion of it had *terrified* her. It had taken years of his support for her fears to subside and even with Reaghan's help, it wasn't something that just went away. Yet she'd barely felt a drop of either anger or fear at Gawan and instead she was just racked with confusion. She ground her teeth even harder at that. *You* should *be feeling angrier. Damn it all, this is the man who killed Dane!*

It was hard to hold back tears as she remembered the day her little brother had crossed the bridge. Dane had fought like a hero at First Nantwyn, wounded though he was, but he'd been no match for Leaping Wolf, who had killed him almost without thinking. *But you were enemies back then, and Dane would gladly have killed Gawan had he had the skill.* The thought brought on a surge of guilt in her and she punched the planks of the heavy tub hard, hurting her hand and sending ripples through the still-steaming water. Why was she defending his actions back then? Why was she even *trying* to understand him right now? What he had done was inexcusable, she should be screaming and swearing in his face, not trying to justify what had just happened. For so long she had blamed herself for what happened with Delyn rather than blaming the man responsible; she should not be making that same mistake again. *But is it really the same thing? A man you trusted raping you while you slept, and a man who dislikes you kissing you and then running off?*

Rhia couldn't make any sense of it, either for him or for her reaction. She tried to hate Gawan for what had happened but found that she couldn't. He was brave and loyal, even noble in his way, and had even slain his own chieftain to keep Baercban from killing her. He'd not done it for *her* exactly but nonetheless, his sense of honour was unquestionable. Once again Rhia felt guilt interrupt her stream of thought as images flashed through her mind, first of Dane and then of Bevan and Marius. For a moment she felt weak as she looked on the faces of the men she had loved, but she banished them with an effort and spoke firmly to herself. *I didn't ask for him to kiss me! I have betrayed no-one.* There had been a time when her inner critic might have mocked her for that but she had learned to fight back against it, and no voice snapped back inside her head. She felt no desire for the man and was not responsible for whatever moment of madness had overcome him just now. But what *had* caused it?

Rhia stamped across the room and grabbed hold of a cloak, slipping into her shoes as she threw it around her shoulders. It was pointless to stand here guessing when the man himself was still nearby. He had clearly been embarrassed but she needed to talk to him, and better to do so now than to wait for things to fester. In all likelihood it had been some flash of foolish lust brought on from anger and grief. Contact and intimacy made people feel alive, and after a day so full of death it was understandable. He would bark something unpleasant at her, she would say something equally cutting to him, and things would be back to normal again. At least, she hoped so.

Rather than walk through the main hall and risk being accosted by well-wishers, Rhia walked into the barrel room and then slipped out through a side door into the darkness of the early evening. The rain had slackened but the wind had picked up and Rhia flipped the hood up on her cloak before venturing further. Gawan would likely have missed the small door and stormed out through the hall, which meant he would be coming out through the main entrance. He had not been gone for long and if he was heading back to where most of the other Gorvicae were settling then he ought to pass by her on his way there. Rhia began walking to the front of the building, the cloak held tight around her shoulders. What exactly she would say to him she still wasn't quite sure, but she knew they had to address this and hopefully he would know that too.

The longhall wasn't large and she reached the main doors in little time, but instead of Gawan coming out she saw Owain and Meg standing there, along with Gregor Galerian and a handful of his guards. The soldiers were looking relaxed and were clearly only there for protocol's sake, but nonetheless the passing Caledon were throwing them uncertain glances. *Can you blame them? Few of us have had good cause to trust a Gaian legionary.* Squinting her eyes Rhia saw that the rest of the soldiers had set up tents not far away, and that the Gaians were eying the Lurians with just as much wariness. *The sooner we get them back on the road the better. They've done us a good turn but now the fighting's done their presence will do more harm than good.*

She put Gawan from her mind for the time being and headed towards the group. Gregor saw her approaching and gave her one of his small smiles. He put his fist to his chest then threw his hand out in salute, but it was only a courtesy, not a necessity. Rhia held no military rank from his perspective but as a patrician *and* an allied commander it was the polite thing to do. As such she returned the gesture, albeit in a slightly hurried manner. She had no wish to seem more Gaian than she had to out here.

'General Galerian.'

'Lady Dessida.'

Back in Tamora it would have simply been 'Gregor' and 'Rhianna', but the days of social suppers in her townhouse were a lifetime ago and besides, it was perhaps best not to seem too friendly. Gregor understood the precarious position she held and didn't greet her with an embrace as he would usually have done, settling for a simple nod of his head. Rhia tried to thank him with just her eyes before continuing in her formal tone.

'General, I...'

But before she could say more the sound of hoofbeats interrupted her and she turned her head in the direction of the noise. A group of mounted figures was approaching through the drizzle, and at a second glance she saw that Alraig was seated at their head. He wore a dark cloak about his shoulders but the hood was down, and water was dripping from his brown-and-grey beard. The light was dim but his expression was clear, and Rhia wasn't at all surprised when his words came out cold as midwinter.

'There are legionaries here, Rhianwyn. Gaian soldiers; armed and armoured.'

Before Rhia could answer him Gregor addressed the headman from beside her. The general spoke almost no Lurian but he had picked out the familiar words, and Alraig's tone had made it clear what he was speaking of.

'Well noticed sir, and you are welcome for the help.'

Alraig spoke good Vulgare and the sarcasm would not have been lost on him, but he ignored the tall Gaian and kept looking at Rhia. His eyes seemed to bore into hers.

'Am I to take it that these soldiers came here at your invitation?'

Rhia flipped back her hood to make sure he saw her face and she thrust her chin out despite herself.

'That they are Alraig, and as you saw they were sorely needed today.'

The mounted chief did not shout but his voice was hard as stone.

'In spite of all our discussion, you have not only permitted but *encouraged* Gaian soldiers to cross Caledon land under arms?'

Rhia matched his gaze and kept her tone as polite as she could. Alraig was no fool, surely he could see that without Gregor's men the day would have been lost?

'In order to save my people bloodshed, yes; I did exactly that.'

Alraig straightened in his saddle and twitched his lip in restrained anger.

'I should have known that you had become more one of them than one of us. It saddens me to see it in the daughter of Carradan.'

Rhia felt her anger rise but Alraig continued before she could answer.

'You have broken your own law Rhianwyn. The treaty which you told us would be for our mutual benefit has been flouted by your actions today.'

Rhia ignored the water on her face as she looked up at him through the rain.

'What I have done is save countless lives Alraig, what else would you have had me do?'

The headman's face was inscrutable.

'I would have my appointed chieftain not keep secrets from her advisors. I would have it that when a decision is made and agreed upon, you did not ignore it for your own ends and disregard your own laws in the process.'

Meg spoke up from behind Rhia, anger and impatience in her voice.

'The Blackbirds saved us all today, what difference does it make?'

Owain piped up in agreement.

'We would have been outflanked and crushed without their help.'

Alraig turned his eyes on them and his words were flat and cold.

'If the law is not obeyed it may as well not exist.' He turned back to Rhia. 'And if a chieftain lies to her people she has no right to call herself their leader.'

Rhia tried to keep from sounding too exasperated.

'All I did was ask for some help to defeat an enemy, help that we dearly needed.'

She gestured towards Gregor as she spoke but the general didn't comment. He might be able to guess what was being said but he could hardly be expected to follow the conversation. Alraig kept staring down at her.

'Today it is the summoning of one legion; tomorrow it will be another legion sent to "secure us" against the Breiryn threat. The next day we will suddenly need more administrators to help us run our affairs. And the day after that we would awake to find another governor in your father's seat, and our lands overruled as they once were.' His eyes flashed though his voice remained calm. 'Well, not while I live.'

The riders around him looked equally determined and Rhia tried to pacify them. Damn it all she was in the right here, and most of her wanted to be shouting her arguments back at them, but she controlled herself with an effort.

'Alraig, I swear to you I have no intention...'

273

But he cut across her.

'Enough! By your own admission you have broken the laws that you yourself set out. You will accompany me back to Bryngarth and remain there in my custody until the headmen and druids of our tribe can be assembled. They will decide what fate best suits you for what you have done here.'

He swung himself from the saddle and those behind him followed. Rhia saw that they bore an array of weaponry on their belts but that only the two archers were carrying anything in their hands. She also noticed that none wore mail or carried dragon shields. They were Alraig's own men then, not warriors of the legion. From their position on the ridge they would have seen the fighting below them but few would have fully appreciated how vital the Gaians had been today. She remembered her own company desperately trying to hold their line, and the Gorvicae on the left beginning to crumble. It was true; without the Blackbirds they would have been crushed. *But Alraig himself must surely understand? Why does he not see that I was right?*

There was no time for contemplation however as the group closed on her, their faces hard. Both Gregor and Meghan stepped forward but it was Owain who placed himself in front of her.

'Rhianwyn is your High Chieftain and I am your First Man. Unless Reaghan himself comes here with the say so, you have no right to make such a judgement.'

The Gadarim held his hands relaxed at his sides but Rhia sensed that he was ready to draw iron at an eyeblink's notice. She put a hand on his arm and spoke to Alraig.

'There is no need for all of this. We will be heading home soon anyway and I can speak to the chiefs then if you wish.'

The lithe headman didn't quite sneer but his mouth twitched slightly and he continued moving forwards, addressing his answer to Owain.

'Merwyn and I were named as her most senior chiefs and advisors. If such a chief believes his chieftain has broken the law he has the right to ask his fellows to hear him out, and Rhianwyn has already *admitted* to betraying us. She may make her case back at Bryngarth to any who might listen.'

A hulking tribesman with arms as thick as Rhia's legs came up to them and reached out to take her elbow. The move wasn't a violent one exactly but it was far from courteous, and it was hardly surprising when Owain shoved him into the mud. Rhia could almost feel the fury in his voice.

'You dare lay your hands on our chieftain like this?'

She opened her mouth to speak but Alraig got there first, his face set and his voice deadly calm.

'We are not on a battlefield now, Owain son of Perlyn. This affair is for chiefs and druids, not for Gadarim, and you will not stand in the way of our justice.'

The big man had risen to his feet and was glaring at Owain, his hand moving to the axe at his belt. Rhia instinctively reached for where Silverbite would hang but then remembered that she wasn't wearing her sword. Owain was of course still wearing his, and the bright iron whipped free of its sheath in a heartbeat. The hulking man looked suddenly hesitant and Rhia tried to seize the initiative before things got any worse.

'For Marna's sake Alraig see reason! I will speak to you all if you...'

But before she could finish the big tribesman seemed to regain his nerve, or embrace his stupidity, and drew his axe free of his belt. He squared up to Owain and the Gadarim levelled his blade at the man's neck.

'Back off boy! Do not make me hurt you.'

The giant ducked to one side and tried to slap the blade down with his axe-haft but Owain was too quick for him, flicking the blade in a half-circle and nicking the other man's chin. It was only a scratch, barely more than he'd have suffered from a long rose-thorn, but it made him jerk his head away and spots of blood flew into the rain. And one of the archers behind Alraig nocked, drew, and loosed before he even straightened up.

Meg and Rhia cried out at once as the shaft thudded into Owain's chest, but only the redhead was wearing a dagger at her belt. As Rhia caught the Gadarim's weight in her arms Meghan launched herself at Alraig's men with a scream that came straight from the Pit, drawing her blade free as she charged towards the archer. Rhia heard Alraig's voice bark out '*Wait!*' but it was too late to stop the bowman as he loosed another shaft. Rhia didn't see the arrow as it entered her friend but she saw the bloody tip emerge from halfway up her back. Meg collapsed to her knees and Rhia's vision turned red. She pounced on the big man and slammed her fists into his ribs, the punches knocking the wind from him and doubling him over. She lashed out at his jaw and felt a crack as the blow made contact, and the tribesman's head snapped sideways before he crumpled to the ground.

Rhia screamed as another man approached with his arms outstretched to grab her, and she flung an uppercut under his pointed chin, the blow taking him clean off his feet. She saw tribesmen drawing weapons and the archer nocking a shaft but she didn't give a damn anymore. Owain and Meg were dead or dying, who cared if she crossed the bridge beside them? Her eyes darted around for another target but the men were standing back. Alraig raised his arms and called out to them.

'Stand off! This is not what we came for!'

Rhia bared her teeth. She didn't give a blighted rat for what they came here for; they had just killed her friends and they would take what was coming to them! She felt a pressure on her arm and spun to strike her new attacker, but pulled herself short as she saw that it was Gregor. Without ceremony he yanked her back towards the building and called out in Vulgare to his guards.

'Form!'

A second later they were surrounded by half-a-dozen armoured men, their short swords held at the ready and their faces blank as masks. Rhia tried to calm herself enough to realise what was happening. A small crowd was gathering around them as people were drawn to the commotion, both tribesmen of the Caledon and the legionaries nearby. No-one really seemed to know what they should say or do, and an eerie quiet fell upon the scene. Rhia bit back a sob as she saw her two friends on the ground, their outstretched hands just inches from each other. The anger and grief at seeing them threatened to overturn her reason but she fought hard to focus her thoughts on what was happening. *This must not go further. It mustn't!* All she wanted to do was to avenge

Owain and Meg but she had to think of her people, however wrenching it might be.

Beside her she saw Gregor pull a tin whistle from his tunic. He spoke to Alraig, his voice steady.

'Stand your men down, right now.'

The headman seemed enraged more than concerned by the threat but he managed to keep his own voice under control. He did not address the Gaian but spoke directly to Rhia, ignoring the men around her completely.

'Would you have more Caderyn die tonight for what you have done?'

Rhia struggled to keep her rage in check but it spilled into her answer.

'I have killed no Caderyn today Alraig! These deaths are on your head, their blood is on *your* hands!'

Her accuser didn't contradict her but he made no apology either.

'I have no wish for more bloodshed. Call off your guards and come with me!'

She heard Gregor whisper in her ear, though it was loud enough for all of them to hear.

'A cohort of my men stands mere yards away, Rhianna. Say the word and we will cut through this rabble and get you out of here.'

Alraig's mouth twitched again.

'Your Gaian friends may indeed help you escape from us Rhianwyn. Most of our people sleep or eat, believing themselves to be safe. You may kill us all and run to Tamora where no Caderyn could follow you.' He leaned forwards and glared at her, moving into easy cutting range of the Gaians and not showing an ounce of concern. 'But it will only prove me right.'

Rhia hated to admit that a part of her was tempted to run. Gregor could get them clear and they could all make straight for Bryngarth. She could collect Lucan and then be on the east road before anyone could think to stop her. What did she have left but her boy anyway? She ground her teeth and balled her fists and tried hard not to think of the two bodies that lay nearby. *Why not go? Why not choose safety in Tamora?* She sighed as her father's face appeared before her eyes. *Because without you and Lucan your tribe will be lost. They may not love you for it, they may even hate you for it, but you are the best chance that they have to live and prosper in a world run by the Gaians. And the one thing you have left besides your son is your duty. You have no choice.*

She looked up at Alraig, the rain still dripping from his beard, and tried to marshal her thoughts through the anger. If she went with him there would be many who might speak against her, but also many who might take her side as well. All the Dragon Legion had seen how needed the Gaians had been today, and there were headmen among the cohorts they'd brought with them. The druids were more of an uncertain factor, but Bael would probably see things her way and if Reaghan appeared from wherever he'd been chances were he would as well. There were no guarantees but there was at least some hope she would be heard.

There was danger in it for her, but far less so than there was to her people if she allowed this to escalate further. She fought back the urge to fight and wreak bloody vengeance for Meg and Owain and took a few deep breaths, praying quietly. She asked every god she knew to stay with her if they would, and then she put her hand gently on Gregor's arm.

'Stand your men down, general.'

The soldier stared at her for a beat but then nodded grimly and addressed his guards.

'Stand down.'

The legionaries sheathed their swords as one and Rhia stepped between the two who stood in front of her. She held her open hands out to Alraig and looked him in the eyes, hoping fervently that he wouldn't see her tears in the rain. Owain and Meg still lay unmoving in the mud, and Rhia fought to keep her voice from trembling.

'I am your prisoner, comrade.'

*

Gawan was oblivious to the wind and rain as he galloped his pony northwards. The water lashed at his face but he paid it no mind, simply gripping the reins hard and snarling at himself. Emeryn, a woman he had loved, was not even laid to rest and already he had betrayed her memory. In a single moment of madness or grief or simple lust he had spat in the face of someone he had once wished would bear his children. He drove his heels harder into the horse's flanks, desperate to gain more distance from the scene of his crime. The beast put on an extra burst of speed as they thudded along the dirt track.

After a lifetime of priding himself on his sense of honour he had thrown it all away, and for no reason. What did all of this say about the man who'd been named the Leaping Wolf; the man who'd sworn to serve the Gods of War with honour to the end of his days? *Did you ever really have honour in your soul to begin with?* His inner voice was dripping with contempt. *Perhaps you were just a youth too bold and stupid for his own good, and the Gadarim mistook it for nobility? Perhaps it was just pride that made you seek fair fights and work so hard to protect your precious reputation? Was it just conceit, or a wish to feel greater than others that made you think yourself so decent a man?*

Gawan couldn't find it in himself to argue back and allowed what he supposed must be his conscience to rail at him some more. *You truly think you were an honourable man before you betrayed Emeryn? What about the tribe that you betrayed in letting the Gaians take Lurian lands? What about the day you killed your own chieftain for the sake of an enemy of the Gorvicae? And today, when you let Tarwyn fight Broad Kellas instead of you and then left Emeryn so exposed that you had to kill her yourself in mercy?* The First Man gripped the leather so tight he felt his knuckles pop.

He only had a vague idea of where he was going but it was roughly north and that was all that mattered. He would probably need to head east a bit to get back on the road towards Nantwyn, but that was something he could worry about later. Right now all that mattered was distance, and he put his head down and spurred his pony on through the rain. Amidst his cursing at himself he found time to damn the old man from the woods as well. It had taken until now for him to realise the full cruelty of Emeryn's dream, and the true nature of the beast that had killed her. He gnashed his teeth and wished the old ghost was here on this road so that he could ride the bastard down, and see how damned ethereal he'd be beneath the hooves of a charging horse. Gawan strongly suspected that the old man had been responsible for the dream, and that his words to him about Rhianwyn had been meant to cause more mischief.

The thought of the Wildcat brought the image of her back to his mind and he detested himself even further as he felt the arousal was still there, nestling within the endless guilt. He took one fist from the reins and struck himself hard on the forearm. The bone ached only a little and he punched it again, harder still, seeking any form of pain to take his mind away from it. *Have you no shame? Even now as you berate yourself you think of that Caderyn bitch?* Gawan had few real memories of his mother, but the golden-haired woman had given him one lesson at least that he had always remembered; if a boy said he was sorry for something it meant he didn't do it again, otherwise the words became empty of their meaning. He scowled as he rode on and hated himself even more, knowing that for all his guilt a part of him was unrepentant.

He forced away his lust and focused on what must happen now. Even if the old man's words had contained some measure of truth, or half-truth, there was no way that he could face Rhianwyn after this. He worried fleetingly if she might tell others of his actions, and if the world would then think of him as he did himself. The Caderyn and the Gaians could boil themselves for all he cared but Boryn was still back there, as were Gwydion and Pryder. What would happen if they found out about what he had done? He shook away the fear quickly enough. Rhianwyn would not be sharing his shame with others. She was likely almost as embarrassed and confused by this as he had been and would be keen to simply forget it. And besides, she had some integrity for all her deceptions.

For a moment he wondered if he ought to have stayed long enough to give some word of support for her regarding her decision, but he didn't dwell on it. She had just won a great victory and saved her people, and the bloody Gaians had been vital in that. She had no need of him there, and in all likelihood he would only have made things worse by his stubborn need to argue about everything. Besides, he couldn't have faced being with her again.

The rain began to grow heavier and a peal of thunder rolled overhead. If Taran was angry at him tonight then Gawan could hardly blame him for it, and if Mabonac opened the earth up in front of him then he had surely earned no better fate. Nonetheless he slowed his pony a little as rocky ground gave way to grass and thickening mud. The beast was sure-footed but continuing at speed was dangerous, and he had galloped for long enough to gain some distance from his shame. *It'd serve you right if he stumbled right now and you broke your bastard neck!* He sighed, agreeing but trying to think beyond his hate. *But it will not serve your people.*

He might have just made the most dishonourable mistake in his wretched life but he was still Gorvicae, and his duty was clear. If nothing else he could hold on to the fact that he still owed all to his tribe, and he could at least still serve them as best he could. He was the First Man of his Gadarim, for now at least, and his people would expect his presence at the moot. What little amends he could make for all this could be made by getting north as soon as possible and helping them choose the best man to lead them as their new High Chieftain. Then he would step down as the First Man and pass the honour on to Duran; he and Gwydion were more worthy to be called Gadarim than he was, and he would be content to follow their lead. *Or perhaps you should go back to making horseshoes and nails?*

He couldn't see the stars above him through the clouds but he locked his gaze ahead and hoped he was travelling the right way. Rhianwyn and the Caderyn could fend for themselves well enough without him, and perhaps in time she would forget the shameful thing that he had done. Ahead of him was the north and the lands of the Gorvicae. Ahead of him lay his duty, and that at least he could try to hold on to.

Chapter 21. Undefeated

Caserach was sorely tempted just to kill Edryd and have done with it. For all his clever plans his promises had led to nothing but disaster, and choking the life out of him might at least make the captive chieftain feel a bit better. He was sitting on the floor of a cramped and leaky hut with a handful of other prisoners, miserable and dejected and ready to punch the next man who tried to speak to him. The great battle that ought to have broken the power of the Caledon had collapsed into chaos just as victory was in their grasp. And now the Breiryn had made peace with the damned Caderyn, and what living Dariniae that Caserach had left were either scattered or else stuck in here with him. *Damn Edryd and his bloody promises!*

His own original plan had been so simple; secure his position as the new chieftain by raiding some Caderyn towns and bring back tribute and glory to Niswyn. It was Edryd and his stinking scheme that had led to his approaching Asrec and his scruffy band of southerners, and turning a plan of raids into a war. In truth Caserach had fairly jumped at the chance but nonetheless, that skinny Gorvic still bore the blame. He had made it sound easy, which perhaps should have put Caserach on his guard. Few things worth having came easy. The idea was that the alliance would break both Rhianwyn and her people, and the prestige it gained him would silence any Darin who might challenge him for leadership. Caserach kicked at his heel, irritated at himself for having been so blindly eager, but he quickly transferred his anger back to Edryd again. He glared at his fellow prisoner with naked contempt.

The Gorvic was sitting across from him, not nervous exactly but avoiding his gaze. He was a man of around Caserach's age, though his blonde hair was already thinning at the crown and his beard was so pale it was almost invisible in some lights. He was slight of build with thin wrists and narrow shoulders, his chin very pointed and his nose very flat. The Darin looked at the man's skinny neck and imagined his hands clamped around it. His enemies might have taken Greyfang but Caserach had killed with bare hands before, and in this case he might actually prefer it.

Another stab of anger hit him as he thought of his sword in the hands of that Gaian-humping bitch. When Caserach had been forced to yield her First Man had taken it from him in a blatant insult to his status. The cocky bastard would not have dared behave so to another chieftain or a fellow Gadarim, and Caserach had only offered it because he'd assumed it would be refused. Yet he had taken Greyfang with barely a word, and handed it to that short-arsed sow as though she'd done something to deserve it. *As if she did anything bold or cunning today! Her precious Gaian friends were the ones who won that battle for her. Likely all she did was suck a few of their shafts to pay for it!* The memory of that black wall charging into them made him want to shiver, and he focused on his anger to chase it away.

Broad Kellas was leaning against one of the earth walls, his long legs stretched out in front of him and his longsword at his side. *He* of course had been treated with the utmost respect, and the Caderyn's First Man had waved away his massive sword when he had offered it. His wounds had been cared for, the lime washed from his hair with hot water and soap, and all he had to suffer for it was to lose a couple of bracelets. *Bloody, bastard Gadarim!* Most people revered the warrior elite like they were some kind of gods but Caserach felt nothing but scorn for them. What were they but good killers with white hair and blue tattoos? What made them so damned special among a whole race of born warriors? Caserach had been a fighter since he could barely lift a blade yet not once had he been told that he was 'worthy' of their rank. And now, when he was High Chieftain of his tribe, they still treated that bumbling giant as if Belenos shone from his arse, and had taken Greyfang from a chieftain without a word!

Caserach tried to calm himself down. In a way it was a good thing that Broad Kellas had been allowed to accompany him, even if the gesture had been two-edged. Most of the Breiryn had simply been sent along their way but, in the most patronising concession to his status the Darin could think of, their First Man had been loaned out to him as an escort up to Bryngarth. It was a hollow and insulting act on both Asrec and Rhianwyn's part, a reminder that Kyran still held him in contempt and that none of his own tribe's Gadarim would join him. What advantage there was in having the big man around was undermined by the obvious slight to him personally. Caserach's resentment was in real danger of boiling over but he fought it down with an effort and simply let his anger simmer, directing it once again towards Edryd.

The Gorvic noticed him glaring and spoke up with surprising confidence.

'There is no use in becoming angry. We knew that this might happen and plans were made in case of it.'

Caserach yearned to cross the room and punch the little bastard in the throat but he reined in the instinct for the moment. He'd not paid that much attention when the Gorvic had spoken of the backup plan. He'd been convinced that the battle would go well. With Asrec's men beside them victory had seemed inevitable, and Edryd's prattling about contingencies had merely bored him. He enjoyed a devious plan as much as anybody but the gods had always loved the strong, so why waste time listening to doubters? Now however he rationalised that a new strategy was called for, and so he forced himself to sit still and listen, though the anger still showed in his voice.

'Tell me then Edryd, what great plan does your master have for getting us out of this? Even if you have trickery of some kind to set us free, we are still in enemy land and with little enough support. Tell me, just how bloody clever is this man of yours?'

Edryd's eyes were fearful but he kept his voice steady.

'He was clever enough to anticipate Gaian involvement through Rhianwyn, and his second plan can take advantage of that.'

The Gorvic shuffled where he sat, leaning forward a little. Caserach and Idwal did the same, though Broad Kellas stayed sitting back, his flat face uninterested.

'Rhianwyn's own people may now do our work for us. Many of her headmen will turn against her because of the Gaians' intervention and they will call her to account for it. And with her ideals of a united Caledon she may well ask to be judged by *all* of them, not just the Caderyn.'

Caserach sneered at that.

'So? Your people fought alongside hers and doubtless plenty are still grateful for her defeat of Lepidus. You can offer no guarantee that the Gorvicae will turn against her.'

Edryd didn't seem discouraged and even shook his head at him. Caserach wanted to grab that chin of his and rip it sideways hard, but he kept hold of his temper and paid attention as the man spoke.

'Some will and some will not, and the same is true of the Caderyn chiefs. But you forget the third tribe of the Caledon.' Caserach frowned for a heartbeat, then his eyebrows rose as Edryd went on. 'Even after your defeat you are Ierryn's only living heir, and until a moot can be called to prove or disprove your rights you are still the High Chieftain of the Dariniae, or the closest thing there is to one. If she wishes to appear to hold all tribes of the Caledon as equals then she must honour your opinion should she be tried. If she refuses to let you speak she will harm her cause by showing prejudice in an alliance that is still in its infancy.'

Caserach felt a flutter in his gut that was equal parts hope and malice, but he kept his answer cynical all the same.

'There is much that is assumed in this clever plan of his and in any case, it still leaves us to rot here until she is tried. *If* she is tried.'

Edryd shrugged.

'He is confident enough that it will happen, though I must be gone from here soon to tell him what has occurred.'

Idwal smiled a nasty smile at the Gorvic and Caserach openly scoffed. The skinny bastard had already tried to flee after the battle but Idwal had cornered him and forced him to come with them. He was not getting away now that they were captured.

'Do you think we are fools? You give us this plan that brought us nothing but disaster, and now you think to leave us and scamper on your way?'

Broad Kellas had still not shown any interest in the discourse, but the Dariniae in the hut glared menacingly at Edryd. The lone northerner did a good job of hiding his fear.

'I have to get back to Graigarw to tell him what has happened. He must know of it before word reaches there by other means.'

Caserach curled his lip and lowered his voice.

'I trust your clever friend less and less the more I hear of him, and since you are the one who landed us in this you can bloody well stay and share the consequences.'

Edryd shuffled a little, clearly sensing the chieftain's wrath, but he kept up his argument nonetheless.

'If I am kept here then sooner or later some other Gorvic will recognise me, and our involvement will become known to all.'

Caserach wanted to tell him that his precious secrecy could go to the wolves, but then he stopped himself as his brain began to work. If it came out that he'd been a part of something like this then his tribe would see him as a conspirer and schemer, rather than as a war leader to be respected. Raiding with the Breiryn at his side was one thing, but having it known that the idea had come from some unknown Gorvic was something else. And if Edryd decided to talk then he might easily make the whole thing seem far worse than it was already, and imply that Caserach was a mere puppet for another man. *Perhaps it would be better just to kill him after all?*

He looked again at that scrawny neck and figured it would not take long to silence him once and for all. He could tell the Caderyn that they had quarrelled and he had killed him in a fair fight, and even if some Gorvic thought he recognised the corpse, the conspiracy at least would be kept a secret. *But what if there is truth in what he says? What if his master can help you to topple this traitorous bitch once and for all?*

The idea of Rhianwyn winning a battle only to fall at her own people's hands had a certain vicious appeal to it. Crimes punishable by death were rare among the Luriae, especially on the mainland, but betraying her own people would surely be one of them? And with Rhianwyn gone the Caledon would crumble, and the old days of raids and tributes would be back before ever they had left. Caserach half-smirked. It was a pity she hadn't fallen into *his* hands after the battle, but if this scheme led to her downfall then it was probably the next best thing.

Edryd might have been a straw-necked little turd but he was clearly a bright enough man because he seemed to follow Caserach's thoughts. He began to stand up as he spoke.

'There is only one man outside. I can slip away easily enough if you can cause a distraction?'

Idwal looked ready to stop him in his tracks but Caserach waved a hand at him.

'Very well. Idwal can distract people as well as anyone.'

The rangy man didn't seem pleased at letting Edryd go but he was somewhat pacified by the chance to cause some mischief. Caserach heaved himself up and enjoyed looking down at the Gorvic. Edryd was still hiding it well but he could tell he was intimidated, and the larger man took him by the throat with one hand. He squeezed a little and looked him in the eyes.

'You can go now. But if you play me false then I swear by Taran's thunder I will find you and feed you your own balls, you understand?'

That was of course, assuming it worked this time. A few years back he'd tried to do it to a Caderyn he had captured on a raid, but the bastard had thrashed and struggled so much as Idwal gelded him that he'd bled his life away before they could get his mouth opened wide enough. *I'll have to be more careful the next time I try that, not that this one seems to have much strength in him for fighting back.*

Edryd was clearly trying to appear unafraid but his words came out in a thready croak.

'I will not betray you. I swear it.'

Caserach sneered and shoved him away as he let go.

'The word of a Gorvic, and a scheming Gorvic at that?' He let out a slow breath through his nose, staring hard at Edryd. 'We shall see.'

The slender man coughed a few times and wisely said nothing, merely stepping towards the door and then waiting silently for Idwal. Caserach gave his fellow Darin a nod and the one-eared man moved to join the Gorvic.

'Do not kill our guard, Idwal. We must give them no excuse to exclude me from a trial.'

The lanky Darin seemed unimpressed but he bobbed his head even so, and Caserach went back to his old spot and sank to the floor. Better that he remain uninvolved in whatever Idwal wound up doing. He longed to fight a Caderyn as much as anyone in that hut, but if things went as Edryd promised he had to appear a well-behaved prisoner. He watched as the Gorvic prepared to leave and hoped to Morannan that he'd done the right thing. Today had been a shambles that might mean his ruin as chieftain, but if things went as Edryd said they would... he smiled to himself again. If all went as the Gorvic said, he might well have cause to be thankful that he had lost a battle today.

Chapter 22. The North

It was a long ride back to Gorvicae land, though it hadn't been as confusing as Gawan had thought it would be. Once he'd found the line of hills that ran up through Caderyn territory he'd got his bearings back fairly well, and had carried on towards the hill of Bryngarth. He'd avoided the town itself of course and had turned north again before reaching Nantwyn, paying a boatman to take him across the Silver Lock rather than ride all the way upriver to the bridge. It was taking that route more than anything else that had led him to this road, the familiar old track that led towards Green Hollow. The place that had once been his home.

The late morning sun shone on green pastures all around him, with fields dotted with grazing cows to his left and a long slope of grass on his right, leading up to a copse of ancient-looking blackwoods. The sky was as clear as it ever got at this time of year and the day promised to stay bright and dry. Camelas was clearly in a favourable mood. Ordinarily Gawan would have enjoyed the beauty of his native land, but it was lost on him today as he plodded along. He had calmed down somewhat over the long days of his ride but he was still fuming quietly at himself for all he'd done.

Day and night he thought of Emeryn, and the way she'd looked at him before the battle. He thought of Tarwyn as well, struck down by Broad Kellas while defending her. *I should have challenged him first. Why didn't I challenge him first?* He would ask himself that question over and over, and then his thoughts would go from Tarwyn back to Emeryn, screaming as her life gushed away, not even seeing him as he gave her what mercy he could. Then Rhianwyn's face would come into his mind, and he would burn with shame as he thought of her body, still wet and gleaming in the firelight. Even now he compounded his betrayal of Emeryn, no matter how hard he tried to force the image from his head. He had focus enough to sense a sword-cut without looking, to quieten his mind when other men were sick with fear, and to feel Mabonac's fire even when his body was drained with fatigue. Why did the Dragon's fire not let him drive away these thoughts?

He tried hard not to keep brooding as he rode, he could not abide men who pitied themselves, but nonetheless it gnawed away at him. Up ahead was the town of Old Cairn, the next settlement along from Green Hollow. Gawan let his pony trundle on and wondered for the hundredth time why he was coming this way at all. His duty lay at Graigarw after all and this detour would not help his people to find a chieftain. He had no desire to see his old home again so why had he not turned back by now? *Because family is a duty as well.* Gawan growled to himself. It was true that until Boryn came back north the moot could not be held anyway, but all the same he felt he ought to be prioritising it over this. Surely that was reason enough to turn around and head to the capital? *No. You are seeking excuses. Have you not done enough to shame yourself already that you now ignore your father when only a town separates you?*

Gawan didn't like that argument but unfortunately it was true. He had come so close to the western road that to not take it and see his father again had seemed discourteous at best, and cowardly at worst. He didn't want to see his brother, or the home he'd once shared with Bronwen, but he had an obligation to show respect to old Dearg, and his honour was already damaged enough. He sighed. It had been a long time since last he'd spoken to his father and they had not parted on good terms. If he was to gain *any* kind of redemption for what he had done then surely a good start would be to reconcile with him? The tribe's

295

moot would not be happening for another few days and he had no excuse at all not to go home. No excuse not to try to make amends. For a moment he thought of Tegwen but he shoved the memory away. Some things were far too broken to ever be mended.

He entered the little town from the eastern side. There were probably around the same number of homes here as there were at Green Hollow but it had always seemed like a larger place to Gawan. Perhaps it was just because he knew fewer of the people living there. For the most part the houses were of weathered grey stone but there were a couple of older ones made from wood and hard-packed earth. A broad street ran along the very centre of the settlement, leading straight through it and then on towards Green Hollow. At the other end of the town Gawan knew there was a wide-flowing stream and he decided not to stop until he reached the water. There the horse could take a drink and he could stretch his legs a while, hopefully without having had to talk to anyone.

There were people in the street and many looked up at the mounted Gadarim but beyond the usual nods of respect they largely avoided his gaze. Gawan wasn't surprised. At the best of times he wasn't a man who invited casual chatter and today was a long damned way from the best of times. Besides, he'd not stopped to bathe or wash his clothes on the long ride north and he was fairly sure his odour would not be a pleasant one. Gawan trotted on in silence as unwelcome memories came to him of the life he'd once lived so near to here, before he'd left to join Graigarw's Gadarim.

Dearg the Smith's eldest son had learned his trade and married young, somehow gaining the hand of the fairest girl in all of Green Hollow. He and his beautiful wife had built themselves their own little house, and they had awaited the birth of their child with joy, the same as any other couple. Gawan had never been a man over-given to smiles or laughter but he'd been happy in that life. He'd been at peace. And then in one day the whole thing had been shattered. His wife had left this world and the best part of Gawan had left it with her, and so great had been his despair and anger that Bronwen's sister had been forced to take charge of their baby girl, Tegwen. Harlen had said he was not fit to be a father and had left Green Hollow with Tegwen in her arms. She had been right. Gawan didn't know where they'd gone. He'd never asked.

Despite himself he pictured Bronwen as the buildings began to thin out. A lifetime of distance and the focus of Mabonac had dulled the pain a little, but it could never truly take it away. He wondered what his wife would think of the man she'd left behind in this life. He had abandoned their child, become a disgrace to his family and his people, and betrayed and killed the only woman who might have made something better of him. Harlen had been right; he would have been a dreadful father back then, but being with Emeryn had made him think it might be worth trying again. But now that chance was gone, and no more than he deserved. He tightened his grip on the reins as he realised he was drifting into self-pity again, but it did little to affect his thoughts. *Hating yourself has turned you into something you detest even more, and knowing it begets more hatred still and so on, ever onwards.*

Hi sighed and thought on as he rode, past the last house and towards the stream. Not so long ago he had found somebody who could help to fill the void that Bronwen had left behind. For so long he had just filled it with the simple joy of battle but it had been a poor substitute, and even back then he had known it. When Emeryn had come into his life he had realised it with even more clarity, and he had dared begin to hope that he might find peace. But

Emeryn was dead, and Rhianwyn was the closest thing there was to a woman in his life. And whatever the old ghost in the forest had said and whatever his own shameful visions, the Wildcat would not be a part of it for much longer. He was alone.

He dismounted and led his pony towards the gurgling stream. His legs ached a little but then they did that more and more these days when he rode for any length of time. He wasn't what a man could really call *old* but even so, he was hardly young any more either. The horse dipped its head to drink and Gawan took a skin from the saddle and eased himself down to one knee on the bank. It only made the ache in his legs that much worse but he grimaced and bore it as he re-filled the flask. The stream felt cool as it ran over his hand and he watched the water for a moment before raising his eyes to the grassy rise beyond. The closer he got to it, the more he felt himself not wanting to ride over that hill and instead to turn north and east, back towards Graigarw. His family didn't want to see him anyway, why inflict himself upon them just to feel better for having done it?

Gawan almost snarled at himself for his indecision and turned his eyes back to the waterskin. It was filled by now and he drew his hand from the stream, stoppering the flask before replacing it on his saddle. It was only as he stood that he saw the white-haired man approaching, leading a decrepit-looking pony by its reins. Just behind him Gawan spotted the familiar old wagon, as grey and weathered as ever but still somehow in one piece. Anryn the Bachelor raised a hand to him in greeting, and before he knew it Gawan had raised his own in return.

Anryn the Bachelor was more properly called Anryn the Brewer, and was famed across half of Gorvicae land as the maker of the finest dark beer in the north. But locals had known him as the bachelor for as long as Gawan could remember since he was apparently... not over-fond of women. When Gawan had first found out about that he'd been wary of him for a while, but it hadn't taken him long to accept it. Anryn was a good man; a fine teller of tales, and a ready friend to anyone who wanted one. The image of what he got up to might make Gawan feel uncomfortable, but he'd decided long ago that what he did in his own house was his own business.

He moved closer to the stream and Gawan saw he had not changed much. He still wore the same cream-coloured tunic that reached to halfway down his thighs, and his brown breeches still sported the same green patch over one knee. Around his waist his broad belt was straining against a paunch but otherwise he seemed as strong and hale as ever. His shoulders were still broad from carrying his casks and the only lines upon his face were the kind a man got from much smiling. Indeed, the only real signs of his aging were his white hair and beard, the former an unruly mop while the latter was trimmed short and neat. He led his horse to water and beamed merrily at the warrior.

'Gawan my boy!' He kept one hand on the reins and clasped his wrist with the other. 'Karanon's blessings.'

Gawan remembered how Anryn's family had come from the other side of the Gedran Range, and how he always paid respects first and foremost to the Mountain Lord. He replied politely.

'And with you, Anryn.'

In his current state of mind he was in no real mood to chat but the older man went on, still smiling broadly.

'How about a drink for our First Man and a hero of Nantwyn? I have some casks of Geidfran Dark that rival any other of my making.'

Gawan tried not to sound rude as he responded.

'I am not stopping.'

Anryn didn't seem to pick up on his lukewarm tone and nodded towards his pony.

'You are stopping long enough for *him* to drink,' he tossed Gawan the reins of his own horse, 'you can stop long enough to share one with me.'

He strode off towards his cart without another word. Gawan let the horses drink for a while and pressed his lips together. Anryn was a decent man and he didn't want to offend him, but at the same time the fact that the brewer thought *he* was a good man only made him feel that much worse. But it was too late to turn him down since only moments later the white-haired man was walking back again, a cask held on one shoulder and a horn cup in each hand.

Gawan led the horses a few paces upstream to where a young willow overhung the water. He tossed both sets of reins over the nearest branch, though he doubted either beast had plans to wander; his own pony was as tired as he was from his journey and Anryn's looked like a swift trot might finally finish him off. The bachelor set down his cask and then propped it with a stone, leaning the barrel over before turning the little tap to fill the cups. He handed one to Gawan without a word and then tipped out a tiny measure from his own cup into the earth. Anryn was an old-fashioned man in many ways and Gawan dutifully copied his gesture, gifting a portion to the gods.

They took their first draughts in silence and Gawan had to admit, it was damned good stuff. It wasn't just that it was strong; it had a rich and heavy taste that made him think of burnt grain, with what felt like a hint of chestnuts in the background. He knew at once that it would go well with some nicely blackened pork and he actually felt his stomach rumble at the thought. He nodded to Anryn who smiled back at him, clearly well aware of how fine his beer was but too modest to say it aloud. Gawan knew he wasn't seeking praise and kept his comment simple.

'It's good.'

The brewer nodded back and they both took a second draught. Gawan surprised himself by feeling almost relaxed as he drank, but the feeling was soon gone as Anryn spoke again.

'So, are you back to see your brother?'

The thought of Rylion wasn't a welcome one and Gawan's answer came out harsh.

'No.'

Once again Anryn either didn't notice or didn't care about the Gadarim's tone and he carried on.

'You ought to go and see him Gawan, it has been a long time.'

Unasked-for advice was one of the many things that grated on Gawan's nerves but he made the effort not to be disrespectful.

'I do not wish to talk of it.'

Anryn took another drink and tilted his head noncommittally.

'You are your own man I suppose, but you remember the tale of Holew and Hylwr?'

As a youth Gawan had enjoyed Anryn's stories but he was in no mood to hear them right now. He vaguely recalled that the tale was about two brothers who had quarrelled and wound up on opposing sides in a war, and by the time one of them decided that he wished to reconcile their differences, his brother was already dead. Of course, with Rylion it wasn't quite so simple. For a start Rylion had always assumed that he was second-best in their father's eyes, even though he wasn't, and Gawan's ascension to the Gadarim had only fuelled his bitterness. On top of this he had once been fond of Bronwen when they were young, and it had broken his heart first to see her wed another man and then to see her die. Added to *that* was his resentment that Gawan had abandoned their family home to go to Graigarw, seeing it as a betrayal of their father for Baercban. *The man you later killed.*

All in all it was no simple story that one talk would easily solve, and Gawan knew that Rylion didn't want to have that talk any more than he did. He tried not to think about the father he'd be letting down if he backed out of going home now.

'I know the tale, and I will speak to my brother when I find the time.' He hated himself for hiding behind it but he spoke before his better self could stop him. 'But I need to get to the moot for the new chieftain.'

Anryn nodded his white head as Gawan growled internally. *What kind of man are you anyway, to run from a simple talk with your family? After all you have done, can you not at least face this?*

The brewer seemed to agree with him, not that Gawan appreciated it much.

'That too is most important of course.'

Gawan knew he ought to say something to acknowledge the agreement but he couldn't think of anything and hid his self-loathing with a drink. The delicious beer had somehow lost a great deal of its flavour, and Anryn continued speaking as he drank.

'You know, I am planning to head over to Graigarw myself; they offer a fine price there for Geidfran Dark. Would you care for a companion?'

For a brief moment Gawan wondered if people might mistake him for Anryn's lover if they travelled together, but he dismissed the idea quickly. If nothing else, anyone who knew enough of Anryn to know his tastes would also know that he and Gelion had shared a house for more than twenty winters, and he was as loyal as any husband to his wife. *And more so than some.* His only real worry was the prospect of conversation on the way, but then that might be something Gawan was in need of. He wasn't about to start bleating to Anryn about his woes but it would at least get him back into the habit of talking again. If he was to be of any use in this moot then he would have to be able to converse with people without dwelling on his own selfish problems.

'I would be glad to have you along.'

He didn't smile at him but Anryn seemed to acknowledge the sincerity, and he beamed broadly enough for the both of them.

'Well that is excellent then. You can hitch your pony to the cart and ride along to spare your legs.'

Gawan nodded, quietly grateful for a respite from all the riding. The pair collected their horses and headed back to the cart, and Gawan removed the saddle and bags before tying his pony to a beam. It wasn't until they were both seated and the wagon's wheels were rolling that Anryn spoke again of his plans.

'Of course, it's not just Graigarw men who love my beer, but almost all that I have here is bound for them.' He nodded at his stock behind them. 'I just need to make one stop along the way.'

Gawan looked at him and knew the answer as soon as the question was asked.

'Where are we stopping?'

'Green Hollow.'

*

They came into sight of the village just as Belenos was passing his zenith. Anryn had chattered a little on the journey but Gawan had not responded in kind. It was not so much in anger at him for his bringing him on this road, but for the reminder that Gawan himself had been so ready

303

to turn back. *So much for your commitment to make amends with your family!* What answers he gave the older man were short and grumbled but Anryn didn't seem to mind, nodding along pleasantly with a smile on his face. Gawan had spent most of the trip so far either wanting to shove him from the cart or else feeling guilty about wanting to do it.

Green Hollow was named for the shallow bowl in which the village lay; a cluster of houses built around a narrow stream that wound down from the hills. Even in autumn the grass was green enough to put Gawan's cloak to shame, and the fields were dotted with sheep and goats as they grazed and bleated in their pastures. A little way from the main huddle of buildings he saw the familiar stone house in which he had been born, with the old workshop still standing beside it, weathered but solid. Dearg the Smith had been the ninth man of his line to take up the blacksmith's hammer, and Gawan knew some of the tools inside were old enough to have been used by his grandfather.

From the lack of smoke emanating from the forge it seemed that Dearg was not at his anvil today, though puffs of grey were coming out of house's chimney beside it. At first Gawan wondered why his father was not working, but then remembered he was not a young man any more. In all likelihood he was leaving most of the work to Rylion by now, and hopefully that meant his brother was away somewhere, trading their iron for silver.

The village grew steadily closer and Anryn slowed the cart.

'I have some casks to deliver to Lann before we can move on. I can meet you by the well once you are done.'

Gawan nodded to him and slid from the seat. The track was firm beneath his boots and Anryn spoke again as the cart rolled on.

'Try not to butt heads with Rylion now, he is your family remember.'

It was maybe a hopeful thing to say, but then Gawan was quietly hoping to avoid him altogether. He nodded his head again at the white-haired man and started off towards the blacksmith's house. He couldn't help but notice the smaller, neglected-looking building opposite the workshop, and a pang of painful memory shot through him. Once, long ago, that house had been a home for a man and his wife; a humble little place but a home nonetheless. Gawan shoved the memories aside and strode towards the larger house with its smoking chimney. He would pay his respects to his father and then leave about his duty. It would not be a pleasant experience, Dearg son of Aur was a stubborn old goat, but it had to be done and best that it be over with quickly, he supposed. He was within ten long strides of the place when the door creaked slowly open, and Gawan bit back a curse as a hard-faced man emerged from within.

He had the same solid build and low brow as Gawan himself, though where Gawan's hair was dark and tangled, this man's was golden blonde and hung straight down past his shoulders. *Like our mother's.* He wore a bluish-green tunic and a pair of checked trews, and on seeing his visitor his face took on the look of a man who'd just drunk his own urine. Rylion barely spared his brother a glance and continued around towards the workshop. Gawan didn't particularly want to follow him but it was too late for avoiding now, and he might as well just grip the thorn and do it. He strode after his brother and spoke to his back, his greeting simple.

'Rylion.'

The younger man only turned around when he reached the open front of the workshop, and that was only to fetch

305

a tin pot from its hook. He eyed his brother with obvious malice but he kept his voice dull and disinterested.

'Come back have you?'

Gawan felt some of his habitual guilt fade away as irritation flared in him. He was an impatient man with most people but Rylion brought it out in him more than anyone else ever could.

'Nothing like coming home to a warm welcome.'

His brother wasn't impressed by the sarcasm and pushed past him on his way back to the house.

'This stopped being your home twenty winters ago.'

Gawan fought to keep himself civil, he *was* here to make amends after all.

'I did not come here for a fight, Rylion. I just wanted to pay my respects to Father before I go to the chieftain's moot.'

The blonde man didn't break his stride and spoke in the same monotone voice.

'Off again of course. Best of fortune talking to da though, he's dead.'

He said it with absolutely no emotion and simply kept on walking towards the house. Gawan's steps faltered. Dead? Dearg had been a strong man his whole life, even after his hair had turned grey. When last he'd seen his father he'd been as robust as ever and that was only... Gawan stopped himself. How long had it been since he'd last come here? How many winters had come and gone since last he'd seen his only parent? Rylion was still sounding disinterested as he spoke over his shoulder.

'I buried him just over there,' he nodded his head vaguely eastwards, 'you can say something to his grave if it makes you feel better.'

Gawan knew that he was doing it to rile him and deny him the simple right to grieve for their father, and he took his brother by the shoulder and spun him around. Rylion glared at him but Gawan was just as angry.

'Why did you not send word to me?'

Rylion sneered and shoved him in the chest. Gawan might be the greater swordsman but Rylion was easily his equal in size, and the First Man was forced back a pace.

'Maybe because you were too busy with your precious chieftain to ever come here, and even after you killed him over some Caderyn bastard you decided to stay with them rather than return to your own people.'

His voice was beginning to gain some feeling. Gawan's first reaction was to be impressed that word of what happened had reached him so quickly, but then it was like their mother had always said; *gossip outruns the wind*. His next reaction was simple anger and he squared up to his brother again, looking him in the eyes.

'Charging Bull was a fine man, he deserved justice.'

Rylion looked ready to spit at the mention of the Caderyn's name, but he settled for another sneer.

'Our father was a proud Gorvic his whole life, the Caderyn were his enemies.' He twitched his lip. 'But then if it meant avoiding your family for the sake of a brawl, I don't suppose you asked too many questions about who you'd be fighting with, Gaians or southerners alike.'

Gawan set his jaw. He had plenty to be ashamed of it was true, but siding with the Caledon was very different to fighting beside Lepidus' legions. He had never truly wanted to in the first place but Baercban had insisted it was the best thing for their people. He had been wrong. Baercban hadn't been a wicked man, but he'd been weak at heart and had sired an even weaker son, and they had grasped at a foolish chance in their weakness. Their deaths were no loss to the Gorvicae. Rylion spoke again before Gawan could say anything, clearly getting into his stride.

'I mean, you let Harlen take away your only child without a thought...'

Gawan's gorge rose further and he shoved his brother hard.

'What do you know of it? What do you know of my thoughts for my daughter?'

His anger was starting to bubble over. He might have let Tegwen go but it hadn't been the easy choice that Rylion was making out. The blonde man righted himself and faced up to his brother.

'I at least know where she is, which is a damned sight more than you know or care!'

Gawan might have been surprised by that but a flash of anger quickly dissipated it. His brother was obviously trying to provoke him, and if that was what he wanted then so be it. He thumped his open hand against Rylion's chest again, hissing out his answer.

'Liar!'

His brother kept his footing this time and shoved back again, just as hard. Gawan rolled with it but all the same he was rocked onto his heels. Rylion's face twisted into a snarl.

'Is it so hard to imagine a man keeping in contact with those of his blood? Or perhaps it *is* hard for you?'

Gawan squared up to him again, baring his teeth.

'You *lie!*'

Rylion gave him a parody of a smile.

'Do I? You could go and see for yourself if you had the nerve; she lives at Ymlan Pass, or did until a year ago.' Gawan blinked and it was enough to make Rylion continue. 'Harlen told me she went off to fight when the Gaians came again, and unlike you I was planning on looking for her. You might not care a dog's turd for your child but *I* wished to make sure my only family is still alive.'

Hate was dripping from his words but Gawan's mind was whirring. Even stranger than finding his father was dead or hearing what Rylion knew about Tegwen, was the notion that she was old enough to *fight*. In his mind she had always been that tiny, featureless bundle that he'd never understood, or else a vague picture in his head of a little girl who wouldn't recognise him if she saw him. But of course Tegwen was no little girl anymore. Gods above she was old enough to be a mother herself by now! And she was old enough to go to war. *Perhaps old enough to die in one.*

Rylion seemed to be enjoying his reaction and carried on, unleashing years of pent-up resentment.

'But then she's been dead in your eyes for years hasn't she, just as da might as well have been? Have you even spared one thought for her or for Bronwen while you've been away fighting for our enemies? Or were you too busy enjoying life as the whipped dog of Baercban and that Gaian bitch...'

Gawan's fist crashed into his brother's cheek before either of them knew what was happening. The older man's face was bright with rage and all thoughts of guilt were burned away as he felt the blow slam home. Rylion was no weakling but the punch caught him off guard and he stumbled into the workshop's wall. He recovered himself in an eyeblink and hurled himself towards his brother. Gawan's hands came up and two heavy blows bounced from his forearms, but then Rylion threw an uppercut that sliced through Gawan's guard to thud hard into his chin.

The Gadarim staggered a pace and Rylion didn't let him recover. The blonde man charged in low and grabbed his brother by the waist, driving him back across the grass. Gawan twisted sharply and hauled him over his thigh, sending him tumbling with the force of his own

309

momentum. The throw was fast but it was clumsy, and the younger man managed to keep hold of him as he fell, dragging his brother down into the dirt along with him. The two rolled a few times and Rylion wound up on top, pinning Gawan down with his legs. The Gadarim managed to keep his arms from being trapped and he held them up beside his head as Rylion hammered blows down on him. The punches were strong but they mostly struck his torso and limbs, and Gawan simply grunted and took the punishment. Rage was still burning in him but Gawan could no more forget how to fight than a bird could forget how to fly, and even pinned in place he knew exactly what he was doing. There were limits to how much damage empty hands could do without striking the head, and when a man was on the attack was when he made himself most vulnerable.

Rylion was pounding down at him for only a heartbeat or two before he left his brother an opening, and Gawan exploited it with ruthless efficiency. One arm, slightly sluggish in withdrawing from its strike, was suddenly grabbed by the pinned man, and before he knew what was happening Rylion was being rolled to his back, and Gawan's elbow slammed into his nose. Gawan hit him twice more and then shifted his position, holding himself across his brother with his weight on the other man's sternum. He pushed one hand down on Rylion's cheek and drove his knee into the younger man's ribs. He could feel his brother coughing but he didn't stop, kicking him again, and then again, forcing more air out of his lungs.

The fight was out of him, it was obvious, but Gawan couldn't stop himself. He swung his leg back across to hold him pinned and started raining blows down into Rylion's face. Didn't he know what he'd been through? Didn't he realise that all he'd ever done he'd done for his tribe and to make their father proud? He'd fought and bled and he'd lost *everything,* and now his own brother was spitting in his face when he came to make amends with his family! Rylion was twitching beneath him but had no strength to defend himself, and bright blood began to drench his blonde beard. Gawan might well have killed him then and there had it not been for that sight.

In a flash he saw Emeryn again, red blood in her golden hair as she screamed her life away, and he rocked back as if kicked by a mule. He toppled sideways and fell awkwardly, coming up onto one knee. He was shaking. Rylion's blood seemed to be everywhere, his hands were soaked in it, and for a moment Gawan thought that he would vomit. *This man is your family. This blood is your blood. After everything you've lost, will you throw this away too?* He stared down at the red on his hands as Rylion groaned softly to himself. *This blood may still live in your daughter as well. Would you greet her by telling her of how you killed her uncle? Is your foolish pride and anger worth so much?*

It took a moment but he managed to steady his trembling limbs and then slowly shuffled back towards his brother. Their father was dead, so was Bronwen and so was Emeryn, and his precious Gadarim honour was in tatters. But perhaps with Rylion he might start to rebuild something of what he'd lost, assuming it wasn't already too late. The blonde man was still breathing, the tough bastard was even starting to move as if to sit up, but he was in no condition to keep on fighting. Ordinarily Gawan revelled in any victory over an opponent, but all he felt now was a sickish feeling laced with shame. For so long he'd been so confident that he could fight his way through anything. *But not everything can be solved by fighting over it.*

Rylion's eyes were swollen but open, and Gawan took care not to seem aggressive. He kept his own eyes locked on his brother's and slowly extended his hand, swallowing his pride as he spoke.

'I am sorry.'

Rylion blinked but didn't move and Gawan kept his hand stretched out to him.

'You are right, I should not have let my daughter go. I should not have left you and Father here, ignored, for so long. And I should not be blaming you for what I have done wrong. I am sorry.'

The younger man kept staring at him and Gawan tried another approach. Anryn had been trying to tell him something earlier but he'd been too stupid and stubborn to listen to him.

'With Father gone all we have is each other. I have made enough enemies, Rylion. I would sooner have a brother instead.'

Rylion kept on looking at him for what felt like a long time but eventually he shifted to a sitting position. He was in pain, he had to have been, but his face betrayed no sign of it.

'Will you see Tegwen, and be a father to her?'

His voice was thick with blood and some of it dribbled from his mouth as he spoke. Gawan felt his stomach twist but he kept his eyes up.

'I shall, if she will have me.'

The idea was frightening, far more so than any battle he'd seen, but he knew it was the only answer to give. He had done enough harm for two lifetimes; it was time to start trying to do some good. Rylion waited for a long breath before clasping wrists with him and squeezing tight.

'If that is true, then you have a brother.'

Gawan felt the beginnings of a smile threaten his face but he held it back as he answered.

'I must still attend the moot, that is my duty, but the moment it is done...'

312

Rylion shook his head and for a moment Gawan thought he would start arguing again, but instead he answered calmly.

'Father would want you to do what is right by the Gorvicae. Go to your moot. But you *will* go to Ymlan once it is done.'

Gawan nodded his head.

'I...'

But Rylion squeezed his forearm tighter and pulled him in close, locking eyes with him again. His face was a mess of blood but his expression was pure resolve.

'And I know that you will go there, because I will go there with you. I am your brother for now Gawan, but if you let your daughter down again then I swear by Taran's hammer you will wish that you had killed me.'

Chapter 23. Graigarw

The mountains to their left had been getting lower for two days before they finally caught sight of Graigarw, and it was most of another morning before they reached it. The Gorvicae's capital was built on a round and rocky hill at the end of the Gedran Range, the last real high ground before the land opened out into a plain. There were some homes at the hill's base but many more were built higher up the slope, where the terrain made them more difficult to attack. There was almost no deep soil at the top and so the town had no ditch around it, instead settling for a palisade of worn-looking wood. Gawan looked up at the town that for years had been the closest thing he had to a home and felt no sense of comfort as he approached. Graigarw had never felt welcoming exactly but for years it had represented the centre of what Gawan believed in; the solidity and strength of the Gorvicae tribe. Now it was just another hillfort full of bickering people, where a bunch of arguing headmen would compete for who would win the chieftain's chair.

He frowned to himself as they passed the first of the houses, lost in his thoughts. It was still strange thinking that his father was gone, but it wasn't his death that was adding weight to the First Man's burden. It was that their last words together had been spoken in anger, and it only made his thoughts of Emeryn that much more raw and painful. To lose them was bad enough, but to have parted like that... Gawan could count on his hands how many times he'd apologised for something, but for those two he'd have done so in a moment had he only known what was to come. But it was too late for that now.

He might have slid into real despair again had he been riding alone, and he was strangely grateful for his travelling companions. The simple act of conversation took his mind from his own roiling guilt, and once or twice he'd even smirked at some comment of Anryn's. Things were still tense between him and his brother but they were at least talking now and then, and Anryn was doing a fine job of keeping them going. When he'd first seen them after the fight he had railed at them both for it, one of the few times that Gawan had ever heard him raise his voice, but after their talking-to he had become his friendly self again, and the three had enjoyed an almost pleasant few days. The old brewer was quick to smile and even quicker with a jest, and had something about him that made him an exception to Gawan's general attitude of impatience with cheery people.

The wagon rolled on along the street between the houses, the sons of Dearg riding their ponies on either side. Gawan was glad they hadn't had to share a seat on the cart together. For all that they were on their way to reconciliation, the real test would come when they saw Tegwen again, and Rylion would be uncertain of him until then.

The ground began to slope upwards and Gawan couldn't help but be impressed by Anryn's pony. The beast looked like its *grandchildren* would be too old for hard work yet it was sure-footed and steady on the rocky ground, drawing the wagon up the hill without any sign of effort. The palisade was set about halfway up the slope but the great gates were wide open, and they passed through them without delay.

As they carried on up towards the main part of the town Gawan's mind went back to some of the conversations he'd had on the way here. Rylion hadn't been friendly with him exactly but his brother had been open and honest enough and had filled him in on all he knew about Tegwen's life so far. It seemed that he and Harlen had kept in contact via her cousin Orel, who travelled through the territory peddling silver trinkets to various clans. Tegwen had lived fairly happily in Ymlan as far as he could tell, with Harlen and her husband raising her as a sister to their own brood. She had not wed so far as Rylion knew but had grown up strong and lively, with a talent for riding and an eagerness for battle. She had apparently been present at the fight against the Gaians at White Ridge, and Gawan wondered if he might have seen her there and not known it, or if she had seen him there but never approached him.

It was so strange. A part of him felt a tiny glimmer of pride that his daughter was a keen fighter, but he scolded himself for daring to feel so. It wasn't as if she'd had him there as an example to look up to. *All Gorvicae are warriors born! She has made herself one with no help from you.* He pressed his lips together and brooded on that a little as they climbed further up into the town. The buildings were clustered close together but he could already see the longhall, set right at the top of the rocky hill. Anryn drew his ancient pony to a halt and jerked his chin towards it.

'I take it you are headed up there?'

Gawan brought his mount to a stop and nodded.

'They will need to know that I am here.'

Anryn nodded back before turning to the other brother.

'Very well. Rylion, you can give me a hand with these?'

He gestured to the casks on the wagon. The blonde man dipped his head.

'Of course.'

Anryn smiled.

'Very well, we will get this lot unloaded over at Estyn's place and meet you later. Whereabouts is your home here again?'

Gawan would hardly have called it a home but he did have a modest little house up near the longhall, and he gestured vaguely in that direction.

'Up at the top just south of the hall, it's the last house before the ground slopes down.'

Anryn nodded again.

'We shall meet you there later then. Camelas guide you at the moot.'

Gawan bowed his head and touched a finger to his lips, more out of respect for Anryn than anything else. The moot would go the way it went and if Camelas was to have a say in it, it would not be via a disgraced Gadarim. He dismounted and tied the pony's reins to the cart, taking only his cloak and sword with him. The top of the hill was unclimbable even for the most sure-footed beast, and Anryn would see it properly housed and watered. He exchanged a brief nod with Rylion, courteous if still not quite brotherly, and turned towards the longhall. The ground became even steeper as he walked this way and soon he was climbing the rough steps that had been hewn in the rocky ground. Behind him he heard the cart begin to squeak away into the town but he didn't look back. He had a task to focus on.

He pushed away the mixture of nerves and excitement he felt at the prospect of soon finding Tegwen, and even shoved down his constant guilt about Emeryn and Rhianwyn. Right now his duty to the tribe had to come first, once he was done with it he could find his daughter and perhaps atone for some of his shameful deeds by becoming a father to his child. *Assuming she will have me.* He pushed that thought away too as he approached the great longhall of his people. Fears and shames and plans could wait, right now he had to keep his mind clear. The steep steps finally came to an end and he trudged on towards the long, low building. There was nobody standing watch outside the door, and Gawan opened it without a pause and stepped inside.

The benches of the long hall had been moved close to the walls, leaving a large expanse of scrubbed wood in the centre of the room. It was well lit by the orange light of the firepit before the high table, though nobody was sitting up there at present and Baercban's chair stood empty. Instead the dozen or so men were standing as they argued, all so absorbed in the discussion that no-one noticed Gawan entering the hall. It seemed the dogs that normally loitered about the place had been taken outside, otherwise at least one of them would have given him away by coming to greet him. Gawan tended to like the dogs here more than he liked most people, and the feeling had always been mutual. He stood and watched quietly for a few moments, recognising the most frequent speakers as the three principle candidates to be the tribe's new chieftain.

The youngest was a man perhaps eight or ten summers' Gawan's junior, middle-sized and brown-haired. His beard was trimmed close to a rather pointed chin and his cheekbones were high and sharp. He was dressed in a grey tunic with his green cloak still slung over one shoulder, a silver pin holding it in place. This was Taliesyn, the headman of Oaken Bridge.

Glaring at him as if he'd just caught the younger man ploughing his sister was the tallest and broadest of the trio of chiefs. He was around Gawan's own age with dark hair, dark eyes and a fearsome scowl. His beard looked as dense as a thornbush and his arms were thick with muscle, his massive fists clenched tight. He wore a sleeveless wolf-fur coat over a brown shirt that strained to contain his chest. Karadoc, the headman of Black Harbour, had the look of a man who was always ready for violence, and was probably keen to get on with it as soon as possible. Gawan almost smirked. He recognised his own kind.

The eldest of the trio was Boryn, looking much as he had done when Gawan had seen him last. The Gadarim hoped quietly that his sudden departure from Moon Ridge hadn't caused any undue problems for the old chief; his face seemed grave enough as it was. The two younger chiefs continued their argument in front of him, with Boryn frowning but not interrupting them.

'You whine like an old woman, Taliesyn. It seems quite simple to me; we have headmen here now, all of them men of good reputation. Let us simply call a moot and have done with this.'

Karadoc's voice was rough and harsh and Gawan could tell that Taliesyn was trying hard to keep his own words calm, even if a touch of sarcasm slipped through.

'I see. And it is coincidence I suppose that most of those men happen to be friends of yours?'

Karadoc shrugged his shoulders.

'It is no fault of mine that *your* friends have been lazy in coming here.'

Once again Gawan saw Taliesyn struggling to hold back an angry answer.

'Most of those chiefs who are not yet here are absent because they went south to fight Lepidus' legions and have yet to return. Many of them lost their lives in that fight.'

Karadoc opened his mouth to comment but Boryn spoke quietly through his thick moustache.

'May they cross the bridge unharmed.'

He placed a hand over his heart and the other men there copied him, echoing the blessing as they did.

'May they cross unharmed.'

Gawan touched his fingers to his chest but merely thought the words in his head. He wanted to keep watching a little longer before he was noticed. The moment the response had been given Karadoc spoke again, the anger plain in his voice.

'Do you say that I did *not* fight? Where were…'

But once again Boryn cut him off. He didn't speak loudly but the big chief stopped and the others turned their eyes to the elder man.

'Peace! No-one is questioning your valour Karadoc. But the fact remains that there are those whose voices ought to be heard in this who are not yet here.'

Karadoc's lip curled beneath his beard.

'I see no reason for all this delay for their sake, the choice before them is obvious.'

Gawan spotted Hywel the druid standing a little way off and the holy man added his voice to the discussion.

'No matter how the choice is viewed Karadoc, each headman of the tribe has a right to be heard, and we will not deny them that right for your impatience.'

Karadoc scowled at the druid but didn't dare to contradict him. Gawan found himself thinking on the choice the headmen would have and despite what Karadoc seemed to think, the decision that faced them would not be a simple one. All three men could claim some kind of relation to Baercban, either by blood or by marriage, all three had proven themselves in combat, and all three were experienced chiefs of their own clans. Candidates at a chieftain's moot were generally selected based on their age, their reputation, and how large a territory they were accustomed to running. Taliesyn might be young but Oaken Bridge was a large settlement and he had been an effective headman there for some years now. Karadoc was more senior but Black Harbour was not nearly so large a place and Boryn, though the eldest of them all, was chief of only a very small clan. Each one had a fairly good reputation and the decision of the druids and headmen would not be easy. And of course, Gawan would have his say as well.

There were rumblings among the other men in the hall, most of them clustered together in two groups on either side of the room. Gawan felt his brow furrow. Lurian methods of choosing leaders were supposed to be simple, but this looked like it might become a complex and divisive affair. *Have they seen too much of the Gaians and their infighting? Have they forgotten what it is to be Gorvicae?* He found his lip twitching in annoyance. Perhaps it had always been this way when a moot was called, and Gawan had just been too blind to see it. He sighed quietly. Say what you would for the Wildcat, she at least encouraged unity in her people.

The thought of Rhianwyn threatened to bring his guilt back to the fore and he decided it was time to show himself. He walked out from the shadow of the door and approached the group of chiefs. Hywel was the first to see the Gadarim and he turned to face him, nodding quietly. The other men saw the gesture and they too looked to the door. Boryn was smiling at him, Taliesyn looked uncertain, and Karadoc's face if anything grew even surlier. Gawan bowed politely to the druid but made a point of not doing so to the chiefs. Until he handed it to Duran he was still the First Man, and it was clear that these bickerers needed a Gadarim to keep them in line. He cast his eyes over the group and spoke in a clear voice.

'Good day, comrades.'

Hywel was the first to answer, closely followed by Boryn.

'Welcome home, First Man.'

'It is good to see you.'

The elder chief walked up and clasped wrists with him as the druid continued to speak.

'We shall be glad of your voice in the chieftain's moot.'

There were more rumblings from the chiefs and Karadoc stepped forward but then Hywel spoke again, this time addressing them all. For a moment it looked as if the big man might cut across him but he held himself back, settling for a glare.

'There is much to discuss but as has been said, not all who ought to be here have yet arrived. We shall speak again tonight about how the moot should be arranged once they are here.'

Both Taliesyn and Karadoc looked like they wanted to add a comment but this time Boryn seized the initiative before they could say anything.

'Well said, father.' He turned to Gawan. 'I hope you will be able to join us, Gawan?'

The First Man knew what was required of him and he bowed his head. He didn't really want to have to listen to more of this arguing but it had to be done and he would do it.

'Of course.'

Hywel gave a tiny gesture that made it clear the current meeting was over.

'Excellent. We shall look forward to it.'

Some of the chiefs in the hall looked annoyed at their discussion being halted so abruptly while others, Boryn among them, looked relieved. Even from the little that Gawan had heard it was clear that nothing had been accomplished so far, and he doubted if any resolution would have been reached had they been allowed to argue on for longer. The little group began to move amongst themselves to share parting pleasantries before heading for the doors. Most of them exchanged nods or clasped wrists with him as they left, some with more enthusiasm than others. His position and reputation had made him a figure of fear and respect, but Gawan knew perfectly well that he was not well-*liked* among the chiefs. Not that he cared; he was hardly that keen on himself.

Boryn's friendly smile was the most genuine of them, closely followed by Hywel, though his expression was far more subtle.

'I would speak to you before we reconvene this evening my friend; we have been most concerned for you since

Moon Ridge. I take it you will be staying at your old house?'

Gawan nodded.

'Yes.'

He wasn't really in the mood to chat with Hywel about where he'd been and why but he was a druid and he could hardly tell him no. The holy man nodded back.

'Very well, I shall visit you shortly if I may?'

It was a rhetorical question but Gawan dipped his head all the same.

'Of course.'

The druid smiled at him a little and began walking towards the doors, his white robe flapping at his heels. Gawan frowned and waited a moment before turning to follow him. A part of him was wishing that Duran was already the First Man and that all of this could just be made his problem, but he slapped himself down for the notion at once. *He* was the First Man of his tribe and he had his duties. However inconvenient they might be.

*

Gawan's house at Graigarw was square rather than round, having been converted from an old storeroom that had once served the chieftain's longhall. It wasn't as warm as most houses but it was spacious enough to have two good-sized rooms, and the four men now sat around the big table in the front one. Ale, chicken and fresh bread had been brought in from the hall, and Gawan, Rylion and Anryn had sat in silence as they ate. Hywel had arrived when they were midway through their meal and they had naturally invited him to join them. The druid had accepted

324

a horn of water and some bread, and seemed contented to nibble quietly until the rest of them had finished. Once they had, Gawan flicked his eyes from the druid to his guests but Hywel smiled, reading his thoughts.

'Your friends may stay as we talk, Gawan. There should be no secrecy in the choosing of our chieftain.'

Gawan thought he detected a hint of impatience in his voice, but it wasn't directed at them. He felt glad that he wouldn't have to ask the others to leave them alone. Anryn was a good friend and he didn't want Rylion to feel excluded. He decided to be direct.

'Alright then father, who do you believe should take Baercban's chair?'

A line appeared between the holy man's thick eyebrows and he pressed his lips together before he spoke.

'It is difficult to say. Taliesyn is very young and I am uncertain of him, while Karadoc is headstrong and stubborn. Since Taliesyn has declared himself in favour of the Caledon and Karadoc is firmly against it, both are men likely to cause division among the Gorvicae. Boryn would of course make a wise chieftain for us all, but for one small problem.'

Rylion asked the question before Gawan could.

'What is that, father?'

The druid shrugged.

'He does not want to be.'

Rylion frowned but Gawan understood. Boryn was only standing at the moot so that a voice of reason might be heard; the old chief was content enough where he was. The two brothers looked down into their cups, neither one quite sure what to say. Beside them, Anryn spoke up.

'Have you *seen* anything regarding all this, father?'

325

The subtle emphasis made it plain what he referred to, and from another man it might have seemed an impertinent question. But Anryn's face and voice displayed obvious respect and Hywel bowed his head a little in acknowledgement.

'I have tried to see into this, comrades, and I confess it is not clear to me. When I look on young Taliesyn my fear is of his being too much influenced by others. With Karadoc I see the danger of his rekindling old enmities as a way to prove his own strength.'

Gawan nodded slowly. Taliesyn, for all his experience, was still very young for such an honour, and if he did indeed favour the Caledon that could be both good and bad. Unity before the Gaians was vital of course, but many would resent the alliance and it would be hard work to convince them of its wisdom. On top of that Taliesyn had fought only a few battles, and with the Dariniae in chaos the Gorvicae needed a strong leader with a good fighting reputation. Karadoc could be just that, but he was a hard and unbending man, and Gawan remembered how he resented not being named to the Gadarim. He would still carry a younger man's need to prove himself which could lead to all manner of trouble.

Rylion interrupted his thoughts but he addressed his words to Hywel.

'You say Karadoc would end our union with the Caderyn, would that be so bad?'

He didn't say it with any anger but Gawan knew he felt strongly about this and was remaining polite mainly for Hywel's sake. The druid cocked his head a little and sighed before he answered.

'It might save us some pride my friend, but if the Caledon means an end to Lurians killing Lurians then it is a thing worth preserving. We have fought with our neighbours since the trees were young and it has gained us little. And if the Gaians go back on their word, I would be glad to know that the southerners would join us in fighting them off again.'

Rylion looked ready to argue back but a gentle gesture from the druid forestalled him.

'I would never claim that the Gorvicae would not fight with great courage on their own comrade, but these Gaians have no concept of honour in war. Alone we would fight bravely and die bravely, that is all.'

The blonde man looked downcast but then spoke again.

'Yet this Caderyn Rhianwyn if half-Gaian. If the Gaians have no honour how can we trust her?'

Anryn nodded his agreement, his white hair flopping down over his forehead.

'I do not know this woman, father, but if she is indeed like the Gaians then Rylion speaks a fair question.'

Gawan felt slightly awkward at the mention of her name but he pulled himself together and corrected his brother, trying not to sound too dismissive.

'She is not half-Gaian, Rylion. Her second husband was a Gaian that is all, and he was a decent enough man.'

Rylion looked unconvinced and Gawan was glad that Hywel decided to take over.

'Rhianwyn is indeed fully Lurian in her blood, though her son of course is not. I know little of her heart but without her General Lepidus would surely have crushed us at Nantwyn, of that I am certain. She understands the Gaians better than any of us and that makes her a leader of great usefulness.' The old man sighed again and Gawan thought he looked weary. 'Though of course, she now has…'

Whatever he was about to say was interrupted by the door opening behind him and the broad figure of Karadoc appearing in its frame. The dark-haired man strode in without even an attempt to appear polite and he gave Hywel only the slightest of nods.

'I need to speak with the First Man. In private.'

Anryn's face flushed and he was halfway to standing when Hywel waved him down.

'There is no need to become offended on my behalf comrade, I had little else to say in any case.' He looked to Gawan. 'Though there are things that you and I must discuss.'

Anryn was still looking unusually angry and Hywel pacified him a little more.

'If Karadoc wishes to speak to Gawan perhaps you and I might walk together a while and talk?'

The promise of a chat with a druid might not have soothed Gawan much but to Anryn it was like offering a child a honeycake. Some of the indignation faded from his face and he bowed his head politely to Hywel.

'I should be glad to, of course.'

He shot Karadoc a disapproving glance before turning to Rylion. The blonde man pre-empted his offer with a shake of his head.

'Thank you but I think I will stay here.'

Hywel paused for a moment and Gawan wasn't sure what he would rather the old man said to that. The Gadarim was as annoyed as any of them by Karadoc's disrespect but if the chief had something of import to say then Gawan wanted to hear it, and Rylion's stubbornness looked like it might cause trouble. The druid moved his shoulders slightly.

'As you will.'

Karadoc opened his mouth to object and Hywel came as close to snapping at someone as Gawan had ever heard him.

'This is Gawan's home Karadoc, and Rylion his brother.'

His voice was quiet but stern and though Karadoc's face twitched in anger he did not argue with him.

'As you say.'

His voice was rougher than ever but the druid matched it with serenity, gesturing casually to Anryn beside him.

'Indeed so. Shall we, my friend?'

The brewer dipped his head and followed Hywel as he made for the door. Anryn closed it behind them and no sooner had the latch fallen than Karadoc was speaking again.

'I am the only choice to lead this tribe and I would have you speak this simple truth to the moot.'

Gawan's eyebrows went up a little. He had suspected that Karadoc would not be subtle in trying to win him over but all the same, this much directness was surprising. He had completely ignored Rylion and Gawan decided to repay his discourtesy.

'Is that so? In my experience very few great men feel the need to convince other men of the fact.'

Rylion smirked but Karadoc bristled, and he clearly wanted to reply with something sharp. Somehow he managed to hold back his temper though, and rather than snapping at his hosts he moved to sit in an empty seat.

'Listen to me, we are both warriors before all else are we not?'

His voice became more reasonable as he sat down but Gawan still saw tension in his shoulders. He nodded his head.

'That is how I have lived so far.'

He said it in a way that seemed only to agree, but Gawan hoped that Rylion understood the meaning of it. To be Gadarim was indeed to be a warrior first but he wanted his brother to know that he was prepared to be more than that. He was prepared to be a family man too. His brother's face remained unreadable but Karadoc seemed to take him at his word.

'Then let us speak plainly. You must know what will happen if Taliesyn is allowed to become our chieftain? The Caderyn will be coming and going here with complete impunity, peddling their shoddy goods and cosying up to the Gaians, all the while robbing decent Gorvicae of their rights to work and trade. And what of the Dariniae? They have already shown how little store they place by the Caledon, but Taliesyn and Rhianwyn would still have us try to be friends with them.' He snorted. 'Though if the gods are good she at least will have learned her lesson soon enough.'

Gawan assumed that meant he thought Rhianwyn would abandon the islanders after the raids of Caserach. He couldn't say he could blame her if she did but he thought it was unlikely. She was stubborn.

'The Dariniae will settle or they will not, but for now at least Caserach's power is broken. You know full well that the true threat to us is the Gaians and that Lepidus would have enslaved us all by now if not for the Dragon Legion.'

Karadoc's eyes were like two dark pits and he met Gawan's gaze, his voice serious as he grudgingly half-agreed.

'There is truth in what you say, and were a Gorvic in charge of all this then perhaps,' he raised a finger, '*perhaps* I would consider remaining, but...'

Gawan leaned back in his seat and cut across him.

'Rhianwyn has not declared herself chieftain over all of us, nor would I have her do so. She is accepted to be a figurehead for the Caledon, that is all; one who can speak for us when agreements are made with the Gaians and suchlike.'

Rylion frowned beside him.

'But if a figurehead is needed then why not a Gorvicae one?'

Gawan tried not to sound impatient with him.

'No reason, but then *every* tribe would want their own chieftain to be seen as overall leader and we cannot all be right. Rhianwyn and Carradan were the first to make this happen and she is still here, combined with her time with the Gaians...'

But this time Karadoc interrupted him.

'That should make her *less* suitable to lead a Lurian tribe, not more.' He waved a hand as Gawan took a breath to answer. 'But I did not come here to speak of her.'

He leaned a little closer and spoke earnestly to them both.

'I am here so that you may know that I am a man of the Gorvicae, first and foremost, and that you should remember this when the moot is called and men ask for your voice. We have been a proud people since the grass became green. I will keep us so.'

He rose to his feet and the two brothers rose as well. Gawan extended a hand to him but kept his words flat as he replied.

'I shall consider what you have said, you have my word.'

It wasn't the answer Karadoc had wanted but he took Gawan's hand anyway and nodded before exchanging the same gesture with Rylion. The blonde man gave him a far more encouraging look and Gawan resisted the urge to roll his eyes. No doubt once Karadoc was gone Rylion would repeat all the arguments he'd just made in the hopes of convincing his brother to speak more favourably of him. Ordinarily he'd have no problem in simply telling someone who did that to mind their own business, but if he was to gain his brother's trust then he would have to be more tactful. He almost growled to himself. Tact was not something he was used to.

The headman of Black Harbour made towards the door but he turned around to face them again before opening it. His dark eyes met Gawan's grey ones and his rough voice lowered to a rumble.

'I have my plans Gawan and I would have you be a part of them. Help our tribe back to greatness First Man, or else stay from my way while I do it.'

Gawan barely inclined his head to him, a gesture of acknowledgement not of agreement, and the big man turned around again and walked from the house. There was silence for a moment and Gawan pondered his last words. Karadoc's cajoling clearly hadn't got the result he had intended and he had resorted to trying to intimidate him instead. *Well, more fool him. He must know that I've killed a chieftain in my time, does he think a headman's glare will make me sweat?* Perhaps he was used to people fearing him for his size and strength, but Gawan had faced soldiers who'd been frenzied by magic, and even Karadoc was a skinny youth compared to Broad Kellas.

The thought of the Breiryn Gadarim brought back a flood of memories of that day, and Gawan felt a sick feeling in his gut as the guilt washed over him again. *It should have been me who faced him. Damn it all Tarwyn, why did you do it?* But he couldn't blame his brother for what happened. *He* had told them to watch over Emeryn and keep southern Gadarim away. *And instead of a kellas cat she met her end at the claws of a wolf.* Shame threatened to overwhelm him again but Rylion's words brought him back to the present.

'He speaks good sense.'

Gawan turned to him, shaking off his guilty thoughts as best he could.

'He speaks *some* good sense.'

He said it as tactfully as he could, some of what Karadoc had said was true after all, and then Rylion proceeded to do exactly what Gawan had feared. The First Man just about managed to keep it more a discussion than an argument, but all the same it felt like two days had passed when a knock sounded at the door. Gawan called out for whoever it was to enter, and noticed from the light outside that it was still only late afternoon. Rylion had managed to make it seem a lot later.

Gawan was not surprised to see that his next guest was Taliesyn, and he braced himself for the young man's arguments. They were not long in coming.

'I will not take much of your time, First Man, but no doubt Karadoc has been here to spin his tale. I only wish to tell my side before the moot.'

Gawan gestured to the seat Taliesyn's rival had lately taken, and the headman of Oaken Bridge sat down. He nodded briefly to Rylion but then fixed his attention on Gawan, his face set in an earnest expression.

'Karadoc would be an unwise choice for chieftain in these times. Speak on my part and I will keep the Gorvicae as part of the Caledon. You have fought against Lepidus, you understand the need for unity among the Luriae.'

His eyes were a very pale shade of green and had a seriousness that seemed at odds with his years. Gawan was thinking of a reply when Rylion answered the chief.

'Even if it means bowing our heads to that Caderyn woman?'

Gawan was glad he'd not used a less flattering word for Rhianwyn, since he would have felt obligated to reprimand him. Thinking about the Wildcat was still confusing at best but she deserved better than to be spoken of disrespectfully. Taliesyn turned his gaze to the blonde man.

'We would not bow to her, we would *ally* with her.' He switched his attention back to Gawan. 'I am told she is still unwed?'

Gawan frowned a little, suspecting where this was leading.

'Marius' blood has barely dried, what did you expect?'

The headman shrugged, ignoring the reproach in his voice.

'If I am made chieftain I would offer to kiss palms with her myself. I am confident she would be eager to strengthen the union with our tribe; what better way?'

Gawan fought to keep the emotion from his face. He told himself it was purely out of indignation for his cheek but he knew that part of him was pricked with jealousy. *For what you fool? A moment of lust that has led to nothing but self-hatred? You barely even* like *her man, what sort of child are you to feel any resentment?* He shoved away his petty thoughts and focused on reality.

'Rhianwyn is unlikely to consent to a marriage she did not propose herself, and even if she accepted you she is not the type to submit to the will of a husband.'

Once again Taliesyn did not seem perturbed and answered him quite calmly.

'I shall make the offer in any case, which is more than Karadoc would do. Should she refuse I shall offer my first daughter as a bride for her son, she might well be more amenable to that.'

The young chief had clearly thought this through and Gawan found himself seriously considering it. Even setting aside his own foolish jealousies this second plan had much more appeal. It would show both tribes that the Caledon was something permanent between partners, not a temporary alliance between rivals. It would be difficult, many Gorvicae would resent a Caderyn man taking a Gorvic wife, but it was definitely a plan worth considering. Though it still had some immediate problems, and Rylion was first to voice them.

'You have no daughter to offer, or not one born in wedlock anyway.'

Gawan nodded.

'And Rhianwyn will not wed her boy to a bastard.'

A child born outside of marriage would not be considered blessed by Camelas and Marna, or at least not in the same way as a child born to man and wife would be. To offer a bastard to marry a chieftain's son would be considered the most terrible insult. Taliesyn waved one hand in an easy gesture.

'I am a man who takes care with his lovers and I've no bastards that I know of.'

Gawan nodded.

'Very well, but then you have no legitimate children either, and no wife to give you any.'

Taliesyn nodded back.

'True, but I know several suitable girls who would be happy to wed me once I am chieftain, and rest assured I shall work hard to gain a daughter as soon as possible.'

The serious man smiled a little, and Gawan noticed how much younger it made his face. Chief he might be but he was still very young for his position, and the First Man remembered how even Hywel had been worried about that. If he became High Chieftain he would need solid advisors around him, which naturally led Gawan to think of Boryn. *If only* he *would take Baercban's chair, we might be spared so much of this nonsense.* Some sense was being shown by both the men who had approached him today, but it said a great deal that Boryn had not come to persuade him at all. The old man knew his own worth and had no desire for power, which probably made him the best-suited man to wield it. Gawan was still pondering this when the door opened once more and all three men turned to see the new arrival.

It was a woman, perhaps twenty summers old and wearing a plain green dress. She was taller than most women, and though her jaw was rather prominent Gawan thought it only served to make her face that much more striking. She had a solid but still feminine figure, and rather straggly blonde hair that hung down past her shoulders. Taliesyn stood up and extended a hand as she approached, his voice lightening a little.

'Ah, welcome my dear. I am sorry to have kept you, we were all but done here anyhow.'

The two brothers stood as well, and the woman took Taliesyn's hand but then stopped as she noticed Rylion. Gawan saw the shock on both their faces and his stomach dropped as he realised who she must be.

'Hello uncle.'

Her voice was rich and calm but her surprise was obvious. Gawan just stared at the face that was at once both familiar and strange as his brother replied quietly from beside him.

'Hello Tegwen.'

Chapter 24. The Gorvicae Moot

On the day of the moot the great hall of Graigarw was host to almost every chief of the Gorvicae. The room was hot, the benches packed tight with grey-bearded men and a smattering of stern-looking women, though Gawan knew there were still several absentees. Some had been unable to come due to illness and others because they had duties elsewhere, but he knew too well what the most common cause of absence was; death. So many Gorvicae had been killed in the war against Lepidus that it was inevitable that chiefs would be among the fallen, and many clans had yet to choose new men to lead them.

Gawan looked at each of them as they listened to the speakers. He recognised many of the people there, like Rhysgon, who sat toying with his plaited beard, or old Dorran with his withered hand resting awkwardly on his thigh, but there were plenty of strangers scattered among them as well. Some of the chiefs here ruled towns that were home to hundreds of tribesmen and had come to Graigarw often to speak with Baercban, others presided over small clans of only a few households each and rarely left their own little communities. But each one would have an equal voice today.

Taliesyn was just finishing his speech, having reluctantly agreed to finally hold the moot. Every chief expected to be there had arrived, but it had been a blow to him when Tostig and Accalon had decided to remain with the legion at White Ridge. They had sent Duran up to Graigarw to speak for them, but it was their persuading voices that he would miss. To make things worse Karadoc had insisted on maintaining the strict law of the moot, ensuring that

Duran could only raise his hand once, despite both of the chiefs declaring for Taliesyn. They were absent of their own will after all, and the law stated that each man of the moot could only speak once. Taliesyn had tried to argue but Hywel had been compelled to agree with Karadoc. For there to be such anxiety over a single hand, it did not take much for Gawan to see that this decision would be a close one.

He tried to listen to the younger headman as he spoke but his mind kept drifting off to think of Tegwen. He'd still had no chance to speak with her, not that he had any idea what he would say. Rylion, clearly as surprised as he was, had simply said; 'this is your father' when they had met, and Tegwen had just nodded dumbly. Perhaps she'd already seen the resemblance between the brothers, perhaps not, but nonetheless the shock on her face had been plain. Neither father nor daughter had known what to say next and Taliesyn had broken the awkwardness by inviting her to leave with him, saying that they could meet and talk later when better prepared. Gawan couldn't decide if he was more grateful or annoyed at the young chief for his actions.

He watched him as he paced about, extolling his own virtues as humbly as he could, and trying to talk down Karadoc without seeming too petty about it. He was doing a fair job. Gawan had to admit he wasn't a bad candidate, but the sight of him with Tegwen had taken some of the shine from the young man. It was well known that he changed lovers the way most men changed clothes and the thought of him treating Tegwen in such a way made Gawan unjustifiably angry. *You've been a stranger her whole life and* now *you decide to become protective? You damned fool!*

When they had left the house he had considered following them out but Rylion had forestalled him, advising him to wait a day or so before approaching her. With his mind half on the moot Gawan might make a mess of all this, and he would not get a second chance at a first impression. Gawan was fairly sure Rylion was taking care of her feelings rather than his but all the same he felt grateful to his brother, who even went so far as to go and see her himself to prepare the ground for the meeting with her father. They had a long way to go, but it was good to know that he and Rylion were becoming a family again. Whether Tegwen would be a part of that was another story of course.

So instead of chasing her down and trying to become a father, Gawan had spent most of his time at the house with Anryn, the older man trying to talk his worries away as they waited for the moot. The bachelor was both a good talker and a good listener and though Gawan had hardly poured out his soul to him, their conversations had helped him to relax. A little. Anryn never pried and was happy to ramble on with some tale or another whenever Gawan didn't feel like talking.

The Gadarim shifted on the bench and focused his mind on the meeting at hand. Taliesyn was winding up his speech and Gawan noticed that Karadoc was glaring murder at him, as if trying to strangle him with just his eyes. He was clearly regretting having taken the initiative by speaking to the assembly first, since he was now forced to watch in silence as his rivals made their arguments. Boryn was watching the speech with what looked like polite interest, occasionally pulling on his moustache but otherwise sitting still and relaxed.

Taliesyn finished speaking and several headmen banged their fists on tables and benches in support. Hywel cleared his throat and rose from his seat beside Baercban's chair.

'Blessings and thanks, Taliesyn son of Cylren.'

The young man bowed his head and strode to an empty patch of bench, where one of the seated chiefs clapped his shoulder as he sat down. Hywel addressed the room again, his voice high and clear.

'Step forward Boryn son of Maldom.'

The elder chief rose from his seat and bowed to the druid before addressing the headmen. He was shorter than either of the other candidates but he held himself with great dignity, and his audience paid attention.

'Camelas' blessing on you all. I am no great speaker and will keep this brief.'

He looked around the room, speaking seriously and gesturing little.

'If Baercban's chair is offered to me I shall do all I can to repair the hurt that has been done to our tribe these last few years. I shall strive to keep peace with our neighbours, listen to advice when it is given, and rule justly and fairly to the best of my ability.'

Beside him, Gawan heard Duran whisper very quietly.

'A fine notion, but not a strong enough view to sway anyone.'

Gawan looked at him out of the corner of his eye, not wanting to seem disrespectful to the speaker. His fellow Gadarim had tied his long hair back at the nape of his neck, highlighting the sharp lines of his face. So far he sported no permanent battle-marks there, but after his service at Nantwyn Gawan felt he had more than earned some. Duran was younger than the First Man but very nearly as experienced, and could boast of heroism in a score of battles. He had fought Dariniae, Caderyn, Gaians, and Sarracs in his time. He had even, long ago, fought alongside Gawan to take down a warrior of the Grenn. Gawan could still remember the great brute today, a monster to rival Broad Kellas in size. Yes, Duran would make a fine First Man once this was over.

Gawan nodded his head subtly and replied in a low voice.

'Boryn is wise. Many older men and druids will support him.'

Duran shrugged and said what Gawan had already suspected.

'True, but his support cannot rival that of either of the other two. Many older headmen are dead and the young ones will want a solid idea to hold on to. The world is changing, brother.'

Gawan resisted the urge to sigh and turned his head back to Boryn.

'Maybe so.'

The elder headman had finished saying what little he had to say and Hywel stood again and bowed to him.

'Blessings and thanks, Boryn son of Maldom.'

Gawan knew what would come next and was already standing up when the druid turned to face him.

'Gawan son of Dearg, First Man of our Gadarim, what say you?'

If anything Gawan was even less of a speaker than Boryn but it was expected of him, and he knew his duty. He bowed to the white-robed men before addressing the benches.

'Druid Hywel, fathers, headmen of the Gorvicae; I have little enough to add to the words already spoken. Each man has made good arguments and any one of them might make a capable leader. But my own first choice to be chieftain of our tribe would be Boryn son of Maldom.'

Both Taliesyn and Karadoc were looking at him with hostility but Gawan didn't care. It might not be the cleverest thing to say, given Boryn's chances, but it was the truth.

'He is the eldest of the three men here and has spoken with much wisdom, and I know him to be a loyal and dedicated man.'

There were rumblings from the benches and Gawan raised his voice.

'Besides which I have fought beside him and know his worth on the field of battle. He makes no grand promises today but he is a fine man and a true Gorvic. Let that be enough to make him our chieftain.'

The hall had fallen to silence as he spoke and Hywel raised his open hand before any muttering could begin.

'Thanks and blessings, Gawan son of Dearg.' He swept his eyes around the room.

'We have heard all that there is to be heard. Now show your hands, and let the Gorvicae make their choice.'

He paused and a silent tension seemed to float through the hall before he spoke again.

'All those who would favour Karadoc son of Ofryd?'

A chorus of 'aye' went up from several throats and Gawan saw hands being raised above heads. None of the druids there had sided with him but the chiefs significantly outnumbered the holy men, and plenty of grizzled Gorvicae had raised their hands for Karadoc. The man himself smirked a little but Gawan could tell it was forced. Young druids were diligently counting the hands but it was plain at a glance that less than half the hall supported him. The robed youths approached Hywel and told him the result, and their senior nodded without expression.

'Very well. All for Boryn son of Maldom?'

More hands went up, including those of several druids, and Gawan raised his own to join them. More chiefs than he would have thought had declared for Boryn but it still looked like fewer than Karadoc had gained. Gawan wondered briefly if his words had swayed any of them to Boryn's side, but then rationalised that Hywel might well have spoken to some of them too. Once again the youngsters counted but Gawan suspected it was the next question that would truly decide this moot. Hywel spoke up for a third time.

'All for Taliesyn son of Cylren?'

Gawan saw Duran raise his hand and voice in support, along with a cluster of headmen and even one or two of the druids. Once again the hands were counted and for a final time the result was given to Hywel. The elder druid frowned but he was not one for dramatics and did not pause before announcing the result.

'Nineteen hands to Boryn son of Maldom.'

A few fists banged onto tables but otherwise the room stayed silent.

'Twenty-six hands for Karadoc son of Ofryd.'

The applause was greater this time and Karadoc's smile widened. The noise died down soon enough though as all eyes turned to the druid. Hywel took a single breath before he spoke.

'And twenty-six hands for Taliesyn son of Cylren'

A few of Taliesyn's supporters tried to make some noise but most of the hall stayed awkwardly quiet. The man himself was sitting expressionless on his bench, watching Hywel and waiting for him to speak again. The white-robed man called out to the hall.

'Will any who raised their hand for Boryn consider declaring for another?'

A nail might have dropped outside and they all would have heard it. Even discounting the draw between Taliesyn and Karadoc, Boryn was so close behind them that it was practically all even. The druids generally liked a new chieftain to be chosen by a large majority, and Gawan doubted if such a close-run moot had been seen in generations. The silence lengthened as nobody offered to change their decision, and Hywel's shoulders seemed to sag a little. It was Karadoc who spoke first.

'Well?'

He was speaking to Hywel but the druid did not reply. The tall chief tried again, this time addressing the moot in general.

'Would you have us choose *no* chieftain? What manner of men are you?'

If he was hoping to persuade more chiefs to his cause he was going the wrong way about it, and Gawan saw Rhysgon fold his arms across his chest, a look of defiance on his face. Taliesyn stood up as well and raised an open hand.

'We cannot end the moot here, we need a decision.'

Karadoc rounded on him.

'If you had not confused the matter with all your damned talking...'

Taliesyn interrupted him.

'*My* damned talking? It is no fault of mine that you cannot...'

But then he too was interrupted as a man beside Karadoc spoke up, closely followed by the headmen on Taliesyn's side of the hall. Boryn tried to step between them but his voice was drowned out by the others. Hywel was still just standing there, a look of pained disappointment on his face. Gawan stared at him. *Just tell them what to do, damn it! No man would refuse you if you told them to accept a decision, and they need leadership right now!* He almost snarled. Druids had such vast power, in more ways than one, yet they were sworn to only assist and advise the chiefs, never to rule them. Gawan wanted to curse him. When the Caledon was formed it had been Reaghan, wisest of the druids, who had created it more than anyone, was that not an exception to the rule? He had not sought to control it but he had seen division and turned it to unity, why would Hywel not do the same?

The voices grew louder and angrier and Gawan knew that if things got any worse there was a real chance of violence ensuing. He had to stop that from happening. The Gorvicae had enemies enough without tearing themselves apart from within. The First Man stepped forward and raised his voice.

'Silence!'

It carried even over the bickering chiefs and most of fourscore faces turned to him. For a moment a spiteful voice in his head told him he had no right to address them so but he ignored it with an effort. Flawed he might be but this needed to be said. He looked around the hall and gave them his second-best glare.

'If you cannot agree amongst yourselves then there is a simple solution; we can call in another voice to force a decision. Since the druids are sworn not to interfere,' Gawan tried not to sound bitter about that, 'our best choice is to bring another High Chieftain here and hear what they have to say. I say we send word to the Wildcat.'

About half of those present looked ready to keep listening but the rest of the chiefs began jabbing fingers at Gawan and arguing all the louder, and the Gadarim took a deep breath to shout them down. Hywel got there first however, his words calm but somehow magnified to a greater volume than any bellow, and Gawan knew that he must have poured magic into his voice.

'Enough!'

The hall became deathly silent as men who'd fought a hundred battles looked with fear at one old man. Druids might not use their power any more than they had to, but the greatest fool of all the tribes knew to respect what they were capable of. Hywel's voice reverted to its usual pitch, though his eyes were still intense as he spoke again.

'You have not made a single choice and the First Man's suggestion is wise. This has happened before now, though long before your time, when a moot has been undecided. There is provision in the law for an outside chieftain to step in to arbitrate, and Rhianwyn daughter of Carradan is the obvious choice.'

Gawan chipped in before any of the more angry-looking headmen could object.

'Baercban declared us a part of the Caledon and only a High Chieftain should have the right to say we are leaving it. Since we have no such man we are still a part of that alliance...'

Karadoc interrupted him, shoving his way towards him through the throng.

'You dare to speak of Baercban? You of all men ought to be ashamed to speak my cousin's name!'

Gawan didn't back down. He knew what he had done, and he knew what he had to do.

'I fought him because he would have prevented justice for a brother Gadarim. I took no joy in it.'

Gawan had always been honest about what had happened that day in Bryngarth's hall but all the same Karadoc looked ready to retort. Boryn spoke up first.

'Does any man here dare to call Leaping Wolf a liar?'

Unsurprisingly nobody answered him. Karadoc might sneer at him but he clearly wasn't prepared to make such a bold statement outright. Hywel nodded politely to Boryn.

'I am sure that no man here would doubt our First Man's word. We all know what manner of man Sedryn was. And we all know that Baercban would still have defended his son. The past is not in doubt, let us look to the future.'

Karadoc took that as a sign that he could start talking again and began before anyone could stop him.

'This woman has no place among us! Caledon or not she is no Gorvic.'

Gawan was fast growing weary of this man's attitude.

'But I am.'

That was enough to silence several would-be objectors but Karadoc was not so easily put off.

'Whatever your notions of justice she killed the son of our last chieftain. You think Baercban would want Sedryn's killer deciding who should take his chair?'

Once again Boryn stepped in to answer.

'Sedryn was justly slain for the murder of Carradan.'

Karadoc looked surly and Taliesyn saw his chance to make a point.

'Baercban all but sold us to the Gaians. He may have thought it the right thing for our survival but he was wrong nonetheless. We cannot bind ourselves by thinking on what he might have said or done.'

Karadoc snarled at his rival.

'He was our chieftain and my cousin, boy! And whatever his mistakes I'll not hear his name slandered in his own hall.'

Taliesyn bristled and Gawan could see that things were beginning to escalate again. He seized upon an idea.

'It was Baercban who agreed to bring this tribe into the Caledon. It was he, Ierryn, Carradan and Reaghan who first began this alliance.'

Karadoc turned to him, ready to argue, but then stopped himself. Several others who had seemed on the verge of adding their voices to his support let out their breaths quietly or looked away, embarrassed. Though he was Caderyn, Reaghan was without doubt the most respected druid in the west, and Gawan struggled to imagine a Lurian who would dare to contradict him. Granted, Reaghan had disappeared on some errand known only to him but that could be dealt with later. If the Gorvicae could be made to agree on this then the Caledon might stand a chance. It wasn't much of a plan but it was all he had.

Yet again it was Hywel who came to his rescue, and Gawan could have sworn he saw a twinkle in the old man's eyes.

'The Caledon was indeed formed by these men and until there is a new chieftain I say that we are bound to it. And the matter of the moot is simply enough resolved: We have here our three candidates. Are you content to bring this to Rhianwyn of the Caderyn?'

Karadoc folded his huge arms and spoke a flat; 'no', but first Taliesyn and then Boryn raised their hands and spoke; 'aye'. The big man scowled at them both but neither one seemed at all discouraged. Taliesyn was trying to hide how pleased he was and Boryn was looking as calm and tranquil as ever. Karadoc turned from them to the druid and made a last ditch attempt at avoiding this outcome.

'Is Rhianwyn not facing a trial of her people for bringing the Gaians to this battle with the Breiryn?'

Gawan blinked. This was the first he'd heard of such a thing. He turned to Boryn who shrugged a little, his face apologetic.

'Forgive me, I thought you knew?'

Gawan shook his head. He shouldn't really have been surprised, he'd been a strong voice in objecting to the Blackbirds' involvement after all, but all the same he was taken aback. The Caderyn must have known that Rhianwyn had acted in her people's best interests? Like him they might not like it but that made it no less true. He pictured the Wildcat being taken back to her father's hall under a guard of her own people, but he quickly drove the image away. He'd felt himself begin to think more of her body than of her plight, and guilt and awkwardness threatened to interrupt his focus. He could ill-afford that right now.

'Whatever the matter is, I am sure it will be resolved easily enough.'

He wasn't sure quite how confident he was in that, given the hard wills of men like Alraig, but he persuaded himself that all would be well. There were a few sceptical glances at him from the chiefs and Hywel spoke again, sounding thoughtful.

'Likely so, though it may take some time. Perhaps rather than sending for Rhianwyn, our candidates might travel down to Bryngarth and speak with her there?'

Predictably, Karadoc disagreed and twisted his face into a sneer.

'Hold a Gorvicae moot at Bryngarth? What madness is this?'

Both Hywel and Boryn raised pacifying hands but it was the druid who answered first.

'I do not say to hold the moot there; merely that the three of you *speak* to her there. If it transpires that she is willing to arbitrate then we would of course bring her back to Graigarw.' He turned to face Gawan before anyone else could comment. 'Naturally, you would be coming with us, First Man?'

Gawan hesitated for a moment. His duty was clear but it would mean an awkward conversation with Rylion. He had promised to speak to Tegwen and if he was sent away south who knew how long it might be before he came back? *But then Tegwen is the lover of Taliesyn, perhaps she will go to Bryngarth with him?* Part of him wanted to play things safe and simply name Duran the First Man here and now, then the responsibility could be his and Gawan would be free to go wherever Tegwen went.

But this plan had been his idea. If he was ever to wipe away his shame he had to accept his responsibilities as a father, but he had no right to avoid this responsibility either. He would have to risk Rylion's anger for this and make peace with Tegwen when he could. He glanced

351

briefly at Duran before facing the assembly. His brother's new honour would have to wait.

'Of course I shall go with you, father.'

Chapter 25. The Prisoner

Rhia's feet thudded dully against the floorboards as she paced back and forth in frustration. The Caderyn's chieftain was hardly heavily built and she wasn't even wearing her shoes, but all the same the wood was creaking in protest as she walked the short distance across her room and back again. She hated the feeling of being stuck indoors, away from fresh air and daylight. Away from her people. She let out a long breath as she spun around for the hundredth time, ready to retrace her footsteps once again. The room was plain and mostly bare, with just a chest for clothes, a pallet bed, a table and a pair of chairs for her to glower at as she walked.

  She found her mind wandering back to her life in Tamora, and not just because the rooms there had been bigger. She thought back to the day she'd seen an animal show at the arena, back before she'd known what such a spectacle would entail. Narbo Galerian, Gregor's brother, had invited her and Marius to come and see a pair of wild boars he had purchased, and she had gone along in complete ignorance of what to expect. Her grasp of Vulgare at the time had been tenuous at best. What she'd seen there had shocked her but, surprisingly, not so much because of the fighting. Animals fought one another all the time and cruel though it was to force them to it, there was nothing intrinsically *wrong* about the violence. It was the fact that they'd first been caged up in tiny metal pens, barely large enough for the beasts to stand up in much less move. Before they fought they had been winched around on a crane for all the audience to see, clearly terrified and enraged by what was happening to them. It had saddened her to see something so unnatural as a wild animal being restrained in such a way, and poor linguist though she was she'd made it *very* clear to Marius that she would not go to a show like that again. She had found renewed sympathy for those beasts in the last few days.

Eventually the pacing worked off some of her fidgety energy and she sat down on the bed and sighed. Ever since Alraig had brought her to Bryngarth she'd been stuck at her father's longhall, with little enough to do but eat, sleep and wander aimlessly about, and it was fast driving her insane. For something so dull she'd found it surprisingly tiring, and was forever alternating between bursts of frustrated activity and periods of lifeless lethargy. There was a loose thread at her left sleeve and she began picking at it absently, mainly to give her hands something to do, and at least she could eat up some time later on by fixing it.

Her mind wandered again as she sat there, thinking over the last few days. After Alraig had made her his prisoner she had insisted on carrying word to the legion about what was happening to her, and being kept updated on all that was happening to them. The headman had reluctantly stopped at Alfwyth for a day while she sent messages back and forth through Bran. At first Alraig had been concerned that she was calling her cohort to rescue her and had kept her under close watch as a result. It was a logical fear, since one word to the Dragon Legion, or to Gregor and his people, and a small army would descend on them and free her from his custody. But he needn't have worried. She was ashamed to admit that the thought had crossed her mind once or twice, but the fact was that escaping was the worst thing she could do. Good Caderyn would likely die in the attempt and all it would prove was that might was right, and Rhia didn't want to lead her people that way. A tear threatened to appear as she thought of Owain and Meg, already dead because of her. She had wept for them both many times already, though she'd taken care only to do so when alone. She had to stay strong before her captors, even if she was so damned weary of being strong.

No, escape of any kind was not an option. To keep herself from being tempted Rhia had agreed to the Caderyn cohort remaining in the south, along with most of her Gadarim warriors. They would be needed there if Asrec and his Breiryn tried to rise again, not that she thought he would. Asrec was not a bold man in the face of hard odds. He had already agreed to return all that had been taken from Three Willows in Caserach's raid, and would be paying tribute to the Caderyn for a whole year's turn. It would have been a response to feel pleased about, had he not also made a gesture to Caserach. For all his deeds he was still the closest thing the Dariniae had to a High Chieftain, and Asrec had offered him a Breiryn Gadarim as a bodyguard fit for his station on the way to Bryngarth. That almost certainly meant Broad Kellas, and though she hated to admit it, the thought of the giant coming here unnerved her.

She channelled her fear into anger and directed it at Caserach, the greedy fool responsible for all this. She hadn't known Ierryn that well, beyond his reputation, but in the brief time they had been allies he had struck her as a brave and loyal man. Ruthless he might have been, but he was dedicated to his people and had supported the Caledon with utter conviction, sending all the warriors he could

355

muster to fight the Gaians alongside them. *Including Delyn...* Rhia shut out that image with an effort and focused on Caserach again.

The Dariniae's would-be leader was as much a prisoner as she was, though he would answer for his actions after she did. All were agreed that he had done great wrong in the killing of Ierryn and had stained his tribe's honour in attacking the Caledon, but it had also been agreed that his own people had to be the ones to judge him. Caderyn headmen might have some way to travel but they were a lot closer than their Dariniae counterparts, and it had made sense for Rhia to face her judgement first. Rhia hoped and prayed that she got through this ordeal in one piece, if only to see that murdering bastard hurled into the sea.

She had hoped her anger at him would be able to sustain her but it soon dribbled away as she thought again on her own predicament. She found herself wishing that Reaghan was here, or Bael who had gone off to commune with him. The senior druid had been a comforting presence in her life for twenty years and she needed his wisdom now more than ever. Even Bael, for all his youth, would have been a welcome sight, since he seemed almost a reflection of his elder. But Reaghan had vanished shortly after Nantwyn and Bael had not been seen for days now. Instead the only druid she knew here was Gryg, who had tried to reassure her but just hadn't been convincing. He wasn't a father to the tribe the way Reaghan had always been. The only real comfort she'd had since getting here had been from her mother and sister, and even that had done little enough to ease her fears.

Alraig had initially said she was to be kept alone until her trial but he had eventually consented for her to see her family. Rhia was glad he had agreed before they'd arrived at the hillfort. Myrna could be fearsome when it came to her children, and Alraig would have had to gather men to restrain her had he tried to keep her from her daughter. Rhia almost smiled. Her mother was such a gentle woman but Carradan had said many times that she had a soul of iron beneath her smile.

She had come to see Rhia the moment they'd returned to Bryngarth, and had come again each day since, sometimes bringing Olla and Lucan with her. From what her mother had said, Rhia understood that there were voices both for and against her actions, but that of those chiefs who'd arrived here, most agreed with what Alraig had said. Her mother had once again advised her to consider marrying a man of the tribe, to show them all she was more Lurian than Gaian. Myrna had intended it as good advice of course but in reality it had just given Rhia something else to worry about. If the Caledon was to thrive then all three tribes had to trust one another, and if she married a fellow Caderyn it would seem that she was excluding the others. Equally she couldn't marry a Gorvic or a Darin for fear of undermining her support among the Caderyn.

Rhia fell back onto the bed and let out another long breath. More than anything she wished that her father was here. He'd been chieftain of the Caderyn since before she was born and knew each headman of the tribe better than their own brothers. He'd been strong and kind and wise along with it, and had he been in this situation... she stopped herself and started wondering. What *would* he have done? Would he have sent for Gregor's help in fighting Caserach and the Breiryn? Would he now marry into another tribe, or arrange for his children to do so? Or

357

would he have risked defeat and death by fighting alone at Moon Ridge, or risked alienating his allies by pacifying the Caderyn? *He is dead,* a hard voice told her in her head, *there is no way to know*.

Tears threatened to wet her eyes and she reached for the thought that she always kept there for times when grief threatened her; she thought of Lucan. He was staying with his aunt at the moment but Olla brought him here most days, and the sight of him always brightened Rhia's spirit. She had her worries for him of course, but mostly when she saw him she saw the source of her joy, and it gave her the strength she needed to push herself onwards through anything.

She closed her eyes and let thoughts of Lucan ease the fears away. She remembered the day he'd been born, and the memory was as sharp as if it had been only yesterday; the pain and the fear and then the sheer unbridled joy of holding her child in her arms for the first time. She remembered watching him play games with his cousins in the great houses of the Dessida clan, or riding his toy horse as he waved around his little sword. *He wanted so much to be like his father*.

Rhia sat up and brought herself back to the present before thoughts of Marius could spoil her new-found calm. The sudden movement made the candlelit room spin for a moment but it soon slowed and she took a deep breath. It would be alright. The chiefs would see that what she'd done had been necessary and things would go back to how they were. Perhaps once it was done she could let Merwyn take care of things for a little and go away with Lucan for a few days? He had never seen the sea, she might take him to Mobryn or somewhere? Bradan would likely feel odd about it but he was a good man and he loved children. He would welcome them. She sighed. *Assuming that all goes well in these next few days.*

For some reason the face of Gawan popped into her head, and she found herself wondering for the thousandth time what on earth had come over him that day. She knew he had lost good friends at Moon Ridge but all the same, it was beyond strange. He had disappeared from the camp that very night and she had to admit, she was concerned for him. Whatever madness that had driven him to kiss her might have led him into some other mischief somewhere else. He was hardly a man who avoided trouble and she hated to think what sort of mess he might have landed himself in.

Despite herself Rhia found that she was smiling. The Leaping Wolf had been her enemy far longer than he'd been her ally, and he had never hidden his animosity towards her, yet here she was fretting over him. *In fairness, he might be a handy man to have around if things go badly here.* Rhia snorted at that as she realised what a foolish thought it was. Gawan was undoubtedly a fine fighter, but in a situation like this she could guarantee that he would somehow make things worse.

*

Rhia realised she must have dropped off because when the knocks sounded from the door she was lying down on the bed again. She sat upright and called for whoever it was to enter, blinking her eyes a few times and stifling a yawn. The door creaked open and she saw Cerridwen standing nervously in the frame. Her young cousin had asked, and been permitted, to stay at the longhall to take care of Rhia's needs. She was tall, or as tall as Rhia's family generally got anyway, and had long hair the colour of horse chestnuts. The room beyond her was lit only by the candle she held, and Rhia noticed that the ones in her own room had burned down by almost a finger. She must have been asleep for some time.

She beckoned Cerri forward but the younger woman shook her head.

'I'm sorry Rhia, I just wanted to make sure...'

She was interrupted by Alraig, who strode past her into the room.

'That you were awake and decent for company.' He nodded his head a fraction. 'And so you are.'

Rhia felt her heart sink a little but she waved Cerri away with the best smile she could manage.

'Thank you Cerri, I will come and help you cook later.'

For a moment it looked as if her cousin might object but then she nodded quietly and stepped away, though she left the door open. Alraig moved closer to Rhia and the candles played strange shadows on his face. He was dressed in his habitual dark clothing, with a legion belt around his waist and a legion dagger at his hip. The light made his brown hair look almost black, throwing the silver streaks in it into sharp relief. He stopped a pace or two from the bed and Rhia stood up to face him. He towered over her somewhat but then most people did, and Rhia had long ago stopped being intimidated by height. His eyes fixed onto hers.

'We await only a few more chiefs and holy druids. Your trial should commence in two days' time.'

Rhia cocked her head to one side. She was in no mood to chat with her captor.

'And you have come here to gloat perhaps? A little soon for that, is it not?'

The lean man's face remained blank.

'I came here to give you fair warning that you must ready your arguments. I will not have it said that I denied you the chance to prepare yourself for your trial.'

Rhia raised an eyebrow and wanted desperately to say something sharp to him. He clearly thought himself the living embodiment of honour for the way he was conducting this, and the urge to slap him down was incredible. But Rhia controlled herself. Alraig was no fool, and if he was as wise and upright as he thought he was he might be willing to listen to some sense.

'You must know what you are risking in this? Without me the Caledon will likely fall apart.'

Alraig's mouth twitched at one corner but otherwise he showed no reaction.

'You think most highly of your own importance, Rhianwyn.'

Rhia again resisted the urge to bite back. It was understanding, not ego, that had made her say what she had. The alliance was still young. And it was fragile.

'I think this because it is probable, Alraig. And if the Caledon collapses we will all be that much weaker the next time we are threatened from without.'

Alraig raised an eyebrow.

'So you admit that the Gaians are still our enemies?'

Rhia paused for a moment to take a breath. The answer wasn't that simple.

'They have the potential to be. Many, perhaps most of them, have no desire to do us harm provided that we cause them no trouble. But we would be foolish not to take care in case another Lepidus comes to power.'

She wanted to go on to say that other threats like the Breiryn and the Sarracs were also good reasons for unity, but she didn't get the chance. Alraig responded instantly, straightening his back and putting his arms behind him.

'They do not need another Lepidus to see us as weak creatures, as something beneath them.' There was a restrained passion in his voice that Rhia hadn't heard before, but he was keeping his features neutral. 'And you brought a legion of them into our lands under arms, defying a law that you yourself had set.'

Rhia felt her patience thinning and half-snapped back her answer.

'They were vital to secure victory against Caserach, you know that.'

Alraig might indeed have known that but it wasn't softening his resolve, and the anger in his voice became even clearer.

'And what happens when another problem arises and you decide the easiest way to solve it is by calling on your Gaian friends? What happens in a year, or two years, when you have become reliant upon them to maintain order in our lands?' He took a small step forward and his eyes bored into hers. 'It will be as if their damned governor never left!'

He practically hissed out the last words and Rhia found herself wanting to back away from him. She had never seen the quiet headman betray emotion like this and it was an unsettling sight to behold. She kept her nerve however and squared up to him, her voice firm.

'We have all of us...'

But he interrupted.

'No!'

It was probably the loudest she had ever heard him speak and it took him a few heartbeats to control himself. The tall man leaned forward, his voice lowering again, dropping down almost to a whisper.

'My family has ruled Penafon for nine generations, did you know that?'

Rhia knew of course, but she simply nodded. Penafon had one of the longest lineages of chiefs of any settlement in Caderyn lands, and the family had always been proud of it. Since time immemorial they had run the silver mine in the mountains there, sending ingots up to Bryngarth to be forged into the Caderyn's coins. Their headman continued to speak.

'While you were in Tamora, eating fine food and ordering slaves to wash your feet, Governor Portunus sent men to take over the production there. He had two dozen enforcers watching over every chip and nugget we mined. Their captain soon saw a chance to line his own purse with our labour and began forcing our people to work harder and faster, while still sending the same amounts to his superiors.'

His voice was growing quieter but harsher at the same time, his face now uncomfortably close to hers.

'When Portunus caught on to this he sent an inspector there, and the enforcers blamed my workers for the theft. I saw a man of sixty winters flogged to death for it, the punishment carried out before the eyes of his wife and children.'

Rhia's breath caught in her throat as she listened. She'd known from Meghan that some of the Gaians had been ruthless or cruel, but the impression she'd had was that most of them had been peaceful. She'd not heard of anything like this happening in her lands. *Yet are you really surprised? Marius and Glaucus were good enough men, but the Gaians look down on anyone who isn't them. 'Barbarians' they call us. To so many of them we are little more than animals.* Alraig continued his tale, his eyes burning into hers.

'I tried to intervene, as any chief would have done, and the enforcers held me fast while their leader threatened to cut out my tongue.'

He opened his mouth and pulled one cheek aside, and Rhia saw that nearly all of his teeth on that side were missing, exposing the dark red gums. He lowered his hand again.

'They settled for a few of those.'

Rhia wanted to say something but she couldn't find the words, not that Alraig was looking for a response.

'After we buried Larryn I understood the true nature of the Gaians. We killed eight of their men that night. Cut their bodies apart and hid them in the hills.'

Rhia's eyes widened. Whatever wrong had been done it was madness to defy the legions. Alraig seemed to read her mind and almost smiled. Shadows flickered across his face as he did.

'We could not fight their armies, but we could fight the men sent to guard us. The next morning we sent a wagon of silver away to Glysger and let them think it had been ambushed on the road. It was over a moon's turn before they began to grow suspicious.'

Rhia couldn't help but ask the question, her voice very quiet.

'What happened then?'

Alraig tilted his head and gave another of his almost-smiles, the expression full of bitterness.

'More than even we had feared. When we were discovered the captain picked out one of our women at random and blinded her with hot irons. When her husband tried to stop them they caved his head in with their truncheons. I can still hear the way that Enfys screamed as they took her eyes. I can still see Baridan's brains in the mud.' He pulled away from her a little, straightening up again as he composed himself. 'That day we killed every Gaian who had set foot in our mines and tossed their heads into the deepest shaft. We all expected Portunus would send a legion to crush us but we didn't care. Justice had been done.'

Once again Rhia found herself struggling for the right words and in the end she settled for another question.

'Why didn't he?'

Alraig shrugged.

'I sent my people into hiding and went to Bryngarth to try to delay him, but then you returned and gave them all something bigger to worry about.' He leaned back and took a tiny step away from her. 'I am grateful for your work in helping us defeat them, truly I am. Because of this I was content for you to become chieftain of our tribe.' His voice hardened. 'But you betrayed us by allowing the Gaians back here again, and that I cannot ignore.'

The tall man turned away from her and walked back towards the door. Rhia wasn't sure what she could say. She knew, or mostly knew, that she'd had no choice and had acted in the best interests of her people. But Alraig's story… after what he had been through he would never be persuaded. When he reached the door he turned back to face her, his expression as blank as when he'd first come in.

'Believe it or not I do not hate you, Rhianwyn. But I *do* hate them. I will trust to the traditions of our people and the judgement of my fellows. If they find you to be innocent I will say no more of this.' His eyes flashed in the candlelight. 'But I will do all in my power to ensure that they do not. At the very least they will ensure that you and your boy never set foot in our lands again. At most?' He shrugged with what seemed a quite disturbing amount of indifference. 'The gods have little sympathy for traitors.'

Chapter 26. A Family Meal

'I tell you it is true, unsettling though it may sound.'

Gawan's eyebrows rose a fraction but otherwise he didn't react. He knew that there was plenty in this world that he didn't understand, and Anryn was a very honest man. All the same, it seemed a little far-fetched. The white-haired brewer went on, gesturing with his spoon and spilling lumps of porridge onto the table.

'He saw the sylph at the woodland's edge and the lust drove him mad enough to follow her in. She walked through twisting paths but still he pursued her until eventually he reached the bower of leaves where her three sisters lay. The fool lay with them until the dawn, and then they drew his soul from his body as easily as they'd drawn his seed.'

Gawan kept spooning porridge into his mouth, but Rylion was smirking at the older man.

'I can think of worse ways to go than being humped to death by a bevy of sprites!'

Anryn frowned at him.

'At the cost of your soul?' He shook his head. 'Foolish boy.'

Rylion wasn't the type to take such a comment from most men but with Anryn he settled for a surly shrug. Gawan took a sip of milk and hoped his affable mood would keep up. He might need his brother on his side today if he was to speak to Tegwen.

They would be heading south soon but he had determined to see her before they left just in case she wasn't accompanying Taliesyn. He might not get a chance to speak to her for months if she remained at Graigarw, and wary or not he knew it had to be done. He also knew that he ought to be planning the right things to say to her but he had no gift for it and soon gave up in frustration. Instead he cocked an eyebrow at Anryn again and tried not to dwell on it.

'If this man was killed in the middle of the woods then how did the story ever reach you?'

Rylion looked up with interest but the brewer was prepared for the question.

'I did not say he was *killed* my friend, only that his soul was drained.' He took a sip of milk before continuing. 'A man can live with only a shred of his soul remaining in him, though it leaves him an empty husk. When this man staggered home he looked to have seen fivescore winters, yet he was only as old as you are, Rylion.'

The blonde man blinked uncomfortably for a moment as Anryn looked at him. The bachelor was getting into his story by now and his voice lowered as he leaned forwards.

'He told his tale to a herbwife he had known all his life and then dropped dead only two days after. With so little of his spirit yet remaining to him, who knows if he even *saw* the Bridge of Souls?'

Anryn looked grave and Rylion shuddered, and even Gawan wasn't sure what to make of it. He'd seen some strange things in his time, Camelas knew that, and he knew that creatures of many kinds still lived in the dark places of the world. But at the very least some of these tales had to be exaggerations, even if a grain of truth lay at their heart. *Or maybe you just* want *them to be fables?* He remembered how nervous he'd been going into the woods below Bryngarth and wondered just how keen Mabonac would be to watch over him now he was disgraced. He shrugged it off uncomfortably. Such knowledge was for the druids. He was respectful to the gods and had learned to take care in strange places, let that be enough. The Gadarim kept his eyes on his breakfast and waved his spoon noncommittally.

'More fool him for going in there anyway. Any idiot knows you cannot trust what you find in the woods, what did he expect?'

He pictured the old man and without thinking drove a knuckle into his open palm for good fortune. In the corner of his eye he saw Rylion make the same gesture and felt an odd moment of kinship with him for it. Anryn tilted his head and shrugged.

'Perhaps he was foolish but generally spirits are more good than bad. They will guard their territory fiercely of course and are wary of strangers, but mostly they are hostile only to those who are hostile to them.' He dipped his chin and looked at them through his brows. '*We* cannot always say the same'

Gawan wasn't quite sure what to say to that and took another mouthful of honeyed oats. Rylion seemed in a similar predicament and so Anryn went on.

'In all my time I have heard of few men indeed who have suffered such fates without somehow earning them. Sprites and Sidhe and suchlike are all reflections of the gods, and many can see a man's heart for what it is, even if his fellow men cannot.'

Gawan began to feel awkward and was glad that Rylion asked the question he wanted answered.

'All the same it's hardly fair to suck out a man's soul, even if he got to plough a few pretty girls first. What if the man had done bad things before but might have gone on to do good things had he lived?'

Gawan wasn't sure if Rylion was speaking generally or making a specific reference to him, but either way he was glad not to have asked himself. Once again, Anryn had his answer ready.

'The gods would *know* that though; they see not only a man's deeds but also what he may yet do. It is his heart that they look upon, not just his history, and there can be no secrets from the gods.'

The First Man wondered if he might take some shred of hope from that, but he was in no mood to discuss his feelings here. He took a last mouthful of porridge before washing it down with some milk.

'So this man you spoke of had it coming to him regardless?'

Anryn shrugged his shoulders again.

'Likely so, though nothing is ever certain where the likes of the Sidhe are concerned. Sometimes they are kindly and guide our paths as they should go. Or it may be he merely trod where he should not have out of simple ignorance and they took offence at it. Wise though most are, some spirits can be fickle.'

For a man stating that he didn't really know something Anryn somehow still managed to sound knowledgeable. Gawan wasn't sure if he was more impressed or annoyed about that and so simply half-smirked.

'Well, the damned fool should have seen the trick and turned back when the sylphs reached for his trews. I can't imagine a bevy of girls wanting to pleasure a stranger on a whim. Bloody dolt ought to have known that.'

Anryn's eyes met his for a moment.

370

'Some things are difficult to resist, even if we know they may do us more harm than good.'

The image of Rhianwyn came to him in a flash and Gawan appreciated just how true that statement was. To his shame he found he still dreamed about her sometimes, with woad on her face and fire in her eyes, or standing in that tub with the water shining on her skin. Then suddenly she would become Emeryn with blood drenching her golden hair, and then Bronwen, then Tegwen, all glaring at him with hatred. He grimaced despite himself and Rylion spoke with what seemed like concern.

'Worrying about Tegwen?'

Gawan nodded.

'Among other things.'

Even with these two he didn't feel like chatting, and Anryn's well-meaning comment just made him grind his teeth.

'You are doing right in seeking to be a father to her. She will respect that.'

Gawan snorted. Would she? And after twenty winters without a father, did she really need one now? He felt Rylion's hand slap his back.

'Even if she is upset at first, it will pass if you prove yourself to her.'

He knew they were trying to be encouraging but all it was doing was making things worse, and Gawan felt himself growing angry despite himself. Both men had good intentions but he was holding back an urge to punch them for it. He forced himself to breathe slowly, focusing on Mabonac's fire at his centre. He managed a few words, though they came out more as grunts.

'I hope so. I cannot know yet.' He poured himself some more milk from the jug. 'I just...'

But he got no further than that. Mid-sentence there was a knock on the door and without thinking Gawan called them to come in. The door opened and for a moment he thought he saw Bronwen standing there. Now that he thought about it there was much in Tegwen's face to remind him of his wife, though he saw a shadow of his own face there as well. As best he knew it anyway. But her squarish jaw somehow enhanced her looks rather than taking from them, and her eyes were so like Bronwen's they were almost painful to look at. She was keeping her expression plain in the same way Gawan did when fear threatened him, and to her credit she was doing a fine job of it. Only the stiffening in her back and shoulders betrayed the fact that she was nervous to be there. She spoke calmly but did not quite meet his eyes.

'I had just come to tell you; I will be riding south with Taliesyn.' She paused for a heartbeat and made an effort to seem disinterested. 'Should you wish to talk.'

The three men stood up and Gawan cleared his throat before replying.

'I am glad.'

He struggled to think of what best to say next but Anryn saved him the trouble. He turned to Rylion with an affected casual air.

'I heard a creak in the rear axle of my wagon the other day, would you help me take a look at it?'

It was a feebly obvious lie to get them both out of the room, and Rylion hesitated for a moment before playing along.

'Of course.'

Gawan suspected that he was a little reluctant to leave the two of them alone for the first time and Tegwen too seemed on the verge of asking him to stay, but neither one said anything and the two men left without another word. Father and daughter stood there in silence for a while, neither one knowing what to say first. Gawan knew he ought to be telling her how sorry he was to have left her but he just couldn't find the words to express it. It was strange. Apologising to Rylion hadn't been nearly this hard, and he felt he'd gladly take another beating rather than stand here in this silence. But then fighting was the only thing he was ever any good for.

It took an effort of will but he shook his doubts aside and said the first thing that came into his head.

'How long have you known Taliesyn?'

As soon as the words were out Gawan realised it was a stupid way to start but it was too late to change that now. Tegwen seemed taken aback by the question but she answered it all the same, her voice even.

'We met when he brought warriors together to march south to Caderyn lands, after the Panthers withdrew to make for Nantwyn.'

Gawan nodded. He and Marius had led a small force of the Dragon Legion to disrupt the Panthers as they moved through Gorvicae land, and their commander had decided to unite with Lepidus in the south to concentrate their army in one place. Taliesyn's warriors had arrived just as Second Nantwyn was ending, though his people had not been idle in the battle. The Dragons had been in no shape to pursue the retreating Lion Legion, and the newly-arrived Gorvicae had maintained pressure on them until the Blackbirds came.

Gawan shoved away the memories and rebuked himself in his head. She was here to speak about the two of *them*, not about her lover. He opened his mouth but Tegwen spoke first, shifting her weight onto one leg.

'I did not look for you.'

Her face was defiant and Gawan didn't know how to answer her. She carried on.

'When I was small I wondered where you were but I did not look for you. Rylion and Harlen always said you did not want me. Is that true?'

Her words were calm but there was pain beneath them and her shoulders were still tight with tension. Gawan felt a fresh stab of guilt and did his best to answer her.

'It was true once. It is not true now.'

It wasn't the answer Tegwen wanted and she cocked her head to one side, anger in her eyes. Gawan set his jaw. *Damn it she wants more than that from you after twenty years!*

'Your... your mother's death hurt me.' Saying it aloud felt like having teeth pulled from his skull but he kept going. 'It hurt me badly. I had no love left in me after that and... I would have been a poor father to you.'

From her face it was clear that Tegwen wanted to snap something at him but she controlled herself, speaking in a voice that was half-curious and half-mocking.

'What was it that changed your mind?'

A flood of images threatened to invade his thoughts but Gawan shut them out.

'I came to realise that I was wrong to leave you. I wish to make amends.'

Tegwen's eyes, so like Bronwen's, grew hard.

'So you are here because you feel guilty and you wish to make that guilt go away?'

Gawan held up a hand. There was truth in what she said but there was more to it than that.

'No, it is...' he floundered for a moment before continuing, 'I have come to think more of my family and I want to do what is right by them.'

He was half-tempted to say, 'ask Rylion', but it would have sounded like a child's excuse. Besides, she almost certainly had already. It seemed he hadn't done much to convince her of her father's sincerity but then again, he might well have tried his best and failed. Tegwen looked at him with that same hard glare.

'I have managed well enough without you so far. Harlen and Garaidh were fine parents to me.'

Gawan spoke without thinking, an edge of anger in his voice.

'But they were *not* your parents.'

Frustrated though he was he regretted the words instantly. He saw Tegwen's nostrils flare.

'They were more my parents than you ever were! I have never needed you before, Gawan, and I never shall.'

She was leaning forwards with her fists clenched and Gawan fought to hold back his own impatience. It was his fault, not hers, that this whole thing was so hard for him, and he pushed away his pride and spoke as gently as he could. Gawan's voice was made for shouting warcries not for soothing women, but he did the best that he could.

'I don't say that you need me.' He paused awkwardly. 'It is I who needs you. Let me be your father.'

Tegwen looked uncertain and Gawan took a breath and swallowed some more pride.

'Please.'

The young woman looked at him uncertainly. Gawan couldn't begin to guess at what must have been going through her mind but the confusion was clear on her face. Her eyes were dry but her brow was furrowed, and she opened and closed her hands a few times. For a moment it looked as if she might say yes but then she thought better of it and spun around without a word. Gawan followed before she'd gone two paces but he didn't catch hold of her.

'All I ask is a chance, Tegwen.'

She reached the door and did not turn around but paused briefly in the open frame.

'As I said I am riding south. Perhaps we may talk again.' Gawan took in a breath but she raised a hand, still not looking at him. 'But not today.'

Gawan realised that trying to dissuade her would do no good and he tried to take comfort that at least he might try again on the ride. All the same when she walked out he felt a surge of grief inside him. He had not started this at all well and if he didn't take care, he would lose his child for good.

*

It was only a short walk between his house and the longhall but Gawan was not walking quickly. His steps were slow and heavy across the rocky ground and the grey skies were mockingly reflective of his mood. He had handled his first talk with Tegwen badly, so badly he had risked there never being a second, and he wished that he could blame someone else for it. He wished he could blame Rylion for not speaking better of him, or Harlen for turning her mind against him in her youth, or even Tegwen herself for being so unreasonable. But he knew full well that he could only blame himself. Rylion had done his best, Harlen had been grieving for her sister, and Tegwen had every right to be angry with him.

He made towards the side door of the longhall, which was nearer, and tried hard to look on the bright side. She had at least suggested that they might speak again, and that was something. *All you have to do is not bugger that up as well.* He frowned at himself as he walked and decided to think on other things. They would be heading off tomorrow and he wanted to speak to both Hywel and Duran before they left. He knew that Gwydion and Pryder would be back as well and he should probably talk to them about his sudden departure after Moon ridge, though what exactly he would say he still wasn't sure.

He reached the side door but found that it was barred and, after giving it a second shove for good measure, he began walking along the side of the hall towards the main doors. His mind wanted to wander back to Tegwen and how best to approach her but he put that aside for now. He had planning to do with the others and he needed a clear head. With a little good fortune Rhianwyn would sort out her difficulties without too much bother and would be ready to receive them by the time they reached Bryngarth. Both Taliesyn and Boryn would be willing to listen to her and combined with some subtle hints from Hywel they might just make this work and keep the Gorvicae from fracturing. Gawan was in no great hurry to see Rhianwyn again but he knew that bringing her into this was the right choice and besides, he could trust that she wouldn't want to bring up what had happened any more than he did.

He reached the main doors, which were slightly ajar, and walked into Graigarw's hall, still pondering. Given the hatred between Taliesyn and Karadoc, he wondered if it was worth asking the Wildcat to throw her support behind Boryn. He might not enjoy the great support that the other two did but neither was he actively disliked by anyone. If he were to be made chieftain there would be only a few objections and the various headmen would soon make their peace with it. If either one of the other two gained Baercban's chair there was a chance the loser would be resentful enough to resort to force to try to seize it. Such conflicts were rare after a moot had made its choice but as Caserach and his father had shown on Niswyn, they were far from unheard of.

Gawan frowned slightly as he closed the heavy door behind him. Even if he were to suggest such a thing, Rhianwyn was hardly likely to listen to *him*. He remembered how she'd trained with Gwydion back when the legion was formed and that the two had seemed to get along quite well. Perhaps it would sound better coming from him? He at least had not tried to force a kiss on her. The memory sent a brief jolt of guilt through him but he battered the feeling down. This wasn't the time.

He walked into the room and found it practically deserted. He had hoped to find Hywel here, giving out some blessings before the ride tomorrow, but beyond a single figure on one of the benches the hall was completely empty. Gawan recognised that it was Boryn though and decided he ought to have a word with him too. If he was going to force the poor man to be their chieftain the least he could do was to talk to him about it. He raised a hand in greeting but saw that the old man was asleep, huddled over a mug of ale that he held in his lap. Gawan was ten paces away when the cold feeling hit his stomach. Another pace and he saw that Boryn's chest did not rise and fall.

The First Man broke into a run and he reached him in moments but it was obvious that he was too late. Boryn's skin was still warm but there was no breath from his lips and no sound from his heart. There was foam on his grey moustache and his face looked peaceful, as though sleeping, but Gawan knew death when he saw it. The Gadarim ground his teeth together, anger and confusion rushing through him, followed quickly by a heavy sense of sadness. Boryn was gone, and with him went all hope of an easy answer for the Gorvicae's troubles.

Chapter 27. Casting Stones

Caserach flicked the pebble with his thumb and missed the cup by a finger's width. Had they been playing in earnest he might have been more annoyed by it but none of the captives were carrying much in the way of coin, and they were only playing the game to eat up time. After countless days of sitting in this cramped hole with the same ugly faces, Caserach was glad of more or less anything that could break the monotony. Idwal went next, squatting across from his chieftain, and his own pebble clipped the edge of the cup but still tumbled to the dirt instead of falling in. The scarred man grimaced but otherwise barely reacted, sitting back on his haunches with a sigh.

Caserach drummed his fingers on his thigh, trying hard to keep his impatience under control. He'd managed to speak to a few of the Caderyn and had demanded to speak with their principle headman. Alraig had apparently agreed to see him but the bastard was probably enjoying making him wait. The Darin drummed his fingers that much harder at the thought. He would pay for his lack of respect soon enough. They all would.

Broad Kellas flicked a pebble and it rattled as it struck the inside of the cup. The giant smiled only a little as he gathered up the tiny handful of copper coins. They had all been around them a dozen times by now and Caserach thought they might as well have been playing for sand for all the difference it made. But then winning was winning, and despite everything he resented having lost. Idwal collected up the stones and tossed them back to their owners.

'You think Edryd ever got back to his chief?'

He addressed the question to no-one in particular but Caserach knew it was mainly meant for him. Broad Kellas was not much of a one for chatter.

'He struck me as a man who was good at wriggling his way out of things.'

Idwal smirked and sat back down again.

'A shame we didn't have a few more useless sneaks captured with us. Taking care of that guard was a nice distraction.'

Caserach snorted out a breath as he remembered.

'I don't doubt it.'

His loyal henchman had leaped on the Caderyn fool standing outside and had barely stopped shy of killing him. Idwal could sometimes get carried away. The three men placed coins before them and the scarred man idly flicked his pebble again, missing his intended target by a hairsbreadth.

'What do you think he really wants out of all this?'

Caserach shrugged as he cast his own stone. It fell just short and clacked from the base of the cup.

'Whatever it is it will mean no good to the Caderyn; that is all that matters.'

Caserach's guess was that the man Edryd served was a chief of some kind, and he would use Rhianwyn's disgrace to undermine the Caledon and make himself High Chieftain of the Gorvicae. Caserach made a note in his head that if things went according to plan, whoever took Baercban's chair would be a man to keep an eye on. Idwal nodded as once again Broad Kellas cast his stone into the cup.

'I suppose. Though if he supports the Caledon we will need to deal with him.'

Caserach hid his annoyance as the big man collected his winnings.

'I doubt if he will. From his actions I'd say he is a man who understands things better than that.'

Broad Kellas gave him a sideways look and Caserach remembered that his giant bodyguard might be fearsome, but he was not exactly a shrewd man. The Darin spoke slowly.

'The world belongs to the strong. Alliances come and go as needed but this Caledon nonsense,' he spat on the dirt in front of him, 'it makes them weaker, not stronger.'

Broad Kellas nodded but did not say anything, settling for adding more copper coins to his little pile and then throwing the pebbles back to their owners. Caserach bit back his impatience with him and was spared from having to explain further by Idwal's voice from beside him.

'What do you think they will do with her?'

He was smirking as he spoke and Caserach wished he could muster as much relish.

'They are a soft people. Likely they will merely banish her.' He held his stone ready to cast but then paused, thinking. 'That said, they still kill the worst of their criminals. They may yet cut her pretty throat.'

Idwal snorted.

'If a Darin chief did what she did we'd have gutted the bastard on the spot and hurled him from Whitespray Rock.' He turned to face Broad Kellas. 'What would the Breiryn do to a chief who led an enemy through your lands?'

The Gadarim met his eyes for a moment and spoke simply.

'Drowned.'

He didn't seem keen to elaborate and turned his attention back to the cup. His stone came close to sinking again but it clattered from the rim at the last moment. *About time.* Caserach spoke as Idwal cast his own pebble. It fell wide again.

'As I say, they are weak.' He smiled wolfishly at them as a pleasing thought came to him. 'You know what my mother's people do to chiefs who betray their tribe?'

Predictably, Idwal leaned forwards eagerly while Broad Kellas sat still and listened. Caserach didn't let his indifference bother him; he was enjoying this. His mother's tribe were a truly savage breed, a vicious race from beyond the Black Mountains whose practices had to be seen to be believed. Even the Gaians had been wary of fighting them.

'The Seiriae would cut his tongue from his head for his deceit, and then force him to eat it whole. They would bind him like a pig for slaughter and then bleed him like one. Then the whole tribe would drink the blood to take a part of the traitor's soul.' The chieftain's smile widened. 'By the time he reached the Otherworld even his ghost would be a shadow of itself, and he would wander the afterlife forever, formless and silent.'

Caserach found himself imagining how it would feel to do that to Rhianwyn. She would try to defy him, try to fight back, and that would make the whole thing that much sweeter. Inexplicably he found himself actually stirring at the thought, though he did nothing to discourage the reaction. *Why not? It's no worse than the stuck-up Gaian bitch has been asking for!*

Idwal was smiling too, but before he could say anything the door to their house was flung open. None of them stood as a Caderyn warrior stepped in, closely followed by the chief called Alraig and a youth so like him that he must have been his son. Caserach held back a grin. He had come.

The chieftain of the Dariniae stood up slowly, ignoring the ache in his legs, and faced the stern-faced Caderyn. Idwal and Broad Kellas followed his lead, but if Alraig was intimidated by any of them, he hid it perfectly. His expression was completely impassive. No, not impassive; contemptuous.

'Well, what do you want?'

Caserach felt his temper rise and he let a sliver of it show through.

'I am High Chieftain of the Dariniae, Caderyn. Does your tribe know no courtesy?'

The youngster seemed a little cowed but Alraig simply raised an eyebrow.

'Forgive me, I ought to have been courteous enough to invade your lands and kill your people before speaking in such a manner. Alas I am not an expert on Dariniae manners.'

His voice was perfectly flat, as if bored, and if anything it made the mockery sting that much more. Caserach held himself back with an effort. He had a plan to focus on.

'I am not an unreasonable man. But as a chieftain I am entitled to better than this.'

He gestured to his miserable lodgings. Alraig's mouth twitched into a sneer.

'You are a man who murdered his own kin. You will take what you are given and be grateful for it.'

Caserach fought back the urge to clench his fists. Idwal was already looking surly but he had to keep his own anger under control. He put on a face intended to depict restrained passion.

'I wept to slay my uncle, but he was leading us into disaster. I...'

But this Caderyn was no Asrec and he held up a gloved hand.

'Spare me your lies. If this is all you brought me here for then go back to your gaming, I have work to do.'

He began to turn away and every fibre in Caserach's body wanted to lunge for him and smash his head into the wall. He managed to settle for a swift pace forwards as the headman and his silent son made for the door.

'Whatever else you may think I am still chieftain of my tribe. There is no other claimant and no other kin to Ierryn.'

Alraig half-turned his head.

'There will be challenges in time, Kyran will see to that. Your Gadarim despise you and your people stay their hands only through fear. You will be judged, defeated, and if your tribe has any sense of honour they will throw you from the nearest clifftop with a stone about your neck.'

The younger man seemed to find his voice and he added it to his father's.

'Rhianwyn should have killed you at Moon Ridge.'

Alraig seemed irritated by the remark, presumably his boy was here to learn, not to talk. Caserach wanted to laugh at him for suggesting the weakling bitch could have come anywhere *close* to harming him, but instead he seized upon the lad's words.

'Since she did not kill me, are you not obliged to honour a prisoner of my station?'

Alraig looked like a man trying to chew on a nettle but he didn't slap the question down.

'Within reason.'

Caserach almost smiled. He had him. From what he'd heard this man loved the law more than most men loved their wives, and with just a little manipulation he could be made into his tool. The Darin kept his voice reasonable.

'Then I should appreciate a better house, and the return of my sword.' Alraig looked ready to object but Caserach continued before he could. 'I may not be Gadarim but such a courtesy would traditionally be extended to a chieftain, would it not?'

Once again the Caderyn looked sour but he nodded his head.

'I shall consider your request.'

Caserach let him turn back to the door before he spoke again.

'My uncle declared our tribe a part of the Caledon, did he not?'

Alraig turned back to him very slowly.

'He did.'

The Caderyn's eyes were fixed hard onto the Darin's but Caserach kept his voice casual.

'And Rhianwyn stated that great tribal affairs were to be discussed by all tribes of the Caledon, in the interests of unity?'

Alraig must have known how fake the curiosity in his tone was but Caserach didn't care. He was beginning to enjoy himself.

'She did.'

Caserach took in a breath, savouring the moment and trying to ignore the stale smell of the house.

'So, would the trial of a High Chieftain not be a perfect example of so great an affair? And should the other chieftains not be involved in such a trial? After all, until Rhianwyn's trial is completed and my own people make their peace, we are both High Chieftains of the Caledon.'

Alraig finally displayed some emotion as his face twisted in distaste.

'You are just as much a criminal as she is, Darin!'

Caserach took a step forwards and beside him Broad Kellas did the same. Alraig was not a small man but he was shorter than the chieftain and a dwarf beside the Breiryn. Caserach had to admit he was puzzled that the headman wasn't leaping on the chance for another voice against Rhianwyn, but then perhaps he hated the Dariniae even more than he hated her. It didn't really matter anyway; he had won this, he was sure.

Not that Alraig was going to comply easily. He glared up at Broad Kellas with obvious distain before turning back to face Caserach.

'Your guard dog does not impress me, Caserach. And threats are rarely the best way to argue one's innocence.'

The Darin held up an open hand and forced a friendly note into his voice.

'I make no threats, I merely offer you facts. If we are to stand by the law as it is then each tribe of this alliance should have a voice in this trial, and I *will* be heard in this.'

Alraig looked torn but his answer was inevitable. He would stick by the law, rigid as old oak. The Caderyn headman took a slow breath before looking into Caserach's eyes again.

'You shall be heard.'

From the sound of them, Caserach would have thought the words had been dragged from his mouth with hot pincers, but they'd been said and that was what counted. His smile became almost genuine and he nodded his head in mock respect.

'My thanks, Chief Alraig.'

The Caderyn looked as if he wanted to say something sharp but then he stopped himself and simply turned away. His son followed him from the house without a word, the guard close on his heels. Caserach almost laughed out loud as he sauntered back across the room. He sank down onto his lumpy straw mattress and leaned his head back with a sigh. That arrogant fool had danced to his tune like a drunken slut, and now Rhianwyn's fate would fall into his hands. Edryd's master would want her dead, as would many of her own people, and the voice of the Dariniae would be the last stone on her tomb. The Gaian bitch would die. Almost without thinking he flicked the pebble that he still held in his hand, and felt a strong sense of satisfaction as it clattered into the cup.

Chapter 28. The Long Road South

The sky above was iron grey but as yet they'd had no rain on their ride through the lands of the Caderyn. The fields around them were still green despite the season, though the scattered trees were fast becoming red and golden brown. Gawan took a deep breath of clean air and tried to relax his mind. He'd been lost in thought for most of the journey and had barely spoken to his companions. Time and again he found himself thinking back to the day he had found Boryn. He had called for Hywel straight away of course, but the old chief had been beyond even a druid's skill, and they had buried him the day before they left. Hywel had said that Boryn's heart must have given out only that morning, but something in his look had concerned the First Man. Something that made him think Hywel had suspicions about Boryn's death that the holy man was unwilling to share. Gawan frowned. He didn't like to think about what that might mean.

Unsurprisingly, though the old man had been respected throughout the tribe, neither Karadoc nor Taliesyn had shed any tears over him. Indeed, Karadoc had tried to persuade the others that there was now no need to travel down to Bryngarth. Without Boryn to outnumber him Gawan had worried that he might get his way, but Taliesyn had been forceful in his arguments against him and Hywel had, reluctantly, weighed in on the younger man's side. Gawan was beginning to become impatient with Graigarw's druid. He continually refused to use his great knowledge and power, even when it would clearly benefit his people to do so. Gawan knew that druids didn't like to become too involved in such things but all the same, if

Hywel suspected something was amiss regarding Boryn's death... the First Man shook his head. It was a struggle to believe that any Gorvic would stoop as low as poisoning, especially when the victim was a man like Boryn. *The north breeds few men so base as that, and the Wildcat killed the last one.*

Gawan shoved it from his thoughts for the time being and tried to lose himself in the ride. They had been on the road for days now and the trip had not been enjoyable. He had spoken occasionally with Anryn and his brother, and even with Tegwen, but he'd had little to share with his daughter and conversation had become sporadic and stilted. The other Gadarim had come along with them and had of course ridden close to their First Man, but they were not the jovial company they had been on the march to Moon Ridge, and he found he missed Gwydion's good-natured mockery. *But then, most of that happy banter had been between him and Tarwyn. It seems Gwydion lost his humour along with his friend.* He and Pryder were riding close behind Gawan but they were not talking, and he didn't look back at them.

The column of riders stretched a long way behind the Gadarim, though it wasn't a war party like the last time they rode together. Taliesyn and Karadoc had brought a few hangers-on with them, and Hywel was accompanied by a pair of junior druids, but beyond that the column consisted only of their modest escort. Duran had decided to bring along fifty warriors of the Dragon Legion. They were not expecting any actual trouble, of course; they were there as a symbol of their chiefs' status, since Karadoc especially would have kicked up a storm if they had not brought a suitable honour guard with them. Not that

390

Taliesyn would have been too pleased in that event either, he would simply have been subtler in complaining about it. He might often seem the better choice of the two men, but Gawan was far from blind to the younger man's faults. *And of course, the fact that he's humping your daughter does nothing to affect your opinion!*

Gawan looked to his right to where Tegwen was chatting with Rylion. He and Anryn had been conversing with her quite happily on the ride, with only Gawan finding the whole thing awkward. He tried to take comfort that she at least no longer seemed hostile towards him, even if she was obviously uncomfortable sometimes. The road led them past a little copse of beech trees and he saw Rylion point a finger towards them.

'Wait for it...' he paused as they passed by them and then continued, 'there; I am now the farthest south I have ever been.'

Tegwen tilted her head, her voice polite.

'Yes?'

Rylion nodded, gesturing west of them.

'Just down that way there's a village where da took me trading once, though that was years ago now.'

Gawan worried that the subject of their father might come up and he was relieved that Anryn spoke next.

'I don't think I have ever come this far either. These Caderyn don't appreciate good brew like we do.'

He smiled easily as he spoke and both Rylion and Tegwen smiled back.

'Well it's a long way further south than I know.' She looked around. 'I couldn't even guess as to where I am.'

Gawan saw a chance to talk about something he understood and he nodded in their direction of travel.

'This road we're on now will take us to Nantwyn, we may even see the town before nightfall.' He twisted in the saddle and pointed east, where the grey outline of distant mountains could just be seen beyond the open plain. 'Over that way is the land of the Bearnicans and the northern part of the Canwyn Range.'

He found himself thinking of the Blackbirds who were probably somewhere that way too, heading back east towards Tamora. Tegwen turned to her father with a curious expression.

'Is it true there are Carrocks living there?'

Gawan felt glad just to have her speak to him and he came dangerously close to smiling. He settled for a nod.

'I've not seen one in many a long year but men have indeed seen them there. Not that they are easy to find; the Carrocks like to keep to themselves.'

That was putting it mildly of course. The dwarf-like mountain folk were very private and fiercely protective of their territory. Gawan had heard more than one story of Bearnicans taking the risk of digging for silver in their mountains, and no mine had ever lasted for long. The workers would begin to disappear in ones and twos, or be found dead in the mornings with fir shafts in their backs. The Gadarim found himself thinking of the haunted woods that grew close to the Canwyn range, and his mind wandered back to the old man and his prophecies. Over the last few days he had finally managed to dismiss them as nonsense and yet here he was now, heading back towards Rhianwyn. Could there have been something in what he'd said about their fates being connected?

Gawan shook the idea away before shameful thoughts of his old enemy could intrude on him. Try as he might they still came to him sometimes; images of her painted face or her gleaming skin, and always followed by a stabbing guilt deep in the Gorvic's belly. Gawan ground his teeth together and told himself firmly that the old man had been nothing but a trickster bent on mischief. Anryn could say what he liked, the beings of the forest could not be trusted.

Tegwen was still looking towards the distant grey haze, barely visible it was so far away.

'I think I should like to see a Carrock someday.'

Gawan wasn't quite sure how to answer that but Rylion took over with some jest about their height. Tegwen laughed and said something back, and the two slipped into an easy conversation. Gawan found himself envying his brother for that and started brooding quietly on his many problems again. The moot was still weighing heavily on his mind, and his new view of Taliesyn wasn't helping that. The man seemed a preferable candidate to Karadoc but his relationship with Tegwen was colouring Gawan's view more than ever. They rarely rode together or conversed all that much, and for the most part seemed only to meet when the column stopped for the day. He didn't like to think too much about what they doubtless did by night.

He furrowed his brow a little. In many ways Karadoc was an admirable man, of sorts. He was an honest warrior and had defended the coast for as long as Gawan could remember. A few summers past there had even been talk of naming him to the Gadarim, but an incident at First Nantwyn had spoiled that for him. Duran had seen him stab an unarmed Caderyn in the back, and though he'd sworn he thought him armed and merely trying to gain ground, the action had been enough for Duran to speak against his recommendation. Whatever the truth of it, he would still make a strong leader for the tribe in time of war, even if he had little patience for living in peace.

Gawan scolded himself for his thoughts. He was putting down Taliesyn purely because of his relationship with Tegwen. He would do right by the tribe by encouraging peace with their neighbours, and safety from the Gaians could only be secured by unity. More and more Gawan was seeing just how much they needed the Wildcat, even if the thought of seeing her was unnerving. He ground his teeth and dragged his thoughts away from her. Taliesyn would be a good choice and with Boryn gone he would give him his support. *Though if I help to make him chieftain I'll make the bastard marry my girl!* Until he handed the honour to Duran he was still the First Man of the tribe, and Taliesyn would know the folly of alienating him. It might be pushing his chances to try to force him into marriage but if he was ever to be a father to his girl then the least he could do was to try his damnedest.

He turned back to face at his daughter again, smiling and laughing with her uncle, and looked forward to when all of this was over. Once a chieftain was chosen and the Caledon secure, and Duran was First Man of the Gorvicae, Gawan son of Dearg would retire himself to a quiet life. He had a family again for the first time in more than twenty winters, it was time to settle down and embrace it.

*

They were in sight of Nantwyn when the news came. Gawan recognised the rider as Elfed, one of the Caderyn's older Gadarim, who he recalled had been left in charge at the eastern hillfort. He was a man of middling size with long, light-brown hair, and the battlemarks on his arms were thick and complex beneath his bracelets. Gawan had noted before that though they ran up only one side of his neck, the sheer amount of them on his limbs, coupled with the various heavy bracelets, spoke of a man who'd no doubt make a formidable opponent. He rode his pony up to the head of the column and nodded his head to Gawan and the chiefs.

'Greetings comrades. We saw you from the hill; is something amiss?'

His voice was calm but his face serious, and Gawan supposed he had every good reason to be. There were still Panthers unaccounted for that might somehow have regrouped and even discounting that, the sight of armed warriors approaching your territory was always a cause for concern. After all, the Gorvicae had been his enemies for far longer than they'd been his friends. Still his manner was polite and confident and Taliesyn tried to dispel any suspicions.

'We are on our way to Bryngarth with our honour guard.' He gestured behind him to Duran's men. 'We are seeking...'

Karadoc cut him off, his voice hard.

'We need to speak to your chieftain. That is all you need know.'

Part of Gawan felt he ought to apologise for Karadoc's attitude but then he could hardly be blamed for wanting their business kept private. The other Gorvicae Gadarim urged their horses closer and Elfed nodded to them before he answered. He frowned at Karadoc but didn't comment on his rudeness.

'That may not be so simple as you think. Rhianwyn is to stand trial before the headmen in a few days.'

He sounded somewhat grieved, and Gawan answered before his chiefs could.

'We had heard something of that kind. I had thought it would be taken care of by the time we reached Bryngarth?'

Elfed's face became graver still.

'Alraig and several others are convinced that she has betrayed the tribe, and Alraig is greatly respected by the other headmen. They will listen to him.' He sighed. 'I fear she will lose her chair, and likely her liberty too.'

He left the rest unsaid. If the headmen decided she was truly a traitor to her people, chances were good it would cost Rhianwyn her life. Karadoc didn't seem particularly disturbed but Taliesyn's eyebrows went up.

'You think so many will speak against her at her trial?'

Gawan added his own voice before Elfed could answer, a hint of anger in it.

'Surely her chiefs owe her their thanks for all she has done?'

The older Gadarim shook his head a little and sighed again.

'Many of them would agree with you, indeed most of the tribe would agree with you, but those who would speak most loudly for her will not be present, and Merwyn may be a good man but he is not the talker that Alraig is. Without Reaghan or Bael to oppose him he will sway many of them.'

Gwydion chipped in, sounding confused.

'What of Owain? He is your First Man and would surely support Rhianwyn?'

Elfed shook his head again.

396

'Did you not hear? Owain is dead.'

Both Gwydion and Gawan spoke at the same time.

'What?'

'How?'

Taliesyn waved a hand at them and spoke more evenly.

'Boryn told me your First Man had been injured when Rhianwyn was taken by Alraig, but he did not say he'd been killed.'

Elfed shrugged his shoulders and his bracelets clanked together.

'He must not have known, but Owain died that very night and with all that is happening, no new First Man has been selected to take his place.'

The Gorvicae Gadarim placed their hands on their hearts and a beat later the chiefs copied the gesture.

'May he cross the bridge unharmed.'

Elfed nodded.

'May he cross unharmed.'

Gawan frowned in the moment of silence that followed. He had liked Owain, as much as he had liked any Caderyn at any rate, but more than that he was concerned that no new First Man had been named. Unlike the complex moots required for the naming of chieftains, the First Man of a tribe was simply chosen by his brother Gadarim, with the chieftain consulted only as a courtesy. Clearly the Caderyn thought they had to wait until this trial was done before they could name a new leader for their warriors, but surely if any time was the right time to make an exception to tradition, it was now? Elfed seemed to read his thoughts and he subtly raised an eyebrow, as though he privately agreed but knew there was little either of them could do. Gawan was a Gorvic and Elfed's duty was at

Nantwyn; what happened at Bryngarth would have to happen without him.

Gawan found his heart starting to beat faster and he took a slow breath to calm it down. With so few to speak for her Rhianwyn could be in real danger over this, and Gwydion spoke his thoughts for him.

'Her guilt in bringing Gaian soldiers into your lands is undeniable, even if she did it with good cause.'

Karadoc snorted.

'Good cause indeed.' The looks that greeted this remark ranged from disapproving to downright hostile but the big man shrugged them off. 'We might as well turn back now if the woman is doomed.'

Gawan strongly suspected that he'd gladly have called her something far worse in private, but with Elfed there as well as several others who would object, it seemed he was willing to convey at least a pretence of courtesy. Taliesyn turned to face him.

'We have come this far, and the situation may yet be resolvable.'

Karadoc gave him a scornful look but fortunately Hywel agreed with the younger man.

'That it may. A few words from us on the matter may help balance out Alraig's accusations. It is certainly worth trying.'

Karadoc stopped just shy of actually arguing with the druid.

'If we are permitted a voice in this then what is to stop Caserach from demanding the same? Will he not counter all that you two might try to say?'

Besides making it clear that *he* would have nothing good to say about Rhianwyn, the point he made about Caserach was concerning. He was after all still Ierryn's nephew, and if Karadoc had reasoned it out like that then no doubt so had he. Hywel said something back to the headman but Gawan only half-heard him. He was thinking hard.

The Gorvicae needed the Wildcat just as much as the Caderyn did, and if she died it would mean chaos for the both of them. But more than that, the thought of Rhianwyn being harmed made him feel sick to his stomach. It was a strange feeling, and it elicited a fresh jolt of guilt from his gut, but it was undeniable. More than any good she might do for either of their tribes Gawan knew one thing for certain; he could not allow her to die. If all went smoothly and Taliesyn could sway her judges then all would be well. If not, they would need another plan.

His thoughts began to race as Karadoc continued to protest about their mission, with Hywel and Taliesyn trying to reason with him. Gawan hated to think it but if all went ill then the only safe place for her would be Tamora. With some warriors and a little help from the gods he could get her out of Bryngarth by force and send her and Lucan back to the Gaians' city. It was madness, and it would destroy his own reputation of course, but then his honour was stained dark enough already, and at least *he* would know he was doing the right thing by saving them.

But what will Tegwen think of it? He grimaced and tried to think positively. Taliesyn would probably understand and he could maybe talk to her. Or maybe not. It pained him to think of losing what little relationship he had gained with her but his own hopes had to come second to saving Rhianwyn and her boy. He set his jaw and focused on the practicalities. He had Duran and fifty warriors of the Dragon Legion who would be loyal to him, and perhaps even loyal to her, but what would their fifty be against whatever warriors Alraig could gather? Besides, he would like this to be as bloodless as possible and a fight like that between Caderyn and Gorvicae could be as great a disaster for the tribes as Rhianwyn's death. He scratched at his beard. There had to be a way, some way to get her out of there if it all went wrong without sparking another war.

A sudden, and very unwelcome, thought struck him and he turned a little in the saddle to look behind him. The idea was risky to the point of foolishness but it was the best one he could think of at that moment, and time was of the essence. He let Karadoc continue blustering as his mind delved into it further, wondering as he did whether he had finally gone mad.

*

Edryd sat quietly on his grey pony, succeeding for the most part in not looking guilty. To the outside observer he was just another rider in the column, waiting around for the chiefs at the front to finish their talking so they could all get on. He fixed his face in an expression halfway between boredom and impatience, while inside he felt as wretched as he could ever remember feeling. He hadn't thought it would be like this. He had gone along with this scheme because he'd thought it in the best interests of his tribe. He'd been assured it was a subtle plan that would weaken their enemies and leave the Gorvicae the strongest of them all once more. And now a Gorvic admired by one and all was dead by his hand, and Edryd was beginning to foster serious doubts.

He could still see the blind trust in the old man's face as he had poured him his applewine. It had been so simple. Faerie's glove given to a man of that age would make it seem that his heart had simply given out of its own accord, leaving no reason to suspect that the elder chief had been murdered. Edryd sighed quietly to himself. Murder. No-one had told him there would be murder to be done. *And yet you did it, didn't you? You could always have said no.* He pressed his lips together hard, trying not to let anything more show on his face. *If I'd said no he would have killed me too and another would have been sent in my stead. Boryn would still be dead, only I'd be in the Otherworld with him.*

A tiny voice in his head wondered if that might not have been better for all concerned but he pushed it away with an effort. Things might still work out. He looked over to where the chiefs and Gadarim were still talking. Everything had gone more or less as predicted; the Dariniae had attacked the mainland, the Wildcat had called for the Gaians, and the Caderyn would now try her for breaking her own law. Now she would likely die at their hands, and Caserach would die soon afterwards. With their nearest rivals leaderless the Gorvicae, under a strong chieftain, would become the greatest of the tribes once again.

Edryd tried to believe in it but it was a struggle. Having seen what he had, he doubted if the new chieftain's ascension would be a clean affair, not with such obvious distrust between the followers of Karadoc and Taliesyn. He slumped in the saddle, his shoulders rounding and his eyes on the ground in front of him. He felt tired and depressed, and somehow stained by his involvement in all this. *But you are in on it now and there is no turning back. Perhaps all will be well and the tribe will thrive because of what you've done?* The Gorvic frowned at the grass as he failed to convince himself. *Or perhaps your actions will only succeed in making a bad situation worse.* He sighed as quietly as he could. All in all that seemed a lot more probable.

Chapter 29. The Detour

Gawan had long given up on counting how many times Rylion had shaken his head on this ride, and was not at all surprised when his brother started grumbling again.

'I still say this is madness.'

Gawan ignored him but then Tegwen spoke up.

'I agree. There is so much that can go wrong.'

The First Man held back a sigh; they hadn't *had* to come after all. He had asked them along mainly to show that they had his trust, and while in some ways he was glad to have them with him, all the same he was growing tired of their attitude. He was tempted to snap something at them about turning around if they wanted but he held his temper in check and spoke to the bachelor instead.

'What do you say Anryn?'

The white-haired brewer shrugged his shoulders a little.

'It may indeed be madness. But if you fear for a friend's life then I can understand your reasons, my friend.'

It was odd to hear Rhianwyn described like that, and it was hardly a statement of support, but Gawan supposed it was the best he was going to get. He nodded at the older man and looked back to the path ahead. They were travelling through a little patch of woodland, barely large enough to qualify as a proper wood but wide enough that to go around it would rob them of precious time. The trees were mostly oak and beech with the occasional red-berried yew growing between them. Gawan, Rylion, Anryn and Tegwen rode quietly for a while until Tegwen spoke again.

'What good will this do anyway?'

Gawan wanted to scowl. He knew this was a foolhardy plan and he didn't need to be reminded of it. They had left the column on the pretext of Tegwen wanting to see the Canwyns closer to, and she probably resented being the focus of the deception. Especially if she felt she had to keep secrets from her lover. It was mainly because of Taliesyn that Gawan had not shared his full plan with her, not that that made him feel any better about it. He didn't want to deceive his only child, but even now that they were away from the column he was hesitant to tell her the whole truth. He doubted if any of his little company would welcome it. *Annwn's blood even I don't welcome it!*

'I will get General Galerian to explain to the Caderyn that his men were already nearby and that Rhianwyn's request for help was barely needed; he would have come anyway when he heard that the Breiryn were attacking.'

Tegwen's brow furrowed and Gawan made sure not to look away. Whether she was sensing the half-truth or just not liking what she'd heard, he couldn't tell. Rylion spoke from behind them.

'I can't see it being that simple, brother. For a start we've no sure idea of where he is, nor any guarantee that he would come with us if we found him.'

Tegwen nodded.

'And might the sight of him not anger the Caderyn, given all that's happened?'

She phrased it as a question but her tone made it clear that she was confident of the answer. Gawan wasn't sure if he was more proud or irritated that his daughter could be so self-assured. *Though she is clearly still uncertain where you are concerned.* You *she still has no idea how*

404

to take. He was spared from having to dwell on that by Anryn's quiet comment.

'Yet he may also be a figure of both fear and respect. He did come to their rescue after all and the Caderyn have seen the effectiveness of his men.' He shrugged his shoulders. 'He may encourage some of them to save Rhianwyn out of gratitude for his assistance, and others may wish to keep her as chieftain out of fear of angering the Gaians.'

Rylion snorted a little at that. He was clearly still of the same mind as Karadoc in his opinions about Caderyn and Gaians. Not so long ago Gawan's opinion would not have been much different, but he had fought against and beside both forces more than once now, and his views on his old enemies had changed. He nodded along, hoping not to provoke his brother into an argument.

'As you say, and as to finding him it shouldn't be that hard. They will be heading back northeast along the road on the far side of these trees. If there are signs of their passing then we follow them, if there are not then we take the road southwest until we encounter them.'

He wished he was as confident as he sounded. This truly was an act of desperation with a very real chance of going wrong. And of course, he hadn't told them his real reason for seeking the Blackbirds. If all went ill and Rhianwyn's life was at stake, there was no better force to take her back to Tamora in safety. The thought of it still made his guts squirm a little. It was wrong in so many ways but he couldn't help but follow through with it, as if compelled by something he didn't fully understand. *Or don't you?*

They rode on a little further and Gawan scowled as he thought on it, though he didn't get the chance to brood too heavily before his pondering was interrupted. Up ahead of them somewhere he heard a noise of rustling in the undergrowth. He couldn't yet see any movement through all the trees and ferns but instinctively he sat up straighter in his saddle, his eyes scanning around him, and a heartbeat later he felt the others tensing as well. Gawan's hand moved to rest close to Heartreaver though he didn't move to grasp it yet. It might be nothing after all. Anryn and Rylion carried only their long knives but he suspected that they too were keeping their hands near to their weapons, and beside him he saw Tegwen wrap her fingers around her axe-haft.

The First Man slowed his breathing and kindled dragonfire in his belly. It didn't burn with the same intensity it once had but the warmth was still there, and he felt it begin to flow into his limbs. The noise grew closer and he flexed his fingers, still ready beside his sword but not yet touching the leather grip. He moved his head slowly from side to side, his eyes taking in every detail of the wood as the sound got gradually louder. When they came, the First Man was ready for them.

A trio of figures burst from the green-brown undergrowth, moving faster than any man had a right to run. They wore plain-looking clothes and their hair and stubble was ragged but even without their inhuman speed, the legion swords in their hands left no doubt as to what they were; they were Panthers. Gawan drew forth Heartreaver and kicked his heels into the pony's flank, taking the beast from a walk into a canter. The magic-maddened men might be moving fast, but he'd been prepared from the moment he'd first heard their noise and he charged the nearest man head-on.

The Panther raised his short blade but Gawan's blow fell just an eyeblink too soon for him, crashing down hard onto his crown. The Gadarim had time to smirk, thinking the bastard was probably missing his helmet, before the second man shoulder-charged his pony from the left, half-toppling the beast and throwing Gawan from the saddle. He rolled clear with Heartreaver still in his grip and brought it up to a guard as he stood. Gawan felt the blood pounding in his veins and for the first time since Moon Ridge all trace of guilt and shame vanished from his thoughts. Mabonac's fire had taken hold of him in earnest, and with a bellowing roar he remembered that for all the terrible misdeeds he had to his name, the Dragon God was still with him; he was still Gadarim!

'Gorvicae!'

He rushed forwards, taking in the situation at a glance. One of the Panthers was heading towards Anryn while the other was sprinting flat out towards Tegwen and Rylion. He saw as he went that the one whose skull he'd split was on the ground and unmoving, though with these creatures you could never be sure what would put them down for good. He was out of the fight for now though, and they could finish him off later.

Rylion was swiping his knife down at the Gaian beside him but the man was too quick and dodged to one side, grabbing for Tegwen's leg as he did. Tegwen hacked her narrow axe into his shoulder but the madman barely noticed as he hauled her from her mount. Gawan saw her land awkwardly but by then he had closed the distance, and with another shout he swung Heartreaver two-handed, the iron crashing into the base of the Panther's spine. Most men would have fallen but Gawan knew from

407

experience that these boys took some hard work to kill, and was unsurprised when he simply stumbled forwards.

Rylion had leaped from his horse and now moved to stand in front of Tegwen. The blonde man's face was pale but determined, and his hand was steady as he held his dagger before him. Gawan followed up on the Panther but then swayed away as the Gaian flung out a blind backhand. The blow clipped him with less than half its power but it stung all the same as it struck the Gorvic's temple. Gawan recovered quickly though and used the momentum to twist on the spot, bringing Heartreaver up in a solid cut that sliced through flesh then bone then flesh again. The Panther's head hit the ground with a dull thud, his lifeless body following a moment after.

Gawan wanted to check on Tegwen but he knew Rylion would be taking care of her, so instead he rushed towards the last of the frenzied legionaries. Anryn had been pulled from his horse and had somehow regained his feet before the Gaian could get on top of him. Both men had lost their weapons but the Panther now had Anryn pinned up against a thick beech, his teeth bared in a bestial snarl. The brewer had him by the wrists and was pushing back furiously, his normally-friendly face locked in a desperate grimace. Anryn was a strong man, exceptionally so for a man of his age, but the Panthers drew their power from unnatural sorcery, and try though he might the effort was in vain.

Gawan reached them just as the Gaian's teeth found Anryn's throat. The Gadarim screamed as he saw the bachelor make one last ditch effort free himself. He dropped suddenly to the grass and shoved the Panther's legs hard, and for a moment the legionary backed off, unbalanced. It was all the Leaping Wolf needed. Gawan hurled Heartreaver with all his might and the iron spun in the air once before impaling the Panther through his chest, passing straight through him to thud deep into the beech tree behind him. Anryn collapsed to his side with blood gushing from his neck and Gawan hurried towards him, keeping one eye on the Panther. He wasn't dead, though he probably had little time left to him, and he was struggling and spitting as he tried to draw the sword out from his sternum. Heartreaver was sharp, and all his efforts seemed to do was slice his hands open on the cold iron. Not that he stopped trying. Pain was no deterrent to the Panthers.

The First Man reached Anryn's side but he knew after barely a look that it was far too late to save him. Scarlet blood was pumping from his neck like beer from a broken barrel, and Gawan knew his friend had only moments left to him. He took him by the hand and tried to look him in the eyes, but they were wide and panicking and darted around without seeing anything. Within five heartbeats his grip on Gawan's hand became boneless, and in five more his eyes were simply staring sightlessly at nothing, his last breath coming out in a wet rattle.

Gawan reached over and closed his eyes, and was surprised he was not angry at what had happened. The comfort of rage was denied to him, replaced instead by a grey sadness that gripped his heart like an icy hand. He sighed slowly and felt more than saw it when his brother and daughter approached. At first they both seemed unsure about what they should look at; their dead comrade or their pinned enemy, and morbid fascination seemed to win over their views. Tegwen especially was looking at the Panther in horror and Gawan saw that her hands were shaking.

He glanced over at the man and almost pitied the poor wretch. Almost. His face was twisted into something that could barely be called human and he was still desperately trying to free himself from the tree. What in Taran's name had Lepidus done to his soldiers to make them like this? Gawan's look hardened. Whatever wrong had been done to him the man was still a mad killer, and if they didn't put him down he might succeed in freeing himself. His wound would kill him eventually, but the magics running through his blood could still keep him alive long enough to cause them trouble.

Gawan spoke over his shoulder to the other two, not wanting to turn back and see the body of his friend.

'This one may still be a danger, we need...'

But a blinding pain in the back of his head cut Gawan off mid-speech and he toppled forwards, dark spots appearing before his eyes. He landed on his face and felt cool mud against his skin, and for a moment he forgot where he was. He tried to turn himself over but a solid kick in his ribs made him double up in pain, and before he knew it he was vomiting on the grass. Another kick rolled him over onto his left side and he felt the stamp of a heavy boot go through his knee. Pain shot through the limb and he almost cried out but another foot into his torso drove the air out of his lungs. He coughed once or twice and then lay still, his eyes closing as blackness beckoned to him. He managed to stay awake with an effort, helped along by the strong scent of the vomit beside him.

A voice came that he knew rationally must have been from nearby but it was faint and muffled, as if he was hearing it through a wall.

'Is he dead?'

A second voice, this one lower, answered gruffly.

'I doubt it, he's a thick-skulled bastard.'

Gawan managed to half-turn himself and opened his eyes slowly. His head was pounding and the sky was uncomfortably bright overhead, but he could just make out the two shadows standing over him. He felt something wet hit his cheek and guessed that one of them had just spat on his face. It still echoed but he recognised Rylion's voice.

'You have no idea how long I have waited for that, brother.' He kicked him again, though mercifully this one glanced from his shoulder. 'Were you really *so* arrogant as to think that a clasped hand and a word of apology could undo twenty winters' worth of hate?'

Gawan wanted to retch again but he managed to hold it in. The images above him were growing gradually clearer but he still felt too weak to move his limbs. Rylion began pacing around his fallen brother, punctuating his words with more kicks every now and then.

'You had the best woman in the world, in the whole damned world, and how did you spend your married life with this goddess among women?' He spat at him again. 'You ignored her for a chief you barely knew, for nothing more than your own stupid pride. And when she died and left you a daughter to remember her by you tossed her aside as if your own child was no more than a broken cup!'

Gawan tried to speak, though inhaling alone was painful.

'Rylion, I...'

411

But the blacksmith thudded another kick into his brother and Gawan coughed out what breath he had left in him, curling up onto his side. What little thoughts managed to penetrate the pain were cold and despairing ones. Rylion was right. Bronwen had been the finest woman alive and he had ignored both her and her child first out of pride and then out of grief. No matter how hard he'd been struck by his wife's death he'd had no right to abandon the daughter they had together. All his life Gawan had thought himself to be stronger than other men, yet with Bronwen he had been the weakest craven that he could imagine.

He heard Tegwen begin to speak from somewhere above him, and the sound of her voice made his heart ache in his chest.

'It was good of you to ask us along on this trip. We have waited for days on end for a chance like this.'

The contempt in her voice was painful to hear; a hate that had obviously been festering her whole life. Rylion snarled from his other side.

'Of course, it's only the *two* of us who have waited mere days for this. *I* have been waiting for this for more years than I can count, I'm almost surprised you didn't see it coming.' His boot found Gawan's injured leg and the First Man ground his teeth to keep back a scream. 'But then how would you have noticed? It's been many winters since you decided that I wasn't worth knowing.'

Gawan's breath was coming out in gasps but he tried to pour some anger into it.

'Perhaps I'd hoped you were above murdering your own brother. You truly hate me enough to fall from the bridge?'

A man who slew his own kin risked angering Annwn, and a fall from the Soul Bridge meant centuries of grappling with the other lost spirits of the Pit as the killer tried to climb back out again. Gawan knew that Rylion had felt resentful towards him, but to do something like this? *How much must my brother detest me?*

Rylion sneered down at him.

'I would dearly love to kill you brother, but I am not such a fool as to anger the gods.' He nodded to where the Panther was still struggling with Heartreaver. 'But if half of what I hear about these sorcerous Gaians is true then eventually he will free himself from that tree.'

Gawan felt a cold shiver run through his whole body, sufficient even to block out the pain for a moment. He was unarmed, weak, and could barely *see* let alone fight. He didn't know how badly his leg was injured but he knew for damned sure that he couldn't put his weight on it. He could barely muster the strength to clench his fist. Memories of White Ridge and Nantwyn came back to him; memories of the dreadful things the Panthers had done in those battles. If this one got free he would rip out his eyes and chew out his innards, at that was likely the *cleanest* death that he could hope for.

On top of that cold fear he felt his shame washing over him again. He would die knowing that his only kin felt nothing but hatred for him. Part of him wanted to rail at his brother, to spend his last breaths defying the man who had all but murdered him, but the thought of his daughter held him back. Tegwen would remember her father as nothing but the coward who never cared for her as a child, nothing but a broken man spitting curses as he lay helpless in an unnamed wood. Unless he spoke to her now, before it was too late. He thought of Emeryn, and the last memory they had shared together, and he knew he couldn't let that happen again.

He saw the pair turning around to head back to their ponies and managed to raise himself onto one elbow and call after them.

'I am sorry Tegwen. For everything. Camelas grant you long life.'

He felt his arm buckle beneath him but he steadied himself with an effort. His whole body ached and his vision was still hazy. He heard Rylion scoff beneath his breath but Tegwen's voice sounded uncertain.

'Is that a trick? Some curse disguised as a blessing?'

Gawan shook his head, regretting it at once as the pounding in it increased. Sprites and suchlike might twist their words but it wasn't his way, and he hoped Tegwen knew that, but nonetheless he left no room for doubt.

'I am no trickster. I wish you a long life, without sickness or grief and full of joy.'

He saw her walk back towards him, her gait slightly clumsy, and though he couldn't really see her face he heard the anger in her voice.

'And I suppose this is the moment where you ask me to forgive you?'

Gawan suspected she had wanted something like that so that she could take some pleasure in refusing him. He could hardly blame her for wanting that but he knew it would do her no good. Bitterness was a weary companion in life, and the least he could do was spare her that.

'No. I do not deserve it. I was afraid to be a father and it is too late to be one now. But I would sooner have it that your last memory of me is with a blessing, not a curse.'

She opened her mouth to speak but he carried on before she could. 'I do not blame you for hating me. I do not blame you for my death.'

Tegwen was silent for a moment and Gawan felt his arm collapsing again. This time he hadn't the strength left to steady himself and he fell onto his side. He heard Rylion's voice from behind her, short and angry.

'You shut your damned mouth! Come along Tegwen.'

Gawan could only just see her but for a heartbeat he thought his daughter hesitated. But then she turned away from him and started limping towards her uncle and the ponies. He heard the distant sound of people mounting horses and the First Man of the Gorvicae let his head fall back onto the earth. He had tried, it was all he could do. Part of him regretted not having done more, and done it sooner, but he put it from his thoughts. He had ended it as well as he could under the circumstances, and Mabonac would know that. Hopefully Taran or the Dragon God would speak well of him to Annwn and Damara, and his dishonours might be forgiven in the end. He closed his eyes. There was nothing more he could do now. Emeryn, Bronwen, Tarwyn and Anryn would all be waiting for him should Annwn let him pass, and he could make his peace with them in the Otherworld.

He felt his breathing slow and wondered if he might die of his headwound before the Panther escaped. It was hardly courageous but a part of him hoped so. Lying powerless while a madman tore at his flesh was not the way he'd pictured himself leaving this world. *But then no man chooses his ending. All is as the gods will it, and the best we can do is to meet them with our heads held high.*

Gawan almost smiled. It was the sort of thing Anryn would have said.

A noise above and behind him broke through his tranquil thoughts and he edged himself around painfully. The Panther had finally pulled Heartreaver from both his body and the tree behind him, and was trying to grip the weapon in his mangled hands. With half his fingers missing and his palms a shredded mess he soon realised it was futile, and Gawan saw him cast the weapon aside. He wouldn't need it anyway.

The Gaian turned his frenzied eyes on the Gadarim and started towards him, shuffling awkwardly. Magically enhanced or not the man had a gaping hole through his chest, and that was plainly enough to slow him down at least. His face was contorted with a mix of agony and hunger, and Gawan wondered if there was any way that one or both of them might die before he reached him. He doubted it. The gods might forgive him his wrongs in the Otherworld but it seemed they were not done punishing him in this life first. *Well, best try to give the bastard a challenge at least.*

Gawan tried to ease up to a sitting position but immediately collapsed back down again, his vision swimming. His head began to pound even harder and the pain in his ribs redoubled. He cursed as the Gaian staggered closer. *Just one punch, that's all. Just let me punch the bastard once and I can die contented.* Once again he tried to lift himself up to sit. *Let me at least tell Annwn that I died with a warcry and not a scream!* The Panther leered at him as he closed the distance and Gawan drew in his will and heaved himself up. His stomach roiled and his head throbbed but he managed at least end up sitting rather than lying. He gasped out a breath. *It will have to do*.

But then something blew past him and he swayed to one side, almost toppling over again. He blinked and saw Tegwen galloping her pony towards the Panther, her axe held high and a shrill cry on her lips.

'Taran!'

She swung the weapon low and it bit into the Gaian's shoulder, spinning him on the spot and almost felling him. He kept his footing though and grabbed the haft as she struck, yanking the weapon from her hand. Gawan's breath caught in his throat as he saw her lose her balance and fall from the saddle but then suddenly Rylion was there, hurtling past his helpless brother. He charged his own pony straight into the wounded Gaian and the sheer weight of it knocked him to the dirt. He lay there unmoving and Rylion leaped from his mount, his arms waving in rage and his voice loud and harsh.

'Damn it all Tegwen! What is wrong with you?'

The young woman didn't answer as she heaved herself up and Rylion shook his head, disgusted.

'So much for fooling the gods.' Gawan saw him draw his knife and start walking towards him, his face set. 'Looks like I'll just have to ask their pardon later.'

Gawan knew there was no point to it but he glared into Rylion's eyes anyway, purely out of his own stubborn pride. He hadn't the strength for anything else. The blonde man closed in on him but Tegwen scurried up and placed herself in between them.

'No! You can't...'

Rylion barely looked at her.

'I can, and I will!'

Gawan had no idea how far Tegwen might go with her sudden change of heart but the mere fact that she had returned for him was enough to cut through his fear. He knew Rylion would either shove past her or try to talk her back into hating him, but as it turned out his brother had little chance for either option. The Panther, his torso drenched in blood and his face as pale as milk, appeared out of nowhere and pounced onto the blacksmith's back, and before any of them knew it he had borne him to the ground. Tegwen screamed and ran for where her axe had fallen, and Gawan simply sat and watched, unable to move, as strong thumbs crushed his brother's eyes into his head. His scream was terrible but mercifully it didn't last for long. The Panther soon sank his teeth into his neck and Rylion's cry was reduced to a rasping gurgle.

Gawan tried to shift his weight but his skull felt like it might burst with pain and he hunched forward with his chin on his chest, his breathing ragged. He saw Tegwen looking around frantically for a weapon but he knew it was already too late. The Gaian was done with Rylion and was almost in arm's reach of where he was sitting. His only hope was that she'd find her axe and slay the monster while it was busy killing her father. It was something at least.

But then a strangely familiar whistling sound went past his ear and the maddened Gaian suddenly stopped still. Gawan had to squint to see the arrow that had grown out of his chest, but then two more whistles came in quick succession and a pair of long shafts thudded into the madman, one in his throat and then another through his cheek. The Panther reeled back but was quite clearly still alive, and Gawan saw him ready himself for a final lunge.

Then another arrow slashed through the air by the Gadarim's head and buried itself to the flights in the dying man's right eye. He slumped to the mud without another sound. Gawan tried to look around to see who had saved them, but all he got was a glimpse of iron mail and pitch black cloth before he keeled over again, and darkness took him.

Chapter 30. The Blackbirds

He'd woken up thrown across the back of his horse and despite everything had insisted that he was perfectly capable of riding. He wasn't of course but that hadn't stopped him from arguing, and he now sat slumped in his saddle with a Gaian scout knee to knee with him, the young man propping him up whenever it looked like he might fall. Which was often. Gawan tried his best to sit up straight but it was easier thought than done, so he swallowed his resentment as best he could and settled for a quiet scowl at his escort whenever he was forced to lean on him. His head felt like his father's anvil must have done after a long day of horseshoes and ploughs, and his body was wracked with fresh agony every time his mount's hoof struck the ground.

The battered Gadarim sighed, though only partly for his pain and injured pride. The image of that monster tearing into Rylion kept playing across his thoughts. No matter what his brother had done, or would have done, he had not deserved to die in such a manner. Perhaps it was that image that was keeping him from hating Rylion for his betrayal, or perhaps it was just that he understood why he had done it. For as long as he could remember Rylion had been resentful of him, both for overshadowing him as a Gadarim and an elder, and for taking Bronwen as his wife. Gawan had never really appreciated to what depths his brother had hated him, but he supposed he had no right to feel surprised. What he did feel was a heavy sadness, like a sodden cloak draped across his shoulders. He had come home to find his father dead and had hoped to build something from that wreckage by making peace with

Rylion and Tegwen. A lot of good that hope had turned out to be.

Gawan's head was still throbbing horribly and he closed his eyes for a moment. He wondered to himself how long ago it must have been that Rylion had first poisoned Tegwen against him. He let out a slow breath as he thought. Rylion probably hadn't needed to try all that hard. He couldn't imagine Harlen speaking highly to Tegwen of her absent father, and even if Rylion barely exchanged a word with his niece he would be building on a solid foundation of anger. *And yet she came back for you.*

He opened his eyes and looked across to her. Tegwen's face was still pale and her ankle looked painfully swollen, but beyond that she looked as relaxed as could be expected under the circumstances. She was in the middle of a group of Gaian soldiers, having just witnessed two fellow tribesmen being torn apart by inhuman foes, yet her face was calm and dignified as she rode. Gawan couldn't help but feel proud to know that she was his daughter. On top of her courage she had come to the aid of a helpless man whom she had every good reason to hate, and had risked her life to save his despite everything. He sighed. Such innate goodness in a person was a rare thing indeed. *She must get it from her mother.*

The young woman looked back at him and managed an awkward half-smile, and Gawan saw through her calm façade to the genuine worry beneath it. He remembered that she had only known the Gaians as her enemies, and the concept of travelling with them was likely more unnerving for her than it was for him. As if she hadn't had a hard enough day already! The fact was that the troop of men, around twenty of them, had been perfectly civil to them both and their optio had spoken enough Lurian to explain that they were being taken to the camp to have their wounds tended. Granted, Gawan had the impression that coming with them had not been a matter of *choice* but the legionaries had done nothing overt to make the two Gorvicae feel like they were prisoners. It was a good sign that no objection had been made to their keeping their weapons, though Tegwen was carrying Heartreaver for the ride. Presumably she had retrieved it after the Panther had been killed and Gawan had deliberately not asked for it back yet. He barely had the strength to lift it and his sword deserved better than to be dropped by a wounded weakling.

His mind began to drift back to the fight he'd barely lived through and despite himself he felt his palms begin to sweat. Gawan couldn't even guess how many times he had been close to death, but it had been many a long winter since he had last felt so helpless before it. He tried to push the thought aside but found himself thinking of Anryn instead, and the First Man shuddered a little. The old brewer had deserved a far better end than that. He would have to send word to Gelion he supposed, though he had no idea at all what he would say. Grief washed over him as he thought of all the stories and legends that Anryn had known and shared; a lifetime of wisdom and learning, all gone in an eyeblink. The image of his friend's last bloody moments flashed before his eyes, horribly vivid, and he turned again to Tegwen in an effort to shove it away.

'Are you alright?'

From the way the Blackbirds ignored them he guessed they either didn't care about their conversation or that most of the legionaries simply didn't speak the language. It was probably both. Tegwen hesitated for a moment before dipping her chin a fraction.

'I shall be.'

There was an awkward pause and Gawan simply asked the question out loud. He could hardly make things worse between them after all.

'How long were you planning it for?'

Tegwen didn't seem surprised but she still took a breath before replying.

'Years, in a way. Though I never really thought that it would happen.' She cast her eyes down but then made herself look back up at her father. 'When I was young, Rylion, he... he told me that we would do it one day. Together. I hated you enough and so I promised him we would. I never knew that we would actually *meet*.'

Gawan nodded. No wonder she had been so shocked when she'd first seen him at Graigarw. Not only was her father suddenly there in front of her, but so was Rylion, and the reminder of the murder they had committed themselves to.

'So you waited until a chance came?'

Tegwen nodded her head.

'Rylion said that you planned your own death for us when you suggested leaving the main column. He said we only needed to wait for Anryn to sleep or make water or something and then we could set upon you. He said we could leave you wounded somewhere to bleed to death or starve, or with talk of Panthers still in the woods we could always blame them for it.'

Gawan felt his eyebrows rise. It seemed a pretty thin plan, but then Rylion had clearly seen it as their best opportunity. His brother must have been desperate to get it done. Gawan frowned again in dismay and considered asking Tegwen why she had changed her mind, but he realised that was both foolish and selfish. She was a good woman and had decided to save her father, there was no need to make her say it out loud. A part of him hoped she had decided that she *wanted* a father now, but he had no right to ask her such a thing. He would offer himself with his actions, not with promises.

The rode in silence for a little while before Tegwen spoke again.

'I...'

But she was interrupted by someone ahead of them barking some words of Vulgare. Presumably it was a sentinel because their optio barked something similar back to him and the little group of scouts passed by without further talk. Gawan noticed that the Gaian gave them a distinctly uncertain look but he said nothing as they rode past him. The Gadarim began wondering just what would happen when they reached the camp, which he assumed was now quite nearby. He had told the optio that he needed to see Galerian but the soldier had simply nodded, neither confirming his request nor denying it. *Well, neither of us is in any state to argue at present. We shall just have to wait and see.*

About thirty paces on from the sentinel the trees began to thin out, and they soon found themselves in open land again. The grassy plain ahead of them was crawling with Gaian soldiers, some wearing mail but most dressed only in the black tunics of their legion. White canvas shelters were being propped up on poles in neat rows beside one another, with centurions and optios striding up and down between them. Gawan didn't have to speak the language to know what they were hollering at their men; he knew criticism when he heard it, and perfect though the shelters seemed to him, the legions' attitude to discipline bordered on the insane. Tegwen looked uncomfortable at best as they moved closer to the Gaians but she hid her fear quickly and turned to face him again. She took a breath and for a moment Gawan thought she was going to say something, but her eyes were fixed on a point over his shoulder and he twisted awkwardly to look. And he understood why she hadn't said anything.

A little way off, but still clearly visible, two men were being nailed to the lower boughs of a pair of ancient blackwoods. They had been stripped naked and what hair they had was matted and unruly, but a glance at their snarling faces was enough to show what they were. The two Panthers did not scream, not exactly, but they gnashed their teeth and growled like beasts as the nails were hammered home into their flesh, spitting and cursing vilely at their former comrades. Gawan felt a sense of morbid fascination wash over him as he watched the legionaries do their work.

It was very efficient. From the strange way they bent it seemed the Panthers' arms had been broken several times, and their feet had been sawn off almost to mid-shin. All that had presumably been done simply to keep them from fighting back as they were dealt with, yet still it was taking five or six sturdy men apiece to nail them up. Three men at least were needed just to hold a prisoner in place while the hammerer drove his iron spikes in between the bones

425

of the forearms, and even without their feet the Panthers tried to kick out at them. Once impaled, the legionaries were bending the heavy nails upwards just to make certain that the Panther could not get free, though with the stumps of their legs dangling a hand-span from the ground, Gawan felt that would be pretty unlikely. *But they're thorough these Gaians. Whatever else you might say about the vicious bastards, they think through what they do.*

The Blackbirds didn't seem to be enjoying their work exactly, but they did seem to be taking a certain amount of professional pride in it. He spotted the odd satisfied smirk or righteous glare from the black-clad men, but for the most part they might as well have been erecting a new barn for all the emotion they showed as they tormented their countrymen. Gawan turned his eyes away from the bloody sight. Men had once called him excessive for mounting heads on spears as a warning to other foes, yet what the Gaians did to their own… he suppressed a shudder. *These are the people you intend to call on for help?*

Gawan clenched his fists on the reins and stalwartly refused to look. The Panthers had done terrible things to innocent people. They were reaping only what they themselves had sown. Gawan didn't want to think too hard about how much he truly believed that and instead just looked ahead as they made their slow way through the camp. Tegwen didn't speak a single word as they rode on, and when eventually the optio halted and asked the two of them to dismount she did so in silence, her face empty and distant. It took a pair of legionaries to assist Gawan from his saddle and one of them stayed next to him as an unwanted leaning post. Needed perhaps, but certainly unwanted.

The First Man tried to hold back his frustration as he looked up at the white shelter in front of them. It was at least five times the size of the other shelters around it, made in an almost house-like shape complete with entranceway and canvas door. There were armed guards posted outside it but they were both standing relaxed. He could hardly blame them for not considering him a threat in his current state. The good news seemed to be that they were indeed being taken to Galerian, and Gawan wondered what exactly he should say, assuming that the general had someone with him who could translate. His grasp of Vulgare was rough at best, and for a conversation like this his limited understanding would not be enough.

Gawan hobbled towards the optio, assisted by his human crutch, but Tegwen stepped in front of him before he could reach the soldier. Her face was still deliberately calm but she bowed her head a fraction as she held out her hands. Heartreaver looked up at him and for a moment Gawan hesitated. He ought to say something to her, shouldn't he? This was an important moment, he knew it, and after what they had just been through he knew he ought to say something to his daughter but he just didn't know where he should start. He accepted the sword one-handed and his Gaian assistant held him steady while he sheathed it at his side. Gawan opened his mouth to say a 'thank you' at least but the words caught in his throat and the moment passed. Tegwen backed away a pace and the pair were quickly ushered towards the canvas door, and Gawan hoped he would be more eloquent when he spoke to the general. They were going to need him.

*

Gawan barely had to duck his head to get through the entrance, and the inside of the shelter was roomy, and spotlessly clean. The afternoon light was filtered through the creamy-white walls, and he could think of plenty of solid houses that were less comfortable to live in. There were a few items of furniture scattered around, all unadorned but obviously well-crafted and solid. At the far end of the space was a wooden cot made up with fresh bedding, with an iron-bound chest set beside it. In front of this was a desk made from a dark-stained wood with a pair of what looked like bronze candles set on top of it. Papers were piled neatly on its gleaming surface and even from this distance Gawan could smell the beeswax polish.

There was a chair on the far side of the table but no-one was using it. The two men already in the shelter were standing, both in almost exactly the same pose; feet shoulder width apart, hands clasped behind the back, chest forward, shoulders back, spine perfectly straight and eyes forward towards their guests. Though they had swords at their belts neither man wore his armour, and sewn over the breasts of their dark tunics Gawan saw the legion's badge of a black raven wreathed in flames.

He recognised the older of the two as General Galerian, and Gawan bit back his pride and bowed his head. The Gaian officers nodded back, their faces blank. Galerian gestured to the man beside him and began speaking in Vulgare, his companion repeating his words in the Lurian tongue.

'Greetings to you. This is Tribune Derrio, he speaks your language better than I.'

Gawan nodded again as he answered, Derrio taking it in before speaking in Vulgare to his commander.

'That is wise.' He did his best to straighten up and was both grateful and irritated by the help of the soldier beside him. 'I am Gawan, son of Dearg.'

Beside him he saw Tegwen step forwards and address the Gaian translator.

'I am Tegwen, daughter of Gawan.'

It was strange, *beyond* strange, to hear those words from her lips but Gawan forced himself to focus on the matter at hand. Galerian dipped his head politely once again and spoke once more through his interpreter.

'I believe we have met before, Tribune Gawan.' He turned to face Tegwen. 'I am General Marcus Galerius Gregorius, commander of the First Legion. You may call me Galerian.'

Tegwen's brow furrowed in confusion, she must not have heard the ridiculous names some Gaians liked to call themselves before, but she recovered herself quickly and nodded back. Gawan tried to think of the best way to begin their conversation but was interrupted by the arrival of two soldiers in gleaming mail, followed by an older-looking man in a frayed tunic. One soldier carried a water-bucket while the other held a pair of camp stools, and Gawan tried to hide his relief when Galerian motioned for them to sit. The general sank into his own chair behind the polished desk and the legionary who'd been propping Gawan up left along with two of the newcomers. The man who remained looked to have seen at least fifty winters, and his hair was the exact same shade of grey as his faded legion tunic. He wore a leather satchel across his body and produced a tiny flask from it before pouring out a cup of wine from a brass jug on the table. He added a measure of something from his flask to it, watching it very closely as the liquid trickled in. The general didn't seem to notice him and continued speaking as though he wasn't there.

'So, beyond getting your wounds looked at after your run-in with those Fourteenth dogs, what is it that you wished to see me about?'

The man in the greying tunic offered Gawan the cup of wine and Galerian gestured absently with one hand.

'You should both drink it; he is here to help you.'

Gawan wanted to hesitate but he knew better than to show fear before an enemy, and he took a deep draught without pause. If these Gaians meant them harm they could have easily left them to the Panthers. The wine was thick and rich and made him think of blackberries, with something else in the flavour that he couldn't quite identify. Almost instantly he felt the pain in his knee begin to soften a little, though it continued to throb. He passed the cup to Tegwen, who drank just as boldly as he had, and then turned his attention back towards Galerian. The general gave a tiny half-smile.

'I trust you do not object?'

Gawan shook his head a little as the grey-haired man took a moistened cloth and started dabbing at his aching skull. It stung but the pain was receding, and Gawan suspected it would be a struggle to keep his concentration. No killer of pain came without a price. He managed to kindle a little of Mabonac's fire in his centre and used it to help maintain some of his focus.

Even though he knew he was here to ask a favour of the man, Gawan couldn't help but comment on the butchery he'd seen outside.

'Rhianwyn won't like what you're doing out there.' He jerked his head towards the door-flap, provoking a tiny jolt of pain that he tried to ignore. 'Not on Caledon land.'

Galerian tilted his head a fraction before answering through Derrio.

'Are they not her enemies?'

He gestured for his junior to pour them each a cup of wine and he sipped it casually as Gawan answered him.

'Hate them she might, but she won't hold with tormenting them like that. It is not her way.'

Gawan could hardly call himself an authority on what *was* her way of course, but he liked to think he was right in this case. She was as fearless as he had named her in the face of her enemies, but he had never seen cruelty in her nature. Galerian shrugged his shoulders.

'Regrettable though it is to offend her, these are our soldiers and we will deal with them as we see fit. They have betrayed the Emperor, Gaivia, and the honour of the legions.' He pointed in their general direction with his cup-holding hand. 'Thus ever for traitors.'

His face was hard and Gawan tried not to think of how Rhianwyn might be punished if her people believed such things of her. Lurians might not be as savage as the Gaians were but for a crime such as that, the penalty would be severe. The grey-haired man began wrapping cloth bandages around his head and Gawan did his best to ignore him as he worked.

'As you will. I came here... to ask a favour of you.'

431

The general raised an eyebrow but gestured politely for Gawan to continue.

'Rhianwyn has been made a captive by one of her headmen, they...'

Galerian waved his hand irritably, his brow creasing.

'Yes, I know. He took her away after the battle.'

Gawan looked at him quizzically and he answered the question before it was asked.

'I was there when it happened. I offered to take care of the situation for her but she told me to stand down. I assumed that meant she was able to resolve it herself?'

Gawan felt a spike of annoyance, both at Galerian and at Rhianwyn, but he supposed he saw her point. At the time it must have seemed something more manageable, and if Owain had already been harmed then no doubt she would have wanted to avoid more bloodshed. The old man finished with his head and began strapping up his knee, binding it so tight it was an effort not to wince, despite the wine.

'She did not fully understand what was happening. She did not know that those who might support her would not be there at her trial. She has underestimated Alraig and if Caserach is permitted to speak against her as well, then the danger to her life is very real.'

Galerian looked at them seriously as Gawan's words were translated for him, and Tegwen added her voice to her father's.

'We would have you come with us and say to the Caderyn chiefs that you were already in Caledon land, and would have assisted Rhianwyn whether she had asked for help or not.'

Gawan nodded his head in agreement. Galerian watched them for a moment before he answered.

'I hold Lady Dessida in high regard and would of course have come to her aid regardless of request.' He paused and raised a finger. 'But the fact is that she *did* send me such a request, and I will not bear false witness in a legal trial.'

The old man continued working without a word, finishing with Gawan's leg and moving on to start on Tegwen's ankle. His wine was still powerful enough to blur Gawan's vision a little but he regained his focus with a moment of effort.

'I would not ask you to lie, General Galerian. I only ask you to swear before your gods that your intentions were not hostile, and that you *would* have come to her aid anyway.'

The Gaian officer regarded them thoughtfully once again.

'There is more to this though, is there not?'

Tegwen turned to face her father, looking puzzled. In a way Gawan was relieved to see her eyes were a little distant. He had not relished the prospect of her hearing this. He faced the general.

'Should it go ill, we would need men to get her out of Bryngarth in safety. If my cohort attacks the Caderyn it could mean war between us. The Gaians rescuing their own however...'

For all the wine's effect Tegwen was looking at him with shock but Gawan shoved away his guilt for the moment and kept his eyes on the Gaians. Galerian's brow furrowed again and when he spoke, it was slow and careful.

'You ask much. Such an action could just as easily spark a war between the Empire and the Caledon.'

Gawan nodded. The last war against the Gaians had not been against Gaivia itself, merely a rogue general and his sorcerous ally, and even then it had almost cost them everything. Should the Caledon face the Empire they would be crushed, plain and simple. Gawan tried to keep his voice confident.

'A war that you would likely win in the long run. But right now you are one legion, far from any reinforcement.' Galerian's expression hardened and Gawan quickly continued. 'But neither one of us wishes for conflict. War with the Empire would be in no-one's best interests.'

It sounded odd, even to him. The Gaians were the *enemy*, damn it all! But then these were strange times, and he had to keep Rhianwyn from harm. Galerian looked at him noncommittally.

'I concur, but still this is difficult. Taking Rhianna with us when she was first threatened is one thing, but to actively attack Bryngarth is another.'

Both Galerian and his interpreter pronounced the town's name terribly, so much so that Tegwen was fighting back a smile. Or perhaps that was the pain-killing wine. Gawan watched the Gaian closely and decided to play the only way he knew how.

'Let us put it like this; if you do not help us, and Rhianwyn dies, then I will use my influence as First Man to make Karadoc the new chieftain of the Gorvicae.' Tegwen's would-be smile vanished as she stared at him but Gawan forged on. 'He is a headstrong man with no love for your people, and under my influence he will lead the Gorvicae against Tamora. Such an attack would

434

probably fail, but not before your legion has been made to bleed so heavily that every tribe on this continent will feel ready to chance their hands against you.'

Galerian's face was turning pale with anger but Gawan kept going. He simply didn't have anything else to trade with.

'Of the three legions first stationed here, one has been destroyed and another badly damaged and disgraced. Your Empire would almost certainly come back and destroy us all, but not before many Gaians had been killed, and your reputation dealt a hammerblow from which it may never recover.'

Gawan wondered just what his own reputation was worth now, especially since he was sitting here and negotiating with the enemy, but if it saved Rhianwyn and her boy then it was worth it. If he was honest with himself Gawan didn't even know *why* that made it worth it, just that it did. Derrio finished his translating and Galerian's eyes bored into Gawan's.

'Are you threatening me, Tribune Gawan?'

Gawan met his gaze.

'Yes, I am.' He paused for a heartbeat before he went on. 'But I do not want any of that. It would mean ruin for my people. Bring yourself and some men to Bryngarth, speak for Rhianwyn and be ready to rescue her and the boy if needed, and I swear by Taran's thunder and Mabonac's fire that I will do all I can to make Taliesyn our chieftain. He is a man who will want unity and peace and he will live as a good neighbour to you.'

Gawan's self-hatred for having to do this was eased a little when Tegwen looked at him again. She wasn't smiling exactly but there was something in her face that was *almost* a smile, and he hoped it wasn't just the wine addling her wits. He doubted it somehow. She didn't seem the sort of girl whose wits were easily addled.

He looked at Galerian. The Gaian's face was a mask but he must have been both angry and conflicted underneath it. It reminded Gawan of how Marius used to hide his emotions so well. *Even when you used to provoke him.* Galerian pondered quietly for a while before taking in a slow breath.

'Stability is in all our interests. Regardless of my own feelings, the Empire would not want Lady Dessida removed from her position, and the boy Lucianus is the last male heir of an ancient name. It is right that he be kept from harm.'

He glared at Gawan again, and though the First Man matched his gaze he suspected most men would have been cowed by it. The man had a stare like solid granite.

'I do not appreciate threats, Tribune Gawan. But under the circumstances I shall forget your tone. This time.'

He turned to Derrio and said something to him that the junior officer didn't translate. Instead he strode to the door-flap and called out something to the soldiers outside. Galerian kept looking forwards and when the tribune came back he spoke through him again.

'I shall give orders to strike camp and head back west.'

Gawan felt a tiny jolt in his stomach and wasn't sure exactly how to respond, but he nodded respectfully to the other man.

'My thanks.'

Tegwen was still looking uncertain beside him and Gawan hoped she would understand his actions. Before he could say anything to her the Gaian general was rising from his seat, and Gawan rose awkwardly as well. His knee felt better than it had done but his head was still feeling heavy, and for a moment he thought he might fall. But then he felt Tegwen's hand on his arm and he leaned into her a little to steady himself. That gesture, more than anything she might have said, gave him a glimmer of hope. Galerian took a sip of his wine before speaking again.

'I shall make sure your mounts are made ready; you had best go on ahead of us, I think.'

Gawan nodded his agreement and, with Tegwen's help, began hobbling towards the canvas doorway. He had almost reached it when Galerian spoke to him directly for the first time, his Lurian rough but surprisingly understandable.

'Threaten me again, Gawan son of Dearg, and you will regret it.'

His voice was flat and cold, and far more unsettling than it would have been had he shouted. Gawan met his eyes for the last time and dipped his head in a shallow bow of acknowledgement before turning and leaving the shelter. The two Gorvicae stepped out into the afternoon sun, and Gawan wondered if he had just taken the first steps towards fixing this mess, or if he'd just made the situation that much worse.

Chapter 31. Visitors

For the first time in days Rhia actually felt at ease, and even managed a short laugh as her mother told her story. She noted, as she often had, how Myrna still looked so much younger than most women of her age, despite the smattering of silver in her black hair. She gestured with her steaming cup as she told the tale, and the smell of rosemary leaf was heavy in the air. Rhia waited for her to take another sip then leaned forward in her seat.

'But what did *you* say?'

The older woman shrugged.

'What else could I say but yes? The man had just swum the White Rush for Marna's sake, and only days before midwinter too.'

She shook her head with a rueful little smile and Rhia smiled back at her. She could well believe that her father had been fool enough to do something so daring. Wise leader though he was there had always been a feeling of youth and vitality about Carradan, and the notion of him risking his life to impress a pretty girl fitted perfectly with her idea of his character. A little jolt of grief struck her as she remembered how much she missed him but she put it to the back of her mind and tried to enjoy the story about him.

'But he must have almost killed himself, diving into the river at that time of year?'

Myrna smiled at her daughter.

'His main objection seemed to be how much the cold had shrunk his manhood.' The older woman winked. 'Of course, once we got him warmed up again...'

Rhia half-choked on her drink and couldn't help but dribble a little as she spoke, her voice mock-frantic.

'I don't want to know!'

They both smiled quietly at that for a moment, remembering how Myrna and Carradan had liked to tease their daughter by talking of such things. The memory made Rhia think back to her first wedding, when she had kissed palms with her dear Bevan, and it was an effort to hold back a tear as his face appeared in her mind. She shook it off quickly enough but Myrna saw her pain.

'You have suffered so much, dear.'

The older woman placed a hand on her daughter's knee and Rhia put her own hand on top of it. She didn't really know what she could say in response to that but her mother spared her the trouble, her voice soft and comforting.

'It is of little solace I know, but I am so proud of the woman you have become, in spite of all.'

Once again Rhia felt herself lost for words and just nodded her head quietly. They sat in silence for a while and sipped at their leaf until Rhia brought up the matter she had been putting off talking about.

'Mother, should it go badly for me in this trial...'

Myrna cut across her, slashing her hand dismissively as she spoke.

'You need not fear, my child. All the Caderyn have great love for you, I have seen it.'

Rhia frowned.

'Alraig does not seem to share their view.'

Her mother tutted.

'He is a hard and brittle man but he is not the whole tribe. Have faith in your people. They have faith in you.'

Rhia wondered for a moment if they were misplaced in that faith, remembering how she'd ignored the dire warnings of the man in Glyscoed all those years ago, and how she'd once allowed herself to be seduced by the easy life of a Gaian patrician. Her judgement might have grown a little better in the meantime but all the same, she'd made some damned foolish mistakes. She swallowed.

'I do have faith in them, but I would be doing wrong by Lucan if I didn't make plans for him just in case.'

Myrna clearly wanted to argue back with some more words of encouragement, but she stopped herself and simply nodded her head.

'Of course. What would you have me do?'

Rhia had thought this through a dozen times and she had her answer ready.

'If the family is not drawn into all this then take him to Olla at Penafon. He and Siriol love each other and it might be wise for you to go there with them.'

The older woman nodded again. Penafon might be Alraig's territory but Olla was married to his only nephew and, provided that the family were not to be punished for her actions, the headman would almost certainly allow them to live there in peace.

'And if we are drawn into it?'

Rhia frowned. There was always a chance of her actions resulting in the whole family facing banishment, though she hoped and prayed it would not come to that. Her first choice in that event would have been to send Lucan to Junia in Tamora. She would take good care of her grandson and he had friends of his own age in the city. He might even welcome a return to Gaian life. But getting him there would be a challenge, especially if Alraig decided to make things difficult for them. After that she had considered sending him to Bradan on the coast. It would be strange for him but Bevan's father was as fine a man as his son had been, and he would take care of Lucan like he was his own child. But even that might prove impossible if the Caderyn chiefs chose to be harsh.

Her final option had come as something of a shock even to her, but at least it would guarantee her son's safety if she... well, Rhia didn't want to think about that 'if'. She had faced death before, she'd even considered taking her own life in the past, but dying in disgrace at the hands of her own people, and leaving little Lucan without a mother, was enough to make her hands shake and her stomach squirm with dread. Her mother held her hand tighter and Rhia pulled herself out of her fear.

'If you are cast out of our lands then get yourselves to Graigarw. Find Gawan son of Dearg and he will take care of you.'

Myrna's eyebrows went up and Rhia could hardly blame her for it. The idea had only come to her the night before and try though she might she couldn't find a better plan. He might not be a friend exactly, she didn't really know *what* he was, but Gawan was a man she knew she could rely on to do what he felt was right. If Alraig and the chiefs made it impossible to get him to Tamora, then Lucan would be safest with Rhia's fellow Gadarim. Myrna bit back whatever comment had first come to her mind and patted her daughter's hand.

'As you say, so long as we are all of us kept together.'

Rhia felt glad and she nodded in agreement. Her family, once so large, had grown much smaller over the last few

441

years and they would need one another more than ever were they cast out of the tribe. She marvelled sometimes at how her mother had coped with it all. Even without the dreadful loss of her husband, of the two sons and three daughters that Myrna had raised only Rhia and Olla remained. Yet Myrna had stayed strong enough to be a rock for her children still, shedding tears but never falling into despair. Rhia envied her for that. She looked at the unassuming old woman and felt proud to know that this was her mother. *What I would not give for half of her strength.*

The older woman kept up her smile as she went on.

'The boy has been pining for you, you know. When he's not running riot with his cousin that is.'

Rhia frowned for a moment.

'He doesn't know about...'

But Myrna shook her head.

'No, no. He knows that you have chief-like things to do and they are keeping you here for now. He misses you, but so long as he has Siriol to cause mischief with he is happy enough. Both Olwyn and I together are struggling to keep control of them.'

Rhia managed a small smile. Lucan was never truly *naughty* but he could be a handful sometimes, not that Myrna was really complaining. She and Olla both loved Lucan and would be glad that he had made friends among his own people. Rhia took some comfort in thoughts of her son, and looked forward to Olla bringing him along to visit. She sat quietly for a while sipping leaf with her mother, and found her resolve strengthening as she drank. She would come through this for him, there was no other way. All would be well... all would be well.

*

Rhia leaned back in her creaking chair and sighed with something close to contentment. Olla had brought along not only Lucan but also a steaming pot of her excellent chicken stew, and both mother and son had found the meal delicious, but filling. There was still half a loaf of bread left over on the table but Rhia couldn't bring herself to finish it. She was happily full, and had just spent a pleasing hour doting on her boy. She'd been a little sad when Olla had returned to take him home but he would visit again tomorrow and that was enough to give her some hope. Lucan had resisted leaving her at first, his devotion fairly melting Rhia's heart, but he'd been tired from a day of chasing dragons with his cousin and Olla had worn him down before too long.

Rhia reached up with an effort and took her cup of milk from the table. It was still quite cool and she sipped at it quietly, her eyes on the fire crackling in the little hearth. The flickering light caught on the bright guard of Silverbite, leaning sheathed against the wall beside it. Rhia's mind wandered back to that day at Broken Stream when she had taken the weapon from Sedryn, the son of Baercban. Everything had been so much simpler back then; the Gorvicae had raided them and the Caderyn had beaten them back. Their enemies had accepted their defeat and they had all gone home again. Warriors had died or been wounded of course, and she remembered all too clearly how much she'd hated her enemy at the time, but at least it had been something that they all understood. Ever since the Gaians came the world had become so much more complicated. *Either that or it was always so, and only now are you old enough to understand that.*

She might have dwelt on that thought for a while as she stared into the flames but a knock on the door caused her to look up, and she called out for whoever it was to come in. Cerri opened the door and bowed her head in greeting.

'I'm sorry to interrupt Rhia, but he said it couldn't wait until morning.'

Rhia wondered what new problems were about to face her this time but she kept her face blank and waved a hand at her cousin.

'It's alright Cerri, let him in.'

She nodded again and stepped aside to let a young man enter the room. He seemed to be around Rhia's own age, and it took only a glance for her to realise he must be the son of Alraig. Besides his hair being fully brown he was almost a copy of the man, though his eyes were nowhere near as hard as his stern-faced father's were. Rhia tried to place his name, she was sure she must have heard it at some point, but he saved her the trouble by introducing himself.

'Hello. My name is Tydfyl, I am...'

Rhia finished the sentence for him.

'Alraig's son, yes I know. Did he send you?'

She spoke more abruptly than she normally would have but then her quiet evening had just been interrupted by an enemy. The young man looked vaguely apologetic and shook his head quickly.

'I told your cousin that he had, but no. I am here on my own account.'

He paused awkwardly and Rhia felt her temper fraying even more. It was true that she had nothing *but* time in her captivity but all the same, she had been enjoying a rare moment of relaxation.

'And *why* are you here on your own account, Tydfyl?'

The young man shuffled his feet for a moment. He might have had Alraig's face but he had none of the headman's composure.

'Well you see... I was thinking that perhaps... for the good of the tribe and... well...' he blurted out the last words in a rush. 'Would you marry me?'

It took Rhia a couple of heartbeats to fully take that in and when she did she couldn't hold back a snort of laughter.

'Has anyone ever told you that your seduction method needs some work?'

The young man dropped his eyes and fidgeted with embarrassment. Even in the firelight Rhia could see his face reddening and she did her best to hold back her amusement. But it was ridiculous! The man's father would happily see her dead or banished from her lands, and now his son was asking her to kiss palms with him? What kind of fool was he? Tydfyl cleared his throat, straightened his back, and tried again.

'It would be for your own sake. You will likely lose in the trial to come but if you marry me I am sure I can persuade Father to be lenient with you. It would show him, and all of them, how much you value your own people.'

Given what the man himself had recently told her, Rhia was far less confident of that than Tydfyl seemed to be.

'Alraig thinks I have betrayed our people. I doubt if climbing into your bed would change his mind about that.'

Once again the young man shuffled awkwardly, and Rhia suspected she might have been wrong in guessing his age. His beard was dark but still quite thin along his jaw, and now she regarded him more closely she saw his face had a very boyish look. Chances were that he was several summers younger than she was, and the uncertainty of youth came out in his voice.

'If you also swore to have no contact with the Gaians again, and left all such matters to Father or to Merwyn in future, I think it would be enough to persuade him.'

Rhia decided to nip this idea in the bud.

'It is a kind offer Tydfyl, but I am the one the Gaians will want to deal with and besides, I intend to win this. My people know that I have acted only in their best interests.'

Tydfyl's brow furrowed.

'It is the headmen, not the whole tribe, who will decide your fate.'

Rhia shrugged.

'Merwyn will speak well of me.'

The young man nodded.

'Perhaps so, but that is it.'

Now it was Rhia's turn to frown.

'I have others who will support me. Bradan...'

He cut her off.

'Bradan has been sent back to Mobryn. Alraig thinks the Dariniae may still be a threat to the coast.'

Rhia felt her confidence falter a little but she carried on.

'When Bael comes...'

But once again he interrupted her.

'Bael has still not returned, and none have heard any word of him.'

The fire was warm but still Rhia fought back a shiver. With Owain dead she had no First Man to speak for her Gadarim, who she knew would be behind her to a man. Aedan's son, she couldn't recall his name, would probably take her side, but the young headman of Nantwyn was barely more than a boy and would not be taken seriously by the others. She knew of the remaining chiefs there were some who would support her, but she couldn't think of any who were senior enough to make a real difference in the argument. She put on a brave face.

'My people know my quality.'

She said it with more confidence than she felt and either Tydfyl wasn't fooled or he was planning to continue anyway.

'Perhaps. But this will not be down to Caderyn chiefs alone.' Rhia began to feel cold again as the young man carried on. 'Caserach has twisted your words and claimed that since his tribe is part of the Caledon, his voice should be heard in this as well.'

Rhia wanted to snap something angry at that. Involving the Gorvicae would have made things difficult enough but *Caserach*? She ground her teeth. *I should have seen this coming from that slippery bastard!* She kept her temper controlled with an effort.

'Kyran will speak for me.'

Tydfyl shrugged his shoulders.

'That he may, but how much will he be listened to by our chiefs? Besides, Caserach will be speaking for his tribe and will no doubt be making veiled threats to sway them.'

Rhia felt her temper flare.

'The Caderyn are not easily cowed!'

It had been an instinctive response but there was some truth in what Tydfyl had said. If Caserach somehow managed to hold on to his position he could cause endless trouble for the Caderyn. He might not be able to challenge them directly but small settlements and villages all along the coast would suffer for Caserach's spite, and her headmen would know it. Tydfyl spoke again, trying hard to hide his nervousness.

'I mean no disrespect to our tribe. But Caserach is a real threat to us and may mean ruin for you. If you marry me that can be avoided.'

For a moment Rhia wondered what would happen if she accepted him. Tydfyl seemed an earnest sort of man, and for all his bitterness if Alraig gave his word on something, he would keep it. If it kept Lucan safe it might even be worth it. But Rhia shook her head almost at once. It would not serve her people to try to wriggle out of this and contact with the Gaians was vital, both for her and for Lucan. She could not agree to such terms. Besides, she could not bring herself to marry again for mere politics and safety rather than love. And pleasant though he was Tydfyl had nothing of Bevan or Marius about him. *Not even of Gawan.* That thought surprised her for a moment but she pushed it away and looked up at her guest.

'It was kind of you to come, but the answer is no. If nothing else, the tribe would see my actions as being born of fear, and I will not have that.'

Tydfyl leaned forwards, his face serious.

'I can assure you that...'

But Rhia interrupted him. She didn't want to hurt his feelings but this was not a matter for discussion.

'I can assure *you* that the Caderyn will support their chieftain. I can assure you that my son and I are the best hope we have of a lasting peace with the Gaians.' She rose to her feet. 'And I can assure you, Tydfyl son of Alraig, that your father will be proven wrong in this, and I will continue to serve this tribe as your High Chieftain long after this trial of his has been forgotten.'

The young man seemed taken aback but still he tried to argue his point.

'Those are bold words, but they are all for nothing if this trial costs you your life. And brave though they are, our people can feel fear as well as love. They fear the Gaians and they fear the Dariniae. They fear the changes that you may bring to their world.'

They were not alone in feeling fear but Rhia stamped hers down before it could show. Fear and shame had been companions of hers for many years but she had learned how to conquer such petty emotions. She looked Tydfyl in the eye and her voice was calm and steady.

'Then let Alraig play on their fears for his argument. I shall rely on their love. And we shall see which quality the Caderyn most possess.'

Tydfyl plainly wanted to say more but he must have known it would be futile. The young man simply bowed his head respectfully and took his leave of her, striding from the room and closing the heavy door behind him. Rhia stayed standing for a while and turned her gaze back to the fire. She knew her people loved her, she *knew* that was true, but that didn't mean she felt as confident as she had sounded. She sank back down onto her creaky chair and kept staring into the dancing orange flames. Worries were running through her head like a herd of hunted deer but the firelight was hypnotic, and in spite of all she began to doze. She had done all that she could, and made preparations for Lucan in case everything went wrong. Now the matter lay purely in the hands of the gods, and time would decide it all. She sighed. *One way or the other.*

Chapter 32. The Trial Begins

The hill of Bryngarth was not as steep as the one at Graigarw, but in his battered state the ride was still a chore. Gawan grimaced as he peered up the long slope through the spitting rain. They were not that far from the top, and his aching body was glad for it. The old Gaian who'd tended to his head and strapped up his leg had done a remarkable job all things considered, but the First Man was still in damned poor shape and couldn't wait for this journey to be done. It was not long after noon but the heavy clouds made the light pale and grey, turning the normally bright hillside into something plain and dull.

Gawan turned in his saddle to see that how Tegwen was doing. The hill might not be that steep but if the weather had been much worse he'd have recommended they dismount. Sure-footed though their mounts were, there was much more scope for damage in a fall from a slipping pony than there was from a fall when on foot. She seemed to be managing well enough though and she gave him a little smile. Gawan nodded back at her before turning to face the hilltop again, keen to get this done.

The First Man tugged at the hood of his cloak and urged his pony on. According to a farmer they had met on the plain below, the Gorvicae column had already reached the Caderyn capital, and Gawan was keen to speak to Duran and the others. He could not expect them to be a part of Galerian's rescue attempt, should it be needed, but it was only right that he was honest with his brother Gadarim. They would understand, even if some might not strictly approve. They were all veterans of the legion that Rhianwyn and Marius had founded, and they would want her kept safe as much as he did. Well, almost as much. He scowled at himself. Even now he sometimes dreamt of the Wildcat for all his efforts to put her from his mind. *I am risking everything to keep you safe, must you still disturb my sleep?*

After what seemed like far too long a time for so short a journey, the two Gorvicae reached the broad top of Bryngarth's hill. Gawan sensed the inevitable and waited for Tegwen to look back at the view of the plain below. Even in dismal weather the sight was impressive, and he allowed her a few moments to appreciate it. Before long Tegwen turned back to him and gave a half-apologetic smile, and Gawan let his lip twitch in acknowledgement. He took a quick look around the top of the hill to orient himself, and then urged his pony in the direction of the longhouses where the Gorvicae had slept on their last visit. Hopefully Duran and his cohort had been put there again, and Gwydion and Pryder would presumably be staying with them.

Tegwen followed him in silence, which left Gawan to his thoughts. He wasn't particularly glad of that, as memories of walking this hilltop with Emeryn came back to him as they rode. He had been happy then, and had lost it all by his own fault. He shoved the thought away. He had resolved to right his wrongs as best he could and self-pity would serve no good to anyone. There was work to be done. As he rode past various houses he found himself mentally planning an escape route for Rhianwyn and the Gaians should it be needed. How much he would involve himself he still hadn't decided, but he knew that if he had to he would lend Heartreaver to her cause. He had done before. He didn't like to think what that might mean for his, and Tegwen's, future in the tribe, but if Taliesyn became chieftain he would understand the necessity. Probably. It was in the Gorvicae's best interests for Rhianwyn to live, even in exile, since she would still be a voice for the Luriae in Tamora. Gawan just wished that was his only reason for helping her.

There were few people about and the silence grew almost oppressive, so much so that he was glad when Tegwen decided to speak.

'Do you think they may have... '

But that was as far as she got before another voice cut across her.

'Leaping Wolf? Where have you *been*?'

For some reason the tone reminded him of his mother and Gawan twisted in his saddle, curious as to what person who knew his name would dare to scold him in such a way. He could not think of many, and what he saw surprised him.

Walking briskly towards them was a dignified-looking woman in a long blue dress, and after a moment Gawan recognised her as Carradan's widow. Trailing behind her was the boy Lucan, looking anxious and confused. In the corner of his eye Gawan saw Tegwen holding back a smirk, clearly enjoying the sight of a woman reprimanding him. A part of him wanted to bristle at her tone but he found himself nodding his head.

'We were delayed. Has the...' He'd been about to say *trial* but a glance at the boy made him hesitate. 'Has it begun?'

The Caderyn matriarch nodded impatiently.

'That it has, and you need to get yourself there. My daughter needs the voice of a Gadarim.'

Gawan doubted if Rhianwyn would *welcome* him exactly but with Owain gone and Kyran an islander, his voice was likely to be the one more listened to by the Caderyn chiefs. He dipped his head to the chieftain's mother, then again to the boy beside her. Lucan nodded back but did not speak.

'I shall go there now.'

He wheeled his mount's head in the direction of the longhall and Tegwen made to follow him, but the woman stepped in front of her pony, her words softening a little.

'The headmen and druids are in private conference my dear, but you can come with me.' She nodded at Lucan. 'I'm sure we can find something useful for you to do.'

Like her father, Tegwen seemed to obey the older woman without thinking. She dismounted at once, walked up to her and nodded respectfully. The Caderyn passed her Lucan's hand without a word and ushered them both away towards the houses. She glanced back at Gawan and jerked her head towards the longhall.

'I said you are needed there.'

Gawan blinked, wondering how he'd have reacted had someone like Karadoc spoken to him like that, but then he dug in his heels and urged his pony into a trot, heading for the Caderyn's hall. What few people were wandering the town scattered from his path and Gawan focused his gaze dead ahead. The trial was already underway, and he was needed.

He left his pony with a young lad and strode boldly into the hall, the warmth of the air inside hitting him pleasantly as he entered. His green cloak was dripping and he lowered the hood and then undid the clasp, both without breaking his stride. He tossed it over an empty bench as walked across the room. The sight in the hall was very much like the moot he had seen at Graigarw, though with fewer faces that he readily recognised. Taliesyn and Karadoc were there of course, with Hywel sitting tactfully in-between them. The skeletal-looking Caderyn druid was there, along with a couple of others Gawan didn't know, but as he had expected, neither Bael nor Reaghan was present. Most of the benches were occupied by various Caderyn chiefs, and though Gawan knew most by sight he knew few of them by name. Merwyn, their elder, was sitting quietly at the high table, while Alraig was on his feet, and had been speaking until the Gorvic had walked in. Rhianwyn was standing in the middle of the hall, ignoring the stool that had been set there for her comfort.

Their faces all turned to the Gorvicae's First Man, and he concealed the little jolt he felt as Rhianwyn's eyes met his. She was clearly surprised to see him but he saw, or perhaps *hoped* he saw, a tiny glimmer of approval in her gaze. He noted that she still wore her sword at her hip and was reassured a little that they were at least honouring her status as a Gadarim. He nodded his head to her, and then to the rest of the assembly, and strode across to where his fellow tribesmen sat. It was only when he reached them that he saw Caserach sitting on a bench near the high table, the giant Broad Kellas beside him. He knew he shouldn't have been surprised to see them but all the same he couldn't help but comment on it.

'What is that craven dog doing here?'

Caserach's face reddened at once and he sprang to his feet, but Alraig waved a hand at him.

'Caserach is here because he is part of the Caledon.' The headman's voice could have cut through stone. 'As are you.'

It would have been clear to a blind man that Alraig resented their presence and a glance around showed that he wasn't alone among the Caderyn. Nonetheless no-one else voiced an objection to it and Gawan sat down with a grumble, Caserach following his example a heartbeat later. His face quickly shifted from angry to smug, and Gawan felt his right hand yearning to reach for Heartreaver. Broad Kellas had watched the exchange with the bored but confident expression of a man who knew that if trouble started, he could handle it, and Gawan couldn't tell which one of them he most wanted to tear in half. The image of Tarwyn's face and the sound of his voice came to him in a flash, and the urge to avenge his brother burned hot in the First Man's gut.

He might have stood up and charged the big warrior and damned be the consequences, had Merwyn not spoken from the high table.

'We thank you for your presence, Leaping Wolf. Our chieftain will appreciate your voice, I am sure.'

Gawan wouldn't have sworn to that but he remembered why he was there and decided vengeance could wait, and the Gadarim let his hands relax and nodded to the white-haired headman. Merwyn dipped his head back to him and gestured with one hand for Alraig to continue. The younger headman went back to speaking, his face grim.

'We come here to decide the fate of Rhianwyn daughter of Carradan; to determine firstly if she is fit to remain as High Chieftain of the Caderyn and, if not, what punishment is to be levelled should she be found guilty of betraying the tribe.'

He was making sure to cast his eyes around the hall when he spoke, addressing each headman and druid almost directly.

'She led us well at Second Nantwyn and has succeeded in making peace with our neighbours in the process. Yet she would make many changes to our way of life, changes that fly in the face of some of the ancient traditions of her people.'

Merwyn spoke politely from the high table.

'With respect comrade, Rhianwyn's record of law-making is not on trial today.'

There was a roughly equal amount of nodding and frowning in response to this, but Rhianwyn kept her face blank and Alraig maintained his composure.

'They are not, yet they are connected to the matter at hand.' He turned back to his audience. 'It is one of these laws, as set down by Rhianwyn herself, that our chieftain has flouted and so broken faith with her people.'

Alraig paced across the room to where a short-haired man was sitting nervously in a corner. Gawan recognised him as one of the Gaian scribes left at Bryngarth by the governor before he fled. Rhianwyn had been utilising them in helping to organise the Caledon and had adopted the Gaian practice of marking laws down on 'paper'. Most people had deemed it to be a waste of time but some headmen had learned the art of reading during the occupation and had found it to be useful to them. Gawan didn't really see the point, since if chiefs and druids couldn't *remember* a law then it probably wasn't worth keeping, but it wasn't for him to judge such things. Alraig took a creamy-white piece of paper from the scribe and held it aloft for a moment.

'For those who were not there or do not recall this law, it is recorded here. It states clearly that no Gaian legion, nor Gaian troops of any kind, may enter Caledon land under arms.'

He faced Rhianwyn, paper in hand.

'Do you deny the creation of this law?'

It was a pretty pointless question, given that most of those in the hall had been there when the law was made, but he asked it anyway. Rhianwyn's voice was calm and steady as she answered.

'I do not.'

Alraig nodded his head and turned back to his audience.

'And yet when our own legion marched towards Three Willows Rhianwyn ignored this law by summoning the Blackbird Legion. She demonstrated contempt for the laws set out for the Caderyn. What is that if not a betrayal of her tribe?'

Merwyn spoke again, a hint of impatience in his voice.

'And what else should she have done when Caserach invaded our lands?'

He made a point of looking directly at the Dariniae chief when he mentioned him, and plenty of other faces were joining him in frowning. Caserach looked relaxed, though Gawan suspected it was an act, and Alraig answered smoothly, clearly prepared for this.

'She could have sent the Dariniae to clear up their own mess, or else placed more faith in her fellow Caderyn. Instead she reached out for the hand of the invader.'

The first hint of emotion Gawan had heard from the man seemed to flicker into life on that last word. Rhianwyn was keeping quiet, her face composed, and Merwyn spoke again in her defence.

'Chief Rhianwyn had little choice, given the numbers that Caserach and his ally had brought to attack us.'

Alraig frowned.

'A Caderyn chief ought to have faith in her people. She should have trusted us to defeat this threat ourselves.'

Merwyn's temper seemed to be thinning and he pointed a finger at Caserach.

'You mean *that* threat? The one you have allowed to be seated here among us?'

There were rumblings of agreement and even Alraig seemed to speak through gritted teeth.

'It was another of Rhianwyn's laws that all the Caledon be involved in great matters of the tribes.'

He seemed about to continue but Taliesyn spoke up from the Gorvicae bench.

'Yet Caserach attacked the Caledon? How can he be both a member of it and an enemy to it?'

Rhianwyn looked quietly pleased at the comment and several Caderyn chiefs nodded their heads. Gawan suspected it was more in disapproval of the Darin than in approval of the Gorvic but it was support nonetheless, and Gawan was glad that Taliesyn had spoken. Alraig gave him a look that might have withered corn but it was Caserach who spoke first. He stood up from his bench and raised his hand in what was clearly a false gesture of respect.

'May I speak?'

It was plain that neither Merwyn nor Alraig was keen for him to, but after what he had just said Alraig could hardly refuse him now.

'Speak.'

Caserach nodded to the headman and addressed the room.

'I swore no oath to the Caledon. I raided another tribe, as we all have done since our grandfathers were young. Had we fought as we ever have before then there would be no need for this; one side would have called for enough and so ended the battle. Tribute would have been paid, and we would all have gone home again.' He pointed at Rhianwyn and his voice gained some heat. 'But she brought in a Gaian legion that slaughtered Darin and Breiryn alike, in defiance of the traditions of our people. Caledon or not I demand to have my say in this matter. Rhianwyn has betrayed her own people and by extension, all the Luriae. Let her pay for it with her life.'

Gawan was not alone in scowling at him for that and Rhianwyn broke her silence, staring straight at Caserach as she spoke.

'You speak poison! You took joy in butchering our people and would have continued to do so with your southern friends because killing is all you are good for.' She looked around. 'Have we all of us forgotten that this is the man who murdered Ierryn?'

She shot Broad Kellas a hard look as well but the big Gadarim simply looked back at her, uncaring. Alraig's head whipped around to face her and his words were quick and waspish.

'Rhianwyn, you will be kind enough to keep silent until you are called upon to speak.'

The Caderyn's chieftain did not argue back, but beneath her calm facade Gawan was certain she wanted to strike him. He knew it because the same urge was bubbling up in him. The various other chiefs seemed uncertain how to react and Alraig spoke into the silence before anyone else could think of what to say.

'Caserach's actions, and his right to rule, will be resolved later, and with his own people. For today he accuses Rhianwyn of attacking his raiding party with Gaian soldiers and this she has undoubtedly done, and in defiance of the law. The penalty for this can and *must* be severe.'

Gawan could see that Taliesyn was ready to speak again but he was hesitating. The easy confidence with which he'd spoken at his own tribe's moot was perhaps somewhat muted in this room of former enemies, and having made his first point he seemed wary of interrupting again. *Karadoc wouldn't hesitate to share his opinions with them, but then Rhianwyn is likely better off if he keeps them to himself.* For good or for ill Gawan got to his feet and projected his voice to the assembly.

'This was no mere raiding party but an army bent on destruction. Without the Blackbird Legion we would have lost that battle, and badly.'

The statement cost him a little pride but it was true for all that. He tried not to think of Emeryn when he spoke again.

'Many more Lurian warriors would be dead were it not for Rhianwyn's decision.'

His words caused something of a stir but Alraig cut through it.

'You forget your place in interrupting us, Leaping Wolf.'

Gawan matched his icy stare with a glare of his own.

'I am the First Man of the Gorvicae Gadarim.' Alraig seemed ready to respond but Gawan forestalled him. 'But I do not speak only for myself.' He gestured to the bench. 'Taliesyn son of Cylren would address you formally.'

The young headman got to his feet, hiding his annoyance well at having been forced into speaking.

'If this trial is one for the Caledon, and if a Darin is permitted a voice in it, then so too should the Gorvicae.' He gestured towards Caserach. 'If we must listen to him then let us all have our say, and it is custom that both chiefs and First Men may have their voices heard in trial.'

Karadoc was looking more sour-faced than ever but did not contradict him, and Hywel gave the room a subtle nod of agreement. Taliesyn continued, regaining a little of his usual poise as he went on.

'I believe I can agree with what was said by the First Man of my tribe; that Rhianwyn made a hard choice but it was perhaps the right choice to make for the Caledon. Her life should not be forfeit for an action that had such good intent.'

Caserach spoke up with a sneer.

'And do the interests of the Caledon allow her to ignore the law?'

Taliesyn looked at him and Gawan saw more confidence ease into his voice and posture.

'It is only the interests of the Caledon that allow you and I to speak here. It might be wise of you not to undermine them.'

Caserach's nostrils flared but Taliesyn was now looking at the assembled chiefs.

'The question of the Caledon in general can be answered tomorrow. Today we are speaking of Rhianwyn's actions. Shall I be heard?'

Merwyn spoke from the high table.

'I have no objection to hearing the views of our northern neighbours, Taliesyn. We are all comrades here after all.'

The old chief gave Caserach a very cynical glance, and Alraig raised his shoulders in a tiny shrug.

'As you say, if we are to hear from one ally we must needs hear from the other.'

He didn't sound enthusiastic but at least he hadn't objected. Taliesyn nodded politely to the two Caderyn.

'In that case, since we have only just arrived here, I think it best that my comrade and I be given a little time to discuss this with your headmen and with Chief Rhianwyn. From what I have heard so far her actions may have been warranted, but it would be unjust to give an opinion without hearing all the facts.'

Alraig's already pale skin seemed to grow whiter beneath his beard but a glance around the hall told him there was no point in arguing. Though Caserach looked ready to leap from his bench and strangle someone, most of the other headmen present were either nodding or hadn't reacted. Beside him Gawan heard Karadoc mumble; 'more bloody talking....' but he did not raise his voice. He too must have known it would be fruitless. Gawan allowed himself to feel a little glimmer of hope. *Perhaps this will all go smoothly after all.* Rhianwyn was betraying little feeling from where she stood but he could see by the set of her shoulders that she had relaxed somewhat.

Alraig too was keeping his emotions hidden, though there was a definite note of impatience in his tone.

'Very well. We shall continue this tomorrow to give you time to speak with the other headmen. We shall hear your views and then Rhianwyn will speak for herself before this assembly.'

The look he gave Gawan was hard as flint, and both Karadoc and Caserach were glaring at the First Man but Gawan didn't give a damn. He sat back and surreptitiously drove a knuckle into his palm. With a little good fortune Taliesyn would counteract the influence of Caserach, and Rhianwyn would leave the trial with her life at least, even if it meant the loss of her station. *And far better that than the alternative.* The Gorvic took a slow breath and allowed himself to hope. They may not need Galerian's help after all.

*

Rhia sat in her rooms and decided that all in all, it could have gone worse. She had walked into the longhall prepared to hear nothing but Alraig's damning testimony, but Merwyn had been convincing in his defence of her actions and the surprise arrival of the Gorvicae had been almost miraculous. She leaned forwards in her seat and put her elbows on her thighs, pressing her fingertips together with her eyes towards the fire. *But I mustn't get too cocky.* Plenty of chiefs had been listening to Alraig's words with interest, and it was hard to escape the fact that nothing he had said was untrue. If she was very fortunate Caserach's current attitude might wind up doing Alraig's cause more harm than good, but then he had yet to speak to the other headmen to make his various threats.

Rhia sighed. However well she defended herself Alraig's arguments would still stand, and as far as the law was concerned she was guilty as charged. The support of Merwyn and Gawan would likely mean her life was spared, but it seemed almost inevitable that she would lose her father's chair. *And then what? Banishment?* She tried not to think about the other plans she'd made and concentrated on the new hope that had come.

Seeing Gawan again had been a shock but the young chief he'd brought with him had spoken well for her. If he could be counted on to continue as he had done then she might just stand a chance. She found herself thinking about the Gorvicae's First Man. Part of her hoped he would come to speak with her, and perhaps give her an answer about what happened that night, yet most of her was keen to avoid that conversation. It would be difficult and awkward to say the very least, and at the moment she had other things to worry about.

Even as she thought these things she heard footsteps outside, and when Cerri opened the door and ushered in some guests, Rhia wondered at just how strange the gods' sense of humour must be. It was Gawan. He walked in, his head up but his eyes not quite meeting hers, and gave her a quick nod of greeting. He was closely followed by the chief who had spoken for her at the trial, and Taliesyn bowed his head a little more deeply than the Gadarim had. The young chief was of middling size with brown hair and a sharp chin. He had green eyes and high cheekbones and was quite handsome in a sallow sort of way. He was dressed in a light grey tunic and dark trews and wore a cloak of Gorvicae green over his shoulder. He wore no jewellery besides a couple of yellow-gold bracelets and the pin on his cloak, and a plain-handled sword hung at his hip. He stopped a few paces from where Rhia sat and Gawan fell in on his left.

'My name is Taliesyn son of Cylren, I am the headman of Oaken Bridge.'

Rhia tipped her own head in response.

'Good evening to you. I hear you are a candidate for Baercban's chair?'

Taliesyn nodded.

'Myself and Karadoc are the two contenders for it, with equal hands shown by our headmen. We had intended to come here to request that you arbitrate at our tribe's moot.'

Rhia gave him a wry half-smile.

'You have not timed things as well as you might have done.'

Taliesyn shook his head.

'It seems not.'

There was silence for a beat and then Rhia spoke again.

'Well, since you have volunteered to take part in this trial in the meantime, I take it you are here to discuss that with me? Am I to expect Karadoc as well?'

She saw Gawan try to suppress a snort before Taliesyn replied a little more tactfully.

'I doubt if he will care to join us.'

Rhia frowned, not liking this.

'Why is that?'

The young chief looked hesitant to comment and Gawan spoke for him, still avoiding Rhia's eyes.

'Karadoc has no love for the Caledon. He had no great wish to come here in the first place and will not be eager to defend you against Alraig.'

Rhia tried not to look concerned, or to show the awkwardness she was feeling at conversing with Gawan.

'Will he actively speak against me?'

Gawan shrugged.

'I do not know.'

Rhia felt a squirming sensation beginning in her gut but she shoved it away as Taliesyn regained his tongue.

'I do not think that he will, but we should be prepared for Alraig or Caserach to try to influence him.'

Gawan folded his arms.

'He doesn't strike me as a man who is easily influenced. Especially by someone of another tribe.'

Taliesyn looked sideways at him.

'Perhaps not, but if they play a tune he likes he may still dance. We cannot afford to assume anything.'

Gawan seemed to begrudge it but he nodded in reluctant agreement. Taliesyn turned back to Rhia.

'I am willing to lend my voice to your cause Rhianwyn, in the hopes of our making an agreement for the future.'

Rhia had lived in Tamora for five years and had seen more than her share of politics, but even she had rarely heard an ultimatum stated so courteously. But that was what it was all the same. She resented having to do it but she knew she'd have to hear him out. The good he had done her today could be very easily undone, especially if Karadoc lent his voice to her opponents. She gestured with an open hand and he continued.

'I would naturally hope that my support for you here would be remembered when you are called upon to arbitrate at the Gorvicae moot?'

It was a predictable enough request and perfectly reasonable too, but Rhia suspected there would be more to it than that. And she was right.

'You may also want to consider marrying me once this is over.'

Rhia almost laughed. A second proposal in what was it, four days? Though Taliesyn at least hadn't mumbled his way through it. She couldn't help but glance at Gawan who was still watching them blank-faced, but she could tell that underneath he was uncomfortable. The memory of their kiss flashed up in front of her for a moment and she quickly dragged her focus back to the present. Taliesyn was looking at her expectantly and she decided not to waste words.

'My thanks for the offer, but no.'

She had expected him to react poorly to her answer but the young man simply shrugged and carried on.

'I did not really think you would accept. Therefore consider my next offer carefully; you have a son and as soon as I am chieftain I shall marry and have children of my own. The first daughter that I have will marry Lucan and thus bind our tribes closer together.'

And bind the two of us *closer together too. Not a bad position for you if I manage to remain head of the Caledon.* Rhia pressed her lips together. Whichever tribe Lucan wound up marrying into, it would inevitably cause resentment in the other two. The simplest solution to that of course would be for him to marry a Gaian girl and tie the Caledon closer to the Empire. *And so offend* all *of the Lurian tribes equally!* It was a tough predicament, and Rhia had no idea at all how she would solve it. She frowned as Taliesyn pressed on.

'The children of their union could then marry among the tribes, and even into Gaian families should you wish it, and so promote unity for all in the long term.' He leaned a little closer to her, his green eyes fixed onto hers. 'You know that my offer is the best that you can hope for. For the both of you.'

Rhia knew he was probably right but she still didn't like the idea. She turned to Gawan.

'What would happen if Karadoc became your chieftain?'

If Taliesyn was offended he didn't let it show. Gawan answered her confidently.

'It could be messy. He would undo much of what you have done to unify us. I would not be surprised if he provoked fresh conflict between our tribes.'

Rhia nodded. Gawan might have his faults, and she had her uncertainties about him, but he was honest and he knew his people. If he said that Karadoc would be a danger to them then he would be. And he probably had her best interests at heart. Even before their... encounter after Moon Ridge, he had killed his chieftain to give her justice for her father and of course, he had named her to the Gadarim after Nantwyn. She looked at him directly and this time he met her gaze.

'What do you think of this plan?'

Taliesyn glanced at him but Gawan kept his eyes on Rhia.

'If you are to keep your chair then I think it is your best chance. Karadoc will make no such offer and there is no-one from the Dariniae save Kyran who will speak for you. With your own chiefs divided you are best served in siding with him.'

He tipped his head towards Taliesyn. He hadn't sounded enthusiastic about the recommendation but he'd spoken promptly and honestly, and Rhia bowed her head in acknowledgement.

'Thank you.'

She turned back to look at Taliesyn and tried not to let her doubts show. This was likely for the best, and it was probably her only chance at this point, but all the same she felt hesitant to do it. Lucan was her boy, she didn't want to use him as some tool to secure her chair, but nor did she want to cause resentment within the Caledon. *But it's too late now to try to come up with a solution to please everyone. You have made your decisions and now you must choose from the options you have left.*

Rhia got to her feet and took a step closer to the headman of Oaken Bridge. She looked into his eyes and extended a hand, and the Gorvic copied the gesture. They traded grips and she spoke formally, the better to hide her apprehension.

'Very well, Taliesyn son of Cylren. We have an accord.'

The chief bowed his head with a little smile but Rhia did not smile back. She might be agreeing to the deal but that didn't mean she had to like it. But then, right now it seemed the only choice that remained to her. Rhia sighed, and prayed quietly both to Gron and to Camelas that her choice would turn out to be the wise one.

Chapter 33. The Judgement of the Caledon

Gawan sat on the bench beside Hywel and watched the trial unfold, half lost in his thoughts. He tried to pay attention but his mind kept travelling back to the night before, in particular his irrational resentment at Taliesyn's proposal. It was senseless; the plan had been perfectly reasonable, damn it all he had practically *recommended* it, and Rhianwyn hadn't even accepted it anyway. He had no claim over her and had no right at all to feel jealous of her. And yet he was. He had decided that morning that he still intended to support Taliesyn at the moot, but what with this and his relationship with Tegwen to boot, Gawan was developing an irrational dislike of him. He tried to convince himself that there was something off about him anyway; that his bargaining with Rhianwyn went against proper Gorvicae pride, but he knew it was an empty thought. He was becoming prejudiced against the young chief very much for his own reasons.

The man himself was up and speaking at the moment, putting across the arguments for Rhianwyn, and Gawan ground his teeth as he watched the two of them. His thoughts of Rhianwyn always rubbed at the still-raw wound of his betrayal of Emeryn, and with concerns for Tegwen's future with Taliesyn added onto that, his mind was extremely distracted. He fought back a grimace and tried to marshal his thoughts. *He said he'd marry once he was made chieftain. If he didn't mean to my Tegwen then he and I will be having some strong words.*

He had spoken to his daughter the night before and had, as subtly as he could, questioned her on how she felt about him. Tegwen had hardly been gushing but it had been plain that she was very keen on Taliesyn, somewhat to her father's dismay. Gawan frowned to himself as he thought on it. It had felt odd to talk to her in a way that any parent might talk to his child, and to have the same worries that any other father would have for his daughter. It was comforting in some ways but very strange in others. *Especially since two moons ago you couldn't have picked her out from a crowd. And a few days ago she almost left you to die!* He shook himself free of such thoughts. Once the trial was over he could begin to get to know her properly, and concerns like these would feel perfectly normal.

He went back to concentrating on the proceedings in the hall. It was going as well as could be expected, all things considered, and Gawan still hoped things might yet be resolved without the need to call in Galerian. He knew he ought to have told Rhianwyn about that part of his plan the night before, but he'd felt sullen after Taliesyn's talk of marriage and had just wanted to leave as soon as possible. He didn't like the idea but he knew that he would have to tell her today. Galerian was probably still a day or two's march away but it would be far better for her to know that he was on his way, even if she didn't need to know exactly why.

He looked across the longhall to where Caserach and Broad Kellas sat. A pair of Dariniae chiefs had arrived during the night and now sat beside their would-be chieftain, watching the trial with interest. Gawan locked gazes with the Breiryn giant and thought back to Tarwyn, but Broad Kellas looked away after a heartbeat, untroubled by the Gorvic's grey stare. Alraig and Merwyn were sitting at the high table with the slender Caderyn druid, all three listening carefully to Taliesyn.

'It has been attested by both Gawan son of Dearg and by Kyran son of Kelian that the Blackbird Legion was vital to their victory at Moon Ridge.'

Rhianwyn nodded quietly but didn't speak. Once again she had elected to stand rather than sit, and she was holding herself straight-backed and proud, her posture so confident that it bordered on arrogant. Gawan thought of how strange it had been to actually talk to her the night before, and for all his resentment of Taliesyn he was glad that they hadn't been alone. He hated to think what their conversation might otherwise have involved. The chief continued speaking.

'Since last night I have spoken to several others who were present at that battle. I have accepted the sworn testimonies of Eifion son of Owen, Dewi son of Derion, Omren son of Rhisiart, Struen son of Rhisiart...'

He went on to name some half-a-dozen other men, and since the legion was still down south, Gawan assumed they were all Caderyn who had been among Alraig's section in the battle. The sour look that flashed across the older chief's face confirmed his suspicions. *Clever boy.* The various headmen continued to listen as Taliesyn finished reciting his list.

'All of these men agree that had Rhianwyn not acted as she had, and the Blackbirds had not come, then what began as a battle would have become a slaughter at the hands of this man before you.'

He pointed at Caserach who kept his composure despite the anger in his eyes. He clearly wanted to say something but Taliesyn kept going before he could.

'Speak truly comrades; how many of us would think it just to cut off the hand of a man who had stolen a loaf to save his starving child? Desperate times sometimes call for desperate actions.'

A few men shook their heads but mostly the room remained quiet and motionless. It was Alraig who broke the silence.

'If a man is a thief he is a thief. And a man whose child is starving should go to his chief to ask for aid.' He paused and looked around him. 'He should place his trust in his tribe.'

There were more nods to this than there'd been shaken heads at Taliesyn's question, and given how Alraig had put it, Gawan wondered if the time had come for Taliesyn to sit down again. Persuasive though he could be he was still a Gorvic addressing Caderyn after all. Rhianwyn seemed to have come to the same conclusion because she took a small step forwards and placed a hand on Taliesyn's arm. Gawan felt a jolt of absurd jealousy but he kept it from showing on his face.

'Your point is well made Taliesyn, thank you for your words.'

The Gorvic took the hint and bowed his head before walking back to the bench. Gawan shuffled up to make space for him. He had lain some good foundations for her but the First Man was still uncertain. Some of the Caderyn chiefs were trying to hide their nervousness, and Gawan assumed that Caserach had spoken to them, threatening those near the coast if they dared to oppose him. Karadoc had stayed silent for now at least, neither helping nor hindering either party, and Gawan supposed that counted as good news for them. Rhianwyn looked up to the high table and began to speak.

'I do not deny that the law I have made has been broken, if looked at with the strictest eye.' Alraig glared a little but didn't comment. 'I also know that some of you are wary of our alliance with the Gaians and are concerned about how my leadership might change our way of life.'

There were a few murmurs of agreement but no statements were made. Rhianwyn held up three fingers and looked around the hall, taking in each face.

'I would say three things to you in answer for all this. Firstly, I say that any changes made to the Caderyn or the Caledon would only be considered if I thought them beneficial to our people, and I vow to never introduce any Gaian practice that is objectionable to my headmen. Always I will consult them before such an action.'

Gawan approved of her tone. She was speaking with an easy confidence, as if her remaining as chieftain here was a foregone conclusion.

'Secondly, as Taliesyn has made clear, the assistance of the Blackbird Legion was vital to our victory at Moon Ridge and without them many lives would have been needlessly lost.'

Caserach received a few unpleasant looks but he weathered them easily, affecting a look of boredom.

'And thirdly,' Rhianwyn continued, 'the law exists for the protection of the people. And to manipulate a law that was broken for a good cause merely to inflict harm upon a leader, is as Gaian an act as any invasion of legionaries.'

For the first time Gawan thought that Alraig might lose control. His face flushed red and he stood up with pure murder in his eyes. Caserach was also staring at

Rhianwyn, his nostrils flaring and his hands clenched into fists. Yet many, if not *most*, of the chiefs seemed to approve of what she said, and old Merwyn was actually smiling. It was easy to imagine what they were all thinking; Rhianwyn was indeed a credit to her father. Of course, that was when it all started to go wrong.

Before either Alraig or Caserach could give vent to their anger, the heavy doors at the far end of the longhall were thrown open. Like everyone else Gawan turned to see what was happening and he almost groaned aloud at what he saw. A young man, who looked so like Alraig that he must have been his son, was leading a pair of armoured men into the hall, and every headman in the room stood up from his bench to stare at them. General Galerian and Tribune Derrio marched in perfect unison, their eyes fixed ahead of them and their backs arrow-straight. Almost at once voices of disapproval came from the crowd of chiefs, and Merwyn and Alraig both had to pound their fists against the table until they quietened. Eventually the assembly took their seats again but Gawan remained on his feet. He wanted to make sure that he spoke before Alraig could say anything.

'Comrades, I present to you General Galerian of the Blackbird Legion. I have asked him to come here to give us his account.'

Gawan saw Derrio quietly translating his words to the general as Caserach pointed a finger at the Gaians.

'He has no voice here!'

Gawan took a tiny step towards him and fixed him with a glare.

476

'But I do. I am First Man of the Gorvicae and I say he is an important witness to this trial. Do you or any other man here dare to call me a liar?'

Gawan made no effort at all to hide the threat behind his words, though he suspected it would not win him many favours among the chiefs. From Rhianwyn's blank expression it was hard to tell if she was more relieved or annoyed by Galerian's arrival, and once again Gawan worried that this might all have been a terrible mistake. He had reached out to the Gaians in panic when he had thought he'd need men to rescue Rhianwyn. With so much of that threat nullified by the words of Taliesyn, he got the sinking feeling that the Gaian's presence would now damage her cause more than help it. But the stone was cast now, and there was no summoning it back. He saw Alraig turn his way.

'I would not call a Gadarim a *liar* Leaping Wolf, but this trial has already admitted men from tribes outside our own. You ask too much of us to allow an invader to speak in it as well.'

The headmen murmured agreement but Merwyn shook his head, leaning forwards with his elbows on the table.

'A witness vouched for by a chief, a druid or a First Man is generally permitted to speak during a trial.'

Alraig turned to his fellow chief.

'Generally, yes. But this man is not Caderyn, he is not even *Lurian*. Never has such an outsider spoken in judgement over one of us before.' He curled his lip a little at the soldiers. 'At least, not legitimately.'

Merwyn made to speak again but Hywel placed a hand on his arm. *Come on damn you, involve yourself!*

477

'What else is a trial but a search for the truth?' He addressed the Gaians. 'Will you swear by your gods to speak no falsehood under this roof?'

It took a moment for Derrio to translate and Gawan half-expected Alraig to continue his objections, but it seemed he was unwilling to argue with the most senior druid present. Once he'd heard the words from the tribune Galerian looked up at the high table to answer. He placed a hand over his heart and Gawan just about followed his words.

'I swear by the justice of Gron Camelas, the wisdom of Cassio Marna, the courage of Vulco Taranis and the purity of Sulis Mehine; I shall speak the truth.'

The oath was unfamiliar to Gawan but it sounded impressive enough, and he saw Rhianwyn nod slightly in approval. Galerian had clearly asked the right questions before coming here, and including both his own and the Lurian gods in his vow would make the chiefs more willing to trust him. As much as they ever would, anyway. Hywel nodded his head and turned to face Gawan.

'Leaping Wolf, will you vouch for this man's honesty?'

It took all his willpower not to hesitate before answering. Galerian was an enemy but this was for Rhianwyn, and mistake or not he had to see it through.

'I shall.'

There were looks exchanged all around but Gawan ignored them and gestured for Galerian to come forward. He bowed his head both to Rhianwyn and to the chiefs. Alraig gave Merwyn a glance of serious disapproval but he opened up his hands and sighed.

'Speak your piece, Gaian.'

Once again Galerian bowed politely and proceeded to speak through Derrio.

'Greetings, honoured lords of the Caledon. What I have to say will not take long.' He gestured to Rhianwyn with one hand. 'I should like first to express my admiration for Chief Rhianwyn. I know and respect her well and I am confident that, under her leadership, the Caledon and the Empire may thrive together in a brighter future.'

The chiefs were watching him stone-faced, and Gawan hoped they were taking in his words and not just waiting for a chance to object to them. Galerian kept on talking, seemingly oblivious to his audience's lack of reaction.

'I will also state, under oath, that as commander of the First Legion and de facto ruler of Tamora at the present time, I have no hostile intentions of any sort towards the Caledon Alliance. I have only the greatest respect for your tribes and for the Dragon Legion, and will make every effort to encourage that same respect among my people.'

Gawan saw the odd look of approval from the headmen but most still watched him without much expression. The General had only paused in his speech to let Derrio catch up properly but Alraig leaped in as soon as the translation was complete. He stood up from his bench holding what looked like the same paper that he'd had the day before, and he approached the Gaian general with the document held out. Galerian took it and presumably read the words.

'Given that you have been vouched for I will not doubt your word General Galerian.' The blatant cynicism in his tone made the title seem more like an insult. 'But be so kind as to tell me; what does this paper say?'

The Gaian looked up at him and Gawan saw Alraig's lip twitch in half a sneer.

'You must forgive us ignorant tribesmen. We are unaccustomed to reading your words.'

Galerian resisted the taunt and spoke plainly.

'It states that no Gaian force may enter your lands under arms.'

Alraig nodded and placed a finger on the paper.

'And is this your mark, here?'

Galerian's face remained blank.

'It is.'

Alraig moved his finger to another point.

'And this is Rhianwyn's?'

Galerian looked down at it.

'This is indeed the signature of Lady Dessida.'

Alraig almost smiled.

'Then is it not true that by your own laws as well as ours, Rhianwyn is foresworn?'

The Gaian was fighting back a grimace as he replied and Gawan felt his heart sink.

'That is so. However...'

But before Derrio could even complete the translation, Caserach was on his feet.

'By his own lips! Even her Gaian friends say she is false!'

Rhianwyn's face hardened and she spun to face him.

'*You* dare to speak of falsehood?'

Both Alraig and Merwyn began speaking at the same time but they were drowned out when Karadoc stood up from the Gorvicae bench.

'I have stayed silent until now but this has swayed me. Rhianwyn has betrayed us all and must face punishment for it!'

At least a dozen Caderyn chiefs began shouting objections at him, even as others raised their voices in agreement. Gawan saw Alraig and Merwyn engaged in furious conversation while Rhianwyn and Caserach continued to argue. Galerian seemed not to know how to undo the damage he had done and remained silent, listening as Derrio translated choice snippets of the discussion. Not that he couldn't have worked it out for himself; the tone was very clear. Gawan scowled as the hall descended into chaos. He'd thought he had done the right thing in summoning the Gaians but he had simply made the situation a hundred times worse. *Damn it all she was swaying them until Galerian came marching in! What were you thinking you damned fool?* But he knew what he'd been thinking. He'd been thinking more of rescuing her by force and the men he might need to do it. He should have sent messages to Galerian to stay away until he knew more, and to come only at some given signal. He sighed. *Well, I may need his soldiers now after all.* But before anything else this hall needed order.

He began banging his fist on the table and calling out for quiet, and was almost grateful when he saw that Alraig was doing the same thing. It did little good however, until Merwyn appealed to Hywel and the druid stood up from his seat. The slender Caderyn druid stood with him and as one they raised their staffs and cracked the ends down hard against the wooden floor. The effect was immediate. Gawan didn't know what magic it was that the druids channelled through them, but the oaken staffs struck the boards with a sound like Taran's thunder, and every soul in the hall fell silent as a graveside. Gawan's heart was hammering fast but he slowed it with an effort. Only fools had no fear of druids, but he knew full well that they did not mean to do harm. All the same, it was always unnerving to see their power in use. The two holy men stood still for a moment, casting piercing eyes around the hall at the various headmen, until the Caderyn man gestured towards Merwyn and Alraig. Both men bowed their heads deeply to the druids before turning towards the assembled headmen. Merwyn spoke first.

'This bickering is pointless.'

Alraig nodded beside him.

'I agree. And it seems to me that all that can be said has been said. I say we end this now by show of hands. Does any man here object?'

Gawan looked around at the assembly. There were plenty of men who would clearly prefer to go an arguing but most seemed to realise that more talk would do little good. No objection was raised. Alraig nodded politely to Merwyn, who raised his hands for a moment.

'Comrades, take your seats.'

Gawan joined the others in returning to the bench, and even Rhianwyn consented to sit down for a moment. The thin druid addressed them, his voice raspy but clear.

'All those who would call Rhianwyn innocent of wrongdoing, and would have her remain as our chieftain, show your hands.'

All around the hall hands went up, including Gawan's own, along with Taliesyn's, Merwyn's, Hywel's and Kyran's. Gawan couldn't really tell but it seemed that about half of the chiefs in the hall were for Rhianwyn. A pair of younger Caderyn druids walked about to count the hands but Gawan kept his eyes forward. It was generally considered bad form to be seen trying to guess at a result.

The young men went up to the high table and spoke quietly to the Caderyn druid, who nodded to both of them before speaking again.

'All those who would call Rhianwyn guilty of wrongdoing, and would have her surrender the chieftain's chair, show your hands.'

Unsurprisingly Caserach and Alraig both showed their hands, as did Karadoc and no small number of Caderyn headmen. Once again Gawan tried not to count the hands in his head but the numbers looked more or less equal. *What will happen if they are exactly matched? Will Hywel and the Caderyn man make the decision?* Not for the first time he found himself wishing Reaghan was still with them. But wishes were for children and fools.

The counting seemed to take forever but eventually the skeletal druid gave the nod to his disciples. Like Hywel he did not waste time with suspense.

'Thirty hands declare that Rhianwyn is innocent.' Gawan was sure he heard him sigh. 'Thirty-one hands declare her guilt.'

Caserach's mouth widened into a shark-like grin and even Alraig looked pleased, even if he didn't smile. Gawan felt as though he'd just swallowed a bowl of eels and when he looked at Rhianwyn her face was composed, but deathly pale. For a moment it seemed that more talking would ensue, either to gloat or to complain, but Hywel stood up first, his hands held up to encompass the room.

'Comrades; since this verdict was so close a decision, I would advise that whatever punishment is to be inflicted be as lenient as possible to reflect the views of the chiefs.'

He turned to the thin man. 'Brother Gryg, would you agree?'

The thin man nodded gravely. Gawan couldn't decide if he was grateful to the Gorvic druid or angry with him. *Bloody advising again; just* tell *them what to do damn it!* Caserach stood up but Merwyn spoke before he could argue.

'I suggest that the sentence be her removal as chieftain and her banishment from the town of Bryngarth.'

Even to Gawan that sounded soft and he wasn't surprised by the angry voices that responded to him, Karadoc's foremost among them.

'Not good enough! I say to keep her life after such betrayal would be too lenient, but at the very *mildest* she must be cast out of all Caledon lands forever!'

Given Karadoc's antipathy towards the Caledon Gawan thought that was pretty rich coming from him, but then he was just angling for a harsher punishment. Alraig spoke up next.

'From Caderyn lands at the very least, and still I would call it merciful!'

Merwyn argued back.

'So long as she and her son are no longer permitted *here,* neither one can claim Carradan's chair or have their voice heard in a moot. That is enough to show that her power has been taken from her.'

Gawan saw a flash of emotion pass across Rhianwyn's face as she watched the elder chief defending her. So many hard men were against her and yet this mild old man still pleaded her cause. Caserach was the next to voice his opinion, and predictable though it was it still made Gawan want to break his teeth.

'It is my people and the Breiryn who have suffered at the hands of her Gaian friends. The sentence *must* be death!'

Gawan couldn't stop himself from taking a few paces towards him.

'You suffered nothing you did not earn. Now hold your lying tongue before I nail it to the wall!'

He glared first at him and then over at Broad Kellas, but the big warrior hadn't even stood up from his bench. He was watching the proceedings without any sign of interest. Caserach stepped towards Gawan, his eyes blazing.

'Say that again you dog-humping bastard!'

The Gorvic squared up to him.

'I told you to hold your lying tongue before I nail it to the wall. Whether you are still attached to it or not.'

Caserach took a step closer and Gawan saw his hands flex open and shut. The First Man didn't move but he put his focus into his centre and kindled the dragonfire, subtly softening his knees as he readied himself to attack. He folded his arms in front of his chest but he held them there loosely, ready to reach for Heartreaver in an eyeblink if he had to. Hywel must have seen what was coming because he crossed the floor faster than any man his age had a right to, and before either man knew it the white-robed druid was standing between them. He said no words but his eyes spoke his thoughts for him, and Gawan took a step back with a nod. No warrior could force a druid to step aside, no matter how much he might want to. Caserach seemed on the verge of shoving the holy man anyway but he controlled his temper and settled for glaring at Gawan around his shoulder. The Gorvic turned his back on him.

The rest of the room had quietened to watch their confrontation and Gawan seized the initiative before anyone else could speak.

'Barely more than half of you wish for *any* punishment to be levelled. If any respect is to be shown for the tribe as a whole then the sentence given must be a lenient one.'

There were a few mutterings of agreement and Gawan shot a quick glance at Rhianwyn. She was still holding on to her proud mask but he thought he detected a shadow of gratitude on her face. It was gone again in an instant and replaced by irritation as Caserach spoke again.

'Nonsense! A chief who betrays his tribe must pay for it with his life.'

Karadoc, along with a few others, lent his voice in encouragement but Merwyn shouted them down before more arguing ensued.

'Enough!' He looked first to Karadoc and then to Caserach. 'None know more of life and death than the holy brethren of druids. We your seniors shall withdraw and confer with them.'

Alraig turned to his fellow Caderyn.

'Presumably by that you mean yourself, Karadoc, Taliesyn, Caserach and I?'

Gawan didn't like the sound of that but Merwyn nodded.

'Yes, we five will discuss it with Gryg, Hywel and their brothers, and let the wisdom of the druids guide our actions.'

A couple of headmen grumbled quietly but none of them dared disagree. Gawan furrowed his brow, wondering if this discussion would be good or bad for Rhianwyn. On the one hand, three of the five chiefs present would be hostile to her, and one had actively called for her death.

On the other, druids rarely approved of shedding blood unless there was no other choice, and Hywel at least would be on Rhianwyn's side, along with Taliesyn. It would be close, and Gawan couldn't help but think on the many times Hywel had settled for *advising* rather than taking action. Traditions or not, if a druid gave an actual *command* the chiefs would have no choice but to follow it. But then it was such a central part of their creed that they never used their power directly. Gawan resisted the urge to clench his fists. Wise they might be, but sometimes he wondered what the point was of a man having power if he refused to use it.

The five chiefs and the handful of druids began moving towards the door beside the high table, leading to the back rooms of Carradan's hall. Gawan wondered if they would decide their chieftain's fate in the room where he had once killed his. The headmen remaining began to talk amongst themselves, and Gawan saw Kyran begin to cross the hall towards him. He knew he should probably talk to his fellow First Man but his attention was fixed on Rhianwyn. She had not moved from her spot and was standing suitably silent, with her back straight and her chin thrust forward. It was a fine act, and damned near everyone would have been convinced by it. But even if he couldn't see it with his eyes, Gawan knew what lay behind that mask. There would be a modicum of fear for her own position and safety, but two other things would be filling the Wildcat's mind right now; Rhianwyn was always one who thought of others before herself. She would be wondering how the tribes would cope in this new world without her help. And her heart would be breaking as she wondered what fate these men would choose for her son.

Chapter 34. Awaiting The Verdict

The house was still damp, the food was still bland and the mead was barely worthy of the name, but none of it took the shine from Caserach's mood. He took a draught from his cup and leaned back against the wall, ignoring the thin flavour as he smiled to himself. She had lost. The damned druids had taken their sweet time in deciding what had to be done, but eventually the old fools had come to an agreement. Rhianwyn was to be banished from all Caledon territory, never to return to the lands of the Caderyn, the Dariniae or the Gorvicae upon pain of death. It wasn't the sentence Caserach had argued for of course, but it had stripped her of all power and protection, and how long could one woman and her whelp hope to last without her mighty Dragon Legion to keep them safe?

He leaned his cup against his leg and let out a sigh of contentment. Once dawn came the headmen would be recalled and told of what the druids had said. At the very least they would be compelled to agree with their verdict, and then when Belenos was high the whole tribe would be told of the sentence. Caserach smirked. If he glared hard enough at the weaker chiefs in the morning they might even be convinced to petition for her death again, not that it really mattered. She was abandoned, helpless, and powerless, and with her went all hope of the Caledon's survival.

Across the room from him he saw Idwal, idly picking at his nails. The rangy man jerked his chin at him but didn't stop what he was doing.

'You seem in a fine mood, all things considered.'

It was a fair point. Caserach had surprised himself by how satisfied the result had made him, but then that was probably due to relief that the damned Caledon hadn't fallen for Taliesyn's smart talking. He and Merwyn had argued long and hard and had been in danger of persuading the soft-hearted druids to sympathise with Rhianwyn, but in the end they had been shouted down. Alraig was clever and Karadoc was belligerent, and with Caserach's help they had made certain that the Gaian bitch would fall into disgrace. He shrugged his shoulders at Idwal.

'Her power is broken. That is what matters for now.'

Idwal nodded slowly.

'You think she will try to make for Tamora after it is done?'

Caserach nodded back.

'In all likelihood.'

Idwal was quiet for a while before he spoke again.

'A long ride to make alone.'

He spoke casually and Caserach smirked a little. It was good to know that they were of one mind. He was about to speak again when another voice made his hand twitch in surprise. In all their time in the little house Broad Kellas had never spoken unless spoken to, and hearing his booming voice unasked-for almost made Caserach spill his drink.

'Am I to leave now that the trial is done? Or am I to stay until you return to your people?'

The Darin chief guessed from his tone that the Breiryn didn't really care either way, but with a voice like his it was difficult to tell. In truth, Caserach had been growing weary of the big man's lack of interest and probably didn't need his sombre bodyguard anymore. On the other hand however he still had his own chiefs to contend with and keeping the giant around might be sensible for now. He might make for dull company but Caserach knew he could show enthusiasm enough when it came to violence. *Well, I don't need him here for his conversation.*

'You will remain for now. Once I have dealt with my chiefs and am ready to make for home you may return to Breiryn lands. It should not take long.'

As expected the big Gadarim showed no real reaction and simply nodded quietly. Idwal raised an eyebrow.

'There might still be trouble with some of them, chief.'

At the word 'trouble' Caserach could have sworn he saw a tiny spark of interest in Broad Kellas' eyes but it died away when the chieftain answered.

'With one or two perhaps, but once I have been seen to break the power of the Caledon they will be less keen to oppose me. And should…'

But he stopped himself. He'd been about to say that should Kyran try to stir up problems then he could always be dealt with the same way Ierryn had, but he held his tongue at the last instant. Broad Kellas was a brute but he would not take kindly to the idea of their murdering a Gadarim, regardless of what tribe he was from. Caserach had always hated that about the warrior elite. They were more than happy to butcher each other when a chieftain told them to, but then they would pretend to be close as brothers the moment a battle was over. It was ridiculous. A man who was your enemy when the sun arose was still your enemy when it set. Just because he had beaten you in the fight or you had beaten him, that didn't change the facts of who you were.

Caserach might have let that stream of thought ruin his good mood, but Idwal gave him a knowing smile which reminded him of his victory today. He put his thoughts of Gadarim aside and leaned back on his bed, enjoying the new straw mattress that had been sent at his request. He couldn't decide what he enjoyed more about it; the fact that it was comfortable, or the searing resentment with which Alraig had granted it to him. The Caderyn fool was a slave to his traditions and had consented to improving his prisoner-guest's conditions as a result. Caserach smiled. *Being treated well by one who you know hates you is truly one of life's greatest pleasures.*

He put his head on the soft straw and let out a contented sigh. In fairness to Edryd, his predictions had come true. Caserach had guessed that Karadoc was the master the little man had spoken of, and it seemed that he would soon be the new High Chieftain of the Gorvicae. Once Rhianwyn was banished Taliesyn's reputation would be marred forever for having defended her, and it would be known that Karadoc had been the man to insist that justice was done.

Caserach struggled not to laugh out loud. Karadoc had spent his life fighting off Dariniae raiders, and now he would play his part in making his enemies' lives that much easier. When the Caledon collapsed, as he would no doubt ensure it would, raiding would be plentiful all along the coast again, only now with both Gorvicae and Caderyn so frightened of the Gaians that neither one would dare to mass their warriors in the west. Caserach had lost his battle but the war would be won by the Dariniae again and again, and that victory would be of his enemies own making!

He settled quietly onto his bed with a smile on his face. Accidents would have to be arranged for a few of his chiefs, and for Kyran of course, but it would all fall into place easily once the Caledon had crumbled away. He let his hand drop to the hilt of Greyfang beside the bed. There would be good fighting to be had once he had the tribe at his back, and Ierryn was long forgotten. The coast would be his to ravage at will and not a damned thing the mainlanders could do about it. Rhianwyn had been doomed by the hand of her own people. And the fools had doomed themselves into the bargain.

Chapter. 35 Defeat

Rhia tried for the fifth time to reach for her cup but her limbs just didn't want to respond. Even in the midst of her fear she had kept up the hope that her people would rally behind her and now... now she would never be among them again. Her whole body felt numb as she sat slumped in her chair, and it was all she could do to keep her face a blank mask. She remembered how much it had irritated her that Marius and patricians like him had hidden their emotions away like that, but today she was glad some of their habits had rubbed off on her. Her heart ached badly enough as it was without the guilt of dragging Lucan down with her.

As it happened he was occupied with something else at present anyway. The boy was sitting at her feet, focusing furiously on trying to untangle a knot he had made in the strap of his shoe. Rhia almost smiled as she watched him. He clearly thought she hadn't noticed and was hunched over his foot, convinced that he was hiding it from her as he worked to loosen it. She didn't have the heart to break the illusion. She didn't have the heart for much at all.

Once again memories of earlier that day ran through her mind, and her stomach felt sick and hollow at the thought of it. She saw again the sadness on Merwyn's kindly face, and the vaguely apologetic look on Taliesyn's. Merwyn, his voice full of sorrow, had been the one to tell her that she was to be banished. And for all her preparation it had struck Rhia like a slap in the face. The chiefs would still have to approve but given that the druids had supported this, they could hardly disagree. If anything, Caserach might be able to threaten some of them into making the sentence even harsher. Rhia ground her teeth together as she thought back. Karadoc and Alraig had both looked satisfied when they had returned to the near-empty hall, but Caserach had looked so smug she'd have thought he'd just come from a virgin's bed, not a council of chiefs. Gregor had still been there and had merely looked at him with disapproval, but Gawan had seemed ready to leap for his throat.

Rhia sighed. Gawan. Part of her wished he *had* leaped for him. Part of her wished they *both* had, and that Heartreaver or Silverbite might have hacked the smirk from the Darin's face. But it would have done no good. She looked down at Lucan, frowning in furtive concentration as he worked at the knotted strap. Had they simply attacked Caserach it would have made matters that much worse, and her boy might now be left without a mother. *Instead of just without a home.*

Rhia held back a tear as she watched him. He would be staying the night with Olwyn, as usual, but had been permitted to spend a little time with his mother beforehand. She hadn't told him anything of what had happened. She didn't know how to. Soon, for the second time in a year, his life would be turned upside-down and there was nothing she could do about it. Her only real choice was to take him back to Tamora. She still had a house there after all, assuming Livilla hadn't found some way of selling it, and Lucan had family and friends in the Gaian city. He might even prefer it there; he'd spent much more of his life in Tamora than he had at Bryngarth after all. But he had made friends here too and had grown close with his cousins and, more than anything, he had become a part of his tribe. If they went back to the city she might as

494

well call him a Gaian and have done with it. After the defeat of Lepidus she had always pictured him *visiting* the city, even staying for a while to gain a Gaian education, but to live there and never return? What would it do to his identity? *What will it do to mine?*

She shook her head a little. That ought to be the *least* of her cares. The name Dessida still carried weight in Tamora's society and her banishment, and especially Lucan's, would be seen as an insult to one of their oldest families. What peace there was with the Empire was fragile at best, and it was only a matter of time before some ambitious general began to look west once more, and now he had that insult to justify himself. Rhia closed her eyes and wished guiltily that she had never become chieftain. She wished that Carradan was still here to lead them and that she could simply follow him and not have to worry about great things. She balled her fist and forced away the thought. It was unworthy of her. Wishes were for fools and she had her duty to do. She just didn't know how she could do it now.

Anger at her helplessness welled up inside her and she tried to focus it elsewhere, which was harder than she'd thought it would be. First she tried to hate Alraig but it was a struggle; he did what he did for good reasons after all. Then she tried to direct her anger at Karadoc but even he was probably acting only out of fear for his people's welfare. She tried to hate Gawan for being fool enough to bring Gregor to the trial and antagonising the headmen, but he too had clearly done so with good intentions. It was only when she thought of Caserach again that her rage found a worthy target. That selfish, vicious, ignorant bastard was destroying the best hope for the Lurians' survival and for no better reason than for his own vanity and greed. She let anger burn away some of her sadness and fear but then let it go again as Lucan looked up at her. His little brow was furrowed and he tilted his head to one side.

'What's wrong mama?'

Rhia didn't really know what to say. So *much* was wrong but she couldn't burden a child with it. All the same she didn't want to lie to him.

'There are some problems that need fixing, that is all.' He didn't seem particularly satisfied with that so she changed the subject before he could say more. 'Do you ever miss living in the city house?'

Lucan blinked and thought to himself for a few moments, still subtly keeping his foot hidden from view.

'Sometimes.'

Rhia nodded.

'Would you like to go back there?'

Once again she saw his brow furrow in child-like thought.

'Can Siriol come with us?'

Rhia had no idea what would happen to the rest of her family but there was a good chance they would be ostracised in some way or another. Whether she could bring them to Tamora was another question but it was worth a try. She could at least ask Olla and their mother what they thought.

'Maybe, we'll have to see.'

Lucan nodded thoughtfully and then looked up at her again.

'And Aunt Olla?'

Rhia smiled at him.

496

'Perhaps.'

'And Grandmother?'

Rhia touched his arm.

'Maybe. We shall have to wait and see.'

'And Gawan?'

This time it was Rhia who frowned. Lucan's only memory of Gawan would be the time the Gorvic had slapped him for disobedience.

'Why him?'

Lucan shrugged.

'Just wondering.'

Rhia didn't know what to make of that and put it aside for now. Gawan was a confusing enough subject as it was without adding this on top of everything else. She forced another smile.

'We shall see.'

She didn't want to tell him that this plan was assuming that things went well the next day. There was always a chance that Caserach would threaten enough chiefs to demand them to reconsider her death. She fumed quietly. There were few enough options open to her to try to stop him. He'd been a clever bastard in bringing Broad Kellas with him.

Rhia felt despair threaten her spirit again. She hated herself for her weakness but she just wanted to take her boy in her arms and go to sleep for a year. *I am so tired of being strong, is that so bad?* Once again Lucan looked up at her with concern.

'Mama?'

Rhia looked down at him. His face was determined and her mind went back to the day they and Marius had been overtaken by Gaian scouts, back when they'd been fleeing from Tamora past the Canwyns. All had seemed lost and this tiny child had picked up a stick and stood ready to defend his mother against her enemies. Her brave boy. *So like his father.* She reached out and stroked his hair.

'Just tired, my sweet. Just tired.'

He seemed to accept that as an answer and after a couple of heartbeats he sat back, leaning his head against her leg. Rhia kept stroking his hair, trying her best to hide her fears. It had reached a point where the very best she could hope for was that she could return to Tamora and never see her home again. Lucan would grow up as an exile, in a place where men would someday plan to invade his former home. *But will it be with his mother, who can at least teach him who he is? Or will he grow up there alone, orphaned by his own people?* Lucan's hair was soft beneath her stroking hand, and it was all Rhia could do to hold back her tears.

Chapter 36. Walking

Gawan was walking more out of habit than because he had to be anywhere. He'd found before that the simple act of putting one foot in front of the other often helped to clear his head in times of stress. Not that it was helping him tonight. Tonight he had already walked two circuits of Bryngarth's defences and still his mind remained in turmoil. Rhianwyn's cause was lost. Her chiefs would banish her at best, and with her would go the best hopes of both the Caderyn and the Gorvicae. And once she was gone he would never see her again. It was that more than anything else that was making his head spin. Guilt at having failed his people or for having caused harm to a chieftain, those were things he could understand. His own feelings however were a mess of confusion and try though he might, he couldn't struggle through them.

He found himself back at the spot where he had started and changed his direction without really thinking about it, plodding down the hill in a lazy spiral. The strange thing was that he couldn't even blame his reaction on a simple moment of lust any more. To his shame he still thought about Rhianwyn's body sometimes but he knew it was more than a simple yearning for flesh that was making his heart so heavy. More than the thought of never seeing her again, he felt weighed down by the knowledge that she was about to lose so much, having already suffered more than any soul her age ought to have suffered. She loved her tribe with an almost blinding fierceness, and Gawan dreaded to think of the beating her spirit would take from this banishment. When the verdict had been spoken he had seen the look in her eyes, and mask or not it had been clear to him that she was crushed. *And what did you do to help her?*

Gawan kicked angrily at a stone and watched it bounce down the hillside in the grey moonlight. Hopefully the sentence would not be worsened tomorrow, but there were no guarantees. Caserach had until Belenos reached his zenith to spread poison among the headmen, and who knew what mischief the bastard might cause in that time? Was it worth speaking to Galerian about having men ready in case of trouble? If the Darin succeeded in intimidating enough people then Rhianwyn's life might still be in danger. *Even if he doesn't, that murderous bastard won't be letting her ride away quietly to Tamora.* The general would surely agree to escort her on the road, but there would be plenty of chance for Caserach to arrange some harm to her before then. Did he dare return to his plan to remove her from Bryngarth by force? The Gadarim scratched irritably at his scalp. Involving the Gaians had caused enough damage already, but if it meant saving Rhianwyn, was it a risk worth taking?

He trudged down the hill, feeling lost and defeated. He'd been so sure that Taliesyn's words would sway them. The young chief had probably expected the same thing. Tegwen had been waiting for them both when they left the hall but Gawan hadn't found it in him to do much more than nod to her, and he had left it to her lover to explain what had happened inside. Tegwen had tried to speak comfortingly but neither man had been particularly amenable to it, though Taliesyn had tried his best to seem positive. Gawan had simply grunted and wandered off upon his walk.

He meandered down the slope, his eyes on the ground. Whether by the hand of her people or by Caserach's scheming, Rhianwyn would be in danger from the moment she left the longhall tomorrow. If he asked Galerian to take her from the town by force the Gaian would almost certainly do it, but what might that lead to? If Alraig sent word to Nantwyn for the Dragon Legion to take her back again then it would mean war, and not just with a renegade general this time. This time it would be war with the whole Gaian Empire, and with Karadoc and Caserach's undoing of the Caledon the tribes would be all but helpless. Rhianwyn would not want to be saved if that was the cost of it. Gawan knew he had his answer and that as her brother Gadarim he should respect her wishes. But the thought of her dying made his stomach turn and his palms sweat, and he found himself thinking that he didn't give a damn about what she wanted. *He* wanted her alive! He slashed his hand at a nearby sapling and cursed himself for his weakness. This was no way for a son of Mabonac to think.

He reached the base of the hill and looked away northwards. The moon was bright, even through the clouds, and he could see the beginnings of the woods clearly enough. Without thinking he walked towards them, half-wondering if he might find another forest spirit in there. The last time he had wandered at night, alone and confused, the old man had found him and spun riddles to confuse him further. If he found a sprite in the woods tonight he wouldn't be waiting to hear his fortune told. He would take it by the throat and strangle some answers from it, and magic and curses be damned! Not that he really expected to find anyone. To meet one spirit was rare

501

enough, and he had disappointed the gods enough by now; they were unlikely to encourage a second meeting. Or not a peaceful one anyway.

He plodded slowly across the open land until he reached the treeline. A fresh wave of guilt washed over him as he remembered the last time he had come to these woods, with a woman who had loved him by his side. He almost growled. Maybe everyone would be better off if he just walked in here and didn't come out; if he found himself a spirit and it tore him apart. He had failed his fellow Gadarim, he had failed Emeryn, he had failed his father, his brother, his daughter and his friend. He had failed Rhianwyn. He had failed his people.

He strode into the trees, careless for what might lie beyond them. Let Jarinn and Echan and all their goblins come and find him if they would, it didn't matter. The leaves crunched under his feet and ferns swished past his legs but otherwise the woods were silent. Once into the trees the moonlight became faint, and strange shadows leaned this way and that between the trunks. Gawan wandered on in no particular direction, no real thought to where he was going or why he was going there. He didn't care anymore.

After a while he stopped moving and looked around him. The trees loomed overhead and the undergrowth lurked darkly between them but otherwise there was nothing much to see. There were no sprites in the trees, no cryptic old men, no cackling goblins, no tempting sylphs. The wood was empty and silent, and completely indifferent. For some reason Gawan found his misery giving way to anger and he lashed out at the nearest branch. It splintered beneath his knuckles but didn't break, and Gawan ignored the hot pain in his hand as he shouted out to the darkness.

'Well? Have you nothing to say?'

He didn't know what he had expected to happen when he came in here, but the wood's refusal to yield anything but silence was infuriating. He tried to think of the gods he most respected like Taran and Mabonac, but even they seemed to have abandoned him. He roared out his challenge to Mehine or Karanon, or whoever else might be lurking in the black-and-grey trees.

'Damn you all then! Damn you all with your tricks and omens!'

He felt blood pumping hard through his limbs and kept staring into the trees, half-hoping for some sprite or another to appear so that he could attack it. Rhianwyn had given everything for this land, and her gods had abandoned her just as surely as they had abandoned him. *Let something of their world step forward, just* something *that I can call to account for all this.* He sighed. *Something I can blame besides myself.* The thought threatened to douse his anger and he fought to keep it going, but a voice from the dark distracted him from his rage.

'Hello?'

The Gadarim spun around with his fists clenched and ready, but even halfway through the turn he was slowing himself down. The voice had been quiet, timid even; not the voice of a being about to confront someone. All the same it was hard to conceal his shock when he saw young Lucan half-hidden behind a beech, his face pale in the silvery light. For a heartbeat Gawan was struck for words and the boy shrank away a little. The Gorvic shook his head, trying to clear it.

'So,' he began, and he faltered a little before continuing. 'You did not learn much from that smack I gave you last time?'

Lucan stayed behind his tree and looked down guiltily, but then he managed to give a little shrug. Gawan approached him slowly.

'What in Taran's name are you doing out here?'

The boy kept his eyes on the ground but did not back away.

'I slipped off when Auntie Olla thought I was asleep.' He gestured weakly with one hand. 'I was looking for a spirit to help Mother. She thinks I don't know but she's afraid.' He looked up at Gawan, his face distraught. 'She's *never* afraid.'

Gawan sighed. The boy had a good heart but none of his parents' wisdom.

'You want to be careful out in the woods my boy. Dangerous things live here.'

Upset though he was Lucan didn't seem afraid and he shrugged his tiny shoulders again.

'They seem friendly. And they'll want to help my mother.'

Gawan frowned at him as some of his anger came back and the boy shifted a little closer to his tree.

'Woodland sprites can be vicious.'

Lucan shuffled his feet a little but then looked up at the warrior.

'Father said the gods were good if we are good to them. Spirits too.'

Gawan remembered how Anryn had always said similar things, not that he'd seen that much evidence of it. All the

504

same it wouldn't do to crush the boy too much and he softened his voice as best he could.

'It is true that some creatures are kind or guiding, but plenty are still dangerous to little boys.'

And to grown men. Lucan nodded, looking downcast, and Gawan moved closer to him, squatting down slowly so as not to tower over him. He had no real experience with children but he did his best to talk without scaring him.

'Whatever they are, you cannot solve anything by running off to seek godly help. Your mother needs *you* more than she needs some woodland sprite. You make her strong.'

Gawan thought back to the cocky girl he'd met the first time he'd come to Bryngarth, and the grown woman who had returned there with her son. Marius had probably been a part of what changed her, and Mabonac had likely done much to give her courage, but everything that he had seen of her told him Lucan was the true source of her strength. He wondered sadly if knowing Tegwen earlier on might have made *him* a stronger man but he pushed the thought aside. Now was not the time.

He stretched a hand towards the boy and spoke as gently as he could.

'Come along.'

Lucan hesitated for only a heartbeat before stepping away from the tree, and he placed his hand into Gawan's, wrapping his whole fist around just three of the big man's fingers. It was an odd feeling but not unpleasant and Gawan looked around to get his bearings before leading the boy away. Though it wasn't easy in the dark he roughly traced his own footsteps through the trees, only occasionally having to stop to check his way. Lucan stayed unusually quiet as they trudged through the undergrowth and Gawan found himself thinking on what he'd just said to the boy. It was true that the gods couldn't solve their problems, but trying to solve everything by fighting was just as foolish a method. Damn it all, but he had learned that the hard way. *Maybe the only way left is to use your mind and your will alone, and draw what strength you can from those around you.* After all, Lucan made Rhianwyn stronger than he had ever been. Gawan resolved that no matter what else he would do all he could to be there for Tegwen, even if he still had no idea what he could do to help Rhianwyn.

They were not far from the treeline when Lucan spoke up again.

'I heard some people talking.' He looked up at Gawan. 'Has my mother done something bad?'

He said it in a way that suggested such a thing was almost impossible, but Gawan heard the tiny note of doubt in his voice. His first instinct was to defend her, to give him the reasons for why she'd done what she'd done and explain that she had acted with best intentions. But a child couldn't be expected to understand something like that and it would only confuse the lad further. All the same it didn't seem right to just give him a simple 'no' and so he considered for a moment before he answered.

'Your mother always does what she thinks is right, no matter what anyone else may think. Sometimes people have to make hard choices to do that. And then they must stick by them.'

Lucan nodded, though Gawan wasn't sure how much he had understood, and once again he found himself pondering on his own words. *Tarwyn made a choice as well. And he stuck by it.*

'He did indeed.'

The voice almost made Gawan jump out of his skin and his hand flew to Heartreaver's grip. It had come from ahead of them and when he looked he saw a figure in white who seemed to have appeared out of nowhere. He was approaching them slowly with his hands clasped in front of him, and it took Gawan a moment to recognise the sombre young druid. It was Bael. The holy man nodded to Lucan, who did not seem at all surprised, before turning back to face Gawan. His blue eyes were piercing but still kindly.

'As did Emeryn, and as did Rylion. We all make our choices and we all have to live with them.'

The First Man felt a prickling of fear run down his back. The druid had read his *thoughts*! Bael's mouth twitched up at one corner before he spoke, but most of the smile was coming from his eyes.

'You are many things my Gorvic friend, but a fast learner is not one of them.'

Gawan didn't know what to say to that. The words themselves might sound like an insult but they were said with no distain, and if anything the young druid seemed fondly amused for a moment. Then his voice became serious once again.

'Choice is all. You are not a blameless man, Gawan son of Dearg, and you do have ill deeds to atone for. But much of that for which you blame yourself was done by choices that were not your own. You did not make Tarwyn or Emeryn fight at Moon Ridge. You did not make Rylion nurture his hatred for you instead of embracing his own life. You did not draw Rhianwyn into her current predicament. You have made mistakes, as have we all, and some of them have had costs.' He took a step closer and his gaze contained wisdom far beyond the young man's years. 'We all of us make choices Gawan, and then we live with them.'

For a moment the Gorvic was certain that he was speaking of someone else but then the holy man reached out to touch his arm. Despite the chill of the night his hand was warm, and something very like dragonfire began to ease its way into the Gadarim's blood. Gawan completely forgot what he'd been thinking as the heat flowed through his body. It was the same, and yet not the same; the same warmth that he found in Mabonac's fire but without the searing heat of war that always came with it. Once again the druid smiled with just his shining eyes and he gestured towards the treeline.

'Come.'

He turned and started walking, his bare feet making no sound on the grass, and Gawan started following, not sure what else to do. Lucan stayed by his side, still completely unconcerned, and they soon reached the edge of the shadowy woodland. He saw Bael pick up a staff from where he'd leaned it against an oak and he cast his eyes towards the hill of Bryngarth.

'Courage may soon be needed along with wisdom and guile.' He turned back to look at them. 'We may yet help Rhianwyn resolve what has come from her own choices.'

Chapter 37. The Druid

The warmth of Bael's magic had almost worn off by morning, though Gawan still felt its remnants flowing through him. Even given time to grow accustomed to it, the sensation was still strange. It was as if Mabonac's fire had been softened without losing any of its power; the heat without the fury. It had been a long time since he last felt dragonfire while his mind was calm, and he felt almost at ease. Almost at peace. The druid had said little enough about his plan but Gawan knew that he was coming to Rhianwyn's aid, and he embraced that quiet hope as he waited outside the longhall.

The morning light was still gentle but already the headmen were gathering to hear the decision of their seniors. The rest of the tribe would have to wait for the announcement at midday but that hadn't stopped dozens of Caderyn men and women from loitering in the area, all eager for some whisper of their chieftain's fate. Gawan liked to think that most of them would be hoping for leniency for Rhianwyn, but beyond their obvious anxiety it was difficult to tell what they were thinking. Just as jittery as anyone was Tegwen, who was trying not to fidget as she waited with her father. She stamped her feet a few times, more in impatience than to ward off the morning chill.

'How much longer must they delay?'

Gawan shrugged at her.

'Who can guess what goes through the mind of a Caderyn?'

She tried to smile but it wasn't convincing. She was probably uneasy on behalf of Taliesyn more than anything;

if Rhianwyn fell from grace his reputation would be in tatters. Not for the first time that morning Gawan's thoughts went to his own reputation. He had convinced himself that it had been destroyed by his various ignoble deeds but the more he thought on it now, the more he realised that it was mostly within his own mind that he'd been ruined. He had torn into himself for all he had done but for the most part, the three tribes still held him in high regard. And he wasn't quite sure how he felt about that.

He still felt ashamed for all that had happened and a part of him felt he did not deserve to be well thought of by anyone. But thanks either to Bael's words or his warming magic, he found that he was hating himself far less than he had been. The guilt was still there but it was bearable somehow; something he could use to fuel his efforts to make amends rather than the crushing weight on his soul that it had been. He would re-earn the right to call himself a Gadarim of the Gorvicae, and his remorse at his mistakes would spur him on to it.

Something of his new hope must have shown in his face because Tegwen looked up at him oddly.

'What is it?'

Bael had told him to keep quiet about his return to Bryngarth and Gawan did his best not to lie to his child.

'There may be hope yet, I think. That is all.'

She kept looking at him quizzically and he changed the subject before she could question him.

'I forgot to ask, how was it taking care of young Lucan yesterday?'

It wasn't much as new conversations went but it was the best that he could think of at a pinch. Tegwen didn't seem to mind it however, and her mouth quirked up in a smile.

'He's a talkative lad. And wilful.'

Gawan almost smiled back.

'That he is, my girl. That he is.'

He was wondering what he ought to say next when the hall's doors were thrown wide and Merwyn stood in the opening. The old man seemed to have aged ten winters since the trial began but he spoke clearly to the little crowd.

'Headmen, you may enter.'

The various chiefs began shuffling inside and Gawan saw Taliesyn approaching through the press. He looked down at Tegwen.

'Wait for us here. This should not take long.'

She nodded to him and took a pace backwards to make room for the headmen. Gawan nodded back before following them into the hall, holding on tight to the quiet hope inside him.

He made his way towards the bench that the Gorvicae had occupied the day before. The other men filed in after him, with Taliesyn among the last to enter. Gawan was surprised to see that Galerian and Derrio had been permitted to join them and had moved to stand a little way apart from the group of Lurians, though still close enough for Derrio to hear them. Presumably it was Merwyn who had extended them such courtesy, unless Alraig wanted them there to witness their ally's fall from power.

Taliesyn approached the bench and nodded to Gawan before sitting down. Though he kept his back straight he was looking crestfallen, and Gawan wondered if he was more concerned for Rhianwyn or for himself. He looked around the room and saw similar looks of defeat on the faces of Merwyn and Hywel. Both Karadoc and Caserach were looking pleased with themselves but Alraig simply seemed satisfied. It was he who addressed the assembly, face stern and voice clear.

'Comrades, we your seniors have reached an agreement.' What little chatter there had been died away almost instantly. 'It has been accorded that Rhianwyn daughter of Carradan is indeed guilty of allowing our enemies to cross Caledon lands, in defiance of her people and of her own laws. When Belenos reaches his peak on this day the verdict of her people shall be announced to the tribe, and her sentence carried out.'

He paused for a moment and cast his eyes around the room. The air seemed to hum with expectation and Alraig gave them another heartbeat before he continued.

'I would remind you all that not only chiefs but holy druids have decided on this, and those who speak for the gods...'

But he was interrupted by three loud bangs that echoed through the hall, and all eyes turned to the door. Even Gawan, who'd been expecting something like this, whipped his head around to look as the heavy doors creaked open and Bael walked into the longhall of his tribe. His white robe swished impressively and the rings on his staff jangled as he strode towards the high table, his eyes fixed straight ahead of him. The hall seemed to brighten as though bathed in fresh sunlight, and power radiated from the young man like warmth from a blazing hearth. The whole room held its breath but Gawan found himself holding back a smile as he watched. Old Reaghan had also enjoyed a good dramatic entrance!

He saw Caserach's face darken with suspicion just as Rhianwyn's seemed to light up with hope. Gawan felt his heart swell to see it. Bael did not look at either of them however and simply bowed his head at the high table, stopping just short of it with his staff planted on the boards.

'You are most kind, Alraig son of Galchoran. But I would not say we speak *for* them. I prefer to think that the gods see fit to speak *through* us. On occasion.'

Most of the room was still looking on in shock but Alraig recovered himself the fastest.

'Your pardon, Druid Bael. I am no expert on the will of the gods.'

He managed to apologise while still giving the impression that the other man was wrong, though he was careful to keep his voice respectful. Bael gave him a small smile, understanding and ignoring the undertone.

'Do not concern yourself, comrade.' He looked around him at the crowd. 'But it is true that the gods commune with us through our methods, and both Druid Reaghan and myself have meditated heavily on this matter with them.'

Gawan could almost *feel* the chiefs around him leaning forward to hear more. The man could enthral a crowd, he'd give him that.

'We are agreed that the law made by Rhianwyn was wise, and made for the protection of our people.'

Alraig tilted his head, confused, and he wasn't the only one to do so.

'Well... indeed.'

He glanced uncertainly at Merwyn who looked just as puzzled as the rest of them. Alraig addressed the druid.

'My thanks Druid Bael for having meditated on this matter. If that is all then we...'

But Bael held up a hand, the gesture gentle but unmistakable, and Alraig stopped speaking.

'That law was of course made to prevent Gaian troops from *entering* our lands in order to threaten our people. As I understand it, the Blackbird Legion was already *in* Caledon lands, hunting down the remnants of our mutual enemy, the Panther Legion.' He spread his hands. 'To my mind, the law remains unbroken.'

An excited murmur went around the room but Karadoc spoke through it.

'With respect you speak of a mere word of difference, and Rhianwyn has already spoken of her distain for technicalities. Has she not at least broken the *spirit* of the law?'

Bael looked first at the Gorvic and then at Alraig.

'I was given to understand that it was by those words that she was judged, was it not? I should say that the spirit of the law was the protection of our people, and in that Rhianwyn has acted only as she saw best for our tribes. Such an action is little different than those which led to the formation of the Caledon. Had I been present to show my hand, I would have shown it in her defence.'

Several sharp intakes of breath followed his statement. His hand would have equalised the verdict, and had Reaghan been there as well and been of the same mind... Gawan held back a smile and saw that Rhianwyn was doing the same. Alraig was not a man easily swayed however and he stopped just shy of scowling at the holy man.

'But you were *not* here. And her guilt has already been decided both by chiefs and by your fellow druids. Would you overturn our decision?'

It was a serious question, and Gawan saw Hywel looking gravely at the younger man. Druids were not to interfere in such things unless requested to, and Gawan knew all too well how much Hywel was reluctant to break that tradition. Bael bowed to the headmen.

'I shall of course respect your decision, as would Reaghan were he here with me.'

Alraig looked almost pleased and Caserach's face lit up with a vicious smile. But Gawan knew that Bael was not done yet.

'But as I understand it, Rhianwyn's sentence has not yet been carried out, nor even announced to the tribe? I would never seek to contradict a verdict made by my tribe's headmen and my honoured brethren,' he nodded to Hywel and the Caderyn druid, 'but I would offer my advice as regards her sentencing, both for my own part and in Reaghan's name.'

Gawan could tell that every man in that room was aching to ask why the senior druid was not there himself, but none of them dared to question Bael. If he had planned to tell them he would have done so already, and he carried himself with such a presence that it was difficult to doubt him when he said he spoke for both of them. And besides, druids did nothing without a reason. He looked around the room.

'Therefore at Belenos' height I say we declare that Rhianwyn be made no longer the chieftain of the Caderyn.'

Gawan saw Rhianwyn looking confused and was feeling very much the same way himself. Merwyn spoke to the druid.

'And what then?'

Bael gave a tiny shrug, and Gawan couldn't help but compare him to the Caderyn druid at the high table. While the older man was skeletally thin and had remained silent and grave through all of this, Bael was young and confident, and even through his white robe the shrug had shown the size and strength of his shoulders.

'She will remain in Bryngarth and a moot will be called for a new leader, as is proper. The chiefs will of course speak from their hearts and who knows, if the gods choose to inspire them so, she may even be made chieftain again? The most important thing will be that all the tribe will have seen that she is truly answerable to her people.'

Alraig's eyes widened and Karadoc was looking livid, but it was Taliesyn who spoke first.

'And what of the Caledon?'

Bael turned to look at him.

'Rhianwyn has been acknowledged as a figurehead for now, but a moot of all three tribes should be called to elect a genuine leader. Not to rule them of course,' he added, forestalling the inevitable objections, 'but to represent the tribes and to serve and guide all three.'

There were some approving nods though most of the room seemed uncertain. Caserach of course had no doubts.

'You think to change a just decision to banish a traitor into her election as supreme leader of us all, is that it? Well no Darin will ever support her or her damned Caledon nonsense, and nor should any right-minded Lurian!'

His tone was shockingly insolent but Gawan had to admit he had a point. Plenty of chiefs would have their objections, and the Darin could influence or intimidate many of them. But Bael had been ready for this.

'That will be for their own hearts to decide, though few of the Dariniae with whom I have spoken would seem to agree with you.'

Caserach seemed to falter and Bael addressed the room in general.

'I have not been idle in my absence from you, comrades. I have travelled to Niswyn and have spoken to many Dariniae headmen and Gadarim, listening to their views and offering my council. Most are of the opinion that the man who killed Ierryn the Black, *and* led many Dariniae warriors to their deaths at Moon Ridge, ought to be brought back to Ynlwyd with all speed to face the judgement of his people.' He looked at Caserach, a tiny touch of iron entering his voice. 'Perhaps they will merely banish you, Caserach son of Heuryn, but they will not be threatened by you. And nor will anyone else.'

This time Gawan actually *did* smile, though he bit it back a moment later. It was subtle, but he saw several Caderyn faces brightening as well, and assumed that these were the men from the clans nearest the coast. Karadoc and Alraig were stone-faced, and Hywel was still looking solemn, but most of the hall seemed to be quietly satisfied. Caserach's face turned crimson but Taliesyn was the first to rise to his feet.

'This man speaks with great wisdom, and wisdom should always be heeded. I am with the druid.'

Merwyn rose from his bench a heartbeat later.

'As am I.'

A dozen headmen at least rose to their feet within an eyeblink, closely followed by a dozen more. Gawan added his voice to theirs and soon Kyran was doing the same. He saw Karadoc calling out objections but no-one heard what they were. So many were shouting support that even Alraig could see there was no use in counting their hands. He had lost.

Gawan felt a warmth in his chest as he watched Rhianwyn trying to maintain her composure. She looked ready to burst into song as she saw how many chiefs were standing for her now that Caserach's threats had been undone. Bael was keeping a dignified silence but Gawan saw satisfaction in his face as well, a quiet pride that he had achieved what he had come to do. With such support Rhianwyn might lose her father's chair for a day but she would have it back again, and they all knew it. That was when Caserach overturned his table.

The noise was deafening as the heavy oak crashed onto the boards, the cups on it clattering across the floor. Gawan noticed that Broad Kellas hadn't moved which meant the Darin must have done it alone, and he felt a new respect for the man's strength if nothing else. Silence descended over the hall and Caserach half-bellowed to the assembly, his eyes wide with boiling rage.

'Then I accuse her *directly* of attacking my people by foul means! I say that Rhianwyn daughter of Carradan has wronged me and my tribe by her actions, and druid or no druid, I *demand* that this be settled in Trial by Iron! Let justice be done in the eyes of the gods, in person or between my First Man and hers.'

Gawan was as shocked as anyone. Trial by Iron was a rare thing to say the least, but to demand it in contest of a druid's decision was completely unheard of. *What sort of madness has seized him?* It was Kyran who broke the silence, fists clenched and eyes blazing.

'You'll find sapphires up your arse the day I fight for you, you piss-drinking goat-shafter!'

Caserach glared at him.

'I will make you regret those words, make no mistake.'

Kyran stepped forward and looked ready to spring across the fallen table. Gawan moved in ready to restrain him but Caserach raised a hand and continued speaking.

'But it is not you that I need. Broad Kellas was assigned to my protection by the chiefs of the Breiryn.'

The giant rose very slowly and folded his arms, his expression as blank as ever. Bael turned to face the Darin and his voice was calm.

'Caserach this is foolishness. The situation is resolved. Let it be, and face the consequences of your actions like a man.'

Any other chief would have backed down, but Caserach did the unthinkable; he shouted at a druid.

'I will not be cheated! Either I am given satisfaction or I shall take this as a snub against my people *and* the Breiryn. We are bloodied but not broken, and we will fight to defend our honour. Two thousand Breiryn await my word at Reed Marsh and they will avenge this insult if I am denied.'

Gawan had no idea where that was but he assumed it was near the border with Caderyn lands. Not that it mattered. It might be an empty threat but even half such a number would do irreparable damage to the battered Dragon Legion. He jerked his chin at Caserach.

'Can those two thousand Breiryn hear you? I hope so for your sake because you're as close to Reed Marsh as you're going to get!'

He heard approving noises from nearby, though most of the chiefs were still reeling in shock at how the Darin had spoken to Bael. Caserach just sneered at him.

'You would not dare!'

Of all people it was Alraig who answered him.

'You are still here as a prisoner of the Caledon, to whom your uncle swore an oath. We have every right to hold you here until your own people take you for trial.'

Caserach simply nodded to Broad Kellas, who began removing one of his bracelets.

'I am no Caledon. I have broken no vow, nor have my people.' He tossed the bracelet at Rhianwyn's feet. 'Take my sword instead if you wish, but I will go where I will.'

Gawan saw her shake her head, but it seemed more like a reflex than a considered decision. Defeated Gadarim would always offer a victor their swords, and it was tradition for the gesture to be refused and some other offering accepted instead. Gawan frowned in thought. Broad Kellas had presumably gone through this ritual when initially captured but now he was making a point of it in front of everyone. Rhianwyn had declined to take his sword, which meant he could leave the hall right now as a free man. Assuming Caserach was not bluffing, Broad Kellas could take word to his allies at Reed Marsh even if the Caderyn kept Caserach as their prisoner. And if they tried to prevent the Breiryn's First Man from leaving too it would mean an insult to the whole tribe, and who knew how many warriors would come north to avenge that?

Rhianwyn's frown and Caserach's smirk told Gawan they were both thinking the same thing he was. Bael spoke again.

'The Caderyn has no First Man to face your champion, Caserach.'

The Darin shrugged.

'Then I shall fight her myself.'

Rhianwyn squared up to him and put contempt into her voice.

'I shall be *happy* to kill you for all you have done.'

Gawan knew she was putting on a show of more bravado than she felt. She was a competent fighter but Caserach had strength and reach on his side, and even if she was his equal in skill, those advantages would be significant. If she fought him, chances were good that she would die. Gawan heard his own voice before he even thought of speaking.

'I will do it! Either with you or with that ugly hillock there.' He nodded at Broad Kellas, who had gone back to looking indifferent again. 'I will prove the innocence of Fearless Wildcat in the eyes of all the gods.'

Alraig and Caserach both spoke at once but they were saying the same thing.

'You are not Caderyn!'

Rhianwyn was looking at him oddly as well but Gawan didn't pause.

'But I *am* Caledon.'

Alraig's voice was that of a man addressing a dim-witted child.

'The Caledon has no First Man, and without a leader such a thing cannot be made.'

Gawan fumed for a moment but then Merwyn spoke from behind the high table.

'If the Breiryn are willing to let Broad Kellas fight for another tribe, cannot the Gorvicae allow their First Man to fight for the Caderyn?'

He looked to where Taliesyn and Karadoc stood, and before they opened their mouths Gawan knew what they would say.

'Yes.'

'No.'

He frowned. There might be no official High Chieftain for his tribe but if both candidates had approved then even Alraig would have been forced to accept the decision. Gawan clenched his jaw. If he let Rhianwyn fight Caserach then her blood was on his hands; he had to be the one to take this trial. Broad Kellas was strong but he *knew* that he could beat him. But without the approval of the chiefs he would never be allowed to. He considered rushing Caserach and killing him right now but at best it would only buy them some time. Once it was done, and once Gawan had been cast out of the Gadarim, Broad Kellas would take news of the murder to the Breiryn and then there would be war. Gawan flicked a glance at Galerian, who had watched all this in silence as Derrio mumbled in his ear. He might still call in the Blackbirds to take Rhianwyn away, but if she was seen to cheat the trial there was a chance that that too might lead to war with the southerners.

Gawan racked his brains for a way around it until an idea came to him that was so simple, and so terrible, that for a moment he could not bear to say it aloud. It was unthinkable. But then he thought of seeing another woman choking on her own blood because of something he had done. Or not done. And the decision was made remarkably easy.

'Then I set aside my tribe! I shall no longer be Gorvicae!' He turned to face the Wildcat. 'Rhianwyn daughter of Carradan, may I be Caderyn?'

The hall went dumb with shock and he saw faces turning pale, and he would not have been surprised if his own face was just as white. His stomach felt hollow and his legs were weak, and a coldness seemed to clutch his heart like the fingers of death itself. But Rhianwyn was smiling. In smiling her face went from merely attractive into something beautiful and Gawan felt warmth returning to his blood.

'Of course you may, my brother Gadarim. The Caderyn would be proud to count such a man among our number.'

She lifted a hand as she looked around at the druids and headmen.

'Leaping Wolf was once the First Man of the Gorvicae; I say let him be First Man of the Caderyn.'

Caserach spat from behind his fallen table.

'You are no chieftain to say such things!'

But Bael's mouth twitched up at one corner, his eyes knowing.

'She is until Belenos rides to his summit today. As both High Chieftain and a Gadarim herself, I say it is for Rhianwyn and her brothers to decide such a thing.'

The young druid gave Gawan a look that he could have sworn contained something like pride before he turned around to face Kyran.

'Bloodhound, First Man of the Dariniae, do you raise objection to this?'

The hard-faced Darin nodded to Gawan and gave Caserach a malicious half-smile before he answered.

'I do not.'

Bael bowed his head in thanks.

'And Broad Kellas, First Man of the Breiryn, do you raise objection to this?'

The big man shook his head at the druid, though his eyes were fixed on Gawan as he replied.

'I do not.'

Bael looked around to address the whole hall.

'So speak the greatest warriors of the Gadarim here present.'

Gawan felt his heart flutter in his chest. To be Gorvicae had meant everything to him but somehow, in this moment, that didn't matter. Rhianwyn spoke again and the hint of joy in her voice made pride swell up within him.

'Then let Leaping Wolf be my champion, and First Man of the Caderyn from this day forth. May he live and die with honour.'

Both Kyran and Broad Kellas spoke together, one with a hard smile and the other with a face as blank as stone.

'May he live and die with honour!'

Chapter 38. The New Champion

Gawan felt strangely calm as he stepped into the dimming light. The day had seemed to take no time at all. It wasn't a blur exactly; he could clearly remember everything that had happened, from his meeting with Bael to the gatherings of the tribe to the feast at the longhall, but somehow it also felt as if the time had sped past him. He took in a slow breath of cool air, glad that he hadn't had too much to drink. Tomorrow would be a busy day and he had to make sure Heartreaver was properly blessed before he allowed himself to sleep.

He leaned on a post outside the doors of the longhall and listened to the muffled noise coming from inside. It was still almost completely filled with people, many of whom would end up sleeping on its floors, but Gawan had decided to sleep with the rest of the Gorvicae on the other side of town. It would be quieter there and he needed a clear head for the morning. The voices in the hall seemed happy enough as the tribesmen ate and chattered but he suspected the mood in the room was still tense. Men were relieved that a decision had been made at last but they were anxious for the fight the next day, and mixture of fear and uncertainty lay over their half-hearted merriment.

Gawan sighed quietly. It would have been simpler, and quicker, just to have held the trial straight after the sentence was announced. Everyone had been there after all and it would have spared them all this night of uncertainty. But Trials by Iron were rare things and traditions had to be upheld, and one of those traditions required a night to pass. As with the Gadarim trials, Mabonac's rituals were best held away from Belenos' light, and both Gawan and Broad Kellas would want their swords blessed. Druids might bless weapons before a battle regardless of time, but for a trial before the gods such formalities were more important. Before he slept tonight, Gawan would hold up Heartreaver in Leu's silver light and ask Mabonac to be with him on the morrow. *You might have lost your tribe, but at least you are still Gadarim.*

That feeling was still a difficult one to get used to, and Gawan suspected that he never truly would. The reaction it had prompted from others had been unexpected enough, with most of the Caderyn welcoming him and most of the Gorvicae respecting his reasons, but it was the reaction in his own heart that was causing him confusion. He ought to feel more ashamed, shouldn't he? For as long as he could remember the greatest source of pride in him was the knowledge that he was Gorvicae, and he had set that honour aside with barely a second thought. He felt a certain sense of loss, even something like grief, but it wasn't nearly so crushing a feeling as he'd have expected. Perhaps it wasn't so bad because he knew his winning this combat would help the Gorvicae in the long run. With Rhianwyn restored to the Caledon and Taliesyn as their chieftain, his people would prosper far more than if he allowed all this to fall apart, simply for the sake of his own pride. Perhaps this was part of the price he had to pay to atone for all the wrongs that still lay on his soul? When he met Annwn he wanted to be able to say that he had at least tried to do the honourable thing in life.

He let out another sigh, hoping that this was indeed the right thing to do. Besides his instinctive loyalty to the tribe, his one nagging doubt was the impact it would have on Tegwen. They had barely begun to know one another and here he was creating yet more distance between them. But what else could he do? How could he do the right thing by *everyone*? He closed his eyes in thought but opened them again almost immediately as he heard someone approach. He turned to see that, as if in answer to his thoughts, Tegwen had appeared in the doorway of the longhall. She closed the door gently behind her, shutting off most of the noise and heat that was coming from inside. Though they'd sat on the same bench to eat she had not spoken much, not even to Taliesyn, and a glance at her face had shown Gawan that she was troubled. She wore the same expression now and didn't waste time with pleasantries.

'Why?'

He shouldn't have been surprised by her directness but all the same it took him a moment to answer her.

'The Gorvicae are best served by Rhianwyn remaining as chieftain here. We need someone who can deal with the Gaians. And we need Taliesyn in Graigarw.'

She nodded and Gawan hoped rather than expected her to settle for that answer.

'There is more to it than that.'

Gawan nodded back.

'It is the right thing to do. Rhianwyn has done no wrong and I am the only one who could stand for her. We all of us owe her a debt, Tegwen; Lepidus would have destroyed us all had she not united us to fight him.'

He could tell that she'd heard the honesty in his voice but that she still wasn't satisfied. Gawan found himself feeling both proud and annoyed that his daughter was apparently a perceptive woman. Her head tilted a fraction and he saw one eyebrow rise.

'And that is all?'

Gawan didn't want to say it aloud and it took an effort to meet Tegwen's eyes as he answered.

'I would see her safe.'

Tegwen nodded again and then jerked her head back towards the longhall.

'I have heard good things about her. But is she worth your tribe? Or your life?'

Gawan shrugged and tried to avoid answering.

'You think I would lose? I have fought big men before.'

In truth he was as wary of Broad Kellas as any sane man would be, but he was confident in his skills, and in the rightness of his cause. He might not escape unscathed but the Breiryn would lose, he knew that. He had to.

Tegwen's face betrayed her worry, and Gawan felt a confusing mixture of warmth at her concern and guilt for having caused it. Her voice became quieter.

'Perhaps.'

Gawan decided to take a risk and he seized her by the shoulders, looking hard into her eyes. *So like her mother's.*

'Tegwen, I can beat this man. I *will* beat this man and I will watch Belenos set with you tomorrow. I promise you.'

She seemed surprised by the contact but she neither flinched nor backed away from him. She met his eyes for a few moments and seemed about to speak but then lowered her gaze, looking uncertain. Gawan let her go, feeling suddenly awkward, and took a step back. After a tense few moments he decided it was best if he just left her in peace, but she broke the silence just as he turned.

'Don't do it, Father.'

Gawan's breath caught in his chest. Hearing her say it made his heart pound faster than it ever had in the heat of battle. What did it mean? Did she truly want him to be a father to her? If that was so, how could he refuse the first thing she'd ever asked of him as his daughter? He looked on her face and part of him wanted to tell her that he would of course do as she asked; that he would abandon the challenge and take her away with him to some safe place. His name would be disgraced forever, and the three tribes might be plunged into chaos, but that part of him thought it would be worth it if it made his daughter smile.

But more important than making her smile was showing her that her father was a man who stuck by his commitments. A man she could trust. He had let her down before and while he could never go back to her childhood to make amends for it, he *could* show her that he had changed, even if it brought her more pain for now. To do as she asked would please her for a day and might even be his first step towards earning her love, but she was a warrior of her tribe in her own right, and sooner or later she would learn to despise him for running away. And love without respect was no more than pity.

He stepped close to her again.

'I would never wish to cause you pain, but this must be done. I believe you know that it must.'

Tegwen's eyes grew bright but no tears fell from them.

'Perhaps it does. But tell me the truth,' she squared up to him, 'do you do this for the Caledon, or for the Wildcat?'

Gawan remembered how the Gaians had charged them at White Ridge, and that Tegwen had been there too, though he hadn't known it. She had seen the threat that faced them all. She had fought against it the same as he had and she would understand the importance of the Caledon. If he reminded her of that black day and told her that unity was his greatest reason for doing this, there was every chance that she would believe him. But she had called him Father. And fathers should not lie to their children.

'I do this for both. Both are in my heart, and both are worth fighting for.'

For a moment he thought she might say something harsh to him, but then she forced a half-smile.

'As if anyone could talk you out of a fight anyway.'

Gawan could see just how forced it was and he let his own mouth quirk up in response. Perhaps it was what she needed to accept what was happening.

'I never was bright enough to avoid them.'

Tegwen nodded to him and another awkward silence threatened. Gawan knew he ought to say something else to her but she began to turn back towards the longhall before he could think of anything. She placed a hand on the door but then spoke over her shoulder.

'Call yourself what you will and fight for what you will, Father. I will be there.'

It was as close to approval as he was going to get and it clearly hadn't been an easy thing for her to say. He owed her a reply.

'I am Caderyn now and will serve my new tribe as best I can.'

He saw her turn to face him and he tapped his chest with a finger.

'But the Gorvicae will always have a place in here. And so will you.'

Tegwen didn't answer but the smile she gave him wasn't forced this time, and Gawan felt a warmth in him to put all of Bael's magics to shame. They exchanged a final nod before she went back into the hall. Once the door closed behind her Gawan turned towards the town. When all of this was done he would be a father to his child, perhaps even a father that she could love one day. But before he could do that there was a fight he had to win. And for that, he'd need to get a good night's sleep.

*

After his third cup of mead beside the longhouse fire, Gawan told himself he really *had* to get to bed. He had only meant to stay with his brothers for a quick drink before going out to bless Heartreaver, but they had pressed cup after cup into his hands, Duran more than any of them. It had mainly been done in the spirit of friendship of course but Gawan knew the other reason behind the gesture. The fight tomorrow would be close, and they both knew it. Neither had gone so far as to say *farewell*, but this was as close as they were going to come to admitting aloud that this might be their final night together. On this side of the bridge anyway. So Gawan had stayed to reminisce and drink and listen to the friendly chatter. The others were all laughing as Duran finished his story.

'I'll say one thing though; the goats on that mountain are still nervous to this day!'

The group of Gadarim howled with laughter and even Gawan chuckled at the memory. Pryder was snorting his drink out through his nose, which of course only made the others chortle even more. Gwydion lost his balance and toppled sideways as he watched, but then he'd had a lot more to drink than the others had. Gawan smiled at his brothers. They had all of them been through some hard times together, he and Duran more than most, and it was good to share the night with them. Pryder and Gwydion had been listening with rapt attention as their seniors had told tales of fine times and hard fights in years gone by. Neither were exactly inexperienced of course; Gwydion had been Gadarim for almost as long as Duran, and though Pryder was young he'd fought like a hero in half-a-dozen battles. They were warriors who could be justly proud of who they were, but still they had sat in quiet awe as Gawan and Duran told their stories. Stories of twenty winters of raid and battle, of great victories and terrible defeats, and of the countless times the one had saved the hide of the other. Gawan bathed in the memories and would happily have stayed with them until dawn, but he had preparing to do and he needed to get some sleep.

Duran seemed ready to embark on another tale and Gawan raised an open hand to him.

'You will have to tell this one without me, brother.' He tapped Heartreaver's hilt. 'Blessings call.'

He eased himself to his feet and tried to ignore the ache in his knee as he straightened it. Duran nodded in understanding and the others followed his example.

'As you say. But come for a last drink before you sleep. We still have to share the story of that miller's girl in Henderw!'

Both Gwydion and Pryder sat up with interest and even Gawan half-smiled.

'And I take it you won't want to tell it without me here?' Duran grinned.

'Where would be the fun in that?'

Gawan shook his head in resignation and walked away, picking his way through warriors who either slept or chattered on the longhouse's floor.

By the time he reached the door his bladder was telling him he had more urgent business than blessings just now, and he unbuckled his belt to ease the pressure on it. Carrying his belt and sword in one hand he pushed open the heavy door and stepped out into the night. The wind was chilly but if anything it just served to freshen him after the stifling heat of the longhouse.

He wandered a little way before untying his trews and drawing himself out to urinate. The relief was instantaneous and he watched the fluid arc away with a groan of contentment. Apparently he'd drunk more than he'd realised because it took a while for him to empty himself, but by the time he was done he was sighing with quiet satisfaction. His member was still in his hand when the arm wrapped around his throat, and he felt another man rip his sword from his grip while his neck was squeezed between bony forearms.

Gawan kept his head and though he was too slow to keep hold of Heartreaver, his elbow found the first man's ribs before the strangler could take proper hold. He felt the grip weaken and he caught the man by the belt and elbow, hurling him into the path of the second attacker. In the darkness he could barely see his assailants but he aimed a kick in what seemed roughly the right direction and was rewarded by a grunt of pain. Then something struck him in the lower back and his torso arched backwards like a bow. Before he could fully face the new threat a fist had cracked into his jaw, followed swiftly by a pair of body blows. His head snapped to the side and his vision swam, but he managed to stay awake and lifted his arms up, dimly aware of two figures moving in front of him. The guard left his ribs open to more heavy punches but Gawan knew what he was doing; in any kind of fight, first priority was always to cover the head.

Gawan was rocked by the blows but he kindled dragonfire in his gut and quickly replied with a strike of his own, his fist lashing out at a shadowy face. He saw the head snap back and but didn't pause to see if he fell; instead he grabbed hold of the man's comrade and forced up his chin before sending a right cross into his throat. The man fell back, gagging, but before Gawan could follow it up someone was grabbing his arms from behind. He tried to turn but it seemed both of the other men had recovered quickly and had taken hold of an arm each, pulling his limbs out and back and hauling his balance over his heels. A shape in front of him, which looked vaguely like a man who was tall but lean, stepped forwards and hammered blows into his face, ignoring his torso now his head was exposed. Gawan struggled and rolled with the punches as best he could but one of the men behind him was damnably strong. He grabbed a thin-feeling wrist and tried to heave the weaker one off-balance, but even as he stumbled the tall man in front of him came forward, and launched his knee hard into Gawan's groin.

If anything the pain only served to make him angrier, but in the moment of distraction it bought them his attackers dragged him to the ground and pinned his arms above his head. He flailed with his legs and felt one kick crack into a knee, but then the tall man was on him again, battering down at his unprotected head while the others held him still. Gawan felt himself begin to black out and forced himself to go limp beneath the beating. The tall man kept it up for a while but then slowed down and finally stopped. Gawan could hear he was breathing hard and he groaned aloud as he stood up, mercifully taking the weight from the Gorvic's lungs.

Gawan felt anger race through him at the craven attack. He ignored his ringing head and lifted his weight up on one hand, swinging his leg in a low arc that caught the tall man in both calves. He toppled and Gawan was about to spring at him when he heard an odd swishing sound just to his left, and suddenly he was collapsing onto his side. It was only when he hit the ground that the pain began. Only when he saw the ragged stump of his left wrist.

The fire in his belly vanished into nothing as searing pain flashed up his arm, and before he knew it Gawan was screaming. He just had time to see his severed hand on the moonlit grass beside him before feet began stamping down onto his head, and the whole world faded into blackness.

Chapter 39. Wounded

Rhia was worrying about Gawan. What he'd done was incredible as far as she was concerned of course, but what would it mean for the Gorvicae? And for him? The northerners at Bryngarth seemed to have taken it well enough, but then they were here and could see how dire the situation was. Would the rest of his tribe be so understanding about the Caderyn stealing away their most renowned warrior? And then there was Gawan himself to consider. He was a proud and stubborn man and fanatically devoted to his tribe. The Caderyn had been his enemies for most of his life and now he was not only fighting for them but abandoning his tribe to call himself one of them. It must have been having an effect on him. *And he is doing it for me.*

  She thought back to that night after the battle at Moon Ridge. Gawan was no fool. He would know the broader implications of what her banishment would mean and it made good logical sense for him to fight in the trial, but she knew that wasn't why he was doing it. Gawan cared for her. In his own strange way he might even have come to *love* her, though how and why was still a complete mystery. Rhia stared into her cup and felt shame in her heart. She respected Gawan of course, and had even come to like him after a fashion; she admired his finer qualities, cared for his welfare and had been truly touched by his actions today. But she didn't harbour anything like the same feelings that he clearly did. Wherever they came from. *And now you're letting him fight Broad Kellas to save you from having to fight Caserach. You're letting him risk his life for you because of how he feels for you.*

She looked over at Lucan, sleeping peacefully in the little bed that had been brought in for him. At Bael's request he had been permitted to stay the night with his mother, and Rhia had been immensely glad for it. Looking at him, she wondered if he would ever love her the same way she loved him, and if it would even matter if he didn't. Rhia couldn't imagine anything she would not do to keep him safe, and even if he grew distant from her, as she had seen some sons do, she knew that could never affect her devotion. She felt sad at the prospect of something like that happening but even if it did, it wouldn't really matter. Her love for him was constant. Perhaps the only constant thing she had to hold on to.

Bael, sitting across from her, nodded his head in a way that made her think he had read her thoughts, and had understood them. She took a sip of rosemary leaf and reflected on how odd that was. Had it been Reaghan sitting there she might have expected to feel like this; Reaghan had been a father to them all for as long as she could remember, and though his powers had been subtle there was not a man of the tribe who had ever doubted their potency. Bael on the other hand was barely a summer older than she was. Rhia could still remember how they had played together when they were small, yet here he was, grave-eyed and calm and radiating the same energy she had always felt from the elder druid. When he spoke his voice was slightly lighter than Reaghan's had been but it had the same quiet, serious quality to it.

'You need not feel guilty, Rhia. The decision was his to make.'

Rhia frowned slightly and pressed her lips together.

'I know it was, but it still makes me feel... cowardly. To let another fight in my place, I mean.'

Bael shrugged his shoulders.

'Chieftains have often called on champions to fight such combats in their stead. There is no shame in it.'

He took a sip from his steaming cup as Rhia considered that.

'True, and if this had been Madoc or Owain then I wouldn't have thought so much on it. But with Gawan...'

The druid nodded, understanding written across his face.

'You feel he fights for the wrong reasons?'

Rhia bobbed her head.

'Yes.'

Bael took a slow breath before speaking again.

'I take it that the main source of your guilt is the belief that he does this out of concern for you alone?'

From what she suspected of his powers Bael probably knew full well that was the source of it, but it seemed he was being polite by asking her out loud.

'Yes.'

He nodded.

'Gawan does indeed care for you Rhia, but he has many reasons for the choices he has made. I do not say that you were not a large part of his decision, but you did not ask for his help, nor are you responsible for what he chose of his own free will.'

Rhia frowned, not feeling much comforted.

'Perhaps. All the same, it might be best if I volunteered to fight Caserach instead.'

The druid raised his hand in a gesture that was gentle but firm.

'No. I mean no offence to your own skills but Caserach is a gifted killer. Gawan is perhaps the finest fighter in all the Caledon; strong though Broad Kellas is, Gawan stands a better chance against him than you would against Caserach.' He took another short draught of his leaf. 'And besides, whatever else happens you are more important to our survival.'

Rhia nodded again, though she felt uncomfortable. She didn't like to be reminded of how damned vital she was. She was about to say something to that effect when Bael's face suddenly changed. His brows furrowed and his eyes grew distant, as if he could hear something but couldn't quite tell what it was. Rhia tilted her head in concern.

'Are you...'

But his eyes suddenly widened and he cut across her.

'Too late!' He sprang from his chair fast enough to knock it over. 'Damn it all!'

Rhia stood up as well, scared and confused.

'What is it?'

Bael was already heading for the door and before Rhia could speak again she heard voices outside, followed by urgent footsteps on the boards. Bael threw open the door in time to admit Cerri, with a pale-faced Duran close on her heels. The Gadarim saw the druid and called out over his shoulder.

'He's in here!'

The shout caused Lucan to stir in his sleep but Rhia's eyes were fixed on the doorway. Madlen the herbwife had appeared in the frame, tutting at a group of men behind her.

'Blight you all be *careful* with him!'

A few grunts of effort came from the men but none of them spoke. As they entered Rhia recognised Gwydion and another of the Gorvicae Gadarim, along with a white-faced young woman and some warriors she knew only by sight. They had stretched their green cloaks between a pair of spears and on the cloaks, barely awake, lay the First Man of the Caderyn.

Gawan's face was a mess of blood from a score of tiny cuts and a single deep gash, and ugly bruises had swollen his eyes almost shut. His lip was split open and the dribble from his mouth was reddish pink, but it was when she saw his arm that Rhia's breath caught in her throat. His left hand was gone. The stump of his forearm was bleeding heavily through a soaking cloth, and Gwydion's hands were drenched red as he tried to stem the flow of it. Rhia saw Lucan sit up and stare at him in panic and she quickly beckoned Cerri over to her.

'Take him out of here. Take him... I don't know just take him somewhere.'

Her cousin nodded and took Lucan by the arm without a word, half-dragging him from the room. Rhia saw her son still looking at the bloody man on the cloaks, and tears welled up in his eyes as Cerri led him outside.

Bael did not waste a heartbeat and gestured for the men to set their comrade on the table. Madlen quickly cleared it of cups and candles and the men laid Gawan onto it. The old wood creaked but it held firm. The herbwife put pressure on the gash in his head and almost at once Rhia saw blood soak through the cloth onto her fingers. Bael closed his eyes and began running his hands over Gawan's body, his eyes closed but his mind still in the present.

'His time runs short. He will soon be dead if we are not swift.'

Rhia's heart was hammering hard and both she and the pale woman made to approach the table, but Bael waved them away with a flick of his hand.

'Give us space please. Gwydion, Madlen, stay where you are.'

The rest of them backed away and Rhia saw Bael's hands pause over Gawan's midriff, the place where she knew Mabonac's fire could be kindled. Her hands were clenching and unclenching and it was an effort to keep her breathing under control. What had happened? Had Caserach found a way to ambush him somehow? She felt anger building in her but her worry for Gawan conquered it. *This is my fault. If he wasn't my champion he would not have been attacked.* She saw the half-conscious man grimace in sudden pain and tears threatened to blur her vision. Bael's voice cut through her thoughts.

'Tegwen, get a torch and hold it close by. Rhia, get something between his teeth.'

They both hurried to do his bidding, the pale woman fetching the light while Rhia whipped off her belt and folded it over several times. She took Gawan's head in her hands as gently as she could and tried to ease the leather into his mouth. His hair was sticky with blood and he clearly didn't know what was happening but she got it there eventually and the Gadarim bit down on it. He began to thrash and his right arm came flying up, but Bael caught it one-handed and held it firm.

'Duran, hold onto this.'

The Gorvic obeyed and Bael's hands went back to hovering over Gawan's centre. Rhia heard him muttering something that sounded like the Old Tongue, though she was sure she caught the familiar words *Leaping Wolf* in amongst them. Gawan's breathing slowed a little but he still struggled, albeit feebly. Rhia saw that blood was still oozing from his wrist and Gwydion's face was contorted with the effort of keeping pressure on it. Gawan was biting down hard on the belt and Rhia hated to think how much pain Gwydion was causing him. And how the poor man must feel to be doing it.

Bael's eyes twitched beneath their lids and she saw frustration flash across his face.

'Damn it.' He spoke over his shoulder. 'All Gadarim step closer. Place one hand on him and the other on me.'

Rhia saw the same confusion she was feeling on the faces of the others but they all obeyed him without question. Gwydion seemed hesitant to touch his bloody hand to Bael's white robe and the druid spoke without opening his eyes.

'Touch my forearms. It must be skin to skin.'

Gwydion did as he was asked, and Duran and the younger man both placed a hand on Gawan's arm with another on Bael's bare wrist. Rhia kept hold of the side of his head with her left hand and reached out for the druid with her right. Bael's skin felt as warm as Gawan's was clammy. The holy man nodded once.

'You all of you know how to kindle Mabonac's fire. Fearless Wildcat, Flying Hawk, Blue Falcon and Rearing Horse; you must call upon the Dragon God.'

Rhia didn't stop to think about it and shut her eyes tight, focusing as she never had before. She slowed down her breathing and summoned the glowing ball of power into her centre, holding it there just inside her abdomen. She shut away her fears and guilt and forced herself to focus. All around her she felt a humming that didn't come through her ears and somehow she knew that the others could feel it too. Gawan's head was still jerking beneath her hand but she held him steady and tried to ignore his groans of pain around the belt.

Bael's muttering grew faster and then he spoke once more to the room.

'Be ready to release your power. Think only of Mabonac and of the life of Leaping Wolf.'

Rhia kept her eyes shut and thought of the Dragon God, but more than that she thought of her memories of Gawan. She thought of the day at Broken Stream when he had duelled with Madoc, and the insults they had bandied back and forth at the feast afterwards. She remembered how she'd hated him that dreadful day when he'd killed Dane, and the shock and gratitude she'd felt when he had let her fight Sedryn to avenge her murdered father. She remembered the day he'd named both her and Marius to the Gadarim, and the day he'd brought her son home safe after he'd been lost in the woods. She remembered the night after Moon Ridge when she'd felt his lips on hers. All that she knew of him, all that he was, went rushing through her head like a river bursting a dam and it fed into her power somehow, making the dragonfire grow hotter inside her centre.

Bael kept on muttering and though she didn't know the words she knew what it was she had to do. Though she'd no idea how she was doing it, she began to *will* her power towards the druid. She felt it flow from her body's centre, up her arm and into Bael, helped along by a gentle drawing from the core of the holy man. It was a strange sensation

543

and not particularly pleasant, but she knew it must be done and she let go of it willingly. The fire, or the ava or whatever it was, ran slowly away from her, and Bael's chanting grew louder as it did. The process was exhausting and Rhia began to feel light-headed as more and more energy was drained out of her, and it reached a point where she was certain she would faint. Then the druid snarled out a single word.

'Eurai!'

Power, raw and hot and dangerous, flooded back through Rhia like a tidal wave of fire, rushing up her one arm and through her body into the other. She gasped, and she heard the others do the same, and then Gawan began convulsing beneath her hand. Her eyes flew wide and she saw him arch up on the table, his own eyes as open as his swollen face would allow. Rhia's legs felt ready to buckle and the other Gadarim looked just as unstable but Bael kept them steady somehow, the young man's presence as solid as a rock before a storm. His eyes were still closed but his face was set and grim as he willed their precious energy into the wounded man.

The whole thing could not have lasted more than a dozen heartbeats but to Rhia it felt like a month of hard toil. Soon the flow of power waned and she held on as long as she could before her hand left Bael's arm to steady herself against the table. She was breathing hard and her dress clung to her skin with sweat. Her head felt as if she'd been rolled down Bryngarth's hill in a barrel and it was an effort to keep her queasy stomach from emptying itself onto the floor. She stayed there panting for a moment, the other warriors looking similarly drained, but Bael and Madlen continued with their work.

Gawan seemed to be breathing more easily, indeed he seemed to be *asleep*, the leather belt flopping limply from his mouth. The pale-faced woman was still holding the torch and though she looked as white as snow she was maintaining her composure. Rhia wondered who she might be but before she could start thinking clearly enough to speak, Bael had taken the burning brand and was holding it to Gawan's wrist. A smell that was horribly reminiscent of searing pork filled Rhia's nostrils and she felt the bile rise up in her throat, all thoughts of speech forgotten. She would have expected any man to wake from his sleep and start screaming, but Gawan merely shuddered and let out a feeble groan.

Beads of sweat were showing on the druid's brow but his breathing was even as he looked down at the former Gorvic.

'He will live, or should do. The bleeding in his arm and head are stopped, but we will need to take a better look at him.' He turned to Madlen. 'Go to your stores, you know what you will need better than I.'

Whether he was just being humble or genuinely deferring to her experience Rhia didn't know, but the herbwife bowed her head and quickly scurried from the room. Only then did he turn to Duran, who was leaning on the table, his face grey.

'What happened?'

The Gadarim tried to shrug but it seemed that, like Rhia, he could barely move.

'I don't know. We heard a cry from outside the longhouse and came out to find him like this.' He paused for breath and shook his head. 'Whoever attacked him must have heard us coming and fled.'

Even in her exhausted state Rhia found it in her to be angry. *Caserach!* She addressed the druid between gulps of air.

'If it was Caserach... we must...'

But Gwydion weakly raised one blood-drenched hand.

'I roused some of our people. We set them to looking. But in this light...?'

Rhia nodded and then blinked a few times as dark spots appeared before her eyes.

'Then we should check on Caserach.'

Duran shook his head at her, still breathing heavily.

'Also done. A pair of my men went to his hut. If he has moved or spoken to anyone, we will know the truth of it.'

Rhia noticed that Bael did not look particularly convinced but it was hard work to think clearly. She felt as though she'd just fought every battle she'd ever been in, one straight after the other, and then sprinted to the Canwyns and back. It took her a moment to realise that she still had one hand at Gawan's temple but she didn't move it away. The pale woman was hovering just a little way off and it seemed to Rhia that she wanted to approach, but wasn't sure if she should. Rhia didn't know what sort of relationship she might have with Gawan but right now she didn't care.

She beckoned to the woman, who looked maybe five or six summers her junior, and gestured for her to place a hand next to her own. She hesitated for a moment but then walked towards the table and placed one hand on Gawan's brow. Rhia didn't have it in her to say anything so she simply stood there, still breathing hard, and looked down at the face of her old enemy. Even had she not been so

546

exhausted she had no idea at all what she ought to think. She had no idea at all what she ought to feel.

*

It was dawn when Gawan finally awoke, though it took Rhia a few moments to notice. She was finally sitting down after having spent most of the night sending various people back and forth through the town seeking answers to what had happened to her champion, and now she stared at the floor with her eyes unfocused, weariness seeping into her bones. Duran's people had come back and told them that Caserach had not moved from his prison-house, nor had anyone been seen to communicate with him in secret. The last time he'd been outside the hearing of his guards had been during his time at the longhall. Had one of her own chiefs been behind this? Had he somehow bribed or threatened one of the tribesmen waiting outside? That Darin bastard had been behind it somehow, Rhia knew that in her gut, she just didn't know how she could ever prove it to anyone.

Alraig had turned up not long after Duran's man had made his report, mainly to complain that so many people had intruded on his prisoner's confinement. To his credit he had ceased his objections on seeing Gawan's condition but he had offered them no help either, and had declared that no more visitors would be permitted save for Bael, Madlen, and Duran. The druid had requested that he allow the pale girl to remain as well and for messages to be relayed through Duran to those outside. The chief hadn't liked the idea but he had relented after some persuasion.

Now Rhia was finally resting, as were the others, each lost in their own thoughts. So much had happened in so little time that it was difficult for her mind to get to grips with it. Gawan had been ambushed by some unknown agents of Caserach's just as he'd given up his tribe to fight for her. He had almost died and she and the others had engaged in some kind of magic that she could never have imagined in order to save him. And perhaps strangest of all, Gawan was a *father*!

After Bael had insisted that she be allowed to stay, the young woman had introduced herself as Tegwen daughter of Gawan. On top of everything else Rhia had seen tonight the shock had almost been enough to make her start laughing. Of all the things to add to her night of insanity! If she stopped and thought about it she had no real reason to be so surprised. Gawan had never confided anything about himself to her, and for a man his age to have children was perfectly natural. Yet still Rhia had been taken aback; she just hadn't ever pictured him as a man who had a daughter. Tegwen had been fairly tight-lipped as they watched over him but Rhia was curious indeed about what sort of father the man was.

It was Tegwen who gave the first gasp of surprise as the swollen eyes began to flicker and a moan escaped her father's broken lips. Both women were on their feet in an instant, with Bael following close behind. Gawan tried to turn onto his side but then grunted in discomfort and fell back again. Rhia reached the table and heard him mumble something.

'Where…?'

But he began to convulse and Bael quickly seized him by the shoulder and waist and turned him onto his flank, just in time for the Gadarim to vomit onto the floor. The smell was horrible but at least he hadn't choked on it, and both Rhia and Tegwen had stepped back in time to avoid being struck by the fluid. The druid's bare feet and white robe had been liberally spattered but he didn't seem to notice. Rhia wondered enviously if this ava of his might have some use in magically laundering clothes but she dismissed the thought quickly. It seemed disrespectful.

The warrior retched a few more times but it seemed everything that was going to come up had come up. Bael signalled to Madlen to prop him up with some rolled blankets and between them they got Gawan lying on his side, his head supported by a folded cloak. The druid got some water into him and though he dribbled most of it out at least some of it found its way down his throat. It took time but Gawan eventually came to his senses, and Bael gave him a brief summing up of what had happened, so far as they knew. The First Man listened politely, but his eyes kept wandering back to the bandaged stump of his left wrist. Rhia couldn't help but be a little impressed. If *she'd* just woken up to find one of her hands was missing, she'd have been a damned sight less calm about it. *Maybe the fire we sent into him helped in this as well? Or maybe he really is that tough a bastard?*

By the time Bael had finished talking Duran had returned with Gwydion in tow, blatantly ignoring Alraig's earlier command. The older man spoke to the druid.

'How is he father?'

Bael was more than ten summers younger than Duran but he used the honourific quite naturally.

'He will live. And thanks to his brethren and the Dragon God he will regain his strength in time.'

He might have continued but Gawan growled to his brother.

'I *am* here, Duran. I can speak for myself.'

Gwydion smirked.

'How could anyone not notice you?

Duran nodded down at him.

'Indeed. Just be glad you've kept your right hand, I would hate you to lose a limb *and* a lover in one night.'

Rhia tried to imagine anyone else who would have dared speak to Gawan that way and found herself struggling. The wounded man grumbled back at them.

'This arm will send you both to sleep once I get off this table.'

He didn't seem to be directing any malice towards his brothers, but Rhia heard both pain and anger in his voice. She found herself worrying for him. Already his face seemed less swollen and Bael's treatment could clearly work wonders but he was still badly hurt, and all on her account. Gawan blinked a few times and tried to shuffle into a sitting position. He winced in pain and Duran stepped forward to help him, easing his legs from the table and keeping close as his brother sat up. His shoulders were slumped and his head looked heavy, and still his eyes kept moving to the stump of a wrist in his lap. He nodded to Duran and then looked up at the others.

'So, today is the day of the combat then?'

Rhia, Tegwen, Madlen and Duran all spoke over one another.

'That does not...'

'You cannot...'

'You are not...'

'No.'

Gawan scowled at them and Rhia noted with concern that Bael hadn't objected. Gwydion spoke into the pause.

'You are in no shape to fight anyone Gawan, let alone a man like Broad Kellas. Let me go in your stead.'

Duran nodded.

'Or I shall.'

Bael shook his head.

'You cannot.'

Gwydion looked at him defiantly.

'Why not?' He remembered his manners a moment later and dipped his head a fraction before adding; 'father.'

Gawan grumbled at him from the table.

'Because I'm *telling* you you can't, that's why!'

Duran stepped in between them but Bael raised a hand.

'You are neither of you Caderyn; you could not fight this combat in any case.'

He seemed about to say more but Rhia had already begun speaking. She hesitated a little in embarrassment but carried on.

'There is no need. I can fight Caserach.'

Bael's face was grave as he answered.

'You should know better than that Rhianwyn. Once a Gadarim has challenged another there is no refusing it. One of them must die, or else cry enough and yield the fight.'

Rhia felt a cold shiver run down her arms. He was right. Even if she and Caserach agreed to face each other to settle the trial, Gawan would still have to face Broad Kellas by the traditions of the Gadarim. Had it been a simple fight then the wounded man could yield and the victor would be bound to leave it at that. The loser would lose face for himself and his tribe but at least he would

551

live. But this was a Trial by Iron and if Gawan yielded it, her guilt would be seen to be proven in the eyes of the gods.

Tegwen stepped forward and placed a hand on her father's arm. Gawan looked at it strangely for a moment before she spoke.

'You cannot do this.'

He didn't seem to know what to say to her but Duran too was not willing to take no for an answer.

'Indeed he cannot. With Gawan gone I will soon be First Man of the Gorvicae. If I can just persuade Karadoc to...'

But Gawan cut him off.

'You are *not* fighting today! And Karadoc will not be persuaded, you know that. I shall face Broad Kellas and that is all there is to it.' He nodded to Bael. 'The druid has healed me well and I still have my sword-hand.'

Stubborn though he was Rhia could hardly believe what he was saying. His chances had been even at best to begin with but now...? Gwydion moved closer to him and spoke so quietly that Rhia could barely hear him.

'Tarwyn will not rest easier knowing that you died for this, nor will…'

But Gawan silenced him with a glare. Rhia didn't really understand but then she didn't really have to.

'Yield the fight then. I can find some other way to solve all this.'

Gawan looked at her through his brows, his grey eyes intense.

'Tell me honestly, do you think Caserach will abandon his accusation against you because of this?'

Rhia frowned at him, angry at him for being right.

'No.'

Gawan continued.

'And if I yield, and he forces the Caledon to inflict some punishment on you to avoid a war with the Breiryn, will the Gaians be willing to deal fairly with whoever is left in charge?'

Rhia ground her teeth and had to fight back the urge to punch him. She was accustomed to Gawan being unreasonable about things and her being able to argue back with good sense. But she had nothing to argue back with in this. Given time to build up relations the Gaians might well deal fairly with the Lurian tribes, but she would be vital in the building of mutual trust. And duty to her people, *their* people, surely had to come first? She scowled as she answered him.

'No.'

Gawan sat up straight, somehow managing to look pained, weary, and satisfied all at once. But Rhia wasn't about to give up that easily. She appealed to Bael.

'Surely Alraig and Merwyn can be persuaded that this was a foul act by Caserach to stop the combat? They could declare the whole thing invalid.'

The druid looked at her sadly and shook his head.

'They could. But then Caserach will tell them, and the Breiryn, that you were lying to them, and that in fact you had your *own* people attack your champion to invalidate the trial.' Lines of disapproval appeared on his brow. 'It is what he would do in your place.'

Rhia wanted to spit, wanted to curse. Surely no true Lurian could do such a thing to one of their own? *But if any Lurian could, it would be Caserach!* Bael spoke gently to her.

'I would that there were some other way Rhia, but there is not.'

Gawan nodded at his words and spoke again, though Rhia suspected that his confidence was forced.

'I will fight today and that is an end to it. And after Heartreaver has taken that Breiryn bastard's head from his shoulders, *then* you may go on fretting like a pack of old women!'

Rhia saw Tegwen's hand grip tighter to Gawan's arm but she said nothing. Every face in the room was grim, though Gawan had poured anger into his features as well. Rhia sighed. Even in the time since he had woken he seemed to have grown stronger, but even dragonfire could only do so much. Barring some intervention of the gods themselves there was no way that he could win. But the look on his face said that he would brook no argument. It was the druid's nod however, that silenced any further attempt.

'I shall give both you and Heartreaver what blessing I can, but there are limits to what I can do for you in so little time, Gawan.'

The wounded man nodded, and Rhia heard him try to keep the resentment from his voice.

'Druids are not to interfere, I know. You have already done more than many would.'

Tegwen said aloud what Gawan was implying, turning to the holy man with bright eyes.

'Thank you, father.'

Bael bowed his head to her before speaking to them all.

'I have faith in Leaping Wolf, in the gods and in the Gadarim. Let him fight today with honour, and with our hopes and prayers to strengthen him.'

Rhia wasn't alone in not knowing how she ought to respond to that and so she joined the others in nodding her head towards the druid. Gawan sat and stared silently at the wall opposite him and Rhia tried to keep her fear in check. It would only do more harm for him to see she was afraid, and she willed herself to have faith in her champion. Inside her head she whispered a prayer to all the gods she knew as she looked at the man who for so long had been her enemy. And wondered if he would die for her today.

Chapter 40. Broad Kellas

Gawan sat hunched on the little stool and stared blankly at the ground. The morning sun was shining overhead and the grass around him was a vibrant green, but the Gadarim's mind was elsewhere. His hand was gone. It was *gone*. He kept finding himself looking down at his wrist as if he expected to see it there, instead of the bandaged stump that looked back up at him. It wasn't as if it really *hurt* anymore, thanks to Bael all he felt was a throbbing ache in his forearm, but the knowledge that it wasn't there, and that he would never have that hand again, was a difficult thing to accept.

He'd played it down in front of the others of course. As far as they were concerned he thought no more of it than he might think of a bruise or a scar. How many maimings had he seen in his time after all? Why should Gawan son of Dearg be concerned by the loss of one hand, and his left hand at that? Yet he was concerned. He'd been dealt the worst injury he had ever received and he felt more than half a cripple because of it. He sighed. His feelings were switching back and forth so fast he couldn't keep track of where they were. First hot rage would flood through him at the thought of Caserach and his men; of their cowardly attack and the dreadful wound they had dealt him. Then a cold sense of loss would descend as he thought on how badly that wound had damaged him, and the consequences that would follow should it cause him to lose this fight.

Gawan snarled to himself. Now was not the time to lose control of his emotions. If he was to come out of this alive and with Rhianwyn safe, he had to pull himself together. He re-focused his eyes and looked across the grass. They were in a large open space on Bryngarth's hill with houses on two sides of it and one or two small trees at the edges. Presumably it was normally used for festivals and big market days. Every soul in the town, and from most of the clans nearby he suspected, seemed to have gathered there, waiting to watch the Trial by Iron. The area set for the combat had been pegged out with stakes and ropes to form a huge square in the centre of the grass. Gawan sat in one corner, Broad Kellas in the opposite, each man attended by more Gadarim.

Gawan watched his opponent for a few moments but then his head began to pound again and he had to shut his eyes. He knew from experience that he ought to be feeling much worse given the punishment he'd suffered but all the same, he ached all over and would happily have dropped off to sleep. He forced himself to open his eyes and ignore the pain in his head. *It could be worse. You could be dead.* He could remember almost nothing of what had happened the night before but Duran had told him of Bael's magic and just thinking about it was unnerving. Neither of them had ever heard of such a healing being performed before and grateful though he was, Gawan couldn't help but feel wary. Bael was a far more frightening man than he had realised, and he wasn't ashamed to admit it to himself. Even if he'd stop short of admitting it to anyone else.

It wasn't just the druid that had done it of course, and Gawan knew he ought to thank his brother Gadarim for their part in the ritual. And his sister Gadarim especially. He was touched by their actions but he'd known the others long enough to know that they would naturally have come to his aid when he was in need, even in a way that confused and frightened them. He had fought with Duran

557

and Gwydion more times than he could count, and even Pryder was a remarkable and devoted young man. But Rhianwyn? She would have been just as ignorant of what Bael was doing as the rest of them and yet she'd apparently given her help without a thought. And the way she'd spoken to him after he awoke, it was... he didn't know *what* it was, but she clearly cared about his welfare, which was more than might be expected. He chided himself for mooning over her like some lovesick youth but it was difficult not to wonder if that meant she had some feeling for him deep down.

He shrugged it off. Regardless of how she felt, more important by far had been Tegwen's reaction. She had called him Father last night, and today she had been on the verge of tears when she had seen the sorry state of him, only to hear that he must still fight. Was she on the path to forgiving him, even loving him maybe? He couldn't tell. All he knew was that he wanted to speak with her again and find out what all this meant. But he couldn't. Duty had to come before all and he had a fight to win. He had to focus. He tore his mind away from the thoughts of his daughter and looked again at the open space in front of him.

Rhianwyn and the other chiefs were standing in the centre, but he didn't linger long on them nor did he listen to what they were saying. He already knew the gist of it. Instead he looked around at the crowd of spectators. Nearby stood Taliesyn and Karadoc, both wearing their green cloaks and both looking at him gravely. On the far side of the square he saw Caserach and his crony, with two Caderyn warriors standing nearby, their hands ready on the axes in their belts. Gawan snorted. Unbending bastard though he was, Alraig was at least wise enough not to trust him.

Away to his right Gawan spotted General Galerian and his tribune-interpreter, with a handful of bodyguards not far behind them. The First Man thought back on how much trouble had been caused already by these damned Blackbirds but still couldn't help but wonder what the Gaian would do if he lost this combat. Would he follow their plan of taking Rhianwyn away by force? Presumably he had more of his men nearby and Gawan knew well how efficient Gaian soldiers were; it would not take many of them to extricate a woman and child from a town of unprepared people. Gawan tried to take comfort in the thought that she would be safe even if he died, but it didn't work. The wider damage that would occur was too much to think about. *Though not enough for you to send word to Galerian forbidding him to take her. Not enough for you to warn Alraig and so prevent the Blackbird General from starting a war over her.*

Gawan sighed and tried to shove away the conflict. *At least Rhianwyn will live if I die.* It was strange that, given how much death he'd seen, Gawan had never given his own that much thought up until now. For most of his life he had simply assumed that Mabonac would guide him across the bridge, he would meet Annwn, walk into the Otherworld, and that would be that. Then after Moon Ridge he had convinced himself that he did not merit such a thing, and that his soul deserved to fall and climb and fall again into the Pit beneath Annwn's bridge. And now? Now he liked to think that in doing this he would redeem himself, at least a little, in the eyes of the gods, and that his bridge would be wide enough to cross in safety before he handed Heartreaver to the God of Death.

He found himself wondering idly who would be in the Otherworld with him. Would he be allowed to see Belenos and Taran in their true forms, or Karanon the Mountain Lord, or Father Camelas and Mother Marna? Would he be permitted entrance into the Golden Hall and see his brother Gadarim feasting there with the Dragon God? But even if he did, what would he say to him, or to Anryn or his father? Or to Emeryn?

He frowned and flexed his remaining fingers. Anryn and Tarwyn would understand, and after his time with the gods so would his father. Even Emeryn may have learned to forgive him. He would always feel shame when he thought of her but what he'd done at Moon Ridge had been a mercy; he knew that and she would know it too. As for his staring at Rhianwyn, he hoped she would know that it had not made him love her any less. With a stab of guilt he remembered the depth of Emeryn's goodness and kindness. She would understand, even if hearing her forgiveness would break his heart.

The chiefs were still talking in the middle of the square as death continued to dominate Gawan's thoughts. He wondered if Baercban would be there. He had been misguided and selfish but he had never been a *wicked* man, and had done what he thought best for his people. He had died defending his family after all. Gawan was fairly certain that Sedryn, and likely Rylion for that matter, would have to climb the Pit at least once or twice before Annwn took them in. He hoped Rylion's hatred would die down there with all the lost souls, and that they could meet again in the Otherworld as brothers. He'd like that.

Gawan blinked his eyes a few times and forced his mind to stay focused. All these thoughts of death and gods were irrelevant today; they had to be. Better that Broad Kellas spend his time thinking of the Otherworld because Gawan son of Dearg was going to win this fight! He looked up at Belenos as he climbed across the sky and hoped that Mabonac was still on friendly terms with his former godly rival. He wanted the Dragon God to be watching them today, and see the warrior who fought for justice emerge victorious.

He felt the broad-brimmed hat being taken from his head and assumed that meant his hair was dry enough. In the corner of his eye he saw Pryder set the hat aside and he ran a quick hand over the quill-like spikes on his head. The rest of his long hair was tied back at the nape of his neck but he knew the hair on his crown would be shining in the sun, the better to attract the attention of the Gods of War. He sat up straight as Gwydion and Hewin stepped forwards with their bowl, and the two Gadarim began painting over the battle-marks on his bare chest and arms. Hewin was still moving awkwardly but had insisted on joining them, and neither Gawan nor Duran had wanted to tell him no. Just beyond them, on a stool much like his own, Duran was holding Heartreaver across his legs and running a whetstone carefully along the blade. Gawan shut his eyes and took some slow breaths, focusing on his centre each time he exhaled. He would do this. He would win.

He felt Gwydion begin working on the marks that went up his neck, the woad cold and wet on his skin. Without looking he felt the presence of someone else behind him as well, and knew that Hywel had come to join them. He somehow knew it was the Gorvic druid without having to see him, and he tried not to let resentment spoil his concentration. Hywel might refuse to act as directly as Bael did but he was a good man at heart and did what he felt was right. *Besides, you are Caderyn now. Bael and Reaghan will be your druids from now on.* It was a strange thought.

His brothers began applying woad to the marks on his face and he felt Hywel's hand touch his shoulder. The warmth that came from it was subtle, barely more than a simple blessing, but still it made Gawan feel a little guilty for how he'd thought of him. Hywel wanted the best for him, and Gawan gave him a silent nod of acknowledgement. He took the blessing and added it the power he was kindling in his body. His breathing slowed even further as he nurtured the fire, becoming one with it. He prayed quietly in his own head, not bothering to search for poetic words to impress the Dragon God. He had little time for such things. *Mabonac, Father of the Gadarim, be with me today. I fight to honour you and to defend one who is innocent. My cause is just. Bring me victory.*

He felt the dragonfire tingle as if in response to the words and he opened his eyes with a calm breath. The pounding in his head was gone, as were the dozens of other aches and pains through his body. Even the throbbing in the stump of his arm had eased into something barely noticeable. Mabonac was with him. As Gwydion and Hewin stepped back from the stool Gawan saw Tegwen waiting nearby and he gave her a nod. She clearly knew now was not the time to try to speak to him, but he could see the question in her eyes; *must you do this?* He beckoned for her to approach and took her hand in his.

'Do not fear for me. We will speak later.'

She kept her face controlled as she nodded to him, but only just. Gawan stood up slowly and looked down at his daughter. He hesitated for a heartbeat then dared to touch her on one cheek. She did not move away.

'You are so like your mother. I am sorry it has taken so long for you to know your father.'

Tegwen opened her mouth to speak but no words came out. Instead she threw her arms around him and held him close. Gawan couldn't describe how it felt as he was filled with a warmth greater than all the magic that all the druids could ever have made. It was a blanket on a freezing night, the first bite of a meal after a month of starvation. It was the simplest and most important thing in all the world; the touch of a loved one. He hugged her back as best he could and didn't want to let her go, but he forced himself to do so after a few blissful moments. Tegwen stepped away from him and looked into his face, dry-eyed.

'Come back alive.'

Gawan nodded, not trusting himself to speak, and Tegwen bowed her head to him before ducking beneath the rope. Gawan wished that he could bask in the memory of her embrace but there was work to be done, and he cast his eyes across the field. Broad Kellas was still seated in his corner of the square, waiting patiently while fellow Gadarim attended to him. His hair was already whitened and shaped into horns and now Bran was painting over his battle-marks while Kyran sharpened his massive sword. Gawan knew full well that both men would sooner have been standing in his corner but whatever else Broad Kellas was he was still a son of Mabonac, and it was right that he be treated as such. *Even if he's a son of Mabonac that I'll soon be sending to meet him*. He thought of his brother's broken body and felt his resolve hardening. *Giant or not, Tarwyn's killer dies today.*

Gwydion, almost certainly thinking similar thoughts, appeared to his left and began strapping a hook onto his wrist. It was a crude and simple thing and Gawan doubted he would make much use of it, but it would give the arm the same reach it used to have and would be a damned sight better than nothing. Once his brother stepped clear Gawan gave it a few practice swings to test the weight. The iron hook felt solid but not so heavy as to drag his shoulder down, and he gave Gwydion a curt nod. It was clumsy, but it would do. He could not have felt more different when Duran handed him Heartreaver. The sword felt so natural in his hand it might as well have been a part of his right arm, the grip soft and the weight perfectly balanced. He twirled it around his wrist once or twice and the newly-polished weapon shone like silver in the sunlight.

He looked again across the fighting area and saw that the chiefs had now left it, and Broad Kellas was on his feet. Gawan's heart began to quicken in eagerness but he kept his breathing slow. Kyran signalled to them with one arm and Duran signalled back to him. He and the other Gadarim bowed their heads to their champion.

'Mabonac guide you.'

Gawan bowed back to them and then turned to face the open field. Broad Kellas was already striding towards the centre with Kyran close behind him. Gawan started walking to meet him, Duran following close on his heels. As they grew closer Gawan once again appreciated just how massive his opponent was, but he didn't let it discourage him. He was the best of all the Caledon. His cause was just. He would win. *And once it is done, you can be a father again.*

The two pairs halted just outside the range of a long spear-thrust, and three druids approached to stand between them; Hywel, Bael, and the slender Caderyn man. Hywel raised his staff and all the chattering from the crowds died down. His voice carried easily across the field.

'May Camelas, Taran, and Mabonac watch over us today by the light of Holy Belenos. May the gods protect the right.'

The other druids echoed him.

'The gods protect the right.'

The white-robed men stepped back, as did Duran and Kyran, leaving Gawan and Broad Kellas alone. The giant's flat face was completely blank and his dark eyes stared into Gawan's without any hint of emotion. The new Caderyn squared up to the Breiryn and issued his challenge, shouting it out for the whole crowd to hear.

'Face me in justice, I am the Leaping Wolf!'

His opponent answered him in a voice that boomed like thunder.

'Face me in justice, I am Broad Kellas!'

They locked eyes with one another and spoke simultaneously, their sword-hands held over their chests.

'Mabonac guide you safely. May you cross the bridge unharmed.'

*

The first blow came out of nowhere. Gawan knew from the fight with Tarwyn that Broad Kellas had some subtle

565

tricks in his arsenal, but it seemed today the big man was planning on doing this the old-fashioned way; kill the other man before he gets a chance to kill you. His massive blade whipped up in an arc aimed to split the former Gorvic from groin to scalp, moving with ridiculous speed for so heavy a weapon. Gawan barely saw it coming in time. He threw back his right foot and twisted his torso with it, feeling air breathe past his chest as the blade passed a finger's length from his body. He brought up his hook in the same motion and tried to catch an arm as the sword-cut rose, but Broad Kellas withdrew the moment he saw his strike had missed, and he stepped back into a high guard. Gawan saw a thin line of red appear on one of his thick forearms but the giant didn't seem to notice. *You won't take this one apart a piece at a time anyway; take him down fast and hard or he will outlast you!*

Gawan followed his own advice and pressed forwards. Mabonac might be with him but the Dragon God helped only those with the will to help themselves. He hacked Heartreaver quickly right and left, aiming at different heights, then paused half-a-heartbeat before doing the same again; right and left with differing heights. His opponent blocked each cut with ease but then Gawan struck right and then right again, breaking the rhythm and creating a tiny opening. The giant anticipated incorrectly and Heartreaver swung hard towards his bulging neck. But Broad Kellas was quick and he jerked his head back just in time, the blade's tip barely nicking his flat cheek. He controlled his own sword beautifully and brought it back to a middle guard, forcing Gawan to pull up short from following him.

They hovered outside of easy cutting range for a few moments, eyes locked on one another. Broad Kellas' nostrils were flaring and Gawan bared his teeth. Minor wounds or not he had drawn first blood on the big man, and he clearly resented that. Gawan doubted if he was accustomed to fighting men as good as he was, especially men who were also a head shorter and ten winters older. They matched stares for another heartbeat before the Breiryn roared and lunged at him. It was a clumsy-looking move and Gawan was expecting the change of angle even as he parried the thrust. He almost smirked as he was proven right. Broad Kellas twisted the heavy blade as if it weighed no more than a stick and brought it across in a quick horizontal cut. Gawan was already moving and hopped back out of range, but his smugness at seeing through the trick did not last for long. His injured leg buckled on landing and though he managed to stay on his feet, the stagger spoiled the distance of the dodge.

Hot pain flashed across his chest and he kept Heartreaver up as he backed off another pace. He knew by the fact that he could still breathe that it wasn't a serious wound and true enough, when he risked a look down, he saw that the weapon's tip had raked a shallow cut across the muscle, almost parallel to the old scar that Madoc had given him a lifetime ago. It burned but that was all, and he kept his eyes on Broad Kellas' as he began to circle him. The giant simply shifted his feet, watching the smaller man with a look of quiet confidence. Gawan decided to wipe the look from his face.

He let the fire in his gut flow into his limbs and leaped towards the big man, cutting high and low before lunging for his throat. Broad Kellas blocked each strike and then began countering, his blade flashing in the sun in a dazzling series of attacks. Gawan tried to move and parry instead of stopping them cold but it was hard work; the bastard was just so *fast*! His feet danced across the grass as he refused to meet strength with strength, but Broad Kellas was just as graceful as he was and the big man cut off his angles, forcing him to fight him head-on. A heavy cut came down for his head and Gawan had no choice but to plant his feet and meet it square. His whole arm juddered and he leaned into it, bracing his hook-hand beneath Heartreaver to hold off the blow. Gawan grunted with the effort. *Gods alive he's strong!*

Broad Kellas snarled at him as their faces grew closer and Gawan flexed his knees, ready to push him off with the power of his legs. Before he could, the giant's massive left fist crashed into his chest, right in the middle of the oozing cut. Searing pain flashed across his torso and the breath was driven from his lungs. He barely managed to redirect the broad-bladed sword before he had to double over and cough. Broad Kellas' knee met his face as he did and white light blinded him as more pain erupted in his head. He could feel himself falling but he kept hold of Heartreaver, swinging it clumsily in front of him as he toppled. He hit the ground hard and shuffled backwards, still coughing. He could taste blood in his mouth and was pretty sure that both his lip and his nose were bleeding freely. He blinked to see Broad Kellas standing in guard above him and the Breiryn First Man half-smiled in satisfaction.

'Enough, Leaping Wolf?'

Gawan didn't answer him. He thrust away his pain and launched himself at the big man, Heartreaver singing in his hand as he forced the Breiryn onto the defensive. Broad Kellas backed off, slapping the cuts aside but unable to counter quickly enough through the flurry of attacks. Gawan felt his blood roaring as he closed in and swung a vicious cut towards his head. But the giant stepped forwards just at the right moment, avoiding the strike and wrapping his massive arms around Gawan's, pinning them to his sides. Gawan felt his feet leave the ground and his ribs compress painfully as Broad Kellas lifted and squeezed. He was too close to use the sword and he desperately tried to use his hook-hand to attack his captor's back instead. The iron scraped along one shoulder-blade and Gawan head-butted him hard at the same moment. It wasn't much but it was enough to loosen the giant's grip and Gawan felt his feet touch grass again, but then Broad Kellas rammed his own head forward and pain exploded across Gawan's nose. It felt like someone had swung an anvil into his face and he staggered backwards, head spinning.

Broad Kellas followed him, keeping close, but Gawan managed to hook his blade and send a right cross into his jaw. It was hard as rock and Gawan was glad he had shouted as he threw it; it covered what would have been a cry of pain as his knuckles cracked. The punch landed well but the giant recovered in an eyeblink and backhanded him across the face with a massive left fist. Gawan spun and fell, his head snapping around fast enough to make the world a blur. He lost his grip on his sword as the ground rose up to meet him.

The earth beneath the grass was firm enough to knock the wind out of him, and for a moment Gawan thought he would black out. Then he saw the polished iron of

Heartreaver, glinting just beyond his reach. He rolled sideways and grabbed for it, coming up onto one knee with the blade aimed roughly at his enemy. The big man's shape was blurred and Gawan had to blink to clear his vision. His head was screaming at him but he made himself ignore it, clamping his jaw hard and focusing his will. *You must win this. Your cause is just. You must win!*

Once again he heard the rumbling voice of his enemy, like distant thunder turned scornful.

'Enough?'

His body was yearning to say, 'yes, enough' but he forced himself to stand. He spat red onto the grass between them and brought his sword up again. This time Broad Kellas gave him no chance to charge and came at him with a blistering series of cuts and thrusts. Gawan moved as fast as his battered body would let him until, more by chance than anything, the big man's foot slipped as he lunged, just enough to make him over-extend. Gawan stepped in to the right and hammered Heartreaver's guard into the Breiryn's ribs with all the strength of his legs and hips behind it, hooking his enemy's blade again ready to disarm him.

Broad Kellas completely ignored a strike that would have winded most men and clamped a meaty hand onto Gawan's right wrist. The pressure was immense and Gawan writhed in his grip, trying desperately to control the other's blade with his hook. He kicked at his opponent's leg but it was like kicking into a tree-trunk and did nothing more than hurt his own shin. Suddenly Broad Kellas released his wrist and punched him hard in the mouth, and Gawan felt teeth crack beneath the force of it.

He staggered back with Heartreaver raised but the next attack didn't come high, and he saw the heavy sword arc low towards his legs just too late to get fully clear of it. He shuffled back but the timing was off, and he knew it, and the razor-sharp tip carved through the muscle of his thigh. Suddenly the whole leg went dead and crumpled bonelessly beneath him, a heartbeat before the pain began to burn across the wound. Even as he was falling he felt a boot hit him in the chest and Gawan flew backwards over the sunlit grass, seeming to hover in the air before landing in an awkward heap. Black spots danced before his eyes and he found himself gasping, then he coughed out a hard breath and saw teeth amidst the blood that he spat out. A voice was coming from far away but he couldn't make it out. He felt the spirit within him grow cold. He had failed. He had failed the Dragon God, failed Rhianwyn, and failed his new tribe. Broad Kellas would kill him, it was inevitable, and he would never again see Tegwen in this world.

He tried to drag his mind away from such thoughts of despair and heard the voice again.

'Enough, Caderyn?'

Gawan managed to kindle a tiny spark of fire in his gut. He was all but spent, and could not possibly win, but damned if he would cry hold to this Breiryn bastard! He didn't reply, he didn't even think he had the strength to speak, but he heaved himself up and leaned heavily on one leg, whipping Heartreaver into a guard. It was parried away immediately and then a fist sank into his stomach. He coughed helplessly as Broad Kellas trapped his sword arm with one hand and shoved the guard of his sword up under his chin with the other. He felt his weight forced back and then a leg sweep through his calves before his back hit the ground again. He lifted Heartreaver up as best he could but there was no strength left in his arms and the weapon seemed to have grown three times as heavy. He could barely *hold* the iron, let alone block an attack with it.

The voice came again, loud and filled with anger.

'Enough?'

Gawan coughed out some more blood and rolled onto his side. He wanted to lie back down again. He wanted to sleep, even if it meant never waking up. His body was on fire with a hundred pains and his head felt ready to split open. He had nothing left in him. *But you cannot yield. All men must die. What better time and place than in a just trial by the hand of a Gadarim?* It was cold comfort but it was all that he had.

Gawan got his knees underneath him, followed by his good hand. The least he could do would be to die on his feet. His ribs screamed in protest as he tried to push himself up but then an odd sound chased the pain of them from his mind; it was the sound of metal hitting hard earth. A moment later a voice sounded above him, crying out something that made no sense at all.

'Enough!'

Gawan just about managed to stay awake as he heard the pounding of many feet coming towards them. He struggled up to one knee. Voices were shouting from outside the ropes but Broad Kellas drowned them out.

'Enough! The Trial by Iron is done.' He looked down at Gawan with that same blank expression he always wore, then he spoke to the crowd again. 'Mabonac's fire is undimmed in this man. The Dragon God loves his cause more than mine. I yield.'

He reached a hand down to Gawan and met his eyes solemnly.

'I am Belion, son of Cylan.'

Gawan could still hear voices around them but he paid them no mind as he offered his own hand. Talking hurt through his mouthful of broken teeth but the words came out more-or-less understandable.

'Gawan, son of Dearg.'

The big man nodded and got one huge arm under him, then heaved his former opponent up as though he weighed no more than a child. Gawan got his uninjured leg onto the ground and hobbled on beside him as Belion walked him to his corner, ignoring the gaggle of chiefs and druids who had approached. Duran and Hywel helped him onto his stool with Gwydion holding him propped there once he sat. Gawan saw Rhianwyn and Tegwen running up towards him and he felt the warmth of Bael's hand on his shoulder. But before anyone could speak a voice bawled out from the field.

'This is foul!'

The group before him parted a little and Gawan saw Caserach stalking across the fighting area, his face bright red with fury.

'This is a disgrace! The fight is won by my champion!'

Gawan looked up to see Broad Kellas, no, to see *Belion* cross his arms before his chest.

'The trial is over when one fighter cries enough. This has happened. The fight is done.'

Caserach practically screamed at him.

'I will not be made accountable for your cowardice, Breiryn!'

The giant's nostrils flared but Caserach was no longer looking at him. He was staring at Rhianwyn with murder in his eyes. Before anyone could say anything his sword was in his hand and he was pointing it at the Caderyn chieftain.

'I will not have justice denied to me! Rhianwyn daughter of Carradan you have attacked my people by vile means and I challenge you here and now – fight me before the eyes of the gods!'

Gawan tried to stand up but fell back again almost immediately, and it took Bael and Duran both to steady him. Alraig and Merwyn started speaking at the same time but Caserach was already moving forwards. Gwydion drew his sword and moved to stand between Rhianwyn and the Darin, but he barely got two steps before the Wildcat unsheathed Silverbite and aimed it at Caserach's chest.

'Caserach son of Heuryn, you are a liar and a murderer, and I will be glad to send your soul to meet Annwn. I accept your challenge!'

Chapter 41. The Wildcat

Rhia didn't even think as Caserach lunged for her. She sidestepped smoothly and let his blade glance from Silverbite, flicking the weapon back up to a guard as he faced her again, eyes blazing. All around them chiefs and druids were speaking in raised voices, trying to talk one or both of them down, but it did them no good and the talk soon died away. Gwydion or Duran could have stepped in to break it up of course, but Rhia was Gadarim and had accepted the Darin's challenge; regardless of whether it had been wrong or right in the offering it was done now, and they could no more interfere in it than they could have in Gawan's fight.

Rhia frowned as Caserach began to circle to her left. This was ridiculous, she knew that. Caserach was no real danger anymore, what with his threats of Dariniae raiding undermined and Broad Kellas satisfied that the Breiryn had not been wronged. The sensible thing to do would have been to refuse his challenge, let her fellow Gadarim disarm him, and have him bound up in a sack and sent back to his island for his own people to deal with. But she hadn't done that. Gawan had almost died twice for her because of him and this reptile was going to pay for that. Foolish or not she had taken up his challenge, and this bastard's damned ambitions would end today!

Caserach came at her again, more cautiously this time, his blade probing for weaknesses in her defence. Rhia gave away nothing, making minimal movement and keeping her eyes on his, waiting for an opening. Her blood was shouting at her just to charge at him but she controlled herself and focused her mind. She forced herself not to think of the bleeding man behind her who had all but given up his life for her moments ago. She forced herself not to think of the shock she'd felt at the miraculous surrender of the giant who'd come so close to killing him. She even put from her mind the constant thoughts of her boy, now sitting in the longhall under his grandmother's watchful eye. Right now all she had time for was the man standing before her, and she glared at him as she readied herself to attack.

Rhia cut high and followed up with a pair of quick thrusts but Caserach batted them aside and moved forward, using his greater reach to force her backwards. She scurried back a few paces and had to dive to one side to avoid backing into the ropes. The Darin sneered as he pursued her.

'Run and dodge all you like you Gaian bitch, you can't dodge me forever!'

He came after her again, attacking with skill, and it was mostly by blind chance that Rhia managed to whip up a counter-cut. It barely nicked his chin but it made him pull up short and she grinned at him as she saw the blood appear.

'I can do more than dodge, you craven rat!'

Caserach snarled. He must have known he had already lost the bigger battle but he was apparently determined to take her down with him. *Well, let him try!* Rhia blocked his next cut and maintained contact with the blade, sliding in close to rob him of his reach advantage. It was a dangerous thing to do, he was stronger than her after all, but she had to get close if she was to finish this. She pushed forward and waited for him to push back before yielding to it suddenly, twisting aside and leaving her one foot extended. He tripped and stumbled but recovered himself quickly; too quickly for Rhia to send Silverbite through his heart as she had planned.

The Darin bared his teeth and reached for his belt. Rhia barely had the chance to see a purse appear in his hand before he threw the little bag of coins at her, the metal discs flying out towards her face. She raised her hands instinctively and Caserach charged in with a bellow, swiping for her stomach. Had Rhia moved an eyeblink later the blade would have opened her guts but she sprang away to one side just in time, scoring a quick cut across his ribs as he went past. The cut did little more than scrape some flesh before it clattered from bone but he grunted with pain all the same and she saw blood start to soak through his tunic.

Rhia grinned at him again but had no time to savour the moment. Once again the Darin rushed forward, hammering strikes in left and right before closing in on her, guard locked to guard. This time he wasn't fool enough to over-lean his weight and he simply pressed forward and down with brute strength. Rhia almost buckled under the pressure and before she could move with it he twisted his hips and caught her jaw with his sword's pommel. Her head snapped around and she tasted blood, and she stumbled backwards with the force of the blow. Caserach slashed at her legs and she fell into a roll to avoid it, coming up unsteadily as the Darin attacked again, his blade clashing heavily against hers.

The memory of Bael's concerned face at the thought of her fighting him flashed before her eyes for a heartbeat. The druid must have known more of the man's reputation than she had because Caserach wasn't just tall and strong, he was *skilled*. She'd seen little enough of him at Moon Ridge and from his cowardly methods she had assumed that he would be barely competent in a one-to-one fight. She'd been wrong. Rhia felt her confidence falter as he continued to press her back, and gained herself a vital second by feigning a lunge and then leaping away.

Her opponent paused before following her, though he wasn't breathing nearly so hard as Rhia was. They began to circle again and Rhia spotted Gregor and his men in the corner of her eye. She couldn't see his expression, but she knew he would be watching closely and a shameful thought flitted through her mind. A signal from her would bring him and his men charging over the field to hack Caserach apart like so much raw meat. *They* wouldn't give a damn about the traditions of the challenge. They would just want the mother of Dessidus Lucianus to come out of this alive. *Just a wave of your hand, that's all it would take*. Caserach came at her with another pair of cuts and she was pushed back again, parrying as fast as she could. Her heart sped up as she tried to fend him off and the moment an opening came she swiped Silverbite towards his face, just to buy herself some time to move away. *One wave to Gregor, that's all...*

Rhia grimaced and forced herself to put the thought aside. It wasn't an option, not really, not if she was to show her people that she and Lucan were Lurian first and Gaian second. And Lucan could be the great hope of her people, even if she was not alive to see it. Rhia evaded another lightning-fast lunge and flicked Silverbite towards her opponent's eyes. Caserach flinched back reflexively and she reversed the attack, slicing a needle-thin cut across his left biceps. Blood flowed and a cheer rang out from the crowd but the Darin ignored the wound and came at her again, raising his sword high to batter down at her from above. Greyfang clanged on Silverbite as Caserach hammered at her defences, and Rhia found herself shrinking back from them. She tried to keep her focus but she felt fear begin to cloud it, and a moment later it was shattered by a single word.

'Mama!'

Rhia threw herself backwards and looked around her in the heartbeat before Caserach could catch up. Lucan was standing beside the Gorvicae Gadarim, his eyes wide and frightened as he watched his mother fight. He made as if to run forwards but Gwydion grabbed hold of him, and then Caserach was on her again and Rhia could watch no more. She blocked his cuts as best she could as her mind began to race. How the Dis had he given Myrna the slip? Not that it really mattered now. What mattered now was that Caserach had a better than even chance of killing her, and Lucan was about to witness that. *He's already seen too much damn it! He's too young to be seeing more death!*

Her heart began pounding harder than ever and Caserach's attacks just seemed to come on faster. Her movements became desperate as she dodged and parried but it was hard to keep track of the blurring blade in front of her. Rhia didn't even see the strike that disarmed her. All she knew was a sudden jarring pain in her wrist and the sun glittering from Silverbite as it flew from her hand.

Rhia backed off as fast as she could while keeping her eyes on Caserach. The Darin smiled, menacing her with his blade.

'So much for the Fearless Wildcat. So much for all you damned Gadarim!'

Fear prickled down her spine as she tried to think what she could do. She had no weapon and nowhere to run, and Caserach had all the honour of a hungry dog; even if she called enough he would probably kill her anyway. In the distance she heard Lucan crying out for her again. *I won't let him see his mother die like this! Not like this.* Rhia moved without even thinking, and it almost felt as if the Dragon God himself was controlling her muscles.

She feinted left as if to flank him and as Caserach adjusted to it she simply leaped on him, wrapping her arms around his head and her legs around his body. The Darin stumbled a pace and before he could react Rhia sank her teeth into his ear, worrying at it like a dog with a rat. She ripped free a second later, tearing loose a chunk of flesh, and Caserach's cry of pain was cut short when she spat it in his face. He blinked as blood spattered into his eyes and Rhia drew back her arm and slammed an elbow into his nose. She felt it crack beneath the impact and they both fell to the ground, the Darin's sword falling from his grip as they thudded to the grass. Rhia didn't have much time. It had been an insane risk to do this in the first place and if she let Caserach grapple with her then his strength would win the fight for him. So she didn't grapple with him.

Rhia punched him hard in the throat then threw herself away from him, diving for the Darin's fallen sword. He caught hold of her ankle but she kicked at his injured arm and managed to crawl away when he flinched. She reached the sword and rose up to one knee, holding the point towards her enemy as he too began to rise. Black hatred poured from his eyes like tears but Rhia saw something else there as she met his gaze with hers; fear. For all his skill here was a man who only fought if he knew he could win, and only fought *fairly* when he had no other choice. As such she was disgusted but not surprised when the would-be-chieftain raised his hands.

'Enough! I yield.'

Rhia looked at him with naked contempt but said nothing. She heard jeers coming from the tribesmen around the ropes but she didn't look at them. She kept her eyes on Caserach, her heart still hammering hard in her chest. She could do it. This man had murdered Ierryn. He had slaughtered her people. He had almost doomed all of the Caledon through his selfish arrogance. The people around her were almost *willing* her to do it and Rhia's mind flew to the sorry state that Gawan was in; a good man maimed and almost killed twice now for the sake of this bastard's greed. She looked into his face and saw no trace of remorse there, only fear and hatred twisting his expression. *I could do it. People would disapprove but they would forgive me for it eventually. Gods, most of them would* thank *me for it.*

Her intention must have shown on her face because she saw Caserach grow pale, and if anything that only spurred her on to gut the cowardly swine. But then she remembered Lucan. Her only son was watching her, probably weeping with relief that she had not been harmed. Could she let him see his mother become a murderer? Did she want his first sight of her in battle to end with her killing an unarmed man?

Rhia sighed and fought back the urge to spit at her former opponent.

'Enough.'

Neither one of them nodded to the other. Between Gadarim they might have clasped wrists and spoken as friends, and he at least would have been allowed to keep his sword. But Caserach was no true warrior, and he knew she would not treat him as such. Rhia turned her back on him and began walking away, tossing the Darin's sword onto the grass ahead of her. She made towards the corner where Gawan had begun his fight, where her brother Gadarim were waiting and cheering for her. She saw Lucan leaping up and down with glee and even Gawan was on his feet. He was leaning heavily on Broad Kellas but he was standing nonetheless, and he began hobbling in her direction. Behind them she saw Karadoc and Taliesyn, the one frowning and the other smiling, along with the relieved-looking faces of Bael and Hywel. She beamed as she grew nearer and saw Lucan waving furiously at her, and she knew it would all be worthwhile once she held him in her arms. But then the boy's eyes flew wide with terror and the men around him cried out in alarm.

'Look out!'

Rhia turned just in time to see Caserach lunging for her, a short knife in one hand and a snarl on his lips. She saw sunlight flash on the blade an eyeblink before he rammed it into her, and hot pain burned in her flesh. Had she not been mid-turn it might have struck her to the lungs. Instead it scraped up her ribcage and buried itself in her armpit, the narrow point emerging from her shoulder. Rhia gasped and then cried out despite herself as the weapon was ripped free. Blood began pouring from the open wound in violent spurts and Rhia's vision swam. Caserach grinned at her and brought the knife up for another lunge, his eyes alight with vicious pleasure. Rhia watched him helplessly, unable to even focus her eyes, and braced herself for the inevitable blow. It didn't land.

With a warcry, a thud, and a guttural curse something struck Caserach hard in his midriff and bore the beaten Darin to the dirt. Rhia watched in what felt like a drunken stupor as Gawan pinned his victim to the ground, hacked his iron hook into his neck, and tore it out again with most of the Darin's throat still impaled upon its point. Blood flowed and Gawan roared, and Rhia felt herself begin to smile in relief. The crowds begin to cheer again as she felt herself slowly falling, but the last thing Rhia heard was Lucan's voice calling for his mother.

*

When Rhia woke up she was in her own bed. Her arm was throbbing painfully and had been tightly bound up, but otherwise she seemed to be unharmed. She blinked a few times as she lay there. Oughtn't she be dead? The blood pumping from her arm had been the bright blood of her heart, and she knew from experience that wounds like that bled out with terrifying speed. But then Gawan had been close to death the night before, and Bael had brought him back with a little help. Had he and the Gadarim gathered to heal her too?

Rhia sat up in the bed, her injured arm moving awkwardly and her whole body aching with fatigue. The fight with Caserach had been gruelling, and healed or not she was exhausted. More sleep would likely do her good but her throat was parched and she decided to fetch herself a cup of water. She swung her legs from the side of the bed and leaned forward, letting out a long sigh as she did.

The room was only lit by a couple of candles on the table but Rhia could see the water jug well enough, and she just hoped that it was full. But that wasn't all that she saw.

On the chair beside the table was the room's only other occupant, leaning back with his chin on his chest. Gawan's eyes were closed and his breathing was deep and even, accompanied by a harsh, snuffling snore. His face was battered almost beyond recognition and she could tell at once that his nose would never be fully straight again. Rhia looked at the stump of his left hand, now minus the hook, and thought again of all that this man had done for her. And for Lucan.

She half rose from the bed, trying to keep silent, but his eyes opened at the sound of the creaking wood and she sat back down again. He nodded to her.

'You are awake. I should tell the druid.'

Rhia nodded back but Gawan made no move to stand up. She balled her free hand nervously and knew that she had to say *something*.

'I take it I am to thank Bael for this?'

She indicated her bandaged arm. It was swathed well past the shoulder and movement was painful as well as restricted, but she bobbed her head towards it and Gawan took her meaning.

'He and Hywel both. You'd have died right there on the grass if not for them.'

His words were somewhat mangled, presumably thanks to his broken teeth, but he made himself understood. Rhia nodded very slowly and decided to just say it aloud.

'And if not for you.'

The First Man looked away and didn't reply. Rhia knew the least he deserved was a more direct form of thanks but she didn't quite know how to put it. She fidgeted awkwardly for a moment before trying again.

'Gawan I...'

But he had started speaking at the same time.

'Rhianwyn...'

They both stopped and Rhia gestured for him to continue. Gawan took a moment before he spoke again and when he did, his voice was gruff.

'I had meant to say... about before...'

Rhia cut him off. She didn't want to make him say anything, least of all in his condition. She might not really know what to say to him either but she could spare him the embarrassment of an apology at least. It was unnecessary in any case.

'I took no offence. And... I do not regret what happened.'

Gawan's eyes brightened for a moment and yesterday Rhia might have felt guilty for leading him on. But the truth was that she *didn't* regret it. She would never feel for him as he felt for her, and Gawan almost certainly knew that, but it was no lie to say that she cared for him in her own way. He didn't reply at once and Rhia worried that she might have just led them into another awkward silence but then he did something she didn't think she'd ever seen him do before; he smiled. Not a smirk or a snarl or a baring of the teeth but an actual *smile*. It spoke of happiness rather than scorn and, bruised though he was, it completely transformed his face. His harsh features softened and it somehow made him seem younger, as if years of care and hate had been washed away from him. He looked as if he was going to say something back to her but then the door swung open and he tried to cover up his expression with a cough. Unsuccessfully.

Tegwen walked into the room, leading Lucan by the hand and with Bael following on their heels. The boy sprinted to his mother and threw himself into a hug, and Rhia tried not to wince as she hugged him back one-armed. Across the room she saw Tegwen embrace her father somewhat more gently, and Rhia met Gawan's eyes over the shoulders of their respective children. He grimaced for a second and then smiled at her again, the look full of unfamiliar contentment. Rhia smiled back at him, trying hard to hold back a laugh. Some pair of mighty Gadarim they made; unable even to hug without wincing in pain, and then grinning at each other like drunken fools!

Bael spoke to them both, a tiny smile of his own on his face.

'I trust you are both healing?'

The two warriors nodded their heads and Gawan answered for them.

'Well enough, father. My thanks.'

Rhia beamed at him, still holding on to Lucan one-handed.

'And mine.'

Bael nodded knowingly and Rhia remembered his words from before the fight. *'I have faith in Leaping Wolf, in the gods, and in the Gadarim'*. It was that last part that suddenly struck her. Had he known, or suspected, that Broad Kellas would behave so honourably? Had he known that Caserach would then challenge her and that Gawan would come to her rescue? A part of her was tempted to ask him about it but she knew she shouldn't, least of all in front of other people. Bael seemed to sense her curiosity but if he planned on saying anything she never got to hear it, because at that moment the door opened again and Alraig strode in, accompanied by a smiling Merwyn.

The taller man was looking as grave as ever and both Rhia and Gawan left off their embracing. Gawan looked ready for a fight, for all his condition, and Rhia too braced herself for the inevitable conflict to come. But it didn't come. Alraig nodded stiffly to them both and spoke in a steady voice.

'Broad Kellas yielded the fight. And Caserach not only lost but fought foully as well. The Trial by Iron is won, and won fairly.'

Rhia felt relief flood through her but the feeling didn't last as the headman took a pace closer to Gawan.

'I know that you brought General Galerian here with the intention of using him to free Rhianwyn by force should you deem it necessary.'

Gawan didn't look away but he didn't deny it either. Rhia had suspected such a motive for his actions but it was strange to hear them confirmed. And stranger still to hear Alraig speaking so calmly about it.

'But you did not call upon them. I had men watching you all since the moment they arrived, though they took care not to be observed. You could have called on the Gaians any number of times and yet you did not. Even when combat began and defeat seemed certain, neither one of you brought them into it.' He faced Rhia directly and if anything his voice became even more serious. 'You are not one of them.'

Gawan was struggling to hide his shock and Rhia's face probably wore the same expression. This man had done nothing but vilify her since the battle at Moon Ridge and now this? *But then he said it himself; he does not hate you. He hates only the Gaians for what they have done, and for good reason.* Alraig straightened his back.

'The law is satisfied. And so am I. You may depend upon my voice in any moot that is to come. May the Caderyn always be blessed with so devoted a chieftain.'

He bowed to her from the waist and Rhia found herself fighting back tears. She squeezed Lucan's hand and saw that Gawan was doing the exact same thing with Tegwen. She smiled. The situation might be complicated, and there might still be struggles ahead, but for today at least all was well, despite all the odds against her. She had loyal friends, her son was safe, and her tribe's future was looking bright again. Rhia sighed as she bowed back to Alraig before nodding once more to Gawan. It felt so strange, and yet also wonderful. Two men who had caused her so much grief in the past had become two men she knew she would find invaluable in the future. She squeezed Lucan's hand again and allowed her smile to become a grin. Once again she would be able to protect her people, and lead them forward into a new era of peace. Once again Rhia could dare to let herself hope.

Chapter 42. The New Chieftain

It was more than a moon's turn before Gawan once more found himself in the longhall at Graigarw. By the time he and Rhianwyn were in any shape for a long journey the autumn was long over, and winter had begun to show her teeth. It had been a strange experience living in Bryngarth for so long, but he had been made to feel welcome by almost everyone he'd met. He suspected it was only partly because he was Caderyn now, a concept he was still very unsure about; mostly they were welcoming because of what they'd seen him do, and because he was so obviously a friend to their chieftain. He felt his brow furrow in thought. *A friend to their chieftain.* Another odd concept for him to get his head around.

He'd had some time to think on that during his convalescence and still it confused him, though perhaps it was for the best that there had been plenty of other things to keep him distracted. Another moot had been called and Rhianwyn had, unsurprisingly, been made High Chieftain of the Caderyn once more by an overwhelming majority of her headmen. Not only that, they had all grown to know Belion a little better before the Breiryn had returned to his people, and the giant had traded grips and drinks with every Gadarim at Bryngarth; Darin, Caderyn and Gorvic alike. He had even given Gawan his snakeskin belt as a parting gift, and Gawan suspected that the Caledon had just gained a good friend amongst the southerners.

Most importantly of all, Gawan had spent the time growing closer with his daughter. They had shared stories of their lives up until now and he was looking forward to learning more about the years that he had missed. More and more he was learning that she was a daughter to be proud of, and that for all his faults she was proud to have him as her father. He sighed quietly as he looked around the hall. It would be a pity to travel back south again after accompanying her to Gorvicae lands, but he knew his chieftain would have no problem with his visiting her often. He found himself hoping guiltily that the weather would start to worsen and they would be forced to spend the winter in the northlands.

Not that the hall was cold today. A roaring fire blazed in the pit and the room was packed full of bodies. Every chief of the Gorvicae had come to the capital, along with a small herd of druids. Kyran, who had decided to sail home from Black Harbour, was standing as a guest with a mob of Gorvicae Gadarim, Duran foremost amongst them. Gawan looked sidelong at his brother. They had already spoken about his becoming the tribe's First Man and would be performing the rituals with the others later that night. Gawan would miss it of course, he knew that, but at the same time it would be a relief to pass on the honour.

Rhianwyn was standing in the middle of the assembly, speaking confidently to the crowd of headmen. Her arm was no longer slung to her body but he knew she still found it uncomfortable to move much, and was limiting herself to one-handed gestures. He felt a stab of envy that she at least still *had* both her hands, albeit with one of them weakened, but he thrust it aside almost at once. It was as the gods willed, and if it meant atonement for his former wrongs then it was a worthwhile sacrifice.

He turned his attention back to his chieftain and reflected on what they'd been through together. After a month of her company he knew for certain that she would never feel for him the way that he did for her and he had managed, more-or-less, to make peace with that. He still thought of her sometimes, strong and beautiful in the firelight, but he was slowly persuading himself to simply be glad of what they had and to be contented, or almost contented, to call her his friend.

Though for all his efforts it was difficult to look away from her as she spoke now, proud and assured in a hall filled with men who had so recently been her enemies. He almost smiled. He thought back to when he'd seen her fight at Broken Stream so long ago, then at *both* the great battles on the plains beneath Nantwyn. He remembered her leading her cohort at Moon Ridge, and fighting in single combat against that treacherous dog Caserach. *Damn but it felt good to kill him! Now* there *was a man whose bridge will be narrow!* It was a pleasant thought but Gawan put it from his mind and focused on something more positive. Both on the field and off it, the Wildcat seemed to always be reminding him of how right he had been to name her to the Gadarim. She was a credit to the sons of Mabonac.

Rhianwyn paused as Hywel whispered a few words into her ear and then she spoke again, addressing the hall.

'With forty-nine hands to his favour, and in accord with my own counsel, I say that Taliesyn son of Cylren is rightful High Chieftain of all the Gorvicae. Does any man here call this unjust?'

Gawan held back a smirk as he looked around. Though some of the chiefs had clearly hoped for another result, most of them seemed contented enough just to have the matter be over and settled. *Most.* Karadoc was clearly struggling to keep the anger from his face, his jaw clamped and his nostrils flaring, his dark eyes blazing brighter than the fire in the pit. But even he didn't bother trying to contradict her. He'd already been outvoted by a respectable margin and with Rhianwyn's approval as well there was no chance of his being backed up if he objected. So he stood there scowling as if Taliesyn had just ravished his grandmother while Hywel raised his hands to the assembly.

'Then let it be so. May Taliesyn son of Cylren lead the Gorvicae into peace and prosperity with honour, with strength, and with wisdom.'

Men drummed their fists against the benches in applause and his closest supporters cheered as Taliesyn stepped forward from amongst them. He looked quietly pleased, if a little shy of ecstatic. Gawan suspected that he had been hoping for a greater majority of hands in his favour. His seat might be secure but the less obligated he was to Rhianwyn, the better he would feel about his position. It hadn't helped his ego that, though she had agreed to marry Lucan to his firstborn daughter, she had also agreed with Gawan's 'suggestion' that Taliesyn ought to marry Tegwen. Fond of her though he surely was, there was every chance Taliesyn had planned on finding a more suitable match for a man of his status. Besides, Gawan could tell he wasn't a man who liked to be told what to do. The Gadarim felt a little conflicted about trapping him into it, but he comforted himself that things would work themselves out with time. *He's a decent enough man and he cares for her, and Tegwen is mad for him. They will manage.*

Taliesyn approached the high table and bowed his head to the man who had just granted him his wish.

'My thanks, Druid Hywel.'

The holy man bowed back, slightly lower, and then gestured to Baercban's empty chair. The new chieftain approached it and paused for a heartbeat before sitting, as if convinced that someone would take the chair away if he tried to sit on it. He shook the feeling off quickly though and lowered himself into it, and another cheer went up for him. Naturally Karadoc did not join in it. Gawan thought Taliesyn looked a little uncertain still, and he could hardly blame him. It felt strange even to Gawan thinking that it was no longer Baercban's chair in Baercban's hall, and *he* wasn't the one having to sit in it. For all his ambitions it must have felt doubly strange for Taliesyn. But he would get used to it, no doubt.

The young man raised a hand and nodded his head politely.

'My thanks to you also, Rhianwyn daughter of Carradan, and to you Leaping Wolf.' The two Caderyn returned the nod but Taliesyn wasn't finished. 'As my first act as High Chieftain of the Gorvicae I would ask something of you both.'

The hall quietened with curiosity and Gawan tilted his head to listen. Taliesyn cleared his throat a little before continuing. 'I would ask both your leaves that Gawan son of Dearg return to his people, and once more be the First Man of our Gadarim.'

The offer was met with noises of agreement from the headmen and Gawan felt his heart skip a beat. It was an amazingly generous offer. To say nothing of the rarity of a man changing his tribe, Gawan was now a one-handed warrior, and a First Man was nominally the best fighter of his people. *Though experience to pass on to others is always valued as well I suppose, and Taran knows I have my share of that!* He allowed himself to wonder how it would feel to call himself a Gorvic again. He concluded almost instantly that it would feel good. And he could live in his old house, right next to where Tegwen would be. He bit back a sigh as reality interrupted fantasy. The decision had been made.

'I am Caderyn now and besides, I have already named Duran son of Syrwn as the next First Man of the Gorvicae.' He made a small gesture towards his brother. 'Flying Hawk is the best of the Gorvicae Gadarim and we all of us are in agreement. We have only to perform the proper rituals.'

Taliesyn nodded slowly, hiding his disappointment. No doubt he was doing him a kindness by the offer but it was also in the new chieftain's interests to bring a man of Gawan's reputation back into the tribe. *And Tegwen might well have put him up to it too.* It was pleasant to think that she probably had.

'I would never wish to interfere with the rites of the Gadarim.' The chieftain glanced at Rhianwyn and then back to Gawan again. 'But will you consider becoming Gorvicae again?'

It was tempting; so much of who he was had been based on his pride in his tribe, and would the Gorvicae not always be his tribe in his heart? He felt his brow furrow in resignation. *But there can be no pride without integrity.* He had a new tribe now. He had a loyalty. He shook his head and then turned to face Rhianwyn.

'I am your First Man, now and always.'

She smiled at him, and the look suited her.

'That you are, my friend. The Caderyn is glad to have known you, however briefly, and you will always have a home at Bryngarth should you wish it.' She placed a hand on his arm. 'But if you wish to return here to your home then I will not begrudge it you, and with your blessing we will have Elfed become First Man of our tribe in your stead.'

Despite himself Gawan felt a glimmer of hope. Elfed was a solid enough man. But he had made a choice.

'I...'

Rhianwyn stopped him.

'Your loyalty to the Caledon is unquestioned, and that will mean much in the days and years to come. More so than what town you choose to live in and what tribe is fortunate enough to keep you.' She smiled again. 'Your family is here. You have earned the right to be with them.'

There were more rumblings of agreement from the hall, most of them coming from Duran and the other Gadarim behind him. Gawan pictured Tegwen, and how he might be a real part of her life if he stayed, then he looked at Rhianwyn. Her face was as open and honest, and as beautiful, as ever. She had known him well enough to understand his sense of obligation, and she had assuaged his conscience with a few simple words. *She may be young, but she is wise far beyond her years.* He gave her a half-smile before turning back to Taliesyn.

'Then with the blessings of you both, I will accept. Taliesyn son of Cylren, may I be Gorvicae once more?'

The young chieftain bowed his head gravely.

'Of course you may, Gawan son of Dearg, and welcome.'

The rumbles turned to cheers and Gawan found himself lost for words. He was Gorvicae again. Just like that. He

595

didn't feel *different* exactly but he felt... something. He couldn't really describe what it was. Before he could dwell on it he felt Duran's hand on his shoulder and he turned to see his brother giving him a knowing smile. He lifted his other hand and the noise quietened.

'I will raise no objection, Lord Taliesyn, though I would say this; I have never known of a warrior who has fought as First Man for two tribes before, and the duty of a First Man is to train and inspire new Gadarim, as much as it is fight beside them. I would not have Leaping Wolf lost to us.'

Gawan frowned as Gwydion appeared next to him.

'Nor would I.'

Pryder piped up from behind them.

'Nor I.'

Kyran's harsh voice came from his other side.

'Nor I.'

Gawan looked at the Darin in confusion but the hard-faced man gave away nothing. Rhianwyn was still standing close to him and her smile turned almost mischievous.

'Nor would I.'

Gawan opened his mouth to speak but the Wildcat got there first.

'I have discussed this matter with many of our Gadarim brethren, both here and at Bryngarth. We are agreed that you have shown yourself to be the finest Gadarim of the three tribes. We would ask you to be First Man of all the Caledon.'

There was an intake of breath throughout the hall and Gawan felt his eyes widening. It was... it was *unheard of.* He heard fists banging on tables as he tried to make sense of it all. He would have his old tribe back, his daughter nearby him, and now a new and greater honour than he'd ever thought possible. What *was* this?

Rhianwyn hid her wince well as she raised her arms for silence.

'Does any man here doubt the strength, the loyalty, the courage, the focus or the will of Leaping Wolf?'

With an unwelcome jolt Gawan thought about his missing hand, his changing of tribes, and all the many things he'd done to bring shame upon himself. There was *every* cause to doubt his virtues, but it seemed that the men of that hall had either forgiven or forgotten. Not a sound came from them. Rhianwyn smiled that smile of hers once again.

'Then let Gawan son of Dearg be First Man of all the Caledon! And may he live and die with honour!'

Duran and Gwydion alone must have shaken the beams with their shouting, and the rest of the room almost rivalled their enthusiasm. Rhianwyn stepped closer to Gawan and clasped his good wrist. In all the noise she needn't have bothered lowering her voice but she did so all the same, tapping her heart with her other hand.

'You don't have to be Caderyn to be in here, brother.'

Gawan smiled at her and gripped back before tapping his own chest.

'As you are in here, sister.'

Rhianwyn's mouth twitched upwards before she turned back to the high table. She had to shout to get the words across.

'Since Gawan is of the Gorvicae the rites can be arranged at your discretion, Lord Taliesyn.'

The young chieftain brushed aside the title.

'There need be no formalities between us, Rhianwyn. And I shall consult with my Gadarim tomorrow.'

His tone was friendly but Gawan suspected he would have preferred to keep his First Man to himself. But he would accept it, and be glad of it in the long-term. Taliesyn had always believed in the Caledon and he would soon learn that Duran was a worthy replacement to lead the Gorvicae Gadarim. Besides, supporting her father in this would make Tegwen very happy. Gawan tried not to think of how she would show her new husband her appreciation!

The noise began to die down and Taliesyn stood up from his new seat. He took a cup from the table and raised it in front of him, his first drink as High Chieftain of his tribe.

'I welcome Gawan son of Dearg back to the Gorvicae, and once again offer my thanks to Rhianwyn daughter of Carradan for her support today, and for all that she has done for us. May we all prosper in the years to come through the unity of the Caledon!'

There was another cheer as he drank and the assembly of chiefs soon became a throng as Taliesyn and Gawan both were congratulated with hand clasps and backslaps, and Rhianwyn thanked by almost every man there. Even those who had doubted the Caledon were relieved that the Gorvicae would not be sundered by the lack of a single leader.

The Caderyn's High Chieftain smiled at him through the crowd and Gawan found himself smiling back. *Brother* might not be as good as *lover* but he was happy nonetheless. After the nightmare that had begun at Moon Ridge he had somehow woken up with his honour, with duty and with peace, and even the beginnings of a family.

There would still be trials ahead of course, the gods had made life that way, but he knew now that he was once again a man who could conquer them, and that he wouldn't have to do it alone. He looked around at the roomful of chiefs and thought of Tegwen, awaiting him outside, then of his brothers who were slapping hands against his aching back. He thought of Rhianwyn, who no matter what else would be a friend and a sister to him for life. He was not alone. He was surrounded by those who cared for him. And for the first time in a long time, there was hope in his world again.

Epilogue

Edryd's knee was still paining him, but compared to the ache in his heart it was almost unnoticeable. He'd seen more than thirty winters come and go in the northlands and had worked in some way or another since he was old enough to lift a basket. He sighed to himself. And never in all that time had he worked so hard at something and taken so little pride in it. He shivered in the icy wind. Winter had come early this year, and he wouldn't be surprised to see the first flurries of snow in a day or two. Something damp hit his cheek but it was only a droplet of rain, and he quickened his pace before it grew any heavier. It was one thing to feel depressed, but to be *damp* and depressed just added insult to injury.

It wasn't far to walk and before long he was standing before the door. The weather was still holding but Edryd wasn't about to take a chance on it and he slipped through the door almost before he had finished knocking. It might not be polite but his errands were generally important enough for manners to be overlooked. It wasn't much warmer in the little back room but at least there was a fire going and he shuffled over to it, his joints aching. The room's two occupants watched him do it and Edryd made an effort to control his fear. The tall man in the chair could be intimidating enough but the one pouring his drink for him, the greasy-haired little Basian, was frankly disturbing. There was something about his empty eyes, his pointed face, and his strange accent that unnerved Edryd, and he knew he wasn't the only one to think so.

He paused to bow to the man in the chair before continuing towards the flames, his hands extended. If they were displeased enough to dispose of him too, he could at least die warm.

'All things considered, I am struggling for good a reason not to kill you here and now.'

Taliesyn sounded disappointed but Edryd had prepared his arguments. He had done only as he was told after all, and it was no fault of his if Caserach and the Breiryn had seen fit to make a mess of things. The new chieftain looked at him expectantly and Edryd readied himself to answer, but then the Basian, Sagris, spoke up for him.

'In fairness, my chieftain, much of what has happened was no fault of Edryd's. And things have still worked out well enough.'

His voice had a cringing, almost sickly tone, but Edryd knew better than to think him a weakling because of it. He had a will of iron and was the root cause of so much that had lately led Edryd to become ashamed of himself; of all the voices to be raised in his defence, Sagris' was by far the least welcome. More and more these days Edryd found himself wishing they had just left him where they'd found him.

Edryd had been with his chief that fateful day, when their party had stumbled across the Basian slave knifing his former master. The Oaken Bridge men had been too late to fight in the great battle at Nantwyn, but they had proved themselves useful in rounding up fleeing legionaries who might otherwise have escaped the Caledon. And of course, they had found General Lepidus.

His sorcerer had abandoned him it seemed, shortly after he and the general had killed a scouting party of Gorvicae. Sagris had told them how the magicker had disappeared into a green mist and how his master had been enraged by his desertion. Lepidus had threatened to flay his slave alive simply for having witnessed it and Sagris had realised he had no choice but to kill him first. Edryd could still remember the little man scurrying up to Taliesyn and himself, thanking them all for coming to his rescue. As if they'd done anything.

Edryd forced his mind back to the present. The Basian was now standing with his hands cupped before him, awaiting his new master's commentary. Taliesyn spoke over his shoulder, a concerned look on his face. Edryd couldn't blame him. *I'd be worried too if I was sat in that chair.*

'I have no *wish* to kill him Sagris. He has been a loyal man for many years. But after all that has happened...'

He left it hanging in the air and for a moment Edryd considered bolting. He was close to the door to the hall after all, and there might well be people still in there. They would not dare to kill him in front of witnesses, would they? Sagris' eyes met his and he seemed to read the tribesman's thoughts. He shook his head very subtly. Edryd stayed put. He tried telling himself it was out of loyalty to his old chief but he knew he was fooling no-one. The Basian spoke calmly to the chieftain.

'All has gone as intended my friend, or mostly as intended. You *are* the chieftain now after all.'

Taliesyn grimaced.

'Just barely, and with far more complications involved than you led me to think.'

Sagris shrugged his narrow shoulders.

'All life is complicated.'

The chieftain didn't seem comforted, and Edryd couldn't blame him for that either. Sagris had known him a matter of days before coming up with his plan for how to win him Baercban's chair, and damned near everything he had predicted had come to pass with a disturbing accuracy. Just how many *complicated* things did this foreigner know? And how many had he told *them* about?

If Taliesyn was thinking the same thoughts as Edryd, he didn't voice them.

'So, what now for Karadoc? He can still cause us much trouble.'

He was speaking to Sagris but it was Edryd who grimaced. He already had one murder on his soul. *At the least.* The Basian sounded relaxed.

'He will be dealt with, but it cannot be straight away. Murders that benefit a man directly are never wise. It was a risk removing Boryn. We are fortunate so much else has happened to draw men's eyes away from his death.'

Taliesyn's voice became defensive.

'He would have caused immediate problems and besides, he was already old.'

Once again, Sagris answered casually.

'I do not say it was not necessary, merely that it was a risk.'

Taliesyn looked as if he'd have been more comfortable if the Basian had argued. A simple fight would feel fresh after all of Sagris' promises and plotting. The chieftain pressed his lips together and looked first at one of them, and then the other. Edryd didn't like that look.

'And what of the Wolf? And the Wildcat?'

Edryd prayed quietly, to gods who would be quite justified in ignoring him, that he would be given no more murders to commit. He was Gorvicae damn it all, it was not their way! But Sagris simply smiled and bowed his head to the chieftain.

'All in good time. Patience, my friend. Patience.'

About the Author

JP Harker is the pen-name of James Thomas, an obsessive martial artist and a committed geek of various types, who apparently didn't drive his fiancée mad enough with those things and so took up writing fantasy books as well. A proud Welshman with just enough Saxon in him to make things interesting, James hails from glamorous Glamorgan where he currently works in the exciting world of hospital admin.

www.jpharker.co.uk

Printed in Great Britain
by Amazon